Mars, J

SKY TRILLIUM

By the same author

THE SAGA OF PLIOCENE EXILE
The Many-Coloured Land
The Nonborn King
The Golden Torc
The Adversary
A Pliocene Companion

Intervention: The Surveillance
Intervention: The Metaconcert

THE GALACTIC MILIEU TRILOGY
Jack the Bodiless
Diamond Mask
Magnificat

Black Trillium
(with Marion Zimmer Bradley and André Norton)
Blood Trillium

Voyager

SKY
TRILLIUM

Julian May

HarperCollinsPublishers

Voyager
An Imprint of HarperCollins*Publishers*
77–85 Fulham Palace Road,
Hammersmith, London W6 8JB

The *Voyager* World Wide Web site address is
http://www.harpercollins.co.uk/voyager

Published by *Voyager* 1997
1 3 5 7 9 8 6 4 2

A catalogue record for this book
is available from the British Library

ISBN 0 00 224197 8

Set in Postscript Ehrhardt by Rowland Phototypesetting Ltd,
Bury St Edmunds, Suffolk

Printed and bound in Great Britain by
Caledonian International
Book Manufacturing Ltd, Glasgow

For Pat Brockmeyer

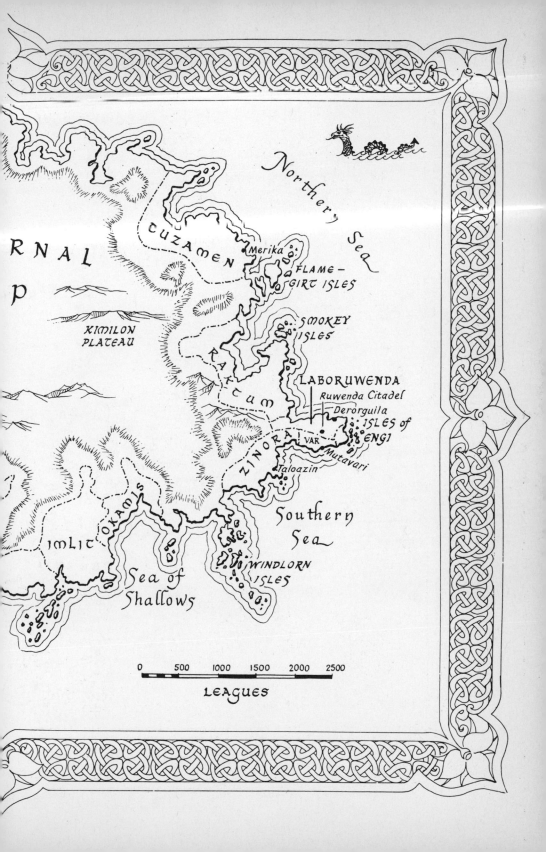

PROLOGUE

The old madman had fallen unconscious at last, prone on the dining room table amidst the remains of the meal. The prisoner let his glittering glass blade descend until its point touched the dark, wrinkled skin of the Archimage's neck.

One thrust. A single movement of his arm and it would be ended. *Do it!*

But the prisoner held back, cursing himself for a sentimental coward, his mind a storm of conflicting emotion. The cup of poisoned wine lay upset near Denby's flaccid brown hand. Dregs puddled on the shining gondawood surface, slowly whitening the varnish beneath. The magnificent table, more than twelve thousand years old, was probably ruined; but its insane owner would survive. At the last, standing over the helpless form of the Archimage of the Firmament with the razor-sharp fruitknife in his hand, the prisoner found it impossible to kill his captor.

Why do I hesitate? he asked himself. Is it because of the old man's crotchety good humour, or his awesome office, that he neglects so scandalously? Do I hold back because Denby Varcour spared my life, even though he sentenced me to share his grotesque exile? Or is magic at work here, protecting this ancient meddler even though he lies vulnerable as a sleeping child before me?

Never mind all that. *Do it.* Kill him! The poison has only rendered him senseless. Kill him now before it is too late!

But the prisoner could not. Not even the power of his Star sufficed to drive the blade home. Denby lay there snoring gently, a smile on his furrowed lips, quite safe, while his would-be murderer fumed and fretted. The reason for the failure was unfathomable but the impossibility remained.

Shaking his head in self-disgust, the prisoner replaced the glass knife on the platter of juicy ladu that was to have been their dessert. With a last uneasy glance at the unconscious madman, he hurried out of the room.

It took only a moment to snatch up the sack of warm clothing and stolen magical implements he had secreted in a cupboard in the salon

9

anteroom. Then he was off, running down the dim, silent corridors toward the chamber of the dead woman, located nearly two leagues away in another quadrant of the Dark Man's Moon.

The prisoner knew he had no time to waste. The sindona messengers and bearers were withdrawn into the Garden Moon as usual, but there was no telling when one or another of the terrible living statues might decide to cross over and seek out their lunatic master on some cryptic errand. Should a sindona find Denby drugged, it would know in an instant what had happened and call out the sentinels.

And if *those* beautiful demons caught up with the prisoner, he would die. The sentinels would discover the new empowerment of his Star, and not even Denby's senile whimsy would suffice to spare his life.

The fleeing man paused for an instant. Clasping the heavy platinum medallion engraved with a many-pointed image that hung around his neck, he called upon its magic to survey his prison. The Star reported that the aged enchanter was still unconscious and no sindona were abroad. The only things that moved in the Dark Man's Moon were the tenders, those odd mechanical contrivances that crept about on jointed legs like great metallic lingits, doing domestic chores.

One of these machines confronted the prisoner now, coming suddenly into view around the corridor's sharp curve. It carried a basket of flameless lamp-globes and moved patiently along, 'sniffing' with one of its armlike appendages, seeking burned-out ceiling lights that might require replacement.

'Out of my way, thing!' The prisoner barged past the bulky device, nearly upsetting it and causing its collection of glowing globes to spill onto the floor. His foot landed on one of the lights and he lost his balance and fell to his knees.

'I beg pardon, master,' the lamp-tender said humbly. 'Are you injured? Shall I summon one of the consolers to treat you?'

'No! Don't! I forbid it!' Sweat broke out on the prisoner's brow. He struggled upright and managed to speak in more normal tones. 'I am not hurt. I command you to go about your normal duties. Do *not* summon assistance. Do you understand?'

Four inhuman eyes studied him. Denby's weird creations were the most solicitous of servants, quite capable of forcing him to accept the medical attention of a sindona consoler against his will if he actually needed it.

Dark Powers! he prayed silently. Don't let it call a sindona. Don't let all my careful planning come to naught and my life be forfeit because of a witless machine!

'It is true that you are unhurt,' the light-tender said at last. 'I will

10

resume my work. I regret any inconvenience I have caused.' It blinked its eyes in salute and began to pick up its scattered load.

The prisoner walked off in a semblance of nonchalance; but when the lamp tender was out of sight he began to run again, feeling fear swell within him. What if the cursed machine summoned the sindona anyway? What if the sentinels were already in pursuit?

He was racing flat out now, his formal dining-robes flapping and his boot-shod feet thudding on the resilient corridor floor. A lump of cramping dread knotted his belly and every breath was now like a sword-cut. Dwelling in this damned place for two years had robbed him of his bodily strength as well as crippling his resolution. But he would mend if he could elude the sindona and finally take advantage of the dead woman's second gift . . .

He was in the disused part of the Dark Man's Moon now, a silent warren of empty galleries and parlours, uninhabited bedroom suites, and abandoned workshops and libraries. It was here that the rearguard of the Vanished Ones had lived twelve times ten hundreds ago while they strove hopelessly to stem the advance of the Conquering Ice.

Denby had willingly given him permission to explore the ghostly rooms, apparently unmindful of what might be found there. Early in his incarceration, the prisoner had come upon the chamber of the dead woman and received her first precious gift. With its help, he had collected his small trove of magical devices; but they were useless, of course, so long as he remained Denby's captive. The Dark Man was invulnerable to ordinary magic.

A long time later, after the prisoner had discovered the truth about himself and about the world's imbalance, he had found the dead woman's second gift: the means to escape this strange prison and its demented jailer. Her third and last gift, without which the other two were useless, he had found just two days earlier. There was no magic in this gift at all, and for that reason Denby had succumbed. The old man had not died, as the prisoner had hoped, but if the profound swoon only lasted a short while longer –

Star Man, where are you going?

Merciful Dark Powers, the sentinels had found him! Their voices rang in his brain like great brazen bells.

What have you done to the Archimage of the Firmament? What stolen goods do you carry in that sack? Answer us, Star Man!

At any moment they might materialize in the corridor with him. They would point their fingers in judgement – and his life would end in a puff of smoke while his naked skull bounced hollow on the floor.

11

Star Man, this is your final warning. Stop and explain yourself!

But he only continued to flee. Suddenly they appeared out of thin air, four of them, less than ten ells behind him and striding purposefully in pursuit. The sindona that were called Sentinels of the Mortal Dictum resembled living statues of ivory, taller than a man and more beautiful than any human being. They wore only crossed belts of blue and green scales and iridescent crown-helms, and they carried golden death's-heads that symbolized their lethal duty. The pace of the sentinels was ponderous and deliberate and he kept well ahead of them, but he was nearly spent. His heart seemed about to burst and his legs were faltering and would not bear him much further.

Where was her chamber? He should have reached it long ago! But the eerie corridor seemed endless, and the sentinels were drawing closer moment by moment. His vision reddened, then began to dim.

I am finished, he said to himself, and pitched forward toward blackness, losing his grip upon the sack. As he fell he took hold of his medallion in a last gesture of futile appeal. The Star seemed to lend him fresh strength. Lying there, he was able to lift his head and open his eyes.

He saw the four pale sindona, golden skulls cradled beneath their left arms, marching toward him. And he also saw that a miracle had been vouchsafed. He lay before a door, massively fashioned of solid metal, marked with a huge, tarnished likeness of the same many-rayed silvery Star he wore around his neck. The portal had neither latch nor keyhole. It was only a few paces away.

Like a dying thing, he crawled with agonized slowness, then lifted his medallion on its chain and touched it to the door.

No! cried the sentinels. Their right arms rose in unison to point annihilation toward him.

The door flew open. There within was the dead woman, seeming to turn her head and smile at him, silently offering sanctuary.

Somehow he was drawn swiftly inside and the door clanged shut behind him. He was enveloped in night – a night spangled with unblinking stars. The room was so cold that the breath was torn from his heaving lungs in a frosty cloud and the sweat coursing down his face turned to crackling ice. An involuntary moan escaped his stiffening lips. He had forgotten that one visited the dead woman only on her own terms.

Near paralyzed with pain and the intense cold, he pulled a cloak from his sack, flung it about himself, and drew up the hood, muffling his face to the eyes. Then he fumbled to pull on fur-lined gloves. Staggering to his feet, he stood with his back pressed to the locked door, fighting to reclaim control of his mind and body.

12

Would the sindona be able to break in and capture him?

The dead woman smiled serenely and seemed to say, *No. Not without the explicit command of the Dark Man himself, and he is still bereft of his senses.*

She sat in a thronelike chair, not really looking at him at all. One entire wall of her chamber was a gigantic window, and her glazed eyes, wide open, seemed to stare with rapt fascination at the scene outside. A shining blue-and-white sphere hung in the midst of a million untwinkling stars. The Garden Moon and the Death Moon were out of sight, tracing their course in the heavens somewhere behind the abode of the Dark Man, so there was nothing to detract from the heart-wrenching beauty of the vision. Uncounted leagues distant, the World of the Three Moons hovered like a massive clouded aquamarine.

The imperilled world. The world that was his home, that he alone could save. The world that had certainly been her home as well, twelve thousand years ago.

She had died with her eyes fixed longingly upon that blue orb, with one hand clasping a Star hanging on jewelled links at her breast and the other holding a curiously wrought little glass phial with a few frozen droplets remaining in it. Her body was perfectly preserved in the deep cold, dressed in rich garments of mournful black. Her hair was dark, streaked with silver. She had been middle-aged but of surpassing beauty, a captive like himself. The archives of the Dark Man had told him some of her tragic story:

Her name was Nerenyi Daral, and she had been the founder of the mighty Star Guild. One who loved her beyond all reason and loyalty had 'saved' her from the fate that had befallen most of the other members of her group, only to see her voluntarily relinquish life rather than evade the Conquering Ice in his despised company. The loss of Nerenyi had driven Denby Varcour, greatest hero of the Vanished Ones and Archimage of the Firmament, out of his mind.

The prisoner bowed deeply before her body, trying to control his shivering. He would not live long in this rigorous place. If the dead woman's second gift proved inoperative after aeons of disuse, he would surely freeze to death before Denby awoke and ordered the sentinels to seize him.

'I could not kill him after all, Star Lady,' he confessed to her. 'Perhaps his magic protected him. But I suspect it was my own soul that demurred, unable to take his life in such a craven manner as he lay smilingly unconscious, replete with good food and wine. Should another day come when he and I meet in honourable magical combat, man-to-man, I will not hesitate to destroy him. Will that suffice?'

13

The voice that might have been hers replied, *It will. Have you found the basic instruments of enchantment – those that will enable you to resume your work?*

'I have.' He lifted the sack. 'My Star eventually led me to all of them, even though it took some time. I am ready now to return to the world, regain the three pieces of the Sceptre of Power, and perform the world-saving task you have commanded.'

The Three will do their best to prevent you.

'Lady, no human being will stop me – not even the one I love. I swear it on the Star.'

When he had first found Nerenyi Daral, some instinct bade him touch his own medallion to hers . . . and the ancient magic of her Guild had done its work, granting him the full potency of the Star at last. It was the dead woman's first gift.

The second gift was a viaduct, one of those wondrous passageways that the Dark Man and the sindona used in order to travel instantly from place to place about the hollow Moons. But this particular viaduct, invisible now, as its kind always were until an adept commanded their opening, led from the Dark Man's Moon back to the world below. Its existence had been revealed to the prisoner on one of his later visits.

Nerenyi Daral had warned him that the Archimage of the Firmament would know instantly if anyone attempted to use the viaduct. And then Denby would either lock it or bid it convey the prisoner to some ghastly new place of captivity. Only if the Dark Man were killed or disabled would the passage lead to freedom.

A tiny glass container in Nerenyi's hand had been her third gift. Sheer happenstance had finally drawn the thing to his attention two days ago and caused him to ask what it contained. When he found out about the poison, he began at once to plan his escape.

'I am ready to go now,' he told her. 'Star Lady, I beseech you to open the world-viaduct for me.'

Do you swear on the Star to recreate my Guild and carry out its great purpose, restoring the balance of the world?

He grasped his medallion with one gloved hand. His fingers were losing sensation and the deadly cold was fast penetrating the cloak as well.

'I do swear,' he said.

Then take my own Star, dear adopted son and heir, and give it to one in whom you place your utmost trust. With the help of the reborn Guild, reclaim the Sceptre of Power. It is still capable of banishing the Conquering Ice. Learn to control its perilous faculties and let the Sky Trillium shine again.

Reverently, he detached her dead fingers from the medallion, lifted the jewelled chain and pendant from her neck, and put it into his sack. 'I will do as you command . . . But now, Lady, I beg you to let me go forth, else I will surely freeze to death on the brink of freedom.'

Go. Viaduct system activate!

A crystalline musical chime rang out and an upstanding ring of light about two ells in diameter sprang into existence to the left of the dead woman's chair. Within it was an area of featureless black from which a musty warm wind flowed.

'Is the viaduct ready to transport me?'

Yes. All you need do is enter. Once it would have led only to the domain of the Conquering Ice, and so it was useless to me. I came here through it, but I could not use it to escape. But in these latter days, when the Sempiternal Icecap is temporarily diminished, the viaduct will debouch in a safe place.

He hesitated. 'May I ask where in the world I will emerge?'

The Star-Voice was stern. *You will go where you are sent, and there you must begin immediately to carry out your mission. Quickly! Denby is about to awake. He will be at the door in a moment.*

'Then, Lady, goodbye!'

Holding tight to the sack, he stepped into the glowing ring and vanished. There was a second bell-like sound and the circle winked out. The remnants of the prisoner's last breath, clouds of minute ice crystals, swirled in the frigid air around the enthroned dead body.

The door of the chamber swung open. The four sindona sentinels marched in, their golden skulls held at the ready. Shuffling after them came a very old man with dark skin and frizzled snow-white hair. He was enveloped in a mantle of golden worram fur.

'Orogastus!' he called. His voice was strong and resonant and might have belonged to a much younger man. 'Are you still here?'

He has departed, one of the sentinels said.

'Well, that's a relief,' said Denby Varcour. 'Now we can get on with saving the world – if it can be saved! A pity he didn't finish me off, but I might have known I'd have to see the thing through to the end.' He flapped one hand at the sindona, ordering them back out into the corridor, then went and stood before the frozen corpse.

'Forgive me, my beloved Nerenyi. It was too good an opportunity to miss. I could not let it be too easy for him, you see.'

As always, her tranquil features smiled.

15

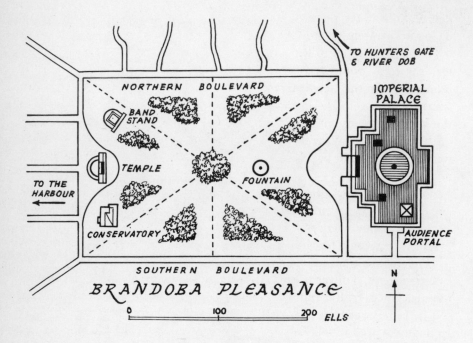

TO HUNTERS GATE
& RIVER DOB

IMPERIAL
PALACE

NORTHERN BOULEVARD

BAND
STAND

TEMPLE

FOUNTAIN

TO THE
HARBOUR

CONSERVATORY

AUDIENCE
PORTAL

SOUTHERN BOULEVARD

BRANDOBA PLEASANCE

N

0   100   200 ELLS

CHAPTER 1

Prince Tolivar lay there in the dark, fully clothed except for his boots, trying desperately not to fall asleep.

He had not dared to leave the silver oil lamps or even a candle lit, for fear someone would see the light shining beneath the door. The only illumination in the chamber came from fitful lightning flashes through the window, and from the clock on the stand beside his bed, an artifact of the Vanished Ones with a face that glowed softly green. It had been a gift on his last nameday from his Aunt Kadiya, the Lady of the Eyes. She was the only one in the world – aside from good old Ralabun – who did not despise him.

Some day he would show them all, especially his hateful elder brother and sister, Crown Prince Nikalon and Princess Janeel. The time would come when they would no longer tease him and call him a useless second prince. They would fear him instead and grant him the respect he deserved!

If he got his treasure back . . .

Lying there, Tolivar gritted his teeth and willed that the slow-crawling minutes go faster. Ralabun would not come until two hours after midnight – if he came at all. 'He must come!' the Prince whispered to himself. But he had not dared to tell Ralabun why he was needed, and the old creature might have dismissed the unusual summons as a boyish whim. He might forget to come, or even fall asleep waiting. Tolivar himself was having great trouble keeping his eyes from closing.

'Holy Flower, don't let me nod off,' he prayed. He was already badly frightened at the prospect of what lay ahead. If he slept – and the awful dream came again – he might be tempted to give it up.

It probably had been foolish of him to hide the treasure out in the Mazy Mire, but the stratagem had seemed necessary. Ruwenda Citadel's ancient stones were themselves permeated with magic, and sacred Black Trillium blossoms bloomed everywhere now on the knoll, thriving beneath the light of the Three Moons. Worst of all, his other aunt – the formidable Archimage Haramis – had taken to visiting his mother too often here in the Summer Capital, which was their childhood home. Tolivar could not

17

risk the White Lady discovering his secret, so he had found a place away in the swamp to hide the precious things.

No one would take them from him. Not ever.

'They are mine by right of salvage,' he reassured himself. 'Even if I am only twelve years old and still unable to make use of them fully, I will die rather than give them up.'

The unwelcome thought stole again into his mind that he might very well perish tonight, drowned in the surging black river.

'Then so be it,' he muttered, 'for if I leave the treasure behind in Ruwenda during the rains, it might be swept away in a great tempest. Or it could be buried in mud before we return next spring, or even found by some stray Oddling and handed over to the White Lady. Then I would have nothing to live for.'

If only the Wet Time had not come so inconveniently early this year!

But Aunt Haramis had said that the world was badly out of balance, and the strange weather reflected it, as did the restlessness of the volcanoes and the increasing number of earthquakes.

The River Mutar that skirted Citadel Knoll had surged to flood stage almost without warning. King Antar and Queen Anigel had decided that the Court of the Two Thrones dared not wait until the end of the month to adjourn to the Winter Capital of Derorguila in Labornok. Instead, the royal entourage must depart within six days, before the mire waters rose too high.

Prince Tolivar, the youngest of the royal family, had reacted to the announcement with panic. So long as the storms continued, the Mutar's current would be too strong for him to paddle upstream alone in the skiff he kept hidden for his secret excursions. He had prayed both to the Holy Flower and to the Dark Powers who aided wizards, begging for just a few dry days and a respite in the flood. But the entreaties were in vain. The time of the royal retinue's departure drew closer and closer until now there were only two days left. Tomorrow the caravan would begin to form. In daylight he would not be able to sneak out of the Citadel without being seen. He had to get the treasure tonight, or leave it behind.

Tolivar tried to banish his desperation as he listened to the rain beating at his bedchamber window. It was a sound that provoked sleep. Several times the Prince found his eyes closing and managed to snap back into wakefulness. But the time passed so slowly, and the raindrops' drumming was so monotonous, that eventually he could not help drifting off.

Once again, the familiar nightmare began.

It had haunted him for the past two years: the rumbling terror of the great earthquake, smoke from burning buildings, himself a snivelling captive, his small-boy fear coloured with the guilt of betrayal. And then miraculous escape! A sudden surge of courage in his heart that had emboldened him to take the great treasure! In the dream, he vowed to use it and become a hero. He would save the city of Derorguila from the attacking army, save his royal parents and all the embattled people. Even though he was only eight years old, he would do it by commanding magic . . .

In the dream, he used the magical device, and they all died.

All of them. Loyal defenders and vicious invaders, the King, the Queen, his brother and sister, even the Lady of the Eyes and the Archimage Haramis herself, dead because of the magic he had wrought! A great pile of bodies lay in the bloody snow of the palace courtyard outside Zotopanion Keep, and he himself was the only one left alive.

But how could it have happened? Was it really his fault?

He fled the horrible scene, running through the devastated city. Snow fell thickly from a dark sky, and the gale wind that drove it spoke with the voice of a man:

Tolo! Tolo, listen to me! I know you have my talisman. I saw you take it four years ago. Beware, foolish Prince! The thing's magic can kill you as easily as it killed the others. You will never learn to use it safely. Give it back! Tolo, do you hear me? Leave it out there in the Mazy Mire. I will come for it. Tolo, listen! Tolo –

'No! It's mine! Mine!'

The Prince woke with a start. He was safe in his own bedroom in Ruwenda Citadel. Thunder was faintly audible through the thick stone walls and the echo of his own terrified cry rang in his ears. He checked the clock on the bedside stand, discovered that it was still too early, and fell back onto his pillow uttering childish curses. The nightmare was so stupid! He had killed no one with magic. His family was alive and well and suspected nothing. The sorcerer was dead, but that was his own fault. Everyone knew that.

'I will retrieve my treasure in spite of the rains,' he said to himself, falling back onto his pillow. 'I will take it with me to Derorguila and continue practising its use. And one day, I will be as powerful as *he* was.'

At last the little clock chimed two. Prince Tolivar sighed, sat up on the edge of the bed and began to tug on his stoutest pair of boots. His frail body was weary after a day spent gathering and packing the things he would take with him to Labornok. The servants had dealt with his clothes, but packing everything else had been his responsibility. Six large brassbound wooden chests now stood ready in his darkened sitting room next door, and four of them were filled mostly with his precious books.

There was also a smaller strongbox of iron with a stout lock that the Prince hoped to fill and tuck in among the other things.

If Ralabun would only hurry!

The clock now showed a quarter past the designated hour. Tolivar put on his raincloak. He wore both a short-sword and a hunting dagger. Opening the casement window and peering out, he saw that the rain had let up, although lightning still flickered in the west. The river was not visible from this side of the Citadel, but he knew it would be high and swift.

At last there came a soft scratching at the door. Tolivar dashed across the room and admitted a sturdy old Nyssomu male, dressed in dark brown rainproof leathers handsomely decorated with silver stitching. Ralabun, the retired Keeper of the Royal Stables, was Tolivar's crony and confidant. His usual aspect was one of sleepy amiability; but tonight his broad, wrinkled face was ashen with anxiety and his prominent yellow eyes seemed almost ready to pop out of his skull.

'I am ready, Hiddenheart. But I beg you to tell me why we must go out in such weather.'

'It is necessary,' the Prince replied curtly. He had long since given up urging Ralabun to bestow a more auspicious mire-name upon him.

'It is a foul night to be abroad in the Mazy Mire,' the old one protested. 'Surely this mysterious errand of yours can wait until morning.'

'It cannot,' the Prince retorted, 'for we would surely be seen in daylight. And early tomorrow the Lord Steward gathers all of the baggage of the royal family and begins forming up the wagon train. No, we must go tonight. Quickly now!'

The boy and the aborigine hurried down a back stairway, ordinarily used only by chambermaids and other lackeys who tended to the royal apartments. On the floor below, a mezzanine overlooking the great hall, was the chapel, together with the small presence chambers of King Antar and Queen Anigel and the adjacent offices of the royal ministers. Guardsmen of the nightwatch were on patrol here, but Tolivar and Ralabun eluded them easily and slipped into a tiny alcove next to the chancellor's rooms where boxes of old royal correspondence filled three tall shelves.

'The secret way is here,' Tolivar said softly. As Ralabun gaped in astonishment, the Prince took out a single letterbox and reached behind it. He then replaced the box, and the entire middle shelf swung soundlessly outward like a door, revealing a black opening beyond. 'Do you have your dark-lantern, as I requested?' Ralabun drew it from beneath his cloak, sliding open the aperture so that light from the glowing swamp-worms within shone out in a wan beam.

The two of them entered the secret passage. Tolivar closed it behind them, took charge of the lantern, and began to walk briskly along the narrow, dusty corridor, bidding the Nyssomu to follow.

'I have heard tales of these hidden passages in the Citadel from Immu, the Queen's nurse,' Ralabun said, 'but never have I been in one. Immu says that long years ago, when the three Living Petals of the Black Trillium were still young princesses, she and Jagun led the Queen and her sister Lady Kadiya out from the Citadel through such a passage when the evil King Voltrik would have murdered them. Was it your Royal Mother who showed you this secret way?'

Tolivar's laugh was bitter. 'Nay. I learned of it from a more obliging teacher. Look sharp! We must go down these steep stairs here and they are damp and slippery.'

'Who then told you of the passageway? Was it Immu?'

'Nay.'

'Did you learn of it then through one of the ancient books you are so fond of perusing?'

'No! Stop asking questions!'

Ralabun fell into a wounded silence as they descended more cautiously. The walls of the cramped staircase were now very wet. In the crevices grew masses of pale fungi that harboured faintly glowing creatures called slime-dawdlers. These little beasts crept along the steps like luminescent slugs, making the footing treacherous and producing an evil smell when they were trodden upon.

'It's not much further,' Tolivar said. 'We are already at the level of the river.'

After a few more minutes they came to another secret portal, with wooden machinery that creaked when the Prince operated it. They emerged into a disused shed full of decayed coils of rope, sprung barrels, and broken crates. A couple of startled varts squeaked and ran away as Tolivar and Ralabun went to the shed's exterior door. The Prince shuttered the lantern and peered cautiously outside. Only a light drizzle fell now and it was very dark. There were no guards, for this quay had been abandoned years ago following the war between Ruwenda and Labornok, and its entrance into the Citadel sealed.

They cautiously made their way over the rotting planks of the dock with Ralabun now leading the way. The Nyssomu's night-vision was much keener than that of humankind and they dared not show a light that might be detected by patrols on the battlements above.

'My boat is yonder,' Tolivar said, 'hidden below the broken bollard.'

Ralabun inspected the craft dubiously. 'It is very small, Hiddenheart,

and the Mutar flood is strengthening each hour. Will we have to go very far upstream?'

'Only about three leagues. And the boat is sturdy enough. I will row with the central oars while you scull with the stern sweep, and together we will breast the current and cross the river. Once on the other side, there will be slack water and the going will be much easier.'

Ralabun grinned. 'I was not aware that you were such an experienced waterman.'

'I am experienced in more things than you know,' the boy said shortly. 'Let us be going.'

They climbed aboard and cast off. Tolivar rowed with all his strength, which truly was not much. But Ralabun, while elderly, had muscular arms after years of heavy work in the stables, and so the boat moved steadily across the broad river. They dodged floating debris, including whole trees uprooted from the Blackmire upstream. Once there was even a log with a huge vicious raffin aboard, that sailed along as nonchalantly as a Trevista tradeboat. The beast roared as it passed less than three arm-lengths away, but it made no move to leave its safe perch and attack them.

Along the opposite shore from Citadel Knoll, which was mucky and uninhabited, the current was much less strong, just as the Prince had predicted. He wearily put up his oars and left the propelling of the boat to Ralabun. They made good headway upstream, and were able to converse above the noise of the rushing water.

Tolivar said, 'There is a very shallow tributary creek that joins the river on the north shore, in the braided section just above Market Pool. That is where we are going.'

Ralabun nodded. 'I know what you're talking about: a nameless waterway clogged with fodderfern and lanceweed. But it is not navigable –'

'It is, if one fares carefully. I have travelled the creek often during the Dry Time, in secret, disguising myself as a common wharfboy.'

Ralabun gave a disapproving grunt. 'That was most imprudent, Hiddenheart! Even so close to Citadel Knoll, the Mazy Mire is not a safe place for a lone human lad. If you had only asked, I would have been glad to take you swamp-romping –'

'I was in no danger.' The Prince spoke haughtily. 'And my business in the mire was both serious and personal. It had nothing to do with the sort of idle funseeking we are accustomed to pursue together.'

'Hmph. What great mystery does this creek conceal, then?'

'It's my business,' Tolivar snapped.

This time the Nyssomu's feelings were clearly hurt. 'Well, I humbly beg Your Worship's pardon for prying!'

The boy's voice softened. 'Do not be offended, Ralabun. Even the dearest companions must have some things private from one another. I was forced to ask your help in travelling to my secret place tonight because of the strength of the river. There was no other soul I could trust.'

'And gladly will I accompany you! But I confess that I am sad that you will not confide in me. You know I would never tell any secret of yours to a living soul.'

Tolivar hesitated. He had not intended to disclose the nature of the treasure to his friend. But he was strongly tempted now to have at least one other person know about the wondrous things he owned. And who better than Ralabun? Tolivar said: 'Do you swear that you will not tell the King or the Queen about my secret? Nor even the Archimage Haramis herself, if she should command it?'

'I swear upon the Three Moons and the Flower!' said Ralabun stoutly. 'Whatever privity you entrust to me I will guard faithfully until the Lords of the Air carry me safely beyond.'

The Prince nodded sombrely. 'Very well then. You shall see my great treasure when I fetch it tonight from its hiding place in the mire. But if you reveal what it is to others, you may forfeit not only your own life, but also my own.'

Ralabun's big round eyes gleamed in the dimness as he made the sign of the Black Trillium in the air with one hand. 'What is this marvellous thing that we seek, Hiddenheart?'

'Something I must show you, rather than speak of,' said the Prince. And he would say no more, for all the Nyssomu's coaxing.

After they had travelled on for another hour the drizzle ceased and a brisk wind began to blow, sending dark clouds speeding across a small patch of starry sky. On the opposite bank the torch-lamps of Ruwenda Market at the westernmost end of Citadel Knoll flickered dim, for the Mutar was now over a league wide. Then they entered the braided section of the river, where there were many wooded islands during the Dry Time. Most of these were submerged now, with the lofty gonda and kala trees that grew on them rising out of swirling black water. It would have been easy to lose the way, and several times the Prince had to correct Ralabun's navigation. Unfortunately, the mirecraft of the old stablemaster was not nearly so expert as he pretended.

'Here is the creek,' Tolivar said at last.

'Are you sure?' Ralabun looked doubtful. 'It seems to me that we must go on further –'

'No. It is here. I am quite certain. Turn in.'

Grumbling, the Nyssomu bent to his oar. 'The jungle round about here is already flooded and full of drifting debris. There's no sign at all of a channel. I really think —'

'Be silent!' The Prince took up a stance in the bow. The few stars gave barely enough light to see by. The water soon became very shallow, with dense thickets of flag-reeds, lanceweed, and redfern between the towering trees. In the respite from the downpour, the wild creatures of the Mazy Mire gave voice. Insects chirped, clicked, buzzed, and made musical chiming sounds. Pelriks hooted, night-carolers warbled, karuwoks splashed and hissed, and a distant gulbard uttered its throaty hunting cry.

When Ralabun could no longer use the sculling oar because of the shallowing water and clogging driftwood, he cried out, 'This can't be right, Hiddenheart!'

The boy controlled his exasperation with some effort. 'I will guide us while you pole the boat along. Go between those two great wilunda trees. I know the way.'

Ralabun grudgingly obeyed, and even though the channel at times seemed hopelessly blocked with brush and hanging vines, a lead of open water barely as wide as the boat stayed always ahead of them. The going was very slow, but after another hour they reached a small area of high ground. Thorn-ferns, weeping wydels, and towering kalas grew about its rocky perimeter. Tolivar pointed out a landing spot and Ralabun brought the boat in to shore.

'This is it?' he murmured in surprise. 'I could have sworn we were lost.'

The Prince leapt onto a bank covered with rain-beaten sawgrass and tied the bow-line to a snag. Then he took up the lantern, opened its shutter, and beckoned for the Nyssomu to accompany him along a nearly invisible path that twisted through outcropping rocks and dripping vegetation. They came to a clearing, where there was a small hut made of hewn poles and bundled grass, roofed with heavy fodderfern.

'I built it,' the Prince said with pride. 'It's where I come to study magic.'

Ralabun's wide mouth dropped open in amazement, displaying stubby yellow fangs. 'Magic? A lad such as you? By the Triune – you are well named Hiddenheart!'

Tolivar unfastened the simple wicker door and gave an ironic bow. 'Please enter my wizard's workshop.'

Inside it was completely dry. The Prince lit a three-candle reflector lamp standing on a makeshift table. The hut had few other furnishings aside from a stool, a carboy of drinking water, and a set of hanging shelves that held a few jars and firkins of preserved food. Certainly there were no instruments, books, or any of the other occult appurtenances one might expect in a sorcerer's lair.

Tolivar dropped to his knees, brushed aside the cut ferns and rushes that covered the dirt floor, and began to pry up a large, thin slab of stone. In the cavity beneath it lay two bags of coarse woollen cloth – one small and the other larger. Tolivar placed both on the table.

'These are the precious things we have come for,' he told Ralabun. 'I did not think it wise to conceal them in the Citadel.'

The old aborigine eyed the bags with growing misgiving. 'And what happens to these things when you reside in Derorguila during winter?'

'I have a safe hiding-place in the ruins just outside Zotopanion Palace where nobody goes. I found it four years ago, during the Battle of Derorguila, when I had the good fortune to acquire this great treasure.' The boy opened the larger bag and slid out a slender, shallow box about the length of a man's arm and three handspans wide. It was made of a dark glassy material, and upon its lid was embossed a silver many-rayed Star.

Ralabun cried out: 'Lords of the Air! It cannot be!'

Saying nothing, Tolivar opened the smaller bag. Something flashed brilliantly silver in the lamplight – a curiously wrought coronet having six small cusps and three larger. It was ornamented with carved scrollwork, shells, and flowers, and beneath each of the three larger points was a grotesque face: one was a hideous Skritek, the second was a grimacing human, and the third was a fierce being with stylized starry locks of hair who seemed to howl in silent pain. Beneath the central visage was a tiny replica of Prince Tolivar's royal coat-of-arms.

'The Three-Headed Monster,' Ralabun croaked, nearly beside himself with awe. 'Queen Anigel's magical talisman that she surrendered as ransom to the vile sorcerer Orogastus!'

'It belongs neither to my mother nor to him now,' Tolivar declared. He placed the coronet upon his own head and suddenly his slender body and plain small face seemed transfigured. 'The talisman is bonded to me by the star-box, and anyone who touches it without my leave will be burnt to ashes. I have not yet fully mastered the Three-Headed Monster's powers, but some day I shall. And when that time comes I will become a greater wizard than Orogastus ever was.'

'Oh, Hiddenheart!' Ralabun wailed.

But before he could continue, the boy said, 'Remember your oath, old friend.' Then he removed the coronet from his head and replaced it and the star-box in their bags. 'Now come along. Perhaps we can get home before it begins to rain again.'

25

CHAPTER 2

'Now!' Kadiya cried out. 'Take them!'

The huge web woven of tanglefoot fell, the scores of ropes that had supported it cut at the same moment by the crew of Nyssomu high in the kala trees. It was deep night, but a searing bolt of lightning lit the moment of the net's landing on the floor of the swamp forest and dimmed the orange-glowing eyes of the startled Skritek war-party.

The ambush had been successful. More than forty of the monstrous Drowners, suddenly trapped in tough, gluey meshes, roared and shrieked amidst the rolling thunder. They tore ineffectually at the web with their tusks and claws, lashing their tails and wallowing on the muddy ground as they became hopelessly entangled. Musk from their scaled hides arose in a noxious cloud. It did not deter their captors from driving long barbed stakes into the soggy soil, securing the net's edges. Those Nyssomu who were not engaged in the task capered about, popping their eyes out on stalks in mockery of their ancient foe, cheering and brandishing blow-pipes and spears.

'Yield to me, Roragath!' Kadiya demanded. 'Your scheme of invasion and brigandage is finished. Now you must pay the penalty for violating the Truce of the Mazy Mire.'

Never! the Skritek leader retorted in the speech without words. He was a gigantic creature, nearly twice her height, and still stood upright with the sticky meshes clinging to his body. *The Truce no longer binds us. And even if it did, we would never surrender to a puny human female. We will fight to the death rather than yield!*

'So you do not recognize me, treacherous Drowner,' Kadiya murmured. She turned to a sturdy little man of the Folk who stood just behind her. 'Jagun. It seems that the night-sight of these addlepate truce-breakers is as weak as their wits. Let torches be brought to enlighten them.'

It had begun to rain heavily again. But at Jagun's command several members of the Nyssomu force struck fire-shells and ignited pitch-dipped bundles of reeds, which they took from their knapsacks and stuck onto long sticks. The captured Skritek warriors hissed and bellowed defiance as flame after flame sprang to life, illuminating the turbulent scene in the clearing. Then, as torchbearers converged upon Kadiya and she slipped off her hoodcape, ignoring the downpour, the monsters fell silent.

She was a woman of medium stature but seemed tall among her cohort of diminutive Nyssomu. Her hair was russet, bound into a tight crown of braids. She wore a cuirass of golden scale-mail over leathern forester garb much like that of her companions, and on her breast was the sacred Black Trillium emblem. Each petal of the Flower bore a gleaming eye – one golden like that of the Folk, one deep brown like Kadiya's own, and one pale silvery-blue with odd glints in its dark pupil, and this last eye belonged to the Vanished Ones.

Now we know you, the chief of the Drowners admitted with reluctance. *You are the Lady of the Eyes.*

'And I am also Great Advocate of all Folk, including you foolish Skritek of the Southern Morass. How dare you invade and pillage these lands of the Nyssomu Folk in violation of my edict? Answer me, Roragath!'

We do not accept your authority! Besides, one greater than you has revealed the truth to us about your spurious Truce. He has told us that soon the Vanished Ones will return and the Sky Trillium shine again in the heavens. Then you humans and all of your cringing Oddling slaves will be destroyed. The World of the Three Moons will be as it was in the beginning: the domain of Skritek alone.

Yes! Yes! roared the other monsters. They began to thrash about and struggle in the net even more violently than before.

'Who has told you this shocking lie?' Kadiya demanded. When the Skritek leader did not reply, she drew from her scabbard a strange dark sword with a tripartite pommel, having a dull-edged blade that lacked a point. Reversing it, she held it high, and at the sight of it all the captive swamp-fiends began to moan in fear.

'You recognize the Three-Lobed Burning Eye that I hold.' Kadiya spoke with an awful calmness. Raindrops streamed unheeded down her face and sparkled like gems on her armour. 'I am the custodian of this true talisman of the Vanished Ones. It can decide in an instant whether or not you have the right to flout me. But understand this, you Drowners of the Southern Morass: If you are judged and found guilty of sedition, the Eye will engulf you in magic fire and you will perish miserably.'

The monsters were muttering among themselves now. Roragath said at last:

We believed what the Star Man said, even though he offered no proof beyond the wonders he worked to demonstrate his command of magic. Perhaps . . . we were mistaken.

'A Star Man –?' Jagun cried in dismay. But Kadiya hushed him with a wave of her hand.

27

'Falsehoods pour easily from a glib and mischievous mouth,' she said to Roragath, 'and fools who are reluctant to give up their old, violent ways may be all too eager to believe liars and charlatans. I know how your people have resisted the Truce. You thought that because you dwelt in a remote corner of the mire you were beyond the White Lady's governance – and beyond my enforcement of her will. You were wrong.'

The huge Skritek gave a groan of furious despair. *Kadiya of the Eyes, leave off chiding us like stupid children! Let your talisman judge us and slay us. At least that will put an end to our shame.*

But Kadiya lowered the peculiar sword instead and slipped it again into its sheath. 'Perhaps that will not be necessary. Thus far, Roragath, you and your band have only been guilty of scattered acts of terror and the destruction of Asamun's village. Nyssomu Folk have been injured, but none have died – no thanks to you. Restitution can be made. If you atone for your hostile actions and pledge to return to your own territory and keep the Truce, then I will spare your lives.'

The great muzzled head of the Skritek leader remained defiantly level for many heartbeats, but at last it sagged in submission and the creature fell to his knees. *I promise on behalf of myself and my fellows to obey your commands, Lady of the Eyes, and this I avow by the Three Moons.*

Kadiya nodded. 'Cut them free,' she said to the Nyssomu band. 'Then let Asamun and his counsellors negotiate the reparations.' She addressed the Skritek leader once again, laying one hand upon the eyed emblem on her breast. 'Do not let your heart contemplate further treachery, Roragath of the Drowners. Remember that my sister Haramis, the White Lady, Archimage of the Land, can see you wherever you go. She will tell me if you dare to break the Truce of the Mazy Mire again. If you do I will come for you, and this time requite you without mercy.'

We understand, said Roragath. *Is it allowed for us to take vengeance upon the wicked one who misled us? He came to us only once and then went away westward into the mountains, out of Ruwenda and towards Zinora. But we could track him down –*

'No,' said Kadiya. 'It is my command that you do not pursue the troublemaker. The White Lady and I will deal with him in good time. Only warn other Skritek to give no credence to his lies.'

Picking up her discarded cape and donning it once more against the unrelenting rain, she beckoned for Jagun to bring a torch and come with her. Side by side, the Lady of the Eyes and her chief deputy set off along the broad trail leading to the Vispar River.

* * *

28

After Haramis, the White Lady, had learned of the rampaging monsters in the remote South and bespoke her triplet sister Kadiya, it had taken ten days to mobilize the small army of Nyssomu and set up the ambush of the Skritek war-party. Now that the expedition had ended successfully, Kadiya was exceedingly tired. The Skritek leader's words had been puzzling and disquieting, but she was in no humour to discuss them now with the Archimage.

Nor was she minded to hear a lecture from her sister, when the White Lady learned of how she had used the talisman.

Plodding through deep mud, sopping wet from head to heel and every muscle aching, the Lady of the Eyes took hold of a thin lanyard about her neck and drew forth an amulet that had been concealed in her clothing. It glowed faintly golden and was warm and comforting to the touch, a droplet of honey-amber with a fossil Black Trillium blossom in its heart.

Thank you, she prayed. Thank you, Triune God of the Flower, for letting the bluff work one more time, for giving me strength. And forgive me the implied deceit . . . If I knew another way, I would follow it.

With the stormwinds inaugurating the premature Wet Time roaring through the tree branches overhead, Kadiya and Jagun spoke hardly a word until they reached the backwater of the swollen river where their boats had been left. The Nyssomu Folk customarily travelled in hollowed-log punts and cumbersome flatboats that were laboriously poled or sculled along. But Kadiya's craft was fashioned in the Wyvilo style, of thin-scraped hide stretched over a lightweight wooden frame. It was drawn up between the buttress-roots of a mighty kala tree, and as she and Jagun climbed into it and loosed it from its mooring two big sleek heads rose from the rain-pocked waters nearby and stared in expectation.

They were rimoriks, formidable water-animals who shared a special relationship – one could hardly call it domestication – with the Uisgu Folk, those shy cousins of the Nyssomu who dwelt in the Goldenmire north of the River Vispar. Since Kadiya was the Advocate of all Folk, including the Uisgu, she also enjoyed the rimoriks' favour. Numbers of the animals, eager to serve her, had left their accustomed territory to live near Kadiya's Manor of the Eyes on the River Golobar, which lay nearly seventy leagues to the east.

The eyes of the aquatic beasts shone like jet in the light of Jagun's guttering torch. The rimoriks had dapple-green fur, bristling whiskers, and enormous teeth that they bared in what was, for them, an amiable expression.

Share miton with us, Lady. We have waited overlong for your return.

'Certainly, dear friends.' From her belt-pouch Kadiya took a small scarlet bottle-gourd. Unstoppering it, she took a sip, let Jagun have his share, and then poured a quantity of the sacred liquid into the palm of her left hand. The animals swam close and drank, lapping gently with their horrifying tongues – whiplike appendages with sharp points that they used to spear their prey.

As the miton worked its benign magic, the four unlikely friends felt a great contentment that sharpened their senses and banished fatigue. When the communion was over, Kadiya uttered a sigh. Jagun slipped pulling harnesses onto the rimoriks. Soundlessly, the great animals submerged and the boat sped away down the wide, dark river, heading for the secret shortcut that would take them all home in less than six hours.

When they were well on their way, with Kadiya and Jagun huddled beneath the shelter of a waxwort tarpaulin and munching an austere supper of dried adop roots and journey bread, she said, 'It went well, I think. Your idea of making a drop-net from tanglefoot was brilliant, Jagun, sparing us a pitched battle with the swamp-fiends.'

The old aborigine's wide, sallow face was masklike and his glowing yellow eyes darted askance at her. It was clear that he was deeply troubled. Kadiya groaned inwardly, knowing full well why. She was able to postpone her sister Hara's reproaches, but not those of her old friend.

For a long time Jagun did not speak. Kadiya waited, eating although she had lost her taste for food, while the rain beat about their ears and the boat hissed and vibrated with the great speed of their passage.

Finally Jagun said, 'Farseer, for four years now you have carried on your chosen work successfully, even though your talisman is no longer bonded to you and no longer capable of magic. No one save I and your two sisters knows that the Three-Lobed Burning Eye has lost its power.'

'Thus far the secret has remained safe,' she said evenly.

'But I fear what might happen if you continue to wield the talisman in your office of Advocate, as you did tonight. If the truth is discovered, the Folk will be deeply scandalized. Your honour will be stained and your authority compromised. Would it not be the greater part of wisdom to do as the White Lady has so often requested, and consign the Burning Eye to her care until it can be made potent once again?'

'The talisman is mine,' Kadiya declared. 'I shall never relinquish it – not even to Haramis.'

'If you simply cease wearing it, no one would dare to question you.'

She sighed. 'Perhaps you are right. I have thought and prayed hard over the matter, but the decision is not easy to make. You saw how the Skritek were terror-smitten by the Eye tonight.'

Her hand slipped to the pommel of the dark sword and she grasped the three conjoined balls at the end. Those orbs were cold now, that once had been warm. The Three-Lobed Burning Eye, created ages ago by the Vanished Ones for their own mysterious purposes, had been capable of dread magic, for it was one of three parts making up the great Sceptre of Power.

Once that talisman had been bonded to Kadiya's very soul, and the three lobes had opened at her command to reveal living counterparts of the eyes emblazoned upon her armour. She had commanded its power, and anyone who dared touch the sword without her permission died on the spot.

But four years ago the sorcerer Orogastus, last heir to the Star Men, stole Kadiya's talisman and acquired through extortion a second one belonging to Queen Anigel. He bonded both devices to himself and dared hope that the Archimage Haramis would give up the third talisman for love of him. Instead, Orogastus lost Anigel's talisman by misadventure; and later, in a climactic battle, he was destroyed by the magic of the three sisters.

The ownerless sword was then restored to Kadiya. But the talisman would no longer unite with her magical amulet of trillium-amber as it had done before, binding itself to her will. The Three-Lobed Burning Eye was apparently as dead as Orogastus.

Nevertheless, Kadiya had continued to wear it.

'I have never deliberately lied to the Folk about my talisman's function,' she said now to Jagun. 'Its symbolic value remains, even if it is now magically useless. You saw the good it did tonight. Without its threat, the Skritek would surely have fought us to the death. With it, I was able to spare them and prevent a great loss of Nyssomu life.'

'That is true,' Jagun admitted.

'The Drowners will return to the Southern Morass and tell others of their tribe how they were conquered and granted mercy by the Lady of the Eyes and her talisman.' She gave a little shrug. 'Thus the Truce of the Mire will hold until the next crisis comes along . . . And there is always a chance that Haramis will eventually discover how to rebond the talisman to me, restoring its potency.'

The little man shook his head, still uneasy. Like others of his race he was superficially human in appearance, having tiny slitted nostrils, a broad mouth with small sharp teeth at the fore, and narrow upstanding ears rising on either side of his hunter's cap. Many years ago he had been Royal Huntsman to King Krain of Ruwenda, Kadiya's late father. When she was but a tiny girl, Jagun had taken her into the Mazy Mire that comprised so much of the little plateau kingdom, teaching her many of its secrets and giving her the mire-name Farseer because of her keen vision. The nickname had proved prophetic when Kadiya became the custodian of the Three-Lobed Burning Eye and the protector of the aboriginal Folk who shared the World of the Three Moons with humankind.

Over the years, Jagun had remained Kadiya's closest friend and deputy. Sometimes, to her chagrin, he seemed to forget that she was no longer a child, upbraiding her for her hot temper and occasional woth-headed stubbornness. The most annoying thing about this habit of his was that he was often in the right.

'You must realize, Farseer,' Jagun now said gravely, 'that this particular conflict with the Skritek was far from ordinary. Roragath's tale of a lying Star Man must have been as great a shock to you as it was to me.'

'The notion of the Vanished Ones returning is nonsense,' she scoffed. 'And only the Lords of the Air know what manner of prodigy a "Sky Trillium" might be. As for the so-called Star Man –'

'What if the worst has happened,' Jagun ventured, 'and the accursed sorcerer himself has come back once again from the dead?'

'Impossible! Haramis' own talisman told her that Orogastus had died.' Kadiya's lip curled in disgust. 'And my silly sister has wept secretly for his damned soul ever since.'

'Do not mock the White Lady's honest emotion,' Jagun said sternly, 'especially when you have never known love's passion yourself. One does not pick and choose whom to love – as I myself know to my sorrow.'

Kadiya looked at him in surprise. For as long as she had known Jagun, he had had no mate. But this was not the time to question him on such a delicate subject. 'Do you think, then,' she asked him, 'that Orogastus might have left others to carry on his impious work? The six acolytes that we know of – the ones he deemed his Voices – most certainly perished. And no more apprentice wizards were found when my brother-in-law searched the haunts of Orogastus in the land of Tuzamen.'

'Such persons might have fled from King Antar's justice when news of their master's doom reached them,' Jagun said. 'And if they were clever and avoided the overt use of magic, then they might also have escaped the White Lady's scrutiny. Not even her Three-Winged Circle can oversee every part of the world, every moment of the day and night.'

Kadiya finished her bread and adop and began to pry open blok-nuts with her small dagger and prick out the meats for the two of them. 'It is more likely that this so-called Star Man is nothing but an imposter, an agent of some enemy of Laboruwenda intent on stirring up trouble for political reasons. It was very clever to arouse the Skritek now, at the beginning of the rains. The court of Anigel and Antar is about to withdraw to the Labornoki flatlands for the winter, leaving behind only a reduced garrison in Ruwenda. That young scoundrel, King Yondrimel of Zinora, would love to see the Two Thrones pulled into a series of ruinous conflicts with the swamp-fiends during the Wet Time. Then his nation might take over Laboruwenda's western trade routes.'

'That is plausible,' Jagun conceded. 'Roragath did say that the Star Man went off in that direction.'

'If Yondrimel is up to mischief, King Antar and Queen Anigel will put a stop to his games in short order. He cannot afford to be caught blatantly undermining the stability of the Two Thrones. Other civilized nations will ostracize him, and he will have no one to peddle his pearls to except the Feathered Barbarians.'

Jagun had been rummaging in their bag of supplies, searching for a corkscrew. Finding one at last, he opened a flask of halaberry wine and filled two wooden cups.

'The Lords of the Air grant that this matter be swiftly resolved,' he said, in a pious toast. Kadiya lifted her own cup and they both drank. When Jagun spoke again, his tone held dire warning. 'But if the Star Guild has truly revived, then not only our own land of Laboruwenda but also the rest of the world may be at the brink of catastrophe. With your talisman useless and that of Queen Anigel lost, there is no possibility of putting together the Threefold Sceptre of Power. And that is the only certain weapon against the ancient magic of the Star Guild.'

Eyeing him over the cup's rim, Kadiya smiled. 'Be of good cheer, old friend. My sisters and I will find out the truth of the situation. Tomorrow, after I have slept in my own bed and refreshed my frazzled brain, we will bespeak Haramis. For now, let us drink our wine and say no more.'

But the next day, when Kadiya had Jagun send the Call to the Archimage of the Land, using the speech without words, there was no reply.

CHAPTER 3

'Iriane!' Haramis called softly into her talisman. 'Iriane, do you hear me? I have very serious tidings to impart to you and I need your advice badly. Please answer.'

But the area within the Three-Winged Circle that she held, looking into it as one would study a hand mirror, remained a formless swirl of pearly luminescence. The plump, cheerful, azure-tinted features of the Archimage of the Sea did not appear.

Haramis frowned in perplexity. 'Talisman, can you tell me why Iriane fails to respond?'

She is shielded by magic.

'Is she in her own dwelling?'

No. She is in the Hollow Isles, among the Mere Folk of the far west.

'Why does she refuse to bespeak me?' Haramis asked the Circle impatiently.

The question is impertinent.

'Bother! Now I suppose I shall have to go and find her.' She took up her harp, which had rested on the carpet beside her, and struck a few slow chords to calm herself and assist fruitful thought. In a large ceramic pot beside the curtained window was a huge plant covered with three-petalled flowers as dark as night, and she gazed upon it and was comforted.

All evening long Haramis, Archimage of the Land, had remained in her study using the Three-Winged Circle to view the conflict between her sister Kadiya and the Skritek. Haramis had been both startled and deeply concerned at the words spoken by the leader of the monsters. No sooner was Kadiya victorious than Haramis cut away from the scene of the ambush hoping to consult with her colleague and mentor, the Blue Lady of the Sea.

Not for a moment did the young Archimage of the Land think of dealing with this present situation all by herself. If another Star Man was at large, bent on carrying out the schemes of his dead master, then the world was once again in terrible danger. As for the idea that the Vanished

34

Ones might return, it was so incredible that Haramis hardly dared to consider it . . .

'Oh, Iriane!' she exclaimed aloud. 'Of all the inconvenient times for you to go off and hide!'

With some effort, Haramis again stilled her agitation by strumming the harp and contemplating the Flowers. She must not let her unruly imagination run away with her. Before undertaking the task of hunting down the flighty Archimage of the Sea, she should first find out just who had fomented the uprising of the swamp-fiends. The Skritek aborigines were notoriously gullible, and the one who had incited them to hostility might be only some common human rogue.

She put down the harp and lifted her talisman once again. 'Show me the person who told the Skritek that he was a member of the Star Guild.'

Obediently, the Three-Winged Circle produced a murky scene of deep night in some rocky fastness, lit by the crimson embers of a dying campfire. Someone lay asleep on the ground.

The vision expanded at the Archimage's command, until it seemed that she stood within it and was able to walk about and examine everything closely, seeing as well as in broad daylight. Lofty mountains reared up on every side, many of them capped by glaciers. There was no snow on the ground in the camp, but a chill wind blew gustily, causing the fire to flare up and then almost expire.

'Where is this place?' she asked the talisman.

In the Ohogan Mountains above Zinora, some nine hundred leagues west of your Tower.

With the darkness abated by the Circle's magic, Haramis could see a large fronial, well cared for and having its antlers bedizened with silver, hobbled near a brawling stream. It was sluggishly cropping leaves from shrubs growing among the boulders. The saddle and other tack, piled neatly at one side of the fire, were of high quality and styled in the Zinoran manner, with pearl-studded silver accoutrements. On the other side of the fire lay the sleeper, wrapped so tightly in zuch-wool blankets that only his nose was visible. Close by him rested a stout pair of what looked like saddlebags – except that they were fashioned not from leather but from exotic birdskin with the red-and-black feathers still in place. Only Sobranians could have made them, those wealthy but rather uncivilized humans who dwelt on the western frontiers of the known world, beyond the nation of Galanar.

Leaning against the bags was an intricate contrivance made of dark metal, and at the sight of it Haramis felt a pang of unbelieving horror and could not help but cry out. Her Sending was imperceptible to the sleeper, however, and he did not stir as she knelt beside the device and studied it.

It was about half an ell in length, flattened and triangular at one end, almost like the stock of an arbalest. From this protruded three slender cylinders or rods, bound tightly together by rings and terminating in a much-perforated metal sphere. Where the upper stock joined the rods was a kind of flared cuff, and behind it numbers of knobs, studs, and appendages of mysterious function.

This particular device was unfamiliar. But the Archimage had seen others like it – in her own Cavern of Black Ice behind her Tower on Mount Brom, and also four years earlier during the siege of Derorguila by the sorcerer Orogastus. The thing in the possession of the alleged Star Man was an antique weapon, one of those artifacts of the Vanished Ones that used to turn up from time to time in the ruins of their crumbling cities. Both Folk and humankind had long been forbidden to possess these fearsome armaments. But Orogastus had acquired numbers of them by looting the cache of an earlier Archimage of the Land, and his Tuzameni and Raktumian warriors had used the weapons to deadly effect waging war on King Antar and Queen Anigel of Laboruwenda.

When the sorcerer's force was defeated, Haramis had caused all of the archaic arms used by the enemy to be collected and destroyed. She had also rendered useless the weapons and other dubious apparatus of the Vanished Ones stored at her own Tower, as well as those remaining in the ancient Kimilon cache partially plundered by the sorcerer. Methodically, over many months, she had used her talisman's magic to visit every ruin and other forgotten spot on the world-continent where operable ancient weapons were hidden away. She had finally destroyed every one of them. The talisman had confirmed it.

Where then, had the specimen at her feet come from?

From beneath the sea, her talisman said, and the Archimage groaned at her own stupidity. Of course! The talisman ever took her words literally, and she had bade it search the land.

The weapon was slightly battered, but quite clean and obviously in working order. Used in some lethal demonstration, it would command respect and fear for its owner among both Folk and humankind in any part of the world, whether or not the wielder was truly a member of the Star Guild. By now, other weapons like it might also have been gathered from submarine hiding places and put to nefarious use.

Haramis arose and stood over the sleeper's shrouded form. 'Talisman, let him turn about so that I may see him clearly.'

A muffled grunt came from the blankets. The man rolled over, and in doing so exposed his face and upper body. He was young and well-built, perhaps two-and-twenty, with nut-brown hair and a meagre beard that he had perhaps grown to lend his rather soft features an appearance of greater maturity. His overtunic was heavy grey silk, tattered and soiled but richly lined with fur. Around his neck, hanging from a beautifully wrought platinum chain, was a disk with a many-pointed Star.

Magnifying her view of it, Haramis saw that the medallion was no counterfeit. It was identical to the one Orogastus had worn, but in her Sending, she could not tell whether or not it invested its wearer with a magical aura.

'Who is this man?' Haramis asked the Circle. 'Where does he come from?'

The questions are impertinent.

'Is he the only one of his kind?'

The question is impertinent.

'What are his plans?'

The question is impertinent.

'Where did he obtain this weapon? Does he have access to more of them?'

The questions are impertinent.

'Why have you given me Sight of him, even though he wears the Star?'

Because he is a novice, as yet without the full powers of his Guild.

Haramis uttered a grim laugh. Well, that was useful knowledge indeed! She now knew for certain that the sleeping man was no imposter but a genuine initiate of the dread body of ancient enchanters – too lacking in training to have shielded himself completely from her scrutiny as his late master had done, but adept enough to conceal his identity and intentions. The talisman's refusals also confirmed the Archimage in her suspicion that the young Star Man had fellows more powerful and dangerous than himself.

Haramis had no desire to take him prisoner, nor would she destroy his weapon. Instead, she intended to oversee his actions with her talisman and hope that he would provide valuable information about the Guild. Dealing with him – and any companions or allies he might have – would have to wait.

'I have seen enough of this vision,' she said.

Instantly, she was back in her study, seated in her chair by the cosy fire with the Black Trillium flowers blooming in the shadowed window-niche. She let the Three-Winged Circle swing free at her breast and sat back, thinking.

So the weapons came from under the sea! She had never suspected that the Vanished Ones might have lived there as well as on the land, nor had the Blue Lady ever mentioned the fact. Easygoing and unsuspicious, Iriane ruled her naive aboriginal subjects with a light hand. Most probably she would not even have noticed the Star Guild quietly seeking out forbidden weapons. Unfortunately, the sweet-natured Archimage of the Sea knew little of the perfidy of humankind.

Iriane's secretive Mere Folk, able to dwell for long periods underwater, would have to assist Haramis in retrieving and destroying those dangerous artifacts that were still hidden beneath the sea. Even more urgent would be Iriane's cooperation in hunting for the home base of the Star Men. It was more than likely that the villains had made their lair in the remote and uncharted western regions of the world-continent, or even on an island.

A chilling idea struck Haramis at that moment. She lifted her talisman. 'Show me a voor's-eye view of the Hollow Isles in the realm of the Blue Lady.'

Again the room vanished. It seemed as though Haramis soared at a great height on the pinions of a mighty lammergeier, those toothed birds of high intelligence who were her friends and helpers. She saw below another peninsula, thrusting seaward from the southwestern margin of the world. Offshore lay a sizeable cluster of islands, some barren and some clothed with unfamiliar vegetation. A few had active volcanoes that steamed gently. In her Sending she flew among the sea-girt specks of land, noting the entrances to many caves. To a human, this was a cheerless and desolate place, pounded by huge waves rolling in from the trackless Western Ocean and blasted by winds that raced for thousands of leagues, unimpeded by land. There were widely scattered settlements of Mere Folk, but she saw no trace of humanity.

'Does the Star Guild abide here?' she asked.

No, the Three-Winged Circle said. Well, that was a relief.

She studied the scene more carefully. This was a region she did not know, for no human beings had settled here – nor, so far as she knew, had any even visited the Hollow Isles. Those of her own race who had chosen not to Vanish, who had remained on the World of the Three Moons and defied the Conquering Ice, inhabited more hospitable parts of the land to the south and east. If any brave souls had ever ventured into the alien purlieus ruled by the Archimage of the Sea, they had not returned to civilized lands to tell the tale. Haramis herself had been too busy with the affairs of her own domain to explore that of Iriane.

'How far are these islands from my Tower?' Haramis asked the talisman.

Over seven thousand leagues, as the voor flies. By sea, as humans would make the journey, it is nearly eight thousand leagues.

38

'Sacred Flower!' the Archimage murmured. 'What a blessing it is that I do not have to rely upon a ship or a bird to carry me there.' She abolished the vision and returned to familiar surroundings.

Her talisman would transport her bodily to the place in a trice, as easily as a Sending. And for this exceedingly useful mode of transport she could thank dear Iriane. By teaching Haramis how to use personal magic expertly, the Blue Lady had enabled her young colleague to command the wider powers of the Three-Winged Circle in ways that Kadiya and Anigel had never been able to achieve with their talismans. Haramis knew that she owed Iriane more than she could ever repay.

'I only hope I can find her quickly.' She stared into the now empty Circle.

Haramis' talisman was not a large thing. The silvery wand had a ring at one end for the chain that suspended it about her neck, and at the other end a hoop slightly more than a handspan wide, topped by a trio of tiny wings. These enfolded a drop of glowing amber with a fossil Black Trillium in its heart, identical to the amber amulets of her two sisters. At their birth, the triplet Princesses of Ruwenda had been gifted with the magical amulets by the late Archimage Binah, who had named them Petals of the Living Trillium and prophesied for them a fearsome destiny and terrible tasks.

Living that destiny, Haramis, Kadiya, and Anigel had faced and overcome many of their own personal weaknesses. All three sisters had taken on responsibilities both awful and magnificent. Were the events now taking place leading them to a challenge greater than any they had yet faced? Like the Holy Flower, they were Three and also one. The futures of Archimage, Lady of the Eyes, and Queen were entwined inexorably whether they willed it or not . . .

Countering the Star Guild threat must then involve Kadiya and Anigel as well as herself – of that Haramis was more than certain. She decided that she would transport herself to Kadi's home immediately after speaking to the Blue Lady. The Three-Winged Circle would then carry her and her sister to Queen Anigel, who was in residence at Ruwenda Citadel. The Queen was four months pregnant, but that would not stop her from working with her husband Antar and the heads of other nations to counter the Star Guild's armed threat to the already faltering balance of the world. Kadiya would have to rally the Folk. With their ability to speak without words to each other across great distances and their intimate knowledge of the land and sea, the aborigines would be invaluable in any quest against the Star Guild.

I will also insist, Haramis decided, that Kadi now give up her impotent talisman to me for safekeeping, as she should have done long ago.

Unbonded, it could be stolen by any sneakthief – or even by the Star Men!

It was bad enough that Queen Anigel's talisman, the coronet called the Three-Headed Monster, should have gone missing during the late war with Orogastus. Losing a second piece of the Sceptre of Power would be insupportable.

Orogastus . . . She had hardly dared speak his name since his death four years ago. What was the connection between the Star Master she had loved so helplessly and this resurgence of the Guild?

Haramis rose from her seat and began to pace before the window. It was a wild night in the high mountains where her Tower stood. Snow fell thickly and a bitter wind from the icecap to the northwest howled round the casements like a chorus of demons from the ten hells. She toyed with her talisman as she brooded over events of the past.

When Orogastus began his last assault on Derorguila, the northern capital of the Two Thrones, he had in his possession not only the Three-Headed Monster and the Three-Lobed Burning Eye, but also a certain glassy container with the Star Guild emblem on its lid that could bind or unbind the talismans. He had used this crucially important star-box to transfer ownership of the Monster and the Eye from Anigel and Kadiya to himself.

The box, like the Queen's magical coronet, had disappeared in the tumult of battle.

For some time, Haramis had been certain that an unknown person had found both of these missing magical items and was now the true-bonded owner of the Three-Headed Monster. Her own empowered talisman, which would readily pinpoint the location of Kadiya's dead Eye (and which had led her without demur to the young Star Man), had steadfastly refused to reveal anything whatsoever about the missing coronet or the box that controlled its bonding.

Iriane had agreed with Haramis that this could only mean that the Three-Headed Monster's magic was fully potentiated. It had cleaved to a new owner.

And yet no great upstart sorcerer had appeared in the World of the Three Moons. The coronet's master was keeping it hidden and unused. Haramis could not imagine why–unless this person was waiting until he could also get his hands upon Kadiya's talisman and bond to it also with the star-box. Owning two parts of the Sceptre of Power, the unknown sorcerer would command magic almost surpassing that of Haramis. If this person should ally with a reborn Star Guild, equipped with the marvellous devices of the Vanished Ones, the world would certainly be lost.

40

'Lords of the Air,' Haramis prayed, 'we have had peace for these four years, and yet it is clear that the world never truly regained the balance that Orogastus upset. Is this my own fault? Is it my love for that dead sorcerer – which I confess has endured undiminished – that has left us vulnerable?'

Or might the unthinkable have happened, as it had once before?

No, thanks be to the Triune! *That* was impossible.

Haramis would remember forever the day she and her valiant sisters had turned back upon the sorcerer the destruction he would have wreaked upon them. The Flower had overcome the Star. There had been unexpected victory for the Living Trillium – and annihilation for Orogastus, even though Haramis had hoped to spare him.

The moment she had inquired of her lover's fate, and the talisman's pitiless reply, were still branded upon her heart. Standing at the embrasured window beside the Black Trillium plant she began to weep. There was a small clear area in the frosted pane. Windborne snowflakes rushed at her, seeming to be fatally drawn to the light within the room, smashing themselves into oblivion as they struck the thick leaded glass casement.

He had also been fatally drawn.

Haramis had wanted to spare Orogastus the ultimate punishment. Before their final encounter, she had placed the black hexagon called the Cynosure of the Star Guild within an ancient prison of the Vanished Ones. This place, a chasm hewn from living rock and lying deep underground, would have held the sorcerer securely no matter what magic he called upon. The Cynosure was to have drawn Orogastus to it like a magnet at the moment he exerted his ultimate powers on behalf of evil. Once in captivity, perhaps reformed by gentle persuasion and their mutual love, she hoped he might undergo a change of heart that would eventually allow her to free him.

But a tremendous earthquake had shaken that part of the world, collapsing the chasm where the Cynosure lay. The device still performed its intended magic, however, drawing Orogastus into airless, rocky chaos at the instant of his defeat.

She had asked her talisman what had become of him, and it had said: *He has gone the way of the Vanished Ones. He is no longer in this world.*

'Dead.' Haramis drew back from the window and wiped a cold hand across her streaming eyes. 'You are dead, my poor flawed sweetheart. And I am left with nothing but my sombre duty, which obliged me to destroy the only man I ever loved.'

41

And now the duties of that office must no longer be postponed. It was time for her to go in search of Iriane, then meet with her sisters. But first . . .

She lifted her talisman and looked into it. 'Three-Winged Circle, show me that which I have been afraid to conjure heretofore: a true vision of my dead love's face. I am sorely in need of comfort, and the refreshment of my memory of him is the only boon that will suffice.'

The talisman came alive, its Circle filled with pale-glowing colours. It said: *The request is impertinent.*

'What?' she cried in shock. 'You deny me this simple thing, you cruel, capricious talisman?'

The request is impertinent.

'Will you drive me mad as well as break my heart? Show him to me!'

No, the talisman replied, calmly. *I cannot show you the dead face of Orogastus because it does not exist.*

'What do you mean?' she asked sharply. 'I know he is ashes, scattered amongst red-hot subterranean rocks. I ask only to renew my memory of his features. If the world is indeed out of balance, then I must embark upon new and parlous adventures. I – I would fashion for myself a portrait of him as a consolation. And perhaps as a warning to myself as well. Surely there can be no harm in that. I command that you depict for me his face as it was during his last days in this world.'

Now your request is one I can fulfill.

The restless eddies of pearly light brightened, became solid. For a moment she saw a head encased within a dramatic silvery headdress, haloed by pointed rays, with two fearsome white stars for eyes.

'No! That is not the way I wish to remember him. Reproduce the face of the one I loved.'

The vision faded, then reformed. The countenance of a white-haired man, haggard and lined and yet strangely beautiful, seemed to gaze directly at her from within the Circle. His jaw was strong, his mouth wryly smiling. His eyes were the colour of her own – the lightest possible shade of blue, with great black pupils holding secret glints of gold.

As she drank in his image, Haramis called upon her personal powers. In her right hand she held the talisman. In her left, something ghostly and crystalline suddenly appeared, flat and slightly smaller than the Circle, glittering like an insubstantial gem.

'A portrait,' she commanded.

The lens of crystal fog darkened and became a likeness identical to that produced by the talisman, delicately painted on horik-ivory and framed in gold. The vision within the Three-Winged Circle vanished, but the sorcerer's picture was real. Haramis put it into one of the pockets of her gown, then left the study to make preparations for her magical journeying.

CHAPTER 4

After giving instructions to her Vispi chatelaine, Magira, and her steward, Shiki the Dorok, the Archimage changed into warmer clothing and put on the long cloak of her office. Its fabric was white, seeming to change with movement into that delicate blue seen in shadowed snow. The cloak was bordered with platinum bands and had on the back the emblem of the Black Trillium. She pulled its hood over her long black hair, then donned gloves.

In the silence of her private apartment she prayed for strength and success. Then, standing on the fur rug at the foot of her bed, she took up her talisman again.

'Transport me bodily to that place in the Hollow Isles where the Archimage of the Sea is.'

Her bedroom dissolved and she seemed to be within some fantastic theatrical set – a cave made of insubstantial diamonds, glittering in a hundred rainbow hues.

An eyeblink later the illusion vanished. She stood inside a genuine cavern, dank and extremely cold. Dripping stalactites hung from the ceiling like the tusks of a gigantic, slavering beast. Beneath them were inky pools into which falling water tinkled and plopped. Rock pillars, water-sculptured shapes like half-dissolved statues, and other strange formations loomed up on every side. Blobs of glowing matter that might have been fungus or even slime-dawdler colonies were scattered about the irregular surface of the cave ceiling, shedding light on the eerie scene.

'Iriane!' she cried. But no one answered and she demanded of her talisman, 'Where is the Archimage of the Sea?'

As if in answer, there came a sudden splashing from one of the larger pools. Three aborigines of a form unfamiliar to Haramis climbed out, shook themselves, and stood in a row, regarding her with luminous golden eyes.

They were of small stature, like the Nyssomu and Uisgu, but had the scaled skin of the taller forest races. Their faces were slightly muzzled like the Wyvilo and Glismak, but were otherwise human in aspect. They had webbed hands and feet with stout talons upon the three digits, and about their upper arms were rows of golden bracelets inset with coloured disks made from fish-scale. Instead of having hair, their round heads were adorned with many parallel crests tending from the brow to the nape. These and their large ears were ribbed, like the fins of fishes, with a translucent membrane connection. They wore no clothing, but the scales of their bodies seemed almost like flexible armour of green and dark blue, giving them a neat and attractive appearance.

'I offer you greetings,' Haramis said. 'I am the Archimage of the Land, and I seek my friend the Blue Lady of the Sea.'

'We will take you to her,' the Mere Folk replied in unison. Their language was unfamiliar; but, as always, her talisman let her understand the sense of it.

'May I ask your names, and to what race of Folk you belong?'

The central aborigine, who wore a necklace of the coloured disks, pointed to his heart and said, 'This one is Ansebado, First of the Lercomi, and these are the Second and Third, Milimi and Terano, also faithful subjects of the Blue Lady. If you would look upon her, follow us.'

Look upon her?

Haramis felt a tingle of apprehension. Could Iriane be ill – or had something even worse happened?

The three Lercomi set off at a rapid pace in single file, the talons of their toes clicking on the wet stone. The cave air became colder the farther they progressed, and as the temperature fell, the numbers of luminescent creatures decreased drastically. After stumbling several times in the growing darkness, Haramis held her talisman high, bidding the trillium–amber within its wings to shine more brightly and light her way.

What a dreadful place, she thought. Except for the glowing lumps, this particular Hollow Isle seemed sterile and lifeless, with no sign that thinking beings had ever made their mark upon it. There was no sign of mineral ore or anything else of value, and the aborigines did not investigate such places for amusement, as humans did. What in the world was Iriane doing here?

Haramis had not seen her friend in some time and realized now that she had greatly missed the Blue Lady's tart good humour and common sense. The Archimage of the Sea was no otherworldly mystic. She loved good food and beautiful clothing (teasing Haramis for her disinterest in either), and she had been the only one to sympathize truly with her young colleague's doomed love for Orogastus.

Haramis thought: Iriane will understand my carrying his portrait, too, while my sisters never would.

Because of her vast age and experience, the Blue Lady would almost surely know whether there was any possibility that the Vanished Ones might return – as the young Star Man had told the Skritek – and what the so-called Sky Trillium portended. Iriane might even be able to obtain the counsel of the mysterious Archimage of the Firmament concerning the rebirth of the Star Guild. The enigmatic Dark Man in the Moon had only grudgingly lent assistance during the late war, and he had ignored every attempt of Haramis to communicate with him since then.

The underground journey beneath the Hollow Isle seemed to be taking hours, leading from cavern to cavern, moving ever deeper into regions of frigid darkness. At last, after they had traversed a cramped, stalactite-fanged tunnel, the Lercomi led the Archimage into a chamber very different from the others. It was full of icy mist that was suffused with a rich blue glow, swirling and billowing like phantom draperies and concealing details of the cave's interior.

'There,' said the aboriginal spokesman, pointing toward the indistinct source of the illumination. 'The Lady is there.'

'Iriane?' Haramis' call was hesitant. She went toward the hazy light, stepping gingerly on the frost-cracked rock floor. All at once the mist thinned, and she saw ahead of her a sight that brought her up short, exclaiming with amazement.

Row upon row of the Lercomi stood in silence, with bowed heads, before what Haramis at first thought was a colossal glowing sapphire. The object was twice her height, with a darker heart. Coming closer, she found she had been mistaken in thinking it a gem.

Within the blue transparency was the ample form of a woman, standing upright. She wore an indigo gown spangled with tiny jewels that pricked out graceful designs of marine growth. A filmy cape of midnight blue fell from two pearl brooches at her shoulder. Her dark hair was elaborately dressed in coils and rolls, held in place by ornate shell combs and hairpins with pearls at the ends.

The plump arms of the Archimage of the Sea were extended in motionless, futile appeal. Her open mouth seemed to have been frozen in mid-scream and her eyes glittered with terror.

'O Triune God, no,' Haramis whispered.

'Yes. Ah, yes!' the Lercomi Folk wailed in heartbroken response.

Haramis ran forward to what she thought was a glass case imprisoning her friend. As she touched it she discovered the truth.

The Blue Lady's eyes moved, ever so slightly.

She was entombed within a great chunk of blue ice. And she was alive.

*　　*　　*

46

'Who has done this?' Haramis asked Ansebado, after some time had passed, during which she tried without success to free Iriane.

'Four humans,' the First of the Lercomi declared, 'came in a small sailboat to our village on Sundown Isle, which is half a day from here by water. Three were men and one was a woman, and they demanded that we summon the Blue Lady.'

'When did this happen?'

'Nearly twelve moons ago. We were most astonished, for the only people of your kind that we ever see are the Feathered Barbarians – and they come very seldom to trade for fireshell, gold, and precious fish-scale, and never during the stormy time of year.

'These human persons were lofty in demeanour and atrociously rude. Each one wore a Star hanging on a chain. When we asked their reasons for wanting audience with the Lady they did not answer, but instead killed several of our old people by means of awesome magic. They repeated their demand, threatening to destroy our children next, and then all of our tribe if we did not hasten to do their bidding. We had no choice but to give in. No choice! Do you understand, White Lady?'

Haramis said nothing. The Mereman continued:

'We explained that our Blue Lady's magical portal is here, in Flyaway Isle. The strangers compelled the three of us to bring them here to the cave. Then . . . this one made the perfidious Call. As First of the Lercomi, it was my melancholy duty. But if I had known what would happen, I would have begged those brutes to slay us all instead.'

He began to weep, and the Second and Third also, and in another minute the entire crowd of little people in the blue misty cavern howled and sobbed in contrition, striking their crested heads on the ground. Haramis calmed them and commanded that the rest of the story be told.

Ansebado said, 'No sooner had the Archimage of the Sea stepped from her enchanted door (which lies right behind her, even now) than the awful deed was done. The female stranger, one having flame-coloured hair, used a magical device that sprinkled the poor Lady with some gelid astral liquid. She froze instantly. Further sprinkling produced the blue ice-block that you see. No fire can melt it. No prayer can banish it. Not even your own magic can overcome it! The name of the Lercomi Mere Folk will stink throughout the Sea Realm forever, for we have condemned our dear Blue Lady to living death.'

'Perhaps not,' Haramis said none too kindly, lifting her talisman to forestall another mournful hubbub. 'This ice is not true magic, but something else appertaining to the Vanished Ones and their science. I cannot free the Blue Lady now, but perhaps a way might be found.'

Ansebado and his people fell on their faces to thank her, but she ordered them to arise, pull themselves together, and answer more questions.

Haramis learned that the human villains were all dressed in the silver-and-black robes of the Star Guild. They were none of them above thirty years in age, were of differing stature, and all save the redheaded woman had hair of grizzled grey or dull white. Each Star Guildsman carried a dissimilar ancient weapon: one killed by boiling the blood, another threw forth a deadly small thunderbolt, the third provoked fatal convulsions, and the fourth, much larger than the others and more complex in aspect, had ensorcelled the Blue Lady.

'The malefactors stayed with us for several days,' Ansebado said, 'questioning us about the underwater regions hereabouts where the Vanished Ones once flourished. Then another sailboat came with two more Star Men. One of them was young, of no special distinction save for his loud and bullying speech. But the other human was different from all the rest. He was much older, and he wore a many-rayed starburst headpiece of silvered leather that concealed his upper face while leaving the back of his head uncovered. His long hair was as pale as the platinum of his Star.'

Haramis gave a low cry. Ice seemed to have congealed in her own vitals. This could not be. Must not be . . .

She found herself asking, 'Was – was he tall?'

'Taller than the others, who gave him great reverence and called him Master. He came into this cavern, stepped into the portal of the Blue Lady, and disappeared. The others waited for some hours, whereupon he reappeared. Then the lot of them got into the boats and went away.'

'Oh, Lords of the Air,' Haramis whispered. With her gloved fingers stiff and clumsy, she drew the gold-framed small picture out of her robe and was barely able to ask her last question. 'And was this the Star Master?'

The little aborigine frowned at the portrait, then replied. 'His face was partly masked by the starry headgear. But, yes. It was he. He had eyes like that. Eyes like yours, White Lady.'

Pain, born in her swelling heart, was spreading like molten metal through the entire body of the Archimage of the Land. It was a jubilant hurting, mingled with stark fear. She spoke in a voice made unsteady by emotion.

'Since the Blue Lady's imprisonment, have the Lercomi Folk visited underwater ruins of the Vanished Ones at the Star Men's behest?'

'Nay,' said Ansebado, 'but we have heard that other Mere tribes have been compelled to do so. They have gathered certain ancient artifacts coveted by the Star Men, but none of them knows what these things might be, nor do we.'

But Haramis knew. 'I will come to you again, Ansebado. Command your Folk to watch by the imprisoned Blue Lady until then. Should any person emerge from her magical portal, bespeak me at once, even if you must lay down your lives to do so. Now farewell.'

She clasped her talisman and commanded her magic to take her to Kadiya.

CHAPTER 5

Queen Anigel stared at the plate of food before her, a simple grilled fillet of garsu fish and a helping of glazed dorun tuber, and put down her knife and fork. 'I confess that Hara's dreadful account of the poor Blue Lady has robbed me of my appetite. It pierces my very soul to know that there is nothing we can do to free her from that hellish enchantment.'

'If Iriane is frozen stiff,' Kadiya said reasonably, 'she cannot be suffering. What good can it do her if you pine and starve yourself?'

'You are ever practical,' Anigel said with a sigh. 'But hard-hearted.'

'Nonsense,' said the Lady of the Eyes, taking a goodly helping of bittercress salad and pouring rich cheese dressing over it. 'One must sympathize with the troubles of others, but not to the point of impairing one's own good health – especially if one has duties of state to perform. Don't you agree, Hara?'

The Archimage inclined her head. 'My talisman refuses to confirm my suspicions, but I believe that Iriane's imprisonment may be only the beginning of a new time of peril for all of us. The return of the Star Guild, and the possibility that Orogastus may be gathering weapons of the Vanished Ones, poses a grave danger to the peace and good balance of the world. It may be that we Three will once again be called upon, and if this be so, then we will need all of the physical and mental strength we can muster. And you, dearest little Sister, have important personal obligations as well.'

Queen Anigel received this admonition in chilly silence. But she began with obvious reluctance to eat.

The triplets were at dinner in Ruwenda Citadel, seated at the high table with the Queen presiding, while others of the court feasted at lower boards in the torch-lit great hall. There were many persons missing—including King Antar and his military advisers – and the usual cheerful conviviality attending the evening meal was absent. Less than an hour earlier, the magic of Haramis had transported Kadiya and herself to the Citadel, where they had reported to the Laboruwendian court not only the misfortune

50

of the Archimage of the Sea but also the apparent resurgence of the Star Guild under the leadership of Orogastus.

The latter piece of news had caused a furore, since only a single day now remained before the departure of the royal entourage on the long journey to Labornok. King Antar, Marshal Lakanilo, and General Gorkain had sequestered themselves in order to make hasty plans for increasing the security of the train, leaving the Queen and her two sisters to speculate upon what the dire events might portend.

'At the present time,' the Archimage said, 'only the Lords of the Air know what Orogastus's long-range plans might be. But we can be assured that they involve the conquest of the world — both by physical means and by dark sorcery.'

Anigel added more crystallized honey to her cup of darci tea and stirred it morosely. 'I find it hard to believe that once again that evil man has cheated death. Who would ever have thought such a thing possible? Hara, how could your talisman have deceived you about his fate?'

It was Kadiya who made the unpalatable reply. 'The talisman spoke true – only the Archimage misinterpreted its words.'

Haramis admitted the accusation with a doleful nod. She brought forth the portrait of Orogastus and put it on the table before them. 'When I requested a view of his dead face, the talisman could not comply. Only when I worded the command differently, avoiding the mention of death, did it show me his likeness so that I could fashion this picture.'

Now the Lady of the Eyes cried fiercely, 'Damn that wizard! For all we know, he has already found the star-box and bonded Ani's Three-Headed Monster to himself!'

'No,' Haramis stated positively. 'My talisman indicates that he has not. Some other person has the coronet and the box – but the Circle will not tell me who.'

Kadiya took up her tableknife and with precision sliced a drumstick from the succulent roasted togar on the platter before her. 'You may wager platinum to plarr-pits that Orogastus will seek out this coy new magician and attempt an alliance.'

'You are probably right, Kadi,' Anigel said. 'And this is all the more reason why you should heed Hara's counsel, and give up your own impotent talisman into her safekeeping so that neither villain gets hold of it.'

'Never!' Kadiya said through her mouthful of meat. 'Even though the Three Moons tumble from the firmament!'

'Oh, Kadi,' cried the exasperated Queen. 'It is the only safe course and you know it.'

'All very well for you to say,' muttered the Lady of the Eyes, pointing

51

in accusation with the fowl's legbone, 'having given up your own talisman to Orogastus in ransom –'

'Thus saving the life of the King my husband!' Anigel exclaimed in high dudgeon. 'Should I have let Antar die in captivity?'

'You did not give Hara and me time to rescue him,' Kadiya retorted, 'but capitulated to the kidnappers with unseemly haste, opening the way to the invasion of your kingdom.'

Very quietly, so that none of the other supping courtiers noticed, the Queen began to weep. 'You are right. I was at fault – but so are you. Your Three-Lobed Burning Eye is sure to be stolen by Orogastus or this unknown wizard sooner or later. My own foolishness and your stubborn vainglory may yet doom us all.'

'For shame, Kadi,' the Archimage said, taking her youngest sister in her arms. 'Have you forgotten that Ani is with child and should not be upset?'

'She is as rugged as a draft-volumnial dropping its yearly calf, for all her fragile looks,' Kadiya remarked callously. 'And do not either of you think to convince me to give up my talisman through this soppy charade.'

Anigel ceased crying. She sat up, wiped her eyes with a napkin, and shrugged. 'It was worth the try,' she said sweetly.

'By the Flower!' the Archimage said, chagrined as much by the Queen's artful deception as by Kadiya's intransigence. 'You two will drive me to distraction.'

'No, dear Hara,' said Anigel, now in deadly earnest. 'We will rather do whatever must be done to help you conquer the Star Men and restore the balance of the world, no matter *what* the personal cost.' She turned to her other sister with a steely glance. 'Is it not so, Kadi?'

'Oh . . . lothok dung!' cried the Lady of the Eyes, flinging the drumstick down onto her plate. 'I suppose I will have to give in. You shall have the Burning Eye, Hara. What matter if my pride is in rags and my confidence undermined?'

'It is for the best,' the Archimage said, with evident relief.

'May I keep the talisman with me until we Three separate, at least?' Kadiya asked.

'Certainly. There can be no danger here within the Citadel. I know for a certainty that there are no viaducts here, through which Orogastus or his agents might enter and steal the Eye.'

'Those triply bedamned magical bolt-holes!' Kadiya exclaimed. 'You had better explain to Ani about them so she is forewarned.'

'Viaducts?' the Queen frowned. 'Do you mean such as carried Hara from the Land of Fire and Ice to the home of the Archimage Iriane, when the Blood Trillium estranged us Three?'

'Yes,' Haramis said. She pushed aside dishes and tableware, laid out a large clean napkin, and touched her talisman to it. There was a faint smell of scorched linen, and immediately the cloth became a wondrously detailed map of the world-continent. 'The viaducts are not truly magic, even though they seem so to us who know little of the science behind their making. Behold the viaduct portals.'

Anigel exclaimed in amazement, for the map became peppered with innumerable scarlet pinpoint dots. 'So many!'

'And now,' said the Archimage, 'since Orogastus stole a certain book belonging to Iriane that explained their operation, they are accessible to the sorcerer and his Star Guild.'

Kadiya said, 'The villains are capable of popping up out of any one of those points like ziklu from a warren, and they can also go to ground through them, escaping their pursuers. Hara is thus far unable to destroy the viaducts or close them with her magic.'

'It seems that the Vanished Ones used these passageways for casual travel about their world,' the White Lady explained. 'To ordinary people, the viaduct openings are invisible and imperceptible. But if one knows more or less where the portal is, it is only necessary to utter the proper arcane command – "viaduct system activate" – whereupon it becomes visible and operative. Some of the viaducts were destroyed in the great conflict between the Vanished Ones and the Star Guild, but these on the map remain. Heretofore, they have been used only by the Archimages of yore and by the sindona, when they venture forth from the Place of Knowledge.'

Kadiya said, 'You'll be interested to know, Ani, that *this* viaduct'– she stabbed her finger at one of the dots – 'opens right into Zotopanion Keep in the Winter Palace of Labornok! It was the way by which both Iriane and the sindona gained access to the keep during the climax of the Battle of Derorguila.'

'Holy Flower!' cried the dismayed Queen. 'Is there no way of getting rid of these abominable tunnels?'

'My talisman says there is,' Haramis replied. 'However, its instructions are given in archaic scientific gibberish and so far I can make no sense of it. When I return to my Tower I will look further into the matter of obliterating the viaducts, but for the present we shall have to barricade them instead. All that are in critical locations must be enclosed within sturdy cages or earthen mounds, and be heavily guarded withal.'

Anigel studied the map intently. 'There are not so many portals in the

Mazy Mire as elsewhere, but here is one not far from the Queen's Mireway. I wonder . . . The trip to the Winter Capital will be so lengthy and tedious in the early rains. If, as you say, there is a viaduct leading directly to Zotopanion Keep –'

'Do not contemplate it for a moment!' Haramis said, aghast. 'Only one adept in the science of the Vanished Ones dare use the things. Sometimes their routing is fixed and one has no control over the ultimate destination. At other times, if a kind of complex magical spell is recited before entry, the viaduct carries the traveller to the location that is specified. But if this spell is not said properly, the person risks emerging within the Sempiternal Icecap or even deep beneath the sea.'

She pointed again to the map, and it was indeed true that some of the scarlet dots were in perilous places.

'Damn,' said the dainty Queen. Her fair hair was bound up with ribbons of a gold so deep it was nearly brown, and she wore a loose-fitting smocked satin gown of the same colour, trimmed with worram-fur and adorned with a collar of trillium-amber. Her pregnancy of four months was still unnoticeable. 'I would have gladly whisked myself and the court by viaduct from here to Derorguila and spared us the long journey in the rain.'

'I could transport you, Antar, and the children,' Haramis offered, albeit hesitantly, 'even though carrying others strains my magic to the utmost.'

But the Queen shook her head. 'It was but a jest, Hara. I would not dream of asking you to exhaust yourself. No, we must go to Labornok with the others of the court entourage, as is fitting.'

'I shall give each of you copies of this map to keep,' the Archimage said. 'Ani, you will have to arrange for soldiers – preferably with aboriginal helpers – to stand guard at those viaduct openings in critical places within Labornok and Ruwenda. I shall command Kadi's Folk to watch the terminals in more remote regions – the Mazy Mire, the Ohogan Mountains, and the Tassaleyo Forest. If members of the Star Guild are seen, the Folk will sound the alarm using the speech without words.'

'What of the viaducts in other nations?' inquired the Queen.

'I have already bespoken a warning,' Haramis said. 'Every civilized country will soon be on the lookout for suspicious persons wearing Stars.'

'The scoundrels can wreak no sorcery without their medallions,' Kadiya explained to Anigel. 'Unfortunately, this does not hold true for their use of weapons of the Vanished Ones, which are not truly magical but partake of the same ancient science as the viaducts and those antique artifacts one may purchase from certain traders.'

'How shall we defend ourselves against Star Men equipped with such dread armaments?' asked the Queen in apprehension. 'If only Hara had not destroyed those weapons that had been deployed by the forces of Tuzamen and Raktum during the Battle of Derorguila! We might have made good use of them ourselves.'

'We still have our magic,' the Archimage said. 'And if the Triune wills it, we will also soon have an alliance of every nation under the Three Moons to counter the much smaller forces of those loyal to the Star. After giving warning to the other nations, I also requested that they dispatch special envoys in fast ships to Derorguila. The delegations should have arrived by the time the royal retinue of Laboruwenda completes its journey to the flatlands. We will hold a conclave of mutual defence there in your capital in forty days.'

'I will gladly assist you and my Royal Husband in rallying the nations,' said Queen Anigel. 'I suppose Kadi will be doing the same work amongst the Folk.'

'Not for some time,' the Lady of the Eyes said, 'for I have been given a larger job to do. Only one state balked at Hara's plan of alliance: Sobrania.'

The Queen assumed a rueful face. 'I might have known. The Feathered Barbarians are so fearful of plots against them by Galanar or the Imlit and Okamisi republics that they resist any pact that infringes upon their much-vaunted independence. Emperor Denombo of Sobrania is an honourable man, according to his lights – but impetuous and short-sighted, and hardly inclined to concern himself with nations other than his own collection of fractious tribes. Will you go to him, Kadi, and attempt persuasion?'

'Yes, may the Flower defend me. Hara has commanded it and I will willingly obey.'

'She will also have another task.' The Archimage spoke more quietly, even though musicians had begun to play the introduction to the night's entertainment, making such a noise that eavesdropping seemed impossible. 'I told you of observing a young Star Man in the mountains above Zinora. He had with him feathered saddlebags of Sobranian make. This could be a meaningless detail . . . or it might be a valuable clue.'

'To the location of the Star Guild headquarters!' Queen Anigel's eyes, blue as the Dry Time sky, sparkled with excitement. 'Have you any other indication pointing to Sobrania?'

'None as yet,' Haramis admitted, 'for my talisman is powerless to descry Guildsmen who are in full control of the Star's magic. It was only good fortune – or the kindness of the Lords of the Air – that enabled me to detect and Send to that young Star Man who incited the Skritek. He was a novice, not yet fully adept in commanding the Star's protection, perhaps

55

undertaking a mission of minor import while his fellows deal with weightier conspiracies.'

They left off talking for a moment while pages cleared the table of earlier courses of food, brought in tarts and fresh fruit, and refilled the wine goblets. Then there was a fanfare of buglehorns. A troupe of Tuzameni acrobats pranced into the hall to much applause.

'But how,' the Queen asked Haramis under cover of the renewed noise, 'will Kadi hope to spy out the Star Men in Sobrania, if your own great magic is powerless to do so?'

'Eyes,' said Kadiya laconically. 'Not Three-Lobed Burning ones, but the two that God set into my head. Wherever the Star Men hide – and it might well be in a backward place like the Land of the Feathered Barbarians – the scoundrels must eat and sleep. And unless they subsist wretchedly as wanderers in the wilderness they require a permanent dwelling of fair size, food to eat, clean clothes to wear, beasts to ride when they are not zipping hither and yon through magical viaducts, and a corps of servants to keep all these things in order. Nor will they go invisible at all times, for that takes much effort. If they are hiding in Sobrania I will find them. If they are not, I will look elsewhere, as Hara instructs me.'

'The Star Men will know that you search for them,' Anigel said baldly. 'They will descry you through sorcery and hunt you down.'

'Have you forgotten,' Kadiya said, pretending to watch the performers with an idle smile, 'how we Three, as young princesses, fled for our lives from Orogastus, his Voices, and the evil King Voltrik? None of those miscreants could seek us out through magic, because we were protected then . . . as we are protected now.'

She drew from the shirt beneath her forester's jerkin a faintly glowing amber pendant with a fossil Black Trillium within, swinging upon a golden chain. 'Only the three talismans of the Sceptre of Power were able to countermand the magic of the Flower.'

'Ah,' breathed the Queen, smiling with relief. 'Of course. I fear that I take its magic too much for granted.' Her hand moved briefly to touch her bodice, where her own amulet was hidden.

Haramis smiled. Her trillium-amber nestled within the silvery wings of the Circle wand hanging about her neck. 'Kadi will be shielded from the oversight of those who would do her harm through magic. The amber has other powers, but that one is perhaps the most valuable.'

'The Star Men or their followers may still recognize my person as I go among them,' Kadiya admitted, 'as I may know them by their Stars. But I will disguise myself and my travelling party well. Perhaps, if I can persuade the amber to obey, I will even be able to go invisible!'

'If you take any of your Mirc Folk with you to Sobrania, you will be conspicuous,' Anigel warned. 'The aborigines of that distant region are said to be much different in appearance from those of the Peninsula.'

'I must take Jagun, for his counsel is necessary, as is his ability to speak without words across long distances and keep me in touch with Haramis. My other comrades on this quest will be human . . . Ani, I ask that you find six of your most valiant young Oathed Companions to accompany me as volunteers. The Wyvilo will take us down the Great Mutar to Var and the sea. I have friends in the Varonian capital who will provide us with a ship and all other things necessary for the Sobranian quest.'

The acrobats did a spectacular turn and the Queen clapped her hands dutifully. 'It seems you have thought of everything. Of course I will find you six brave knights. More, if you wish.'

'I would travel lightly and swiftly. Six will suffice.'

'There is still great danger in the enterprise,' Haramis noted. 'And as you have said, if Orogastus should once again obtain a working talisman, not even trillium-amber would prevent him from viewing and listening to all of us. With a talisman, he could locate you easily, Kadi. I do not know if he could slay you while you wear the amber, but you would ill serve our cause embedded in a block of blue ice like poor Iriane.'

Kadiya grinned at the Archimage. 'It is your job to see that does not happen. Keep me under surveillance as best you can, and warn me of danger if you are able to. I will find the Star Men's nest and smoke them out like night-carolers from a honey-tree.'

'You will act only according to our agreed plan!' the Archimage admonished. 'You must not attack Orogastus or the Star Guild on your own!'

Kadiya sketched a mocking bow. 'Of course not, White Lady.'

'Forgive my abruptness,' Haramis apologized. 'But for the love of God, Kadi – promise me to eschew any rash action.'

'You must take great care,' Anigel added. 'I feel guilty – my own task is so much easier and safer than yours. Dearest Kadi, I would accompany you myself, together with all my knights of the Oathed Company, if I were bearing but a single babe and not triplets.'

'Triplets!' Both Kadiya and the Archimage were astounded.

'Immu has only lately been certain of it,' the Queen said, referring to the little old Nyssomu woman who had been midwife to their own unfortunate mother, Queen Kalanthe, and later the nurse and trusted friend to the sisters.

'Can this pregnancy be another omen?' Haramis wondered. 'Might these also be children of high and awful destiny, as we Three were?'

Anigel placed a reassuring hand on that of the Archimage. 'More likely it is an entirely natural thing. At any rate, Immu says that all of my unborn babes are boys, so the Petals of the Living Trillium need fear no usurpers.'

'Idiot!' laughed Kadiya, and turned in her chair to embrace and kiss Anigel. 'May the Flower bless you and your new sons. Antar must be so proud.'

'He is,' said the Queen, 'and so are my two eldest children. Only Tolivar seems dismayed by the prospect. Twelve is such a difficult age, when a boy is on the brink of manhood and torn by unfamiliar emotions. Poor Tolo has always been plagued by self-doubt and envy of his older brother and sister, and he seems now to resent the impending birth of the babes. But when he sees them, I am sure he will love them dearly.'

Haramis and Kadiya exchanged glances over their sister's head. Young Prince Tolivar was a secretive and jealous boy who had been a thorough-going brat not too many years earlier. He bitterly resented being subordinate to Crown Prince Nikalon, who at fifteen was not only taller and better looking but also considerably more popular with the courtiers and common people. Princess Janeel, a year younger than Niki and clever as a she-fedok, had never been able to resist teasing her little brother, whom she thought deficient in character. Tolo loathed her heartily in return.

Over the years, Kadiya had made a special effort to be kind to the unhappy younger Prince; but she feared he might think she was only taking pity on him. Tolivar seemed to have no real affection for either of his illustrious aunts and had been barely civil when presented to them tonight before dinner.

Kadiya now studied the lad, who sat with the other royal and noble youth at one of the tables not far from the triplet sisters. Crown Prince Nikalon and Princess Janeel were laughing and throwing coins with the others as the acrobats retired, but Tolivar only sat with his elbows on the table, an inscrutable expression on his face.

The boy's mire-name was Hiddenheart. And Kadiya thought that it suited him only too well.

'Tolo needs to be given useful work to do,' she said. 'Ani, have you ever considered cutting him free of your apron strings? Letting him leave the court for a time, so he would not constantly compare himself to Niki or feel belittled by Jan?'

'He was always my baby,' Anigel confessed, 'and since he was restored to me four years ago I have kept him close to me, hoping that my love would suffice to boost his fragile self-esteem. But perhaps you are right. The newborn sons will take all of my attention for some time, and Tolo might possibly feel worse than ever.'

'Let the lad accompany me,' Kadiya said impulsively. 'Perhaps not as

58

far as Sobrania, but at least during the first part of my mission. Jagun and I will keep him so busy he'll have no time to sulk or feel sorry for himself.'

'He is so young,' Anigel said, looking doubtful, 'and his body is not strong.'

Kadiya's expression was sardonic. 'He survived being snatched by pirates and held captive by Orogastus. Even though he is a bit lacking in stature, he is robust enough. Do not overprotect the boy, Ani. We may not deny children the right to encounter and overcome great obstacles. Such can turn even a shy or petulant soul heroic.'

'As I myself know full well,' the Queen admitted, smiling. 'What do you think, Hara?'

'The idea has merit,' said the Archimage, 'provided that the lad is carefully supervised. Is not the retired stablemaster Ralabun his close friend? He is a responsible person, if not overly endowed with brains. Perhaps he could accompany Tolo.'

'Let us put it to the boy himself,' Kadiya suggested. 'I would not take him, were he unwilling.'

'Very well.' Queen Anigel gave in with reluctance. 'But if he accepts, you must promise to send him home before you venture beyond the Peninsula.'

'He and Ralabun can catch a fast Engian cutter to Labornok from Mutavari,' Kadiya said, 'and with fair winds, reach Derorguila not too long after the arrival of the royal entourage. What say we speak to the boy right now?'

'We may as well.' The Queen beckoned to a page, telling him to summon Prince Tolivar to the high table.

CHAPTER 6

Tolo's mouth tightened as the message was given to him.

'Now what trouble have you got yourself into?' Princess Janeel inquired. 'Have you filled too many wagons with boxes of your precious books?'

'Perhaps,' Crown Prince Nikalon suggested, 'he decided to take so many that there was no room for his boots or underwear.'

That set the entire table of young people to laughing. Tolo flushed and lowered his head to hide his anger as he accompanied the page to the high table and bowed deeply.

'How may I serve you, Great Queen and Mother?' he inquired. All expression had now been banished from his features. He was a thin lad with fair hair and skin that was very pale, as though he spent too much time sequestered indoors.

'Your Aunt Kadiya has a proposition to put to you,' Anigel said.

The Lady of the Eyes explained in some detail, not minimizing the hardships of the expedition, for they would travel downstream when the Great Mutar was in flood, and the seas on his journey home from Var would doubtless be wracked by storms.

To Anigel's surprise, Prince Tolivar's listlessness dropped away like the husk of an emergent nas-beetle. His eyes shone with excitement and he exclaimed, 'Oh, yes, Aunt Kadi! Take me and Ralabun with you! I promise to obey you in everything, and never complain or shirk my duties or vex you.'

'Then it is settled,' the Lady of the Eyes said, clapping the boy on the shoulder.

'I only wish you would let me help in your quest against the Star Men,' Tolivar said stoutly.

The three women laughed.

'You are brave, but still too young,' said the Archimage.

'The world must be saved from Orogastus,' the lad said in a low voice. 'I have personal knowledge of his evil and treacherous ways. If necessary, I would give my life to destroy him.'

'It will suffice if you serve your aunt faithfully,' said the Queen. 'Leave graver matters to those older and wiser.'

'Yes, Mother.' The Prince's demeanour could not have been more respectful and docile. He bowed and took his leave from the great hall, saying he was eager to tell the exciting news to Ralabun.

'Poor Tolo.' Anigel's concerned gaze followed her son. 'He was so deeply affected by his time of captivity with Orogastus. He still feels guilty because he believed the sorcerer's lies about becoming his heir and his apprentice in enchantment.'

'He was too immature then to understand the enormity of his actions,' the Archimage said kindly.

But the Queen shook her head. 'He was eight years old, and capable of knowing evil. Again and again he has besought Antar and me to forgive him for repudiating us, and we have tried with all our hearts to reassure him. But his guilt remains unassuaged. Kadi . . . be kind to him. Try to ease his troubled spirit.'

'I will do what I can,' said the Lady of the Eyes, 'but I suspect Tolo's healing will come only with time. And with some atoning action he himself must perform.'

'The times are perilous,' Haramis said with a sigh. 'There will be dangers and challenges and opportunities for heroism sufficient for all of us, even the young Prince. Pray that we will measure up to them, Sisters. Pray with all your hearts and souls, for I cannot help but feel that some fresh disaster will confront us very soon.'

Long after the midnight hour he dared to unlock his iron strongbox, which he had refused to let the servants take away until the very moment of the caravan's departure. He took out the smaller cloth bag, unwrapped the Three-Headed Monster, and held it in trembling hands. The silvery coronet shone in the light of the guttering candle on the bedside stand, shadows making the awful faces carved upon it seem almost alive.

Did he dare? Was there a chance of success if he did?

The unexpected great opportunity had come almost like a miracle, but it would not last long. He placed the coronet upon his head, took a deep breath, and strove to speak without faltering.

'Three-Headed Monster,' he whispered, 'you belong to me! Answer me true: If I obtain the dead Three-Lobed Burning Eye from my Aunt Kadiya and place it in the star-box, will it bond to me?'

For a moment, nothing happened. Then a mysterious voice within his own head replied: *Yes. If you press the coloured gems within the box in*

consecutive order, the Eye will cleave to you alone, slaying any other person
who presumes to touch it without your permission.

'Will the Eye obey my commands?'

It will, if the commands are pertinent.

Tolivar nearly shouted with elation. 'Can – can you make me invisible
so that I may enter my aunt's room without her seeing me?'

The question is impertinent.

The Prince nearly burst into tears of frustration. Not again! Not now!
'Make me invisible! I command you!'

The request is impertinent.

The talisman would sometimes obey his commands – especially when
he asked it simple questions, or bade it give him Sight of some person or
place far distant – but more often it spoke that maddening phrase of
refusal. His attempts at sorcery, undertaken either in the hut out in the
mire or in his other hiding place in the Derorguila ruins, had always been
timid and hesitant and not often successful. Tolivar had good reason to
be afraid of his talisman. Sometimes, for reasons unknown, the power
would turn upon the one who wielded it. This had happened to Orogastus
while Tolivar was his hostage. The sorcerer had not been seriously hurt.

But even though there was danger, Tolivar could not let this fortuitous
opportunity pass by.

'I will not give way to faintheartedness,' the Prince said to himself.
'After all, the Monster did make me invisible once before, when I first
obtained it.' He squeezed his eyes shut, breathed slowly in and out until
he felt calmer, and then spoke to the talisman again, this time choosing
his words with care.

'Instruct me how I may become invisible.'

Visualize the deed to be accomplished and then command it.

Could it be that simple? Was the talisman's operation triggered by his
thoughts, then, rather than by spoken words? Was that the great secret
to successful wizardry? It was a notion that the boy had never considered
before. Had he perhaps done the visualization inadvertently earlier on,
when issuing the successful magical commands?

Let it be! Please, let it be!

With his eyes still closed, Tolivar conjured a picture of himself within
his imagination, sitting on the bed in his room, wearing the coronet.
Keeping the vision clear, he caused his body to fade away like dissipating
smoke. He did not speak until the imaginary bedroom was empty.

'Talisman,' he intoned, 'now render me invisible.' He waited for a few
heartbeats, then opened his eyes. Slowly, he lifted his hand in front of
his face.

He saw nothing but the room and its furniture.

There was a small mirror mounted on the wall near the washstand, and he rushed to it. No face returned his gaze into the glass! The talisman had obeyed him.

He sat down on a stool and pulled off his boots (which immediately became visible once they dropped from his hands), and ran on tiptoe to the door. There he paused as a thought struck him, inspired by the reappearing boots. Would the Burning Eye seem to vanish when he picked it up? If it did not, and if Aunt Kadiya woke and saw it wafting away from her, borne by a magical force, she might lash out with her dagger. Invisible or not, if that happened he might be wounded or even killed.

He experimented, lifting the silver pitcher from its basin on the wash-stand, and uttered a groan of disappointment. Horrors! The thing *did* remain quite visible, seeming to float in mid-air. But then he collected himself, once more closed his eyes, and imagined that the pitcher disappeared. Without speaking aloud this time, he formulated a thought-command:

Talisman, render the pitcher invisible.

He opened his eyes. His fingers still grasped a smooth metal handle and his arm muscles were aware of a weight being held. But he saw nothing. Carefully, he put the invisible pitcher back into its basin. He heard a faint clink, withdrew his hand momentarily, then poked the unseen vessel. It was there, all right.

He found himself smothering a delighted laugh. He was getting the hang of it! Not even speech was truly needed. The thought was what counted in wreaking magic.

'Is that true?' he asked the talisman.

And the voice within him said: *Yes.*

Serious again, he caused the pitcher to reappear. Then he slipped out into the corridor and headed for his Aunt Kadiya's room.

She had kept it, as always, at her side in bed; but when she awoke the next morning the Three-Lobed Burning Eye was gone, leaving only its empty scabbard. Jagun swore to her that no one had entered, for he had slept just outside her door. The Citadel servants and guards had noticed nothing unusual. Nevertheless the Burning Eye had undeniably been stolen.

What was worse, Haramis' Three-Winged Circle refused to show the whereabouts of the magical pointless sword, nor would it say who was the thief.

'This can only mean,' the White Lady said to her two badly shaken sisters, 'that Kadi's talisman is now bonded to another and empowered. There is no use attempting a physical search of Ruwenda Citadel. It is too vast, with countless potential hiding places. Besides, the thief is no doubt long gone with his booty. A search would not only be futile, it would also trumpet the fact of the second talisman's theft and dishearten the people. Only we Three and Jagun must know of this.'

'Now we are surely lost,' the Queen said, her voice heavy with despair. 'All this time, one of my own courtiers has had both the star-box and my purloined coronet! And now he owns the Burning Eye as well. The wretch is probably already on his way to a rendezvous with Orogastus! The situation is hopeless.'

'Don't talk like a fool, Ani,' snapped Kadiya. 'We will carry on – as we did once before when the sorcerer himself owned two talismans. Now *that* was a time seeming to be truly without hope – and yet we prevailed. If the Triune wills, we shall do so this time also.'

On the following day the three sisters said their farewells and quit Ruwenda Citadel.

The Archimage Haramis used her magic to transport herself instantly to her Tower on Mount Brom. There she began preparing proposals for the defensive conference in Derorguila, as well as devising instructions for those Folk who were to be entrusted with the blockade of the viaducts. After that she intended to search her own archives and those of the Blue Lady, in the hope of discovering a way to either control the invisible portals or destroy them. She was not optimistic of swift success.

Kadiya, Prince Tolivar, Ralabun, and six of the Queen's valorous Oathed Companions set off on the first leg of their journey to far Sobrania. The Prince was allowed to bring along a locked iron box of modest size, which he said contained certain of his most valued books.

Lightweight boats drawn by rimoriks would carry them through Lake Wum. After bypassing Tass Falls they were to travel down the Great Mutar through the vast Tassaleyo Forest to the Wyvilo town of Let, where they would take passage on an aboriginal tradeboat bound for the kingdom of Var and the Southern Sea.

The caravan with Queen Anigel, King Antar, and all of their court began the long journey northward to Labornok, which was expected to take at least thirty days. The Wet Time was now well and truly begun, and unrelenting rain poured down upon the long train of coaches, carts, riders, and foot travellers like a cataract from heaven.

In spite of the inclement weather, the advance of the slowly moving royal entourage through the swamp was marked by many a furtive eye.

CHAPTER 7

By the time the travelling court was ten days out of the Citadel, Anigel was bored to death riding in her lumbering great carriage with Immu and the four ladies-in-waiting. The new Queen's Mireway, opened only the previous year, was living up to its reputation as a great marvel of the world. It was as sturdy as any dryland thoroughfare, even in the exceptionally heavy rains that plagued the trip this year, and Anigel saw no reason why she should not go riding up and down the procession visiting and sightseeing, as the King and the royal children and the male members of the nobility did.

The women were shocked at her daring and tried to dissuade her, but the Queen swept their objections aside. After all, it was *her* mireway. For nearly six years she had supervised its construction, eking out funds from a shaky budget, coping with rebellious Glismak road-gangs and other aboriginal problems, and bolstering the confidence of engineers who insisted that certain sections of the thoroughfare could never be built.

Anigel lowered the coach window and called to a page riding hard by. 'Summon the Royal Fronial Master.' She smiled at the perturbed noble ladies around her. 'I refuse to travel shut up in a stuffy coach like an invalid simply because I am with child. It will not harm my unborn babes if I take to the saddle in the honest Ruwendian rain.'

'But such things are not done by pregnant queens!' exclaimed Lady Belineel. She was of an ancient Labornoki family, and only too eager to voice disapproval of the more easygoing Ruwendian customs.

Surprisingly, the old Nyssomu nurse Immu piped up in support of Belineel. 'Your mireway is not Derorguila High Street, my Queen. It traverses some of the most dangerous country in the Peninsula, particularly in this section, and there is a scent of Skritek spawn in the air. I beg you to stay in the carriage.'

'Nonsense,' said Anigel. 'I smell only muck and wet leaves and the spoor of harmless tarenials – and someone's oversweet perfume, which is giving me a headache.' She called out the carriage window to the middle-aged peer she had caused to be summoned. 'Lord Karagil, pray bring me a mount at once, and have my Oathed Companions attend me. I will ride for the rest of the day.'

'This is very unwise,' Immu said grumpily. 'One shouldn't take chances when spawn are about.'

The Fronial Master was equally dismayed at Anigel's decision. 'The Oddling nurse is right about the Skritek, my Queen, for our scouts have come upon fresh sign. It is unusual for the horrid offspring of the Drowners to range this far east, but –'

'Obey me,' said the Queen, her voice low and pleasant but her intent unshaken. 'If my Oathed Companions cannot protect me from Skritek spawn, then it is time they turned in their swords and took up fancy needlework. I shall first visit with my Royal Husband, who is in the advance party.'

'Stubborn stubborn stubborn!' said Immu to Anigel, using the overfamiliar manner of venerable retainers. 'It is indecent for a gravid royal woman to go off galloping amongst a cavalcade of soldiers and teamsters – even if there were no danger from spawn.'

'Nevertheless,' Anigel said blithely, 'I am going.'

Immu besought the noblewomen. 'Will not one of you ride with the Queen?'

But the ladies only made excuses and continued to remonstrate. Finally, Immu said, 'Then I will go myself!'

Anigel looked upon the Nyssomu nurse with some doubt. 'You may certainly ride pillion with me if you insist, dear friend. But I daresay it will be most uncomfortable for a small person such as yourself, jouncing along at my back.'

Lord Karagil suddenly brightened. 'I have an idea that may serve all purposes,' he declared, and rode off. He returned anon with two grooms, one leading a white fronial caparisoned royally for the Queen and the other bringing the she-beast's gentle, half-grown colt, fitted out with an improvised saddle and bridle for Immu.

Happily, Anigel put on boots and a cloak. Accompanied by twenty knights of her Oathed Companions, and with Immu following resignedly on the long-legged colt, the Queen rode forward along the line of march until she reached the vanguard. There she found King Antar and his commander-in-chief, General Gorkain, dismounted at one of the new bridges that spanned a swollen tributary of the River Virkar. They were conferring with two aboriginal scouts clad in the livery of the Two Thrones. Lord Marshal Lakanilo and numbers of other noble officers sat their steeds close by, waiting upon the royal pleasure. They wore only light helmets and cuirasses beneath their raincloaks, as did the Oathed

Companions, the King, and the General. A troop of well equipped men-at-arms and a single knight in full battle-armour had gone down to the riverbank, where they prepared to board a large raft manned by two human boatmen and a Nyssomu guide.

King Antar greeted his wife and the other comers courteously, then showed Anigel the map he and Gorkain and the scouts had been studying.

'One of those infernal viaducts Haramis warned us about lies some six leagues downstream from here,' Antar told her. 'Soldiers under Sir Olevik's command have volunteered to guard it while the main body of our train passes by. They will travel on that raft.'

'But what can our brave men do,' the Queen asked in a low voice, 'if villains should pop through the magical doorway while they are on watch? Soldiers cannot fight magic, and surely there will be no time to barricade the viaduct effectively.'

'No, my Queen,' General Gorkain admitted. 'In truth, all that Sir Olevik and his force can hope for is to divert any invaders for a brief period, selling their lives dearly while their Oddling comrade bespeaks us fair warning.'

'They are brave hearts,' Anigel murmured.

'There is small chance of an attack by Star Men so soon,' Antar reassured her. 'Nor is Orogastus likely to assail a huge, well-armed column such as ours. We are merely taking due precaution.'

'Within two tennights,' said one of the little Nyssomu scouts, 'our Folk dwelling in this part of the Mazy Mire will have secured that viaduct, as the White Lady and the Lady of the Eyes have commanded. We will heap a tall mound of stone and soil over the site and set a guard.'

'It will be very hard for Star Men to emerge unnoticed from a viaduct after this is done,' said the other scout. 'They will have to resort to powerful magic to dig their way out. This we will surely detect, and then sound the alarm in the speech without words.'

Anigel looked again at the map. 'It seems there are no more viaducts near to the road until we reach the mountains. We can be thankful for that.'

A ragged cheer now arose from the Oathed Companions as the raft with Sir Olevik and his men pushed off from the shore. 'May the Flower bless you,' the Queen called, sketching the sign of the Trillium in the air beyond the bridge railing, 'and bring you back safely to our company.'

Those on the raft responded with spirited cries of their own, brandishing their arms. Then the raft rounded a bend and was lost to sight behind a dense stand of trees.

The advance riders resumed their slow progress through the rain, with

Anigel and Antar riding side by side amidst the troop of knights, and Immu trailing behind the Queen. Coming after them at a fair distance was a parade over two leagues in length: volumnial-drawn wagons loaded with baggage of the court, more carts carrying food and supplies, fine coaches and carriages bearing the nobility and civil servants, royal officers and knights on fronial-back, and nearly a thousand other retainers both mounted and afoot. Double files of soldiery plodded along on either side of the main column, and the sound of their singing came softly through the swamp to the ears of those riding ahead.

The Queen was well content now, making proud inspection of her mireway. What had been from time immemorial an indistinct and hazardous track only negotiable in the Dry Time (and then, only by those possessing local knowledge or the secret maps of the Master Traders) was now a handsome paved road. Its elevated bed, formed of alternate layers of crushed rock and massive logs from the Tassaleyo Forest, stood three ells or more above the swamp and was surfaced with cobblestones. Wooden bridges had replaced the old fords over streams and rivers, save for the crossing of the broad Virkar at the edge of the Dylex country, where there was a ferry. Hostels with guardposts, sited a day's journey apart, provided secure places where smaller parties of travellers or merchant caravans might rest; but the huge royal train perforce camped on the road itself, with only the royalty and elderly or infirm nobles taking shelter beneath hostel roofs.

The middle section of the mireway that the entourage now traversed was more narrow than the rest since it had been so difficult to build. Twisting nearly a hundred leagues between Bonar Castle and the Dylex city of Virk, this part of the road crossed a wilderness devoid of human habitation. Soaring trees and dense tangles of thorn-fern, vines, and nearly impenetrable vegetation hemmed in the mireway and even overhung it in many stretches, so that it sometimes seemed to Queen Anigel that they rode through a green tunnel curtained by misty rain.

The advance party made a halt at midday, eating cold food and resting while a welcome sun broke briefly through the clouds, causing the roadway to steam. But by the time the riders remounted storm clouds had returned, together with a rising wind. Nevertheless Anigel found herself dozing in the saddle as the patient fronials moved slowly onward, their antlered heads bobbing, the tendons in their legs clicking, and their splayed hooves clip-clopping on the mossy stones. Overhead, the leaden sky became more and more oppressive, although the heavy rain held off.

The Queen was jolted into wakefulness when occasional whiffs of stomach-turning stench began to contaminate the wind. No one was much

69

surprised when General Gorkain came riding back through the ranks of knights and saluted the King and Queen before delivering grim news.

'A scout reports freshly scoured raffin bones on the mireway ahead, and the cobbles show sign of Skritek spawn. We will halt here in order to close up the gap between our advance group and the main body of the caravan. The Lord Marshal and the Oathed Companions will provide Your Majesties with close escort, and foot-soldiery will come forward to accompany us until the danger is past. I have also sent a messenger to summon Crown Prince Nikalon and Princess Janeel. It is no longer safe for them to range up and down the procession casually with their young friends.'

'Very well,' said Antar. 'You may carry on.'

The General touched his helm-visor in salute and spun his fronial about. But before he could ride away there were shouts from the knights ahead. 'Spawn! Spawn on the road!'

Gorkain swore and spurred his mount forward, drawing his two-handed sword. Marshal Lakanilo and a dozen Oathed Companions closed in around the King, the Queen, and Immu, lances couched, while others of the elite group followed the General.

An excruciating foul odour spread through the air. For a time everyone was quiet and the only sounds were distant hoofbeats, the creak of harness, and the hiss and patter of the rain.

Then Immu whispered, 'See there!' She pointed to a dark slough at the right of the mireway, half-screened by thornless fodderfern twice the height of a man.

Rising from the scummy water were dozens of glistening white shapes, some nearly the size of a human body, others much smaller. They resembled odious fat worms or grubs, lacking obvious heads but having stubby limbs equipped with razorlike claws. Their foreparts lifted as they reached the narrow verge beside the roadbed, revealing wide open mouths with green teeth that dripped venom. The blind monsters swayed from side to side questing for prey, which they tracked with their keen hearing.

For an instant the riders were frozen with horror. Then one young knight exclaimed, 'Zoto's Stones, what detestable things! Like giant corpse-maggots!'

At the sound of his voice the Skritek spawn began humping and wriggling up the embankment toward the road.

King Antar's longsword sang as it left its scabbard. 'Follow me, Oathed Companions!'

He sent his fronial skidding down the steep slope, the Lord Marshal and the knights following closely after, and with a single sweeping stroke he smote one of the leading spawn in two. It disintegrated, splashing vile jelly-like ichor all over the King. The Companions spitted other blood-thirsty Skritek young on their lances or put them to the sword, crying out in anger and disgust as they were also drenched by evil-smelling fluids from the spawn bodies.

Lakanilo's fronial fell to the muddy ground, squealing in agony, its foreleg held fast in poisoned jaws. But the Companions raced to the Lord Marshal's rescue, hauling him to safety, slaying the tenaciously clinging spawn, and granting merciful death to the doomed antilopine steed.

It was not long before all of the larvae were either killed or fled, leaving Antar and the knights beslimed from helm to heel. Victorious cries from the road ahead signalled that the other pod of immature Skritek had also been routed by Gorkain and his men.

'Well done,' cried Queen Anigel warmly.

But the King looked down upon his filthied person with a grimace. 'Only the Triune knows how we shall remove this mess from ourselves, unless we take a headlong leap into the swamp and exchange mud for spawn-slime.'

As if in answer, thunder rumbled overhead and a deluge of rain pelted down. Antar removed his helm, tilted his head so water bathed his face, and laughed. 'Thank you, gracious Lords of the Air! By the time the main column catches up with us, we may almost be fit for civilized society again.'

'Perhaps you should return to your carriage, my Queen,' Lord Marshal Lakanilo suggested to Anigel. He was a tall man of sparse flesh, whose manner was grave and dignified in spite of his befouled appearance. He had been appointed to his office following the heroic death of Lord Marshal Owanon in the Battle of Derorguila.

The Queen shook her head, dismissing the suggestion that she should retire. 'Heavens, no, Lako! With the smell of Skritek now stronger than ever, my ladies will wrap their faces in perfume-soaked veils. Frankly, my nose is less offended by the smell of the monsters.'

Princess Janeel and Crown Prince Nikalon came cantering up with a group of noble attendants and gave noisy greeting to their parents and the Oathed Companions.

'Phew!' cried the Princess, pinching her nose. 'The spawn-reek is much worse up here – *oh!*' She screamed at the sight of the slaughtered creatures.

'They are quite dead, my Lady,' the Lord Marshal said. 'There is nothing to fear.'

Prince Nikalon had drawn his sword and his eyes were alight as he surveyed the noisome remains. 'Are you certain, Lako? Perhaps we'd better reconnoitre the swamp. I'm ready!' At fifteen, he had nearly attained a man's stature and wore a helm and breastplate and military cape.

'Ready ready ready!' Immu exclaimed crossly. 'Your royal parents and the Oathed Companions must now feel very relieved that such a great champion has arrived.'

'Oh, Immu,' groaned the Prince. The knights were laughing, but with good humour for they all were very fond of the impetuous Niki.

'There is no need for us to leave the road,' Antar said. 'Indeed, it would be foolhardy for us to do so, since the water continues to rise.'

'Well, I'm sorry I missed the fight. I never saw Skritek spawn before.' The boy sheathed his sword and began questioning the knights about the attack, and the Lord Marshal sent off for another mount.

Janeel rode closer to her parents and the little old nurse, expressing relief when she was told that the only casualty was a single fronial. 'What horrible things the spawn are! Is it true that they kill their dams at birth?'

'More often than not,' Immu said. 'Adult Skritek have the use of reason – more or less! – but the young are ravening and mindless. If the mother is lucky, she may leap to safety as each larval offspring drops from her womb, and the spawn will feed upon meat she has provided. But it is more common for the offspring to awaken before birth and gnaw their way from confinement through the mother's body wall.'

'Ugh!' said Janeel. Her face had gone white within the hood of her raincape and she would gladly have departed the nauseating scene, were it not that Queen Anigel seemed unfazed. 'No wonder Skritek know nothing of love or gentleness.'

'And yet,' Prince Nikalon interposed with grisly relish, having rejoined his parents and sister, 'the Skritek are the oldest race in the world, and sages say all Folk are descended from them. Even you, Immu!'

'I thought humankind was the most ancient race,' the Princess said.

'We did not originate in this world,' said the Queen. 'Your Aunt Haramis the Archimage learned that human beings came here from the Outer Firmament uncounted aeons in the past. The Vanished Ones were our ancestors.'

'What is even more amazing,' said King Antar very quietly, 'is that the Vanished Ones used the blood of both Skritek and humanity to fashion a Folk-race that might withstand the Conquering Ice.'

'But . . . why?' The Princess, unlike her older brother, had never heard the story; nor had most other people, for the Archimage had decided that it must be kept secret, except among the royal family and its most trusted confidants.

'The ancient humans felt guilty abandoning the world their warring had largely destroyed,' Antar said. 'You see, Jan, the Vanished Ones believed that the ice they had unwittingly created twelve-times-ten hundreds ago would devour all the world's land, save for the continental margins and some islands. They thought the Skritek would surely die, leaving the world devoid of rational beings. But that did not happen. The ice failed to conquer after all, and both the Skritek and the new race of hardy Folk lived on together. So did certain stubborn humans who had remained behind when the rest Vanished into the Outer Firmament.'

'Those aborigines that we call Vispi,' said the Queen, 'the high-mountain dwellers who aided your Aunt Haramis in obtaining her talisman and who are now her special Folk, are the result of that long-ago experiment. They are the true firstborn, combining the Skritek and human lineage. Of course they give birth in human fashion, as other high races of Folk do.'

'But the Vispi are so beautiful,' Jan said, 'while the other races of Folk are –' She broke off, realizing how improper it was to speak thus before the old Nyssomu nurse. 'Oh, Immu, I beg pardon. I did not mean to insult you.'

'I take no offence, sweeting.' Immu was calm. 'To Nyssomu and Uisgu the Vispi appear unattractive. You call them beautiful merely because they most resemble yourselves.'

'But how, then, did the other races of Folk come about?' Janeel inquired.

'Some were engendered through new infusions of Skritek blood,' said the Queen in a sombre tone.

The Princess thought over the horrid implications of this, and she and her brother were silent for some time.

Then Immu added, 'Over the ages, fresh human blood also contributed to the racial mixing. In ancient times, humans often mated with Folk. It is just within the last six hundreds that your people began to call mine Oddlings, insisting that we are inferior beings. In other human kingdoms, the disdain for us persists. Only in Laboruwenda are the Folk acknowledged to have souls, and certain of us are granted the privileges of citizenship.'

'I will see that the nation of Raktum does likewise,' Princess Janeel stated offhandedly, 'when I marry Ledavardis and become its queen.'

'Oh, Jan!' Anigel exclaimed angrily. 'You know I have forbidden you to speak of that matter before your Royal Father.'

'What's this?' Antar glared at his daughter. 'Don't tell me she still fancies that Goblin Kinglet?'

'Ledavardis of Raktum is a brave man,' Janeel said, 'and no more a goblin than Niki is. Even though his body is not handsome, he is noble of heart.'

'So you say!' The furious King spoke to the Princess through clenched teeth, and his blond beard bristled. 'To my mind, the Raktumians are naught but half-reformed pirates, and no daughter of mine will wed their malformed King! How can you forget that Raktum allied with Tuzamen and the despicable Orogastus to make war upon us?'

'Ledo fought and surrendered with honour,' Janeel retorted. 'And he has ever since then commanded his people to change their old lawless ways and behave in a civilized manner.'

'Civilized!' The King's laugh was contemptuous. 'Nothing has changed in the pirate kingdom, except now the Raktumian corsairs commit their crimes on the sly, whereas before they were bold as the vipers of Viborn. You shall never marry Ledavardis.'

The Princess burst into tears. 'You care nothing for my happiness, Father. The real reason why you reject Ledo is your vain hope that I will marry King Yondrimel of Zinora, that scheming braggart. But you will never force me to accept him! Let him marry one of Queen Jiri's daughters.'

'Jan, my dearest!' Queen Anigel hastened to intervene. 'I beseech you to forbear. This is not the place for such discussion. Let us wait until we reach the next hostel, and —'

Her words were drowned out by a colossal thunderbolt. Simultaneously the mireway shook as with an earthquake, and a flash of light blinded all beholders. The rain now fell prodigiously. Shouts arose from the shocked knights, who had withdrawn some distance in order to give the royal family privacy. The fronials shied in terror from the unexpected noise, and the King forgot his anger as he strove to prevent his daughter's crazed steed from slipping off the road into the swirling floodwaters.

Prince Nikalon was similarly occupied with the distraught mount of his mother. Anigel's ramping white beast pawed the savage downpour with its split hooves and tossed its antlered head wildly. The Queen regained control only with difficulty after Niki dismounted and clung to her bridle. Several ells away, the young fronial Immu rode lay on its belly near the road's lefthand edge, shaking with terror, while its rider urged it vainly to rise. But then Princess Janeel's animal escaped Antar's grasp and nearly trampled the colt and Immu as it galloped back down the road toward the main column.

'Oathed Companions!' cried the Queen. 'After the Princess!' And to her son, 'Save Immu! Look — the verge of the mireway near her is crumbling!'

Prince Nikalon leapt back onto his mount and went pounding down

74

the rain-lashed road. Leaning from the saddle, he swept up the little Nyssomu woman just as the fronial colt tumbled down the embankment and vanished without a sound into churning muddy water.

'Bring Immu to me, Niki,' the Queen shouted, 'then aid your father and sister!'

Anigel could not understand why the Oathed Companions had not come to the rescue. Her sight of the knights on the road ahead was obscured by the pounding rain and the growing darkness, but she heard their shouts amidst continuing rumbles of thunder and a strange rushing sound. When Immu was safe on the pillion behind her and the Prince gone to Antar, who had halted Janeel's runaway mount some distance away, the Queen put spur to her fronial in order to fetch the Companions. But the white beast skidded to an abrupt halt after taking only a few bounds.

'Great God, the road!' Anigel screamed, looking down from the saddle.

Between the Queen and her knights stretched a steep break in the mireway over five ells wide. It appeared that lightning had blasted the road asunder. High water formerly impounded on one side of the causeway was now pouring through, laden with downed trees and other floating debris. Before Anigel could recover from her astonishment another brilliant flash and a shattering clap of thunder rocked the Mazy Mire, causing her mount to stagger.

'Hold tight, Immu!' she cried, reining the animal's head far to the right, so that it whirled in tight circles, squealing. But it did not panic this time and she was able to calm it at last, urging it back toward the King and the children.

Then the beast again stopped abruptly. Anigel gasped as she saw a second gap in the mireway, narrower than the first but growing wider every second as swift waters chewed away at the road's foundation.

The Queen and Immu were marooned on a small island of cobblestone pavement in the midst of a raging flood.

'Ani!' howled the King, and Nikalon and Janeel cried, 'Mother!'

Thunder seemed to give a mocking answer. The Oathed Companions stood helpless on their side of the severed road, but several carts and numbers of men-at-arms had finally reached the King. One quick-thinking fellow dashed up to Antar with a coil of rope, and both father and son dismounted and helped to fling it across the water.

Anigel and Immu also slid from the saddle, crouching at the lip of the shrinking section of mireway. Twice the rope failed to reach them; but on the third throw Immu took hold of it, screeching in triumph and nearly falling into the rising flood.

'Come!' the nurse cried to the Queen. 'Knot it about your waist!'

Anigel tried, but at that moment the waters undermined the roadbed beneath and the cobbles under her feet shifted and separated. She fell into a shallow, water-filled hole, her arms and legs entangled in her long raincape. Dropping the rope, Immu scrambled to Anigel and helped to free her. Queen and nurse crawled over the treacherous, dissolving surface while the King recoiled the rope and flung it again and again across the widening breach.

But the line kept falling short, and soon the island of roadway would be entirely washed away.

'Your trillium-amber!' Immu screamed at the Queen above the roar of the storm. 'Bid it save us!'

They were clinging to each other. Anigel took hold of her magical amulet with one hand, holding Immu tightly with the other. Behind them, the white fronial scrabbled and shrieked, consumed with terror. The ground melted under it and it was swept away into the torrent.

A third monstrous explosion sounded at the same time that lightning struck. Stones, broken timber, clots of muddy earth, and roiling mist filled the air, together with shouts from the frustrated rescuers.

Queen Anigel felt herself falling, felt Immu torn away from her grasp, felt strangely painless blows from the wind-flung branches whirling all around her, felt her slow slide into dark, rushing water that filled her mouth and nose, choking off her prayer to the Black Trillium.

Then she felt nothing.

CHAPTER 8

The viaduct on Mount Brom was situated in the Cavern of Black Ice.

Long ages ago it had given the Vanished Ones access to their mysterious storage place deep in the Ohogan Mountains. And now, as Haramis had anticipated, the viaduct provided the sorcerer Orogastus with a means of entry to her Tower. Through her magical Three-Winged Circle she watched him emerge out of nowhere, through a dark disc without thickness that vanished with a loud bell-chime as soon as he was beyond it. He wore his silver-and-black Star Master regalia, including the gauntlets and the awesome starburst headpiece that hid the upper part of his face.

He stood quietly in the very middle of the cavern's obsidian-tiled floor, looking at the vault of quartz-veined granite soaring overhead and at the hundreds of alcoves, compartments, and roomlets on every side. The peculiar illumination of the place, shining from unseen sources, caused the icy extrusions in the rock crevices to gleam like polished onyx.

The sorcerer seemed bemused as he walked slowly toward the exit, perhaps remembering the time that the Cavern of Black Ice and its wondrous contents had belonged to him. The glassy dark doors to the chambers and niches were all open. A few sophisticated trinkets and trifles remained, but were useless to his purposes. The compartments that had contained ancient weapons, or other devices intended to intimidate or harm, were empty.

'So you destroyed them, did you?' He addressed thin air, knowing she viewed him through her talisman. 'And yet you kept the most deadly instrument of all! Did it never occur to you that the other two parts of the Sceptre of Power would be denied their greatest, most awful usage if there were no Three-Winged Circle?'

Haramis said nothing. She *had* thought of it, had even contemplated throwing the Circle into one of the active volcanos in the Flame-Girt Isles when it became obvious that the other two talismans had passed into the hands of a person unknown. But that small silvery wand had been purchased at such a great cost to herself; and the original purpose of the Threefold Sceptre, thwarted twelve thousand years ago, had never ceased to intrigue her. She could not bring herself to cast the talisman away.

Orogastus reached a large wooden door encrusted with hoarfrost and addressed her once more. The set of his mouth had become ironic. 'Do I have your permission to enter the Tower, White Lady? It is mine, after all, even though you have made free with it for these sixteen years.'

Haramis made the door swing silently open. He would be allowed this single visit, during which she would do that which must be done.

The sorcerer bowed his thanks and hurried up the rough corridor that he himself had bored through the mountain with one of the ancient devices. Memories crowded his mind. He had dwelt here on Mount Brom during most of his frustrating association with Voltrik, late King of Labornok, and here he had trained his first three followers. The Green, Blue, and Red Voices (may the Dark Powers grant them eternal joy!) had not only served him faithfully unto death, but had also helped amplify his thaumaturgical vision . . . as had their three less-worthy successors. Now, of course, thanks to the Dark Man and Nerenyi Daral, he needed no help from other minds in order to command the full magic of the Star.

Unfortunately, the Star alone would not suffice to fulfil his ultimate design. For that, he would require the Threefold Sceptre. Obtaining two parts of it would be comparatively easy; but the third piece belonged to Haramis, and taking it from her by force or coercion was very likely impossible.

There was an alternative, and he had come here tonight to explore it . . .

At the tunnel's end he found himself at the lowest level of the Tower's stairwell. He stood on flagstones just across from the main entry, sampling the aura of his former home. It was much different from the way he remembered it, permeated with the Black Trillium's alien enchantment. Now this Tower belonged to Haramis absolutely. For an instant a brief thrust of fear touched him. Would the Star grant him sufficient protection?

In truth, he did not know. But he had come anyway.

On either side were storage chambers, now quite empty, and the stable where he had once kept his mounts, and the small room housing machinery for the bridge that spanned the chasm outside. He was not surprised to discover that the mechanism he had tended so carefully was now rusty and neglected. No one used his amazing bridge any more. The White Lady called upon her preternatural powers for travel, and the Vispi aborigines who were her servants flew wherever they wished on gigantic birds that dwelt among the nearby crags.

Except for the night wind, faintly audible through the thick walls, the Tower was silent. There was no hint of her presence, but he knew she

78

awaited him and he knew where to find her. Climbing the spiral stairs, he wondered if she felt as torn by this impending meeting as he did. He was here on her sufferance. It would have been easy enough for her to destroy the tunnel connecting the cavern and the Tower, so that the viaduct became a dead end. But she had forborne.

The last time the two of them had shared the Tower's shelter she had been little more than a girl, newly possessed of a talisman with powers unknown to her, foolhardy and susceptible to the appeal of a handsome older man. He should have been able to bewitch her as easily as a newborn tree-vart.

Instead, she had bewitched him.

He reached the library, the place where they had shared their first and last kiss, and opened the door. It had been his favourite place, his sanctuary, crammed with the rarest and most valuable volumes in the world. She had not changed it much. Heavy drapes had been drawn across the tall windows on this evening of biting cold. Two highbacked armchairs cushioned in rich red damask were drawn up close to the comfort of the fireplace. Between them was a pedestal table with a flagon of white wine, two chunky cut-glass goblets in the Vispi style, and a plate of small sweetcakes.

She arose from one of the chairs, for a moment nothing but a dark silhouette against orange flames. Then she stepped forward so that the light from the quaint library-lamps of the Vanished Ones showed her clearly, and he felt his heart catch in his throat. Her black hair fell in glistening tresses to her waist. She wore a white velvet gown with silver-blue fur at the wide sleeves and hem, and a belt of soft azure inset with moonstone. Her underdress was powder-blue challis, embroidered with tiny Black Trilliums at the neck, where the wand of the Three-Winged Circle hung on its chain.

'Good day to you, Star Master,' Haramis said. 'Dressed for combat, I see. What a shame! I had hoped for a brief truce while we discussed what is to come.'

And that was a lie. A small one, but the first Haramis had ever told since becoming Archimage of the Land, done deliberately in order to provoke him into the actions that must follow . . .

He said nothing, but deliberately pulled off the silver gauntlets and dropped them on the carpeted floor. Then he removed his headpiece and black cloak, also letting them fall. Doffing his odd vestment of metal mesh with its shining black leather panels, he stood before her clad in a simple tunic of unbleached wool, and trews of darker material stuffed into high boots. A pouch laden with something heavy hung from his belt.

79

'Greetings to you, Archimage of the Land.' His voice, unfiltered by the talisman's magic, was as mellifluous and beguiling as she remembered it to be. But his face was older than the portrait had shown, gaunt and weathered, having deep creases between the pale eyes and on either side of his mouth. 'Behold! I have cast away the habiliments of sorcery and herewith invite an armistice.'

'I accept,' she said, lying for the second time. And in a gesture that was clearly a challenge, she lifted the Three-Winged Circle on its chain from around her neck and placed it on the table.

A breathless silence followed. He came closer and one of his long-fingered hands stretched out and hovered over the wand. The three tiny wings at the top of the Circle unfolded and the glow of the trillium-amber within throbbed a warning.

'Would you really let it slay me?' he asked in a playful tone.

She shrugged. 'If you wish to take my talisman up, Star Master, I grant you permission to do so. It will not harm you, but you will find it as unresponsive as a common fork or spoon. You know it obeys only its bonded owner – and even then, sometimes capriciously.'

He laughed, then took the wine-flagon from the table instead, filling goblets for both of them. 'Capriciously indeed. Let us both pray that whoever now owns the other two talismans experiences as much trouble learning to command them as we did.'

'So you know that Kadiya's Eye was stolen.'

'Yes.'

'Was it taken by one of your agents?'

He smiled enigmatically. 'The thief is no ally of mine . . . yet.'

She ignored the provocation, her eyes fixed upon his Star. 'I have set aside my talisman. Can we not, at least for a little while, forswear magic and meet as man and woman?'

His eyelids lowered, veiling his gaze. Did he dare to face her unprotected? But he was confident that she would never be so base as to violate a truce, just as he was confident that her love for him had endured.

He lifted the Star medallion from his neck and lay it on the table next to her talisman. Then they both sat down, she rather stiffly and he in an easy sprawl, warming his boots by the fire.

'So you have been spying upon my sisters,' Haramis said.

'I cannot see them individually, as you know well enough, because they are shielded by their trillium-amber. But their associates have unwittingly revealed what has been going on. The theft of the Burning Eye is a most vexing development – and a puzzling one as well. One must ask why this mysterious burglar has made no use of the magical loot. Is he a paragon of prudence, content to keep both talismans safely hidden? Is the thief too timid to wield them, knowing that the Vanished Ones themselves were afraid of their terrible power? Or is our wily pilferer merely cautious? Has he been testing the magical devices in unobtrusive ways until he attains expertise and confidence in their use?'

'I think we will find out before long,' Haramis said with dark certainty, 'and to our woe.'

'Perhaps, Archimage,' he said lightly, 'we should consider an alliance against this mutual menace.'

Her smile was cold. 'I am no longer the simple child you hoped to win over to your Dark Powers, Star Master.'

'I know that full well. And you shall discover that I am no longer the man I was when I last contended with the Petals of the Living Trillium and . . . went the way of the Vanished Ones.'

For an instant, ardent hope transfigured her face. But then she looked away from him, lips tightening in unrelenting resolve. 'I can only judge you by your actions, which tell me you are the same as ever: charming, persuasive, and completely ruthless in the pursuit of your evil ambition.'

He threw back his head and laughed, and his brilliantly white hair reflected the fire like high clouds at sundown. His amusement was youthful, heartfelt, having in it nothing of slyness or cynicism. 'You know nothing of my present ambition, dear Haramis, any more than you know where I was held captive while you thought me dead.' His eyes sparkled as he bent closer to her over the table. 'Would you care to hear the tale?'

She nodded, still frowning, not trusting herself to speak.

He sat back then and took a deep draught of the wine. 'It was the Great Cynosure that saved me, of course – that magical device of my Guild that was created as a countermeasure to the Sceptre of Power, drawing to it any wearer of the Star who is smitten with the Sceptre's magic. Twice it has preserved my life. The first time, with the existence of the Cynosure unbeknownst to any of us, I was drawn to the Inaccessible Kimilon deep within the icecap and marooned there for twelve years. I knew not how I had been transported to that Land of Fire and Ice. The Archimage Iriane made off with the Cynosure after it had done its work and in time gave it to you. Cruel Haramis! You intended to use it to imprison me forever in that Chasm of Durance that lies beneath the Place of Knowledge. But death would have been more merciful.'

'I – I hoped you would amend your ways. I could not bear to destroy you, even indirectly.' Her eyes were fixed upon her tightly clasped hands lying in her lap. She felt ashamed, as he knew she would. He was manipulating her feelings again, as he had done before. But this time the outcome would be different.

'As it happened,' he went on, 'another person thwarted your plan. He took the Cynosure from the chasm just before you and your sisters conquered me with the Sceptre for the second time. And thus it was that I awoke to find myself safe abed ... within one of the Three Moons.'

'By the Flower!' Haramis cried in sudden understanding. '*Denby!* And now I suppose he has sent you back to carry on where you left off. Oh, the perfidious wretch! What manner of Archimage is he to play such games with the very balance of the world?'

'In my opinion, the Dark Man is a senile lunatic, but one who nevertheless taught me much. Do you know who the Archimage of the Firmament really is?'

'Iriane told me something of his aloof and vagarious ways. I know he is very old and cares little for events of our world. Yet he did vouchsafe to us the assistance of those sindona called Sentinels of the Mortal Dictum, defeating your army and saving the Two Thrones. Why he saved you –' She shook her head.

'Are you glad that he did?' Orogastus spoke very softly.

She replied, 'Yes ... God help me!' And this was not a lie.

'Even now,' the sorcerer continued, 'I know almost nothing of the Man in the Moon's motives. But I do know who he is. He is that same great hero of the Vanished Ones who both conquered the Guild of the Star and brought about the birth of the Folk. He is Denby Varcour, a man of dusky complexion who is over twelve thousand years old. When the Vanished Ones fled the Conquering Ice, he remained, together with a small cohort of others, hoping to undo some of the damage humankind had wrought upon the world. The Vispi Folk and their telepathic bird friends were created in workshops inside his Moon.'

Haramis was shocked. 'The Moon is hollow? He does not live upon the orb's surface, as we live upon the world?'

'All of the Three Moons are artifacts of ancient magic. The one called the Dark Man's Moon, where I was incarcerated, has every manner of thing necessary for civilized life inside of it, including abandoned workrooms with marvellous tools, and beautifully appointed apartments without a single soul dwelling within. The second orb is called the Garden Moon. Although I was not allowed to visit it, I know that it is a conservatory of plants and animals, and some of our food came from there. It is also the residence of numbers of those damned living statues, who acted as my jailers and served Denby in other mysterious ways.'

'The sindona,' Haramis murmured. She had recovered her composure and now sipped a bit of wine and tasted one of the small cakes.

'The third orb is called the Death Moon. I do not know why. The Three Moons are connected to each other and to this world by viaducts. I escaped two years ago through one of these bizarre passages. Never mind how. Oddly enough, the Archimage of the Firmament has made no attempt to recapture me since then – but of course he is mad.'

'Why do you call him so?'

'Because of his behaviour. He holds conversations with the dead and berates himself for unspecified sins. At other times he seems unaware of his surroundings, as if in a trance. During most of my captivity he was considerate, even jovial, permitting me to roam the entire Moon and study its weird treasures. But on occasion, for no reason I could fathom, he would scream vulgar imprecations and threaten to banish me to the Death Moon, saying all members of the Star Guild deserved no better than to perish under torture. These moods of deranged fury were all the more frightening because he had been the model of sweet reason immediately before.'

'And so you escaped,' she said flatly. 'And for two years you dwelt . . . where?'

But Orogastus only shook his head, smiling. 'I know you are searching for the headquarters of my Star Guild, as is your sister Kadiya. But by the time you find our place of habitation the knowledge will do you no good. The Guild of the Star is reborn to assist me in attaining my great objective.'

She regarded him with a steady and sombre mien. 'So now we come to the crux of the matter, Star Master. Just what *is* your objective? Do you and your Guildsmen intend to conquer the world on behalf of your Dark Powers? Is your barbaric imprisonment of poor Iriane a warning of the fate you would inflict upon me if I oppose you?'

Instead of answering, he poured more wine into his glass and drank. Then he said, 'You carry my portrait, Haramis. Why?'

'Because I am a fool,' she retorted. 'But in spite of myself, I am bound and determined to do my solemn duty as Archimage of the Land and Petal of the Living Trillium – no matter what the personal cost may be. And this time, if my duty encompasses your destruction, I will not hesitate.'

She took the picture of him from an inner pocket of her gown, letting him glimpse it briefly. Then she rose from her seat with abrupt swiftness, strode to the hearth, and cast the framed ivory image into the flames.

He bowed his head, and when he finally spoke again his voice was

83

unsteady. 'I love you, Haramis. You must believe me. Believe me also when I say that my intentions in regard to this world of ours are neither evil nor selfishly motivated.'

She stood with her back to him, staring at the blackening portrait. 'I wish I could believe you.'

'I learned much while I was Denby's prisoner – about the mortal imbalance threatening the world, about myself, about my reason for being, and about you. You think that your life-work is inevitably conjoined to that of your sisters. *I* say that your fate is as far beyond their paltry concerns as the sun is beyond the glow-worms of the Mazy Mire.'

He opened the pouch at his waist and took out a second Star. Its chain blazed with jewels as he held it out to her. 'This is for you.'

She turned and beheld the medallion, and her features stiffened with dismay. 'Never!'

'Together, we can save the world. Dearest Haramis, you and I are wielders of transcendant magic. We are more alike than either of us ever realized. Only look in a mirror! The very eyes in our heads reveal it. Denby Varcour has the selfsame silvery eyes, and so does the woman he loved, whose dead hand aided my escape. We are of the Vanished Ones! Can't you understand what this must mean?'

It was some minutes before Haramis replied. 'The Blue Lady of the Sea, who is my dearest friend, was also my instructor in the high magical arts. She imparted to me all she knew, charging *me* to restore the lost balance of the world – that chaos brought about by you and your crimes. My sisters declared they would assist me, but I believed that the first responsibility was clearly my own. In my perplexity, still torn between my love for you and my duty, I went to the sindona called the Teacher. She provided me with one last precious nugget of guidance: "Love is permissible. Devotion is not."'

He smiled, once again proffering the second Star on its gem-studded chain. 'An intriguing riddle. One that gives me a modicum of hope.'

But she shook her head, speaking hesitantly and low. 'I heard Iriane repeat the aphorism at that awful moment when the Flower conquered you and the Cynosure snatched you out of this world. All throughout the years that I thought you dead and damned for your wickedness, I pondered the saying, unable to discover its meaning. Only now, knowing that you live, have I been able to draw fresh insight and strength from the Teacher's words . . . from that mysterious and terrible saying that can bring no sweet solace to the contemplator but only the wintry satisfaction of duty fulfilled.' She came to the table, took the Star of Nerenyi Daral from his hands, dropped it onto the carpeted floor, and spurned it with her foot. 'Do you understand the meaning of the riddle, Star Master?'

He exploded from his chair and seized her with an emotion akin to ferocity. 'I understand only my love for you – and that you also love me!'

'Yes,' she said. 'I do love you.' The pupils of her eyes had gone wide, and centred in each was a pinpoint of white radiance.

'Haramis!' he groaned, and the eyes looking down at her were also twin blazes of starlight. His first embrace was painful in its strength, but then his arms gentled and she felt his hands cradle her head. His face descended and their lips met.

For uncounted minutes the only sound in the room was the crackle of the fire in the great hearth. But the kiss ended at last and the ineffable light dwindled and was gone. The eyes of both of them saw the real world again. He gave forth a shuddering sigh. She spoke his name for the first time. Her head fell upon his breast, he pressed his cheek to her soft black hair and they stood together motionless until Haramis finally disengaged herself and stood apart. Her face was calm, almost wistful.

'Love is permitted,' she whispered. 'Devotion is not.'

'What *does* it mean?' His voice was harsh with alarm.

'It means that there can be no more than this, Orogastus. No avowed consecration of one to the other. No union within your Star. And above all, no mutual bodily worship . . . for that is what devotion implies.'

'Can you deny the special magic we have created together?' he cried, clasping her hands. 'This is only the beginning, Haramis! You and I –'

'Are antagonists,' she said, pulling away again and turning away. 'We oppose each other – as the dead champions of the Vanished Ones opposed the ancient Star Guild. I am the servant of the human people and the Folk, obligated to guide and assist them through my magic. You and your followers worship Dark Powers and do not scruple at any wrongdoing that would forward your schemes.'

'You don't understand! All that has changed. Why won't you let me explain–'

'I understand Iriane enduring a living death. I understand the provoking of the Skritek by your agent and the misery thereby inflicted upon harmless Nyssomu Folk. I understand that you have terrible weapons at your command that your Guild has used in the wanton murder of innocent Lercomi. And I doubt not that you and your henchmen are guilty of other crimes that have yet to come to my attention.' She turned about to face him. 'Am I wrong?'

'Iriane will be released in good time,' he said. 'I regret the deaths of the little Mere Folk. My followers are of a nation that believes they are soulless animals, and I cannot always control them. But I did ensure that no Nyssomu were killed by the Drowners –'

'Free the Blue Lady now,' Haramis pleaded. 'Destroy the ancient weapons you have gathered. Abandon your plan to conquer the world.'

'I cannot,' he said, 'for it is part of my greater intention that would save it! Iriane would have thwarted me out of ignorance, as would the rulers of the nations if they were not compelled to do my bidding.'

'As every right-thinking person would thwart you!' Haramis said in a voice of thunder. The talisman was suddenly in her hand. 'I knew you would come here, Orogastus. I knew you would try again to win me over as you did before. Deciding what to do has torn the heart from my body and perhaps condemned my own soul to hell. But I have vowed that you shall not go forth from this Tower to resume your evil work. Not while it is in my power to prevent you.'

A sudden billow of smoke, blacker than midnight, enveloped her form. As the sorcerer fell back, stunned by the sudden change in her aspect, the darkness swirled and gathered into three great petals, becoming a looming tripartite shape reaching to the library's high ceiling.

A Black Trillium.

She came forth from the centre of the Flower, suspended above the floor, a woman cloaked and hooded in lucent white that somehow seemed to combine within it all the colours of the rainbow. Held high in her right hand, the Three-Winged Circle enclosed a dark void that the sorcerer could not take his eyes from. The void expanded suddenly, as if it were a great round window opening into a night without moons or stars, hiding the glowing form of the Archimage. But her radiance still shone from within the boiling smoke.

She did not speak, and yet he felt himself impelled to enter that Circle, as though it were some viaduct leading to eternity.

'No!' he cried, unwilling to accept that she would really threaten him with death when he had left himself unguarded for love and trust of her. 'Haramis, you cannot do this!'

The Circle widened further, obliterating all view of the library shelves, the furnishings, the great stone hearth, swallowing the very light in the room. He hung amidst shining smoke with doom only an arm's length away, magnetic and terrible, compelling him to enter into unending night.

He was afraid. Mortally afraid. But as the dread Circle continued its advance his prayer was not to the Dark Powers but to her.

'Haramis, dearest Haramis! You cannot play false to our truce, to your oath as Archimage—to our love. Let me go!'

I know it is unjust to destroy you in this way, Orogastus. I know I have lied to you and broken faith. But by doing so I can spare our world great pain – perhaps even prevent its destruction. Without you, your Star Guild will founder and disappear. There will finally be peace and balance.

'My dearest love, is it you yourself who contemplates this monstrous betrayal – or is it that perfidious talisman? Has it tempted you to impose your own will upon destiny? Denby Varcour knew the peril lurking within the Sceptre of Power! He argued with Binah and Iriane against letting you and your sisters possess the pieces of that dire instrument, even when broken apart from its threefold whole. Do you know why? It is because the talismans can own their owners!'

Haramis was silent, hidden. The enormous Circle drew nearer until it hovered only a finger's length from his paralyzed body. Beyond was nothingness. Extinction. In another moment he would be gone. She would consign him to emptiness everlasting, thinking that by trampling her own conscience she would bring about a greater good.

In the extreme of desperation, he cried out to her, 'Do not trust yourself, nor the talisman! Ask your Flower if you should do this. Ask the Black Trillium if it is right that I die this way! Ask the Flower if this is the way to restore the world!'

He was suddenly blind.

The Circle has swallowed me, he thought, and I am alone in the dark forever, with nothing but my own soul showing me my sins over and over again. Why would she not listen to me? Why would she not let me explain –

He heard her weeping.

Felt the fire's warmth.

Smelled wine and the exhalation of ancient bookbindings, paper, and parchment.

He opened his eyes and saw her, crumpled facedown on the rug before the hearth. The Circle on the chain around her neck was an empty silver hoop, but atop it the trillium-amber shone like a tiny winged sun.

Numb with relief, he was capable only of standing stock-still, daring to breathe again, looking down at her. After a time she drew herself upright, sitting there amidst the white folds of her Archimage's cloak.

'How could I?' she asked him, speaking more like a small child confronted with some horror than like a woman repentant. 'Holy Flower, how could I have contemplated such dishonour, even for a moment? And all the while not ceasing to love you?'

'The answer is in your hand,' he told her gravely.

She lowered her eyes to the talisman. 'I do not believe you.' But her fingers opened and she let the Three-Winged Circle drop, swinging from its neck-chain.

He said, 'While I was Denby's captive I discovered things about the Sceptre – about the magic of the three talismans – that you will have to confront and deal with, Haramis. Let me tell you –'

'Go away!' she said in a voice roughened with misery. Her eyes brimmed. 'You have always been a liar and a manipulator. Now I have become like you. Iriane and the Teacher were mistaken. Our love is a despicable thing and I will root it out of myself or die in the trying!'

She attempted to climb to her feet, but her legs were bereft of strength. He helped her up. Then, before she could protest, he kissed her lips fleetingly.

'We will talk again,' he said, 'when you have meditated upon this meeting further. And when other events have helped to clarify your thoughts.'

'Go!' she cried, holding the Circle between them with both hands trembling, her eyes squeezed tightly shut against the fresh tears that would have poured forth. '*Go!*'

He gathered up his discarded vestments and the second Star, put on his own medallion, and went away.

CHAPTER 9

Lummomu-Ko, Speaker of Let, leader of the Wyvilo Folk, and devoted friend of the Lady of the Eyes, had willingly obtained passage for her and her party on a flatboat owned by his cousin that was bound down the Great Mutar River. Over her protests, he had insisted upon accompanying Kadiya as far as the capital of Var, which lay at the rivermouth on the southern coast of the Peninsula.

Kadiya had been tense and moody during the days they had already spent on the voyage. And now the Archimage had come to her in a Sending, and Lummomu had waited for over an hour outside the forward deckhouse while the two sisters conferred secretly. When the Lady of the Eyes emerged at last, the Wyvilo felt his heart sink. Her body was taut with suppressed anger and the grime on her face betrayed the tracks of dried tears.

'The Sending from the White Lady contained evil tidings indeed,' Kadiya declared. 'I must speak at once with Wikit-Aa.'

'My cousin is at the tiller,' Lummomu said. 'Come with me and watch your footing.'

From behind, the Wyvilo chief had the appearance of a very tall, robustly built man; but his race's sizeable admixture of Skritek blood gave him a face that was pointed like that of a beast, having fearsome white teeth and prominent golden eyes with vertical pupils. Both his neck and the backs of his hands were partly scaled and partly clothed with short red hair. Indulging the proclivity of the Forest Folk for human finery, the Speaker of Let was sumptuously attired. His raincloak was of supple maroon leather with embossed golden borders at the hood-edge and hem. He wore pantaloons and a jacket of ochre brocade beneath a sleeveless jerkin of emerald green milingal-hide. His matching jackboots had platform soles and spur-leathers, even though he had never sat a fronial in his life. The outfit was completed by a glittering gem-studded baldric and scabbard of flamboyant Zinoran workmanship.

To the untutored eye, the young woman trailing the splendid aborigine looked to be nothing more than a servant. She wore drab grey wool and scuffed black leather, and only her magnificent sword and her assured bearing hinted that she commanded the expedition.

Kadiya and Lummomu made their way cautiously to the stern of the big boat, dodging around bales and hampers and casks of cargo. The deck was slickened and treacherous from the endless rain. Mist clouded the air and made the distant riverbanks nearly imperceptible, so that the flatboat's midstream progress seemed deceptively slow. But the Great Mutar was already in full spate and the aboriginal trading craft raced through the turbulent brown water almost as fast as a mounted courier could gallop. It was expected that they would reach the twisting river's mouth, and the Varonian capital of Mutavari, within another nine days.

As she passed the lamplit after-deckhouse, she saw young Prince Tolivar and his crony Ralabun through the thick, bubbly windowpane. They were watching the Oathed Companions and the off-duty members of the Wyvilo crew play game after game of dance-bones to alleviate boredom. Jagun had discovered years earlier that he and Ralabun were not destined to be congenial, and so he spent most of his spare time with the Wyvilo skipper, Wikit-Aa.

Kadiya and Lummomu found the pair in the small pilothouse that gave the steersman meagre cover from the elements. With a little crowding, all four of them shared the shelter.

Jagun beheld the despondent look on the Lady's face and murmured, 'Bad news, then, Farseer?'

'There has been a signal disaster,' she said, and proceeded to describe how Queen Anigel had been swept away in the flooded mire near the River Virkar. 'Antar's warriors and the Nyssomu scouts accompanying the royal entourage have searched for two days. They rescued Immu, who was carried off by the waters at the same time as the Queen, but of my poor sister they found no trace.'

'Surely the White Lady's talisman –' Jagun began.

But Kadiya shook her head. 'It will not show where Ani is, nor reveal anything else about her state, not even if she is alive or dead. Clearly, there is dark magic at work.'

Jagun, Lummomu and Wikit-Aa bowed their heads and intoned, 'May the Triune and the Lords of the Air have pity.'

Kadiya continued. 'Since the Queen's Mireway was ruptured – perhaps by lightning, more likely by the sorcery of the Star Men – the royal caravan has had to turn back to Ruwenda Citadel. It will be impossible to perform road repairs until the Dry Time.'

'And the hunt for the poor Queen continues?' Lummomu inquired.

'It does,' Kadiya said, 'with reinforcements from Bonor Castle and the local Nyssomu settlements. But the search may be futile. Just before my sister disappeared, a party of warriors was sent out from the royal train to guard a viaduct site near the mireway. These men have also vanished utterly.'

'By the Holy Flower!' Jagun exclaimed. 'Then it is virtually certain that the Star Men have abducted them all through that viaduct!'

'Certain as the changing phases of the Three Moons,' Kadiya said with a grimace. 'And the almighty White Lady says she can do nothing about it. Nothing! She has been dallying with that bastard Orogastus, and he has somehow got her all in a swivet, and she says she must *think* over the alternatives before taking action! While she dithers about, my poor pregnant sister and the others could be dying – or enduring torture. And so I will go to their rescue myself, since Haramis declines to do so. We must turn back at once.'

'Lady, no!' exclaimed the Wyvilo skipper, in a voice full of dismay. 'You do not understand the difficulty –'

'I have made up my mind, Wikit-Aa,' Kadiya stated. 'You will be handsomely reimbursed for any losses.'

'That is not the point,' Wikit said. 'I would gladly sacrifice my cargo if it would help to rescue your sister the Queen. But to return to Let the way we came, against the flow of the Great Mutar in flood, would take no less than two tennights. Possibly three.'

Lummomu-Ko added, 'And then it is still nine days or more of travel from Let to Bonar Castle via Tass Falls, Lake Wum, and the mireway. After so long a passage of time, how can you hope to find the Queen alive if the White Lady herself has failed?'

'I will seek them until the Conquering Ice freezes the ten hells!' Kadiya declared. 'As to how . . . the answer came to me moments after the Sending of the Archimage had withdrawn. I shall go to the site of that viaduct with a force of brave warriors, and I will command it to open, using words the White Lady taught me. Wherever the viaduct leads, my comrades and I will go – and at the other end we will find the Star Men's hideaway, and the Queen and the other persons held captive.'

'Your Royal Sister may already be dead,' Jagun said quietly.

'Anigel is alive!' Kadiya insisted. 'We are Daughters of the Threefold – Petals of the Living Trillium. I would know if she had expired. Wikit-Aa, I order you to turn back.'

The Wyvilo skipper said, 'Lady of the Eyes, you must understand that this boat is not suitable for upstream travel against a strong current. It is little more than a massive raft with twin deck housings, as befits a watercraft that must withstand the rigors of vicious rapids and the battering

91

of floating debris while hauling much cargo. It is our usual custom, after descending the river to the capital of Var, to sell the boat for its timber after the cargo is disposed of. We make the return journey paddling small Varonian canoes through the shallows.'

'Then you must put me and my knights ashore at the nearest village,' Kadiya said. 'I will procure other small craft and boatmen to take us back to Ruwenda. Prince Tolivar and Ralabun will remain with you, and take ship from Mutavari as we had planned.'

'There are no human villages in these parts,' Wikit told her. 'Until the Truce of the Mire, the people of Var were too terrified of the savage Glismak Folk dwelling hereabouts to even consider using the Great Mutar as a trade-route. Even we Wyvilo shunned the lower section of the river passing through Glismak tribal territory, and this prevented commerce between the Varonians and us. Now, of course, the merchants of Mutavari eagerly welcome our boats. But human settlements along the river are still almost non-existent because of the uncertain temper of the Glismak. There are only rude outposts here and there where factors of the Mutavari companies trade with tribal gold-gatherers or trappers.' He gestured toward the right bank, which was largely obscured by fog. 'One such trading post is nearby, but it is an unsavoury place –'

'Pull in,' Kadiya ordered, 'and we will review the situation.'

It was mid-day when the flatboat docked. The Varonian factor in charge of the dismal outpost was a stocky bearded fellow named Turmalai Yonz. He wore greasy buckskins and had a suspiciously enthusiastic manner. When Kadiya and her party came ashore, he greeted them cordially and brought mugs of salka, the bitter cider that was the national beverage of Var. He went away then, promising to check into the availability of manned small boats.

The day remained dark and gloomy and the rainfall was unabating, leaking through the ill-thatched roof of the porch attached to the factor's squalid lodge. Kadiya, Lummomu, Jagun, Wikit, and Lord Zondain, the senior knight of the six Oathed Companions, sat waiting on crude stools at a rickety table.

'At least the factor seemed sanguine about being able to assist us,' Lord Zondain said in a hopeful tone. 'Can't say that I like the fellow's looks much, though.' The knight was a burly man of two-and-thirty whose sparse hair was already going grey, a native of the Dylex country in northeastern Ruwenda. His younger brothers, Melpotis and Kalepo, who were also part of Kadiya's company, had remained on the boat with the other three knights.

'This Turmalai has the smile of a brigand,' little Jagun said, scowling. 'I have seen his like skulking about the waterfront of Derorguila and the Trevista trade-fairs. They will promise you anything, but delivery is something else again – especially if you have paid in advance.'

'I doubt any well-found craft can be obtained in this wretched pelrik-hole,' growled Lummomu-Ko. With increasing unease he had been watching the activity down by the dock, where figures could be discerned loitering around the Wyvilo vessel. 'The humans in these regions are poor and lawless. The honest merchants of Mutavari hold them in contempt.'

'That is true,' said Wikit-Aa. 'These river people also hate Wyvilo Folk, since we are so much more hardworking and prosperous than they. We never stop at these sorry outposts if we can help it. And I tell you with all sincerity that we would be wise to quit this one promptly and move on.' He tapped his muzzle with one taloned digit. 'My nose itches – and amongst the Wyvilo, that is a sure sign of trouble ahead.'

'I must find a way to return to Ruwenda!' Kadiya was undaunted. 'I don't need a royal trireme, only three or four dugout canoes to accommodate me and Jagun and the knights –'

'And I myself,' Lummomu appended. 'You require a trustworthy guide to lead you through Glismak country, and can hardly hope to find one here.'

Wikit-Aa tossed salka down his throat with practised ease. 'It will be touch and go for the Lady and her party, even with your redoubtable assistance, Cousin. Would it not be wiser to continue downriver to Mutavari, and there embark with the young Prince on a ship sailing around the Peninsula to Labornok?'

'The sea voyage would take even longer than going up the river,' Lummomu said, 'because of the greater distance and the adverse winds at this time of year.'

'And we would then have to travel overland from Derorguila to Ruwenda in order to reach the viaduct,' Kadiya said, 'crossing the Vispir Pass. With the early monsoons, we could find the pass snowed-in by the time we arrived. No . . . I am determined to return up the Mutar.'

The sagging door of the lodge creaked open, and there stood the beaming factor with a tray, on which stood a steaming crock, a stack of chipped bowls, and a collection of wooden spoons. 'Noble guests! This humble one begs you to partake of a nice fresh karuwok stew. Although the utensils are lowly, you will find the dish both bellywarming and delicious on this dreary day.'

Kadiya frowned. 'That is most civil of you, Factor Turmalai, but we did not order food.'

The bearded man chortled and began setting out the bowls. He nodded at a pair of tall shabby youths who had emerged from some rear door and were carrying a covered cauldron and a big wicker-covered salka jug down the muddy path to the river. 'I have taken the liberty of sending my sons with refreshments for your companions on the boat. The cost will be modest, I assure you. While you eat, my associates are looking into your request for small boats with paddlers.'

'The stuff smells edible,' Lord Zondain conceded, sniffing the portion of stew that had been ladled into his bowl, 'and I for one am famished.'

'Splendid!' The factor rubbed his hands and grinned. 'I'll fetch more salka.' He hurried off into the lodge.

Kadiya stared at her dish without enthusiasm, but Zondain was already eating heartily. 'Dig in!' the Companion urged. 'It's actually quite tasty.'

Jagun lifted his spoon and touched his long tongue to the contents.

His yellow eyes popped out on their stalks and he spat, leaping to his feet and knocking over the table so that bowls and salka cups and the stew crock scattered onto the rotting planks of the porch. 'Sacred Flower – it's laced with yistok root! Don't eat it!'

Kadiya, Lummomu-Ko, and Wikit-Aa flung away their spoons and started up, reaching for their weapons. But Lord Zondain still sat on his stool, head lolling forward on his breast.

'Poisoned!' cried the Lady of the Eyes. 'Oh, the treacherous worram-scat! Lummomu, do what you can for poor Zondain, then go and deal with Turmalai. You others – with me to the boat!'

She went flying down the path, her great steel sword shining in the rain, with the Wyvilo skipper and Jagun following. The dock area was an untidy collection of rickety sheds, baled furs and hides, carelessly stacked lengths of timber, and beached watercraft. The factor's sons were evidently aboard Wikit's flatboat. Three other tatterdemalion Varonians guarded the gangplank, one waving a rusty sabre and the other two holding long knives.

Kadiya screamed to those aboard, 'Poison! Poison! Don't eat the food!' At the same time she swung her blade at the sabre-bearer. He parried her blow clumsily, then rushed at her in an attempt to push her from the dock into the fast-flowing river. She sidestepped and thrust forth her booted foot. As the Varonian howled and lost his balance she clubbed him at the base of the neck with her heavy sword-hilt. He hit the brown water with a loud splash and was swept away.

Wikit-Aa had already disposed of his human foe, running him through with a fine blade of Zinoran steel. His muzzle opened in a hideous grin of triumph. 'I'll see what's happening aboard!' he shouted, and leapt aboard the boat and ran to the after-deckhouse, from which came sounds of fighting.

Kadiya whirled around to help Jagun. He had sliced his attacker's left leg, drawing blood, but the ruffian had backed the diminutive Nyssomu into a cul-de-sac formed by two big bales of tarenial hides. Giggling in anticipation, the human was drawing back his arm to fling his knife into Jagun's throat when Kadiya hacked off the limb below the elbow. The Varonian fell screaming in a welter of blood.

At that moment a human form crashed out through the starboard deck-house window. It was one of the treacherous factor's sons, who hit the boat's rail, clung to it precariously for a moment, then slid screeching into the river as a knight leaned through the windowframe and swiped at him with a bloody sword. There were cheers from inside.

Another Oathed Companion, Sir Bafrik, came to the deckhouse door and yelled, 'We've done for the bastards, Princess! How fare you?'

'Go up to the lodge, some of you! See if Lummomu needs assistance.' As several knights dashed away she turned back to the injured Varonian, who sat clutching his severed arm with an ashen face. 'Will you die, fellow, or shall I tend to your wound?'

'If – if you please, gracious Lady,' he moaned.

The rain had stopped and it was nearly dark. Sir Bafrik and Sir Sainlat brought out a gore-smeared youth and flung him unceremoniously onto the dock next to the dead man, where he lay half conscious. Young Prince Tolivar crept from the deckhouse with the Nyssomu Ralabun, both of them seeming to be dazed with terror, and surveyed the scene. Wikit-Aa gave his crewmen a few orders, then came and stood impassively with Jagun, watching Kadiya minister to the wounded man.

She used his belt to make a tourniquet, which stanched the deadly spurting of blood. Her nearly clean kerchief served to bind the stump. 'Do you have halaka resin among your stores?' she asked the patient when she had finished. 'It is the only thing that will do for treating this kind of injury.'

'I – I know not,' he whispered. 'Factor Turmalai keeps all such medic-aments under lock and key.'

'If there is none, I shall have to sear the stump with fire,' Kadiya warned, 'or you will die of the putrid rot. On your feet, then. The skipper and I will help you up to the lodge.'

With Jagun following, she and Wikit supported the one-armed Varon-ian, who was on the verge of collapse, and dragged him to the factor's dilapidated hovel. Turmalai, alternately bellowing curses and sobbing, had been lashed to a stout wooden chair and was guarded by Lummomu and

Sir Edinar. Kadiya directed the two Wyvilo to put the injured man in another room and care for him as best they could. Then she noticed for the first time that Sir Melpotis and Sir Kalepo knelt beside an improvised pallet in a corner. Lord Zondain rested there, unmoving and with features pale as wax.

'How fares he?' Kadiya asked.

Young Melpotis shook his head. His cheeks were wet with tears.

Kalepo said, 'Lady, our noble brother Zondain has passed safely beyond, borne into glory by the Lords of the Air.'

'May the Triune God grant him mercy,' Kadiya whispered. For a minute she gazed down at the dead Companion. Then her blazing brown eyes lifted slowly and regarded the captive factor, who had not ceased his noisy lamentation.

'Maggot-ridden offal,' she said, striding to confront him. 'Is it your usual mode of hospitality to poison your guests?'

Turmalai Yonz made no reply, but only continued to keen and sob wildly over his lost sons. He had seen the fight on the dock before being captured and tied up by Lummomu.

'Tchaa!' Wikit-Aa exclaimed in contempt. 'The one murderous stripling was only knocked senseless after receiving small wounds, while the other who went overboard was seen to reach shore some fifty ells downstream.'

'My precious boys are alive?' the factor cried. 'Praise be to Tesdor the Compassionate, the Life-Giving!'

Kadiya seized a handful of the factor's dirty hair and hauled his head erect. Her other hand held a poniard. 'You are indeed blessed, you sack of woth-vomit,' she remarked conversationally. 'Your misbegotten whelps have escaped the death they justly deserved.' Her blade's point pricked Turmalai's throat. 'But *you* will face the judgement of your god not two minutes from now unless you give me true answers to my questions.'

The factor squirmed and gave a gargling cry.

'Why did you poison our food?' Kadiya demanded. 'Was it only for merry mischief's sake, in order to rob us . . . or did you have another reason?'

Turmalai's eyes rolled desperately. The sharp steel at his throat drew a threadlike trickle of blood.

'There was . . . an offer,' he croaked. 'To all of us who dwell along the river. If we were able to capture you, dead or alive, and bring you to a certain spot before the next fullness of the Moons, there would be a reward of a thousand platinum crowns.'

'Zoto's Holy Heel-Spurs!' exclaimed Sir Kalepo, for the amount was

96

literally a king's ransom. He and his brother Melpotis left off their vigil beside their dead brother and stood with the Lady of the Eyes.

'Who promised this extravagant largesse?' Kadiya let loose of the factor with a grimace and sheathed her dagger.

'There was no name given,' Turmalai Yonz said sullenly. 'Only the place where you were to be taken, beside the Double Cascade that lies up the River Oda, which has its confluence with the Mutar some twenty leagues downstream from here. I could not believe my good fortune when you came ashore.'

Kadiya reached beneath her cloak and drew forth a folded piece of cloth, which she opened. 'Can you read a map, qubar-dropping?'

'Yes, Lady.'

She indicated a river on the inscribed napkin. 'Here is the Oda. Is this red dot the location where the reward was to be paid for us?'

He squinted at the cloth thrust beneath his nose. 'Y-yes. The very place. You were to be brought there at dawn on any day during this present moon, and those putting up the reward would be waiting.'

'Dawn . . .' Kadiya gave a curt nod, then put away the chart of viaduct sites and turned to the knights. 'Companions, bring Lord Zondain's body down to the dock. We will build his funeral pyre with the trade goods of this pitiful assassin.'

'No!' Turmalai Yonz cried. 'I'll be ruined!'

'Be grateful,' Sir Kalepo retorted, 'that you and your surviving people are not also serving as fuel for the flames.' He, Edinar, and Melpotis bore away the body.

Lummomu and Wikit came out from the other room. 'We found the medication,' Lummomu said, 'and applied it to the rogue's wound. There was also a bottle of fine Galanari brandy, which he consumed to the relief of his pain. He now lies senseless.'

'You didn't give him the last of the good stuff?' the factor wailed.

Melpotis smote him on the ear and he subsided, whimpering.

'What shall we do with this abominable creature, Lady?' Lummomu asked Kadiya.

'Let him stay lashed to the chair until someone comes to free him. If the wounded man does not die, he will awake from his drunken stupor some time late tomorrow.'

'And what of your desire to travel upstream?' Wikit asked. 'There are skiffs here that might serve your purpose.'

'I have changed my mind. Please return to the flatboat and make ready to cast off. Jagun and I will join you shortly.'

Kadiya beckoned to her Nyssomu friend and he followed her out into the darkness. They went off to the side of the lodge and stood beneath the dripping branches of a large ombako tree.

'I would like you to bespeak my sister, the White Lady,' she said to the aborigine, 'and bid her Send to me.'

'Very well,' said Jagun. His luminous eyes closed and his small body became rigid as a billet of wood as he sent out the Call in the speech without words.

An instant later Haramis stood there, so ghostly and insubstantial that one five paces away would not have been able to discern her.

What is it, Kadi?

'Have you watched what took place here?'

No, said the Archimage. *I have been occupied with other matters.*

Kadiya told the tale quickly, whereupon the White Lady became very agitated. *I should have anticipated this! What a fool I have been. Of course they would try to seize you after capturing poor Ani!*

'To exert pressure upon you?' Kadiya inquired grimly.

Beyond doubt.

'And would you surrender your talisman if Orogastus showed you Ani and me embedded in blue ice?'

No, said the Archimage.

Kadiya smiled. 'Good! . . . Obviously I cannot attempt to return upriver through the shallows now, not with every lowborn mudsucker on the Great Mutar lying in wait for me, licking his chops. I shall have to go on as we planned originally, to Sobrania.'

Not long ago I viewed the young Star Man who incited the Skritek taking ship from Taloazin in Zinora. He was bound for Sobrania as well. Whether or not the Star Guild is headquartered there, it is at least a suitable place to begin our investigation.

'What will you do about Ani? . . . I had made up my mind to enter that viaduct in the Mazy Mire in search of her, whether you approved or not.'

That will not be necessary. I have already decided to go through it myself. Pray for me, dear Kadi.

The Sending vanished, but Kadiya stared for some time at the patch of dark foliage where the image of Haramis had been. Finally Jagun put a hand on her shoulder.

'Farseer, they are lighting Lord Zondain's pyre. We should be there.'

'Yes,' she sighed. They set off for the dock together in the dreary rain. After a few moments, she said, 'Jagun, are you willing to accompany me on a journey that may be far more dangerous than a sea voyage to Sobrania?'

'You know that I am. And the five Oathed Companions will surely tell you likewise. Where are we to go?'

'We will discuss it,' said the Lady of the Eyes, 'after bidding farewell to Zondain.'

CHAPTER 10

After Queen Anigel's struggle in the chill water and subsequent plunge through the clangorous void, there was a long interval of complete silence. Then her senses began slowly to return. She lay in some sort of conveyance that moved and jolted along, feeling in many different parts of her body severe pain that ebbed and flowed, blurring the passage of time and making rational thought impossible. She was aware of green twilight through briefly-opened eyelids, and spicy forest smells, and the sound of unfamiliar birds. Someone spoke to her but the words were impossible to understand. She drifted back into unconsciousness.

Then it was night, and she heard hoofs clattering on rock in the darkness. The wagon pitched wildly, aggravating her injuries. She wept in helpless anguish until finally they came to a halt. Rough male voices mingled with the nervous whickers of steeds and draught-beasts and her own feeble sobs, muffled by blankets. Every breath she took produced a stab of pain. Her right leg would not move, nor would her left arm. Suddenly she was shocked by a thunderous explosion, and her wounded body leapt as lesser concussions occurred and the animals shrieked in terror.

Someone shouted a command. The wagon lurched forward once more, resuming its jarring progress. But now it seemed to her confused brain that they had departed from the natural world somehow and travelled instead through the innermost of the ten hells, for she saw through swollen eyes roaring columns of fire, orange against the night sky. The heat was so intense that she thrashed about the wagon bed in an agony of fear, calling out brokenly for her husband.

King Antar did not reply. All she heard was a hoarse shout: 'Faster, damn you! Use your whips. Any minute it'll rain, and that'll be the death of us all!'

The jouncing and tossing movement of the wagon then increased so tremendously that the pain-racked Queen fainted away, once again entering a world of formless dreams. This state continued until a light, so bright that it penetrated even her closed eyelids, flicked briefly over her face and left coloured stars in its wake. She heard indistinct speech. The fire-heat was gone. She was no longer travelling but at rest upon a couch or bed indoors, quite unable to move. Then something hard and dull jabbed at one side of her throat, and once again she lost her senses.

When she came to herself again it was daytime and very quiet. She lay betwixt sleep and waking, unsure at first whether that which she experienced was real.

I am Anigel, she said to herself. I am Queen of Laboruwenda and I was broken and drowned, but now I am whole and alive.

She was not certain how she knew these things, and she had no memory at all of how the drowning had come to pass. She lay flat on her back beneath a thin coverlet. Two unyielding pillows as firm as sandbags prevented her from moving her head, which was slightly elevated. Her hands and feet were also restrained in some manner but she was not uncomfortable. Deep within her abdomen there was an infinitesimal flutter and she smiled. Her babes were also alive.

Anigel could see a low ceiling framed with ancient timbers, and the upper parts of stone walls. On her right was a casement window open to a grey sky, having coarse-woven draperies. The breeze carried a faint, pungent scent that she could not immediately identify.

On the lefthand wall hung a large tapestry done in vivid colours. What she could see of it depicted a female hero with long red tresses, clad below the neck in exotic plate-armour, poised to smite some downed foe with her sword. Tall flames, nearly the colour of the woman's hair, spewed from the rocks on either side of the combatants. In the background, the charred remains of a devastated forest made skeletal black patterns against a lurid sky that was heavy with storm clouds.

Yes. The smell in the air was that of burnt wood, intensified by recent rain . . .

Puzzled and disoriented, Anigel studied the wall-hanging for some time. It was not of woven fabric. What was it made of? What land was it intended to show? And what manner of foe was it that the heroic barbarian woman was about to dispatch? It seemed vitally important to Queen Anigel that she know these things, although she did not understand why. She cudgelled her brain until the answers came.

Feathers. The brilliant tapestry was wrought of intricately layered feathers, and the triumphant woman was about to slay a cringing red-bearded man of oddly familiar aspect. He wore a gaudy cloak and clutched the handle of an ornate battle-axe.

Feathers . . .

Sobrania.

Suddenly she knew beyond any doubt that she was in that country of

101

the far west where the weather was clement throughout most of the year and prodigal numbers of birds inhabited the fertile forests. The Land of the Feathered Barbarians was a scattered collection of little kingdoms and tribes, whose self-styled 'emperor', Denombo, reigned over but did not truly rule the truculent people. But Sobrania lay thousands of leagues distant from the Mazy Mire. The only way she could have been transported there was –

'No!' the Queen cried out. She began to fight against her restraints with all her strength, but to no avail. She was as helpless as a trussed togar lying on a poulterer's stand.

But why, she asked herself, did not my trillium-amber protect me as I fell into the floodwaters?

Was it because she had failed to formulate the prayer in time – or was there some other reason? *Had she lost the amulet?* Had some villain taken it from her? There was no way she could tell, for the coverlet reached to her chin and she was unable to shift it, in spite of her futile struggling.

She fell back exhausted at last and let her eyes close, trying not to weep. Anger, frustration, and fear laid siege to her, but she refused to surrender to them, taking long slow breaths in an attempt to calm herself. She tried to think who might have captured her, and for what reason, but her muddled mind gave no answer and the very attempt at thought made her head ache.

Black Trillium, she prayed in despair, help me! Help me!

For an instant the tripartite Flower seemed to glow behind her lowered eyelids. Then Queen Anigel slipped again into dreamless sleep.

CHAPTER 11

'White Lady, all of us in your household beg of you—do not do this baneful thing!'

Tears brimmed from the enormous inhuman eyes of Magira, Vispi chatelaine of the Archimage's Tower. For an instant, the tall slender body of the aboriginal woman seemed to flicker and disappear, leaving only those ice-green orbs, overflowing with woe and apprehension, shining in the dimness of the Archimage's room. Then the eyes blinked and Magira became visible once more, clad in her filmy scarlet gown with the jewelled collar. Her face was nearly human in delineation, save for the overlarge eyes and the graceful upstanding ears nearly hidden in her pale hair. She and others of her race had served Haramis zealously ever since she had assumed her white cloak of office.

Although Vispi Folk were notably hotblooded, Magira was shivering violently from the intensity of her emotion, clasping her own body as if to fend off deadly chill. 'Forgive me!' she wailed. She disappeared again briefly, as her kind were liable to do when gripped by strong emotion, and when she rematerialized she seemed more composed. 'I beseech you most urgently to reconsider. Do not enter the viaduct that swallowed your sister the Queen.'

Haramis was sitting at a small table in her private sitting room, where she had been making a few last notes on her magical slate concerning a sea-search for ancient weapons to be conducted by the Mere Folk. It was nearly midnight, the time she had selected for her departure. The latest snowstorm to sweep the Ohogan Mountains had blown itself out and the Three Moons shone brilliantly through the chamber window on a night of intense cold, silvering the leaves and flowers of the great Black Trillium plant in its pot.

'Magira, dear friend, my mind is made up,' the Archimage said with kindly firmness. 'You must reassure the others and tell them that I do this only because I have no other choice. I am sorry that you are so distressed –'

Magira interrupted, speaking in a tremulous whisper. 'White Lady, never before, during all the years I have served you, have I presumed to question your wisdom. But this journey you would make into the viaduct is different. You know that we Vispi are the most ancient of Folk, charged with special tasks by our Vanished creators. Over thousands of years, memories of our duties grew dimmer and dimmer, and much was forgotten or passed into legend. But our obligation concerning the viaducts has remained clear: We were commanded to shun them because they are mortally dangerous, and see that no other beings entered them inadvertently. If you go into one of those secret portals, we may never see you again! Only the Vanished Ones understood the way that the viaducts worked. Others who dared to enter never returned. It is said that the most awful thing about the viaducts is that they do not lead an intruder to clean death, but rather to a realm of unending horror where the soul abides alive, in an agony of fear forever, with no hope of escape.'

'I cannot simply remain here, waiting upon events,' Haramis said with determination. 'Every day, I discover new mischief wrought by the minions of Orogastus. I have not yet told you of the latest enormity, which I confirmed only this morning. Seven other rulers besides my sister Anigel have mysteriously vanished: dear old Widd and Raviya of Engi, the Queen of Galanar, the King of Raktum, and the elected chief executives of Imlit and Okamis. All of them disappeared shortly before Queen Anigel was taken. No one in the affected nations would admit to me what had happened – doubtless for fear that the missing rulers will be slain. I only confirmed their absence through my talisman's magic, after my requests to confer with them in person were oddly denied. I have since told the heads of state of Var, Zinora, and Tuzamen what has happened, and I have also cautioned King Antar. They will take stringent precautions against being kidnapped themselves.'

'Do you think that the captured human rulers were spirited away through viaducts, in the same manner as Queen Anigel?'

'Beyond doubt. And this makes it all the more urgent for me to locate the headquarters of the Star Guild myself, and as soon as possible. I can no longer wait while Kadiya takes a long sea-journey to Sobrania. If I do not take action I can only yield the advantage to Orogastus. Do not fret about me, Magira. I shall go invisible into the viaduct that swallowed Queen Anigel, armed with my strongest magic.'

'But if aught goes awry –'

'I am confident that the Three-Winged Circle and the amulet of trillium-amber within it will keep me safe.' Haramis rose from the table, coming to Magira and laying her hand upon the chatelaine's shoulder. 'I have no other choice, dear friend. Kadiya was quite right when she pointed out

104

to me that the viaduct through which Anigel was abducted is our only significant clue to the whereabouts of the villainous Star Men. It must certainly lead to a region not far from the Guild's stronghold – if not within the very headquarters itself. I do not intend to attack the Star Men at this time, nor undertake any other rash encounters. I shall simply observe them. If all goes well, I'll return before morning.'

The chatelaine bowed. 'Very well, Lady. May the Lords of the Air defend you.' Magira left the room.

Haramis went into her bedchamber and donned a sturdy outfit she had had specially made by the Tower tailor, a hooded tunic and trousers of water-repellent white cloth. She also wore leather gloves and boots, and at her belt was a pouch with food and water and a small clasp-knife. Over this garb she fastened her Archimage's cloak. After kneeling briefly in prayer, she lifted the Three-Winged Circle.

'Talisman, I command you to make me invisible to all viewers.' When this was accomplished she transported herself to that viaduct in the Mazy Mire through which her sister the Queen had been kidnapped.

As the usual crystalline vision of her destination attained solidity, Haramis found herself standing on a small patch of high ground in the midst of the flooded swamp. It was night and raining dismally, but her magic gave her clear sight of the locale. She had been here before, of course, seeking clues to Anigel's abduction. The trampled mud round about the site of the viaduct had long since been smoothed by the unrelenting downpour. The only peculiar thing about the place was a nearly imperceptible straight line an ell or so in length that persistently indented the soggy earth. Her talisman would have called forth the viaduct had she made the request, but it was high time that she used nonmagical means for the summoning.

Haramis conjured in her mind a vision of the uncanny portal, at the same time that she softly said, 'Viaduct system activate.'

And it was there, heralded by the usual bell-chime, a tall disk blacker than the shades of night, standing on edge within its notch in the ground and faintly haloed with pearly light. It had no thickness and both its front and back surfaces were identical. It mattered not which way the thing was entered by a would-be traveller.

Haramis remembered from her cursory examination of Iriane's book that the viaducts had two principal modes of operation. One might simply step in and be taken automatically to a preordained destination, as she herself had once travelled from the Kimilon Plateau to Iriane's home in the Auroral Sea. Or, one might enter and simultaneously give a rather complex mental command, asking to be transported to the place of one's choice. Haramis did not intend to risk the latter option until she understood the viaducts much better.

The only sign that this wondrous device of the Vanished Ones was more than an impenetrable ebon cutout was a faint breath of moving air emanating from it. Earlier, when Haramis had experimentally activated this particular viaduct but had not dared to enter, that breeze from nowhere had carried a pleasant woodsy scent. Now, oddly enough, the smell was unmistakably that of baking bread!

She asked her talisman, 'Where does this viaduct lead?'

The Three-Winged Circle replied, *The question is impertinent.*

She sighed. It was as she had expected. The viaduct would yield up its secret only in one way. She stepped inside.

Now she felt again the same horrid suffocation she had experienced while travelling to the Blue Lady's northern realm, the same sense of hanging suspended in nothingness while her mind exploded to the accompaniment of a gigantic, throbbing musical note.

The trip to Iriane's artificial iceberg had taken scarcely a moment. But this passage was more prolonged, bringing Haramis to the edge of panic as the explosion seemed to go on and on, separating the very fabric of her body into its component atoms, scattering them beyond any hope of retrieval, leaving her soul adrift in a hammering void.

Oh, dear God, she thought. Have you abandoned me after all? Am I trapped here in the dark forever? . . .

'Welcome.'

She heard a raspy voice, smelt the wonderful homely scent of fresh bread more strongly, felt sudden warmth and a firm surface beneath her feet, saw –

A very old man with a brownish complexion and silvery eyes with great black pupils nodding at her. He was grinning in delight. Obviously, the talisman had not rendered her invisible to *him*. His white hair was curly, standing out from his pate like sparse zuch-wool. He wore a floor-length robe of dusty black with a hem-border of tarnished diamond glitter, and over it an ordinary cook's apron badly in need of laundering.

She gaped at him, astonished beyond speech. They stood in a kind of foyer, with the standing black disc of the viaduct in the centre and four corridors extending away into dim distance like the spokes of a wheel. The old man beckoned for her to follow him a short distance down one of the hallways and turned into an open door. The chamber was brightly lit, cluttered, and bizarre – but nonetheless recognizable as some kind of kitchen. Along one gleaming greenish wall was a metal counter crowded with baskets of fresh fruits and vegetables, transparent crocks of honey, colourful jars of jam and conserves, and neat little vials of dried spices. Copper pots and pans hung from ceiling hooks, and on cupboard shelves stood smallish machines of unknown function and an astonishing variety of ceramic boxes and containers, all labelled in an unfamiliar alphabet.

In the middle of the room stood an oddly styled table with a stool beside it. It held a large glass bowl covered with a red-checked towel, a greased metal sheet having coarsely ground meal scattered on it, a floured board, a saucer of pale bubbly liquid with a brush in it, a lump of butter on a plate, and a large serrated knife. Against another wall were what appeared to be more storage cupboards, and also several singular doors with little windows in them, one of them obscurely illuminated within Above it a glowing red gem blinked slowly.

'Just in time, too!' the old man giggled. 'I know I should let it cool, but it tastes so much better fresh out of the oven.'

He picked up a pair of padded-cloth potholders and opened the bejewelled wall door, whisking out a sheet with three long, narrow, golden-brown loaves upon it. He slammed the oven door (causing the red light to wink out) and transferred the bread to a wire rack. Then he took off his apron and began to wash his floury hands at a marvellous sink with no pump, which apparently produced both hot and cold water if one simply willed it.

'We haven't met formally,' the elderly man continued, looking at her over his shoulder as he shook off excess water and fumbled with another checked towel. 'I'm Denby Varcour, your celestial colleague.' He spun about, struck a pose, and pointed his right index finger at the smoking bread. 'Can't wait. *Pa-choof!*' He giggled as one of the long loaves executed a kind of skip, rising minimally into the air and then dropping back onto the rack. 'Yes! That's cooled it just enough.'

Taking a handsome wooden tray from a sideboard he began loading it up, opening one cupboard after another. He found two faceted crystal plates and matching mugs, and a pair of small silver spreading knives. He took a glass pitcher of white liquid from what was apparently a magical cold-vault located next to the sink, then grabbed the plate of butter from the table, the big saw-toothed knife, and the loaf of bread he had lately enchanted.

'Do you fancy jam or meat-paste?' he inquired.

She could only shake her head mutely.

'Quite right. Plain and simple's the best, I say! Come along.'

He kicked at a swinging door, which opened wide into a large room of surpassing untidiness that seemed to be a study or library. The shelves contained not only books but also transparent holders full of the magical

107

slates that she knew were the reference materials of the Vanished Ones. Peculiar metal contrivances that might have been scientific instruments stood here and there on stands. Marching ahead of her, Denby plopped the tray down onto a wooden table in front of an expanse of closed blue velvet draperies. Beside the drapes was a tall round door having a very elaborate bejewelled plaque instead of a latch or knob.

A conjuring flick of Denby's finger sent books, papers, and mysterious small black gadgets cascading off the table onto the carpeted floor, giving room for them to eat. He drew out a leather chair and bade her to be seated, then plumped down into another chair opposite her.

'Forgot the napkins,' he observed, twinkling. 'But never mind. One of the tenders will oblige.' He snapped his fingers. In a moment, an amazing little machine like a mechanical lingit with an open box for a body pushed through the kitchen door and crept up to the table. One of its many jointed limbs took two folded linen squares from its back compartment and laid them neatly beside each plate.

'Will there be anything else, master?' the thing inquired in a buzzy small voice.

'Perhaps a cup of tea?' Denby asked Haramis.

She shook her head, still too bemused to speak.

Denby told the machine, 'Pick up the stuff on the floor and put it on the desk over there.' Then he folded his gnarled hands and bowed his head. 'Thanks be to the Source of Eternal Light for this good food.' Seizing the loaf, he gleefully sawed it into slices with the bread-knife. It was still hot enough to steam slightly. He slathered butter on both their portions and filled the mugs from the pitcher. 'It's nice cold volumnial milk. You still drink it down there, don't you?'

'Yes . . .' She picked up her piece of bread, stared at it for a moment, then lifted her eyes to her host. 'You are he. The Archimage of the Firmament.'

His mouth stuffed full, the old man gave a blissful nod.

'Was it you, then, who abducted my sister the Queen and the other human rulers?'

Denby shook his head, still chewing. 'Jus' you. Necess'ry.' The old man downed a gulp of milk, then wiped his greasy fingers on his napkin. 'Temp'rarily changed Oro's programming of the viaduct to bring you for a visit. O' course I'm able to countermand anybody else's transportation directives.'

'Then . . . Anigel and the others are not here?'

'No. But *you* most indubitably are! And to stay – at least for a while.' He began to laugh uproariously, wheezing and rocking back and forth, flinging crumbs in all directions. The small domestic machine patiently began cleaning up the mess.

Haramis was striving to keep control of her emotions. 'What do you mean – "to stay"?'

'Oh, dear child! We'll have such wonderful talks, you and I. You must tell me all about your life – and the lives of your sisters as well. I've been so disgusted with the world below, sunk in melancholic despair. What to do, what to do! I arranged for Orogastus to be born before Binah came up with the new scheme, and from the start I thought that hers was silly and futile. But sentimental Iriane loved it, and between the two of them they bullied me into giving it a try. I couldn't believe three young girls would be able to set things right when *we'd* tried and failed, but you triplets did find the pieces of the Sceptre. It seemed that there might be something magical about you after all – something to do with the way you focused and influenced the threads of worldly destiny. Petals of the Living Trillium combined with the resurgence of the Star! Magical science versus scientific magic! I never did divine the straights of it myself, and now it doesn't matter. You ultimately failed, just as I knew you would. But I'll see that it all comes right in the end. Wait and see.'

'I don't know what you're talking about,' Haramis said in great bewilderment.

He gave a crafty wink. 'It's genuine magic in that trillium-amber of yours – quite beyond the magical science of the Star and the Archimagical College. Most intriguing – and dangerous as well! I was half-afraid the amber might prevent my bringing you here and winding it all up, but everything worked splendidly.'

She decided that he was certainly mad, just as Orogastus had said, but she gave calm reply. 'I am sorry that I cannot accept your kind invitation to stay, Archimage of the Firmament. In plain fact, I intend to leave you at this very instant. Other important business demands my attention.' She grasped the Three-Winged Circle, visualized her Tower on Mount Brom, and awaited the crystalline vision that always preceded her magical transport.

Nothing happened.

The zany good humour left Denby's face as swiftly as a footprint in sand is obliterated by an ocean wave, leaving his countenance grimly triumphant. He stood up, leaning his knuckles on the table, and his voice, formerly cracked and enfeebled, now had a metallic resonance. 'The magic you learned from Iriane won't work here, Haramis. It draws its potency from the land which is your personal archimagical domain. Neither will the talisman obey you, because its power derives from planetary

109

wellsprings, and you are beyond their sphere of influence as well. The only way out of here is through the viaducts that I control – or *that* way.' He chortled, nodding at the round door beside the drapes. It was made of a metallic black material, with a single enormous hinge. 'But that door leads to a release that is eternal, and only I myself will ever pass through it.'

Haramis' face was alight with anger. 'Denby, I warn you –'

'Resign yourself, Archimage.' The condescending smile reappeared. 'I intend that you shall stay with me until the time is appropriate for you to leave.'

'And I say you are wrong! For I can still call upon a third source of magical power that has been mine since my birth.' Haramis touched the silvery wings shielding her trillium-amber and they spread open, revealing a tiny bright light like a golden star. Denby gave a squawk of dismay as she got up and went to the round door. 'You were quite right about the magic of my amulet,' Haramis continued. 'It is independent of the talisman and capable of aiding me in many ways. I regret that I shall be unable to discuss them with you. Suffice to say that the amber will open every lock in this dwelling of yours – including this one.'

Denby leapt to his feet, genuine alarm on his brown, withered features. 'Haramis – wait!' he cried. 'You don't understand! You can't open that! It would be the death of you!' He stumbled to the enshrouded window beside the round black door and pulled the blue velvet draperies back.

Haramis uttered a cry of consternation. Leaning heavily against a chair, she stared at the scene outside. It was a night sky, strewn with multi-coloured stars beyond counting. Three side-lit heavenly bodies hung amidst the profusion of twinkling points – one seeming to be of modest size, coloured blue and white, the other two much larger and silvery, without recognizable features.

'Sacred Flower!' Haramis whispered. 'You've taken me to your Moon!'

'Yes,' Denby said, now almost apologetic. 'You really can't go until I let you. It's *necessary* that you stay, I tell you . . . just as it's necessary for Iriane to remain out of the picture for the time being.'

'What? You know of her monstrous captivity and will do nothing to help her?' Eyes ablaze, Haramis strode to the Dark Man and took hold of his skinny shoulders. 'You doddering lunatic! What kind of silly game do you think you're playing?'

'No game! No game!' he wailed. 'Ow! That hurts. Forbear, young Archimage! I'm twelve thousand years old and my bones are brittle and my poor heart is weak. I may just drop dead on you if you treat me too roughly. Then you'll never get back home.'

110

She turned him loose and spoke in tones of icy contempt. 'Explain yourself, then. Where is my sister Anigel if she is not here – and why have you dared to interfere with me in the execution of my solemn duties?'

He lifted his hands in a placating gesture. 'The Queen is safe enough, along with the other rulers. Orogastus has them locked up in his castle in Sobrania. It's all part of my plan.'

The drop of trillium-amber atop the Three-Winged Circle now began to shine like a tiny sun as the face of Haramis became awesome in its wrathful resolution. 'Denby Varcour,' she intoned, 'I command you, as your fellow Archimage and peer, to send me back to the world at once – or face dreadful consequences.'

His shaken nerves seemed to be mending. He tilted his head, pursing his lips in a teasing grimace. 'What consequences? Do you plan to shake the teeth out of my crumbling skull if I disobey? Or deny your sacred oath and slay me – a feeble old eccentric who only has the best interests of the world at heart? You could easily do so with just your bare hands, you know. But I beg you to hold off, lovely young Haramis. I brought you here for a very good reason.' His expression turned mock-reproachful. 'And I was so sure you'd enjoy the new bread.'

'*What do you want?*' she cried in desperation.

Abruptly, he seemed both serious and sane. 'Archimage, you know that the World of the Three Moons that you love so much is out of balance, threatened with catastrophe.'

'I – I do know that. My sisters and I have tried to restore this balance, as it was prophesied of us. Once we thought all would be well when Orogastus was conquered, but that did not prove to be the case. Now I suspect that only the reassembly of the broken Sceptre of Power will alleviate the peril that threatens.'

'Yes!' the Archimage of the Firmament affirmed. 'It holds the secret, all right. The Sceptre, that damnable instrument capable of both restoring the world and annihilating it. You have one piece, and the other two are . . .' The old man trailed off, shaking his head. 'But there is much more to the matter than that.'

'Then explain,' she demanded.

He essayed a tentative little smile. 'It would help your understanding, I think, if you first allowed me to show you something. Will you accompany me to that Moon over there? There's a viaduct in the alcove next to the middle bookcase.'

She frowned. 'Orogastus spoke of a Garden Moon and a Death Moon.'

'It is to the latter we must go.' As Denby gestured, opening the viaduct, the familiar bell-tone sounded and a dark disk sprang into existence. 'I'm not trying to trick you, lass. I'll go first, if you like.'

He disappeared. Haramis hesitated for a moment. 'The Death Moon! I must be as mad as Denby.' She took hold of her talisman, murmured a brief prayer, and followed.

They emerged and stood side by side on a round piece of transparent scaffolding, suspended in murky crimson twilight. Above them, below them, and on all sides extending as far as they could see into the distance floated a myriad of golden spheres some two ells in diameter, each one tethered to others nearby with barely visible gossamer threads, as though they were caught in an enormous, elegantly woven lingit-web spangled with huge drops of dew. When her eyes became better accustomed to the dim light, Haramis realized that the spheres were transparent, filled with some kind of luminous mist. Inside each one was a human form, motionless, attired in garments of a strange cut.

'Dear Lords of the Air,' Haramis exclaimed, stricken. 'There must be thousands upon thousands of them! Who are they?'

'Those who were unable to Vanish,' said Denby Varcour.

CHAPTER 12

'Are they truly dead?' Haramis asked, overwhelmed with pity and horror at the sight of the countless glowing bubbles and the bodies within them – men, women, and children.

'No,' said Denby. 'They sleep, as they must continue to do, forgotten by everyone except me and the surviving sindona.'

'But why can't you free them?' she cried. 'The poor souls – neither dead nor truly alive! It's dreadful!'

'I've waited twelve thousand years, hoping that the appropriate time would come. But it never did. If these people were revived now –' He broke off, shaking his head.

'What would happen?' Haramis demanded.

'I'll tell it all to you, lass,' said Denby, taking her arm and pulling her back toward the black disk of the viaduct, 'the real story – not the half-truths you got from Iriane during your time of study. But we can't talk here. Not in this accursed Death Moon. Come with me.'

In spite of herself she was drawn away again into ringing darkness. When the passage was complete they were in another place that at first sight seemed ordinary enough, a paved hexagonal eminence a dozen ells in diameter, bordered by a parapet of pierced stone. The sun shone brightly overhead, and for a moment she felt a great surge of joy and relief, thinking that they had returned to the world of her birth.

'Come and take a look,' Denby said, going to the platform's edge and flinging out one arm in an inviting gesture.

Standing beside him, Haramis gave a cry of amazement. She and the Archimage of the Firmament stood atop an enormous pyramid composed of stacked terraces. The level directly beneath was planted with geometric beds of blue and orange flowers, alternating with orchards of small trees laden with many different kinds of fruit. The third terrace from the top had groves of larger trees, meadowlike expanses where some kind of animals grazed, and irregular bodies of water that glistened in the sunlight. Still lower were more green terraces, broad and encircling, that spread far down into the misty depths. Haramis lifted her eyes, looking off into the

113

distance, and was astounded to discover other huge pyramids dimly visible in every direction. There was no horizon, only a dizzying concavity soaring upward, bearing endless numbers of the mysterious prominences. And what she at first thought were oddly shaped dark clouds on the blue bowl of the sky turned out to be more hexagonal shapes, closely spaced, with the 'sun' obscuring the smallest ones immediately overhead.

They were inside a colossal globe studded with pyramidal gardens, having a bright light-source at its centre.

'Once there were dwellings and pleasure-domes and places for games here,' the Dark Man said. 'But their emptiness made me sad, so I had the sindona take everything away but the plantings and the things in the Grotto of Memory.' Again he took her arm. 'We'll go down to the grotto now. But I wanted you to see the Garden Moon from this vantage point first.'

The viaduct had changed into a black circular pit precisely at the centre of the platform. Before she could say a word, Denby stepped nonchalantly into it and dropped out of sight.

'I'll never get used to this,' Haramis murmured crossly. Holding tight to her talisman, she followed the old man.

Instantly, she found herself in a sun-dappled woodland clearing, standing beside her smiling host. A little pool glimmered in the distance. Haramis looked at the peculiar vegetation underfoot, which had a certain familiarity. The grass was very fine and smooth-edged rather than properly saw-toothed, and odd wildflowers with cushiony yellow heads grew here and there in sunny spots. 'The Place of Knowledge had strange plants like this,' she observed.

'Yes. That was the landside floral archive of our university. But mine's much nicer, don't you think?' The old man reached down and plucked a globular seedpuff. 'These are the plants of our original home world, kept in both places for sentimental reasons as well as for their unique genome.' He blew, and the seeds flew off, hanging from tiny parasols. 'Aeons ago, these plants served as foundation breeding stock for the hybrids that are the most valued crops down below. Of course, there were many more varieties before the Conquering Ice came along and destroyed the ecological and geophysical balance.'

'I don't understand.'

'Of course you don't! That's one of the reasons why you're here.' He turned and started off in the direction of the pool, forcing her to trail along behind. 'The Grotto of Memory is over yonder, among those rocks on the other side of the water. It has something interesting inside that I want to show you, and we can sit down and rest for a bit, too.'

Skirting the shore, Haramis admired the pink and white exotic blossoms that grew in the water, surrounded by round flat leaves that floated on the surface like rafts. Strange little green animals crouched on the leaves and watched her with protuberant golden eyes, and a very large four-winged insect darted just above the water's surface, keeping well clear of the leaf-sitters.

'It's time for you to know the history of the World of the Three Moons,' Denby said as they reached the cave mouth. It was broad, but only slightly higher than their heads. 'I know that Iriane told you something about it when you studied with her, but there's much more. Please come inside.'

The cave was almost cosy, the size of a modest cottage parlour. From somewhere in the shadows came the tinkle of falling water. Ferns grew lushly on the walls and ceiling and the floor was carpeted with moss. At the centre stood a low pedestal topped by a ball of stone about an ell in diameter. Behind it was a curved wooden bench.

Denby touched the ball. Instantly it glowed from within, becoming deeply blue with a single irregular area of ochre and dark brown, thickly dotted with azure.

'Why, it's a representation of our own world!' Haramis exclaimed. 'I recognize the single continent from charts in my Tower library, even though its shape on this globe seems slightly different. But where is the Sempiternal Icecap?'

'Ah!' Denby crowed. 'This shows the planet as it was *before* the coming of humanity – when the Skritek dwelt in abominable primacy at the summit of animal evolution.' His forefinger poked at the brown patch. 'You're right about the continent being somewhat different in contour then. The sea was higher, but the land was, too – because it wasn't weighted down by a thick icy mantle covering over half of its surface.'

He motioned for her to sit down on the bench. One of the omnipresent domestic machines called tenders now appeared, tiptoeing discreetly through the viridescent twilight and bearing two glass goblets of reddish-purple liquid in the box on its back.

'You requested refreshment, master,' it said buzzily. 'Will there be anything else?'

'Bring me a schematic diagram of the Threefold Sceptre of Power,' said Denby, giving one cup to Haramis and taking the second for himself. The tender stalked away into the depths of the cave.

Haramis gazed into her drink, as if into a scry-bowl. Its scent was both heady and familiar. It was mistberry brandy, one of the favourite drinks of Ruwenda, her home. 'The Sceptre . . . is that at the heart of the matter, then?'

115

'Oh, yes, lass. It's been both our shining hope and our ultimate menace ever since the world's imbalance worsened. But let me tell the whole story to you properly, in my own way.'

'I presume you also told this tale to Orogastus, during his sojourn here.'

The old man giggled. 'Three Petals of the Living Trillium and the last Star Master . . . Of course I told him! And he learned more delving through my archives, discovering how the imbalance might be corrected. That's why he was born. That's why *you* were born!' And he began to chant:

'One, two, three: three in one.
One the Crown of the Misbegotten, wisdom-gift, thought-magnifier.
Two the Sword of the Eyes, dealing justice and mercy.
Three the Wand of the Wings, key and unifier.
Three, two, one: one in three.
Come, Trillium. Come, Almighty.

'That's the rhyme! That's the secret! The way to call forth the Sky Trillium and heal the ancient wounds of the world! Binah and Iriane thought you three girls would be able to do it, but I put my money on Orogastus. It's impossible to unite all those disparate nations and tribes with sweetness and light, you know. It's against human nature– against aboriginal nature, too. Force! That's the only way to get things done. Crush the opposition! We tried persuasion and reasoning during the war of enchantment, and what did it get us, eh? Disaster, that's what! And in the end, a Death Moon. Could never let 'em wake up into this primitive environment. They'd destroy your simple civilization with their science and high magic – start the fracas all over again.'

He had leapt to his feet during the fevered harangue, his eyes wide and flecks of spittle flying from his mouth. She drew back in alarm.

He *is* insane, she thought. As unbalanced as the world itself –

'I know what you're thinking,' he carolled. His frenzy evaporated and he took his seat once more. After taking a swig from the cup of brandy he stared at the shining world icon and vented a doleful sigh. 'Yes, I *do* know what you're thinking, and you're right. I'm a lunatic. That's why I could never fix things all by myself.' Two great tears rolled down his wrinkled dark cheeks.

Haramis spoke gently. 'You were going to tell me the story. Please begin.'

* * *

116

Oh, very well [said Denby Varcour]. The trouble started twelve-times-ten hundreds ago.

In those days, the whole world looked just like that globe. The continent had a myriad of lakes with islands scattered upon them, and that's where we built most of our cities. You've seen some of the ruins, deep in your Mazy Mire: gorgeous places like Trevista, laced with canals and adorned with verdant parks and gardens. We modified the original planetary flora to suit our needs, and worked over some of the animals, too – although they were already compatible with our basic biology.

The settlement was a success for many hundreds. Then we were abruptly left on our own when the outside political ultrastructure crumbled and it became dangerous to sail the firmament. For some other worlds, that spelled calamity, but not for us. Oh, no! Our planet was small but it was completely self-sufficient, and our population was stable, enlightened, and contented. We lived as long as we liked, then passed safely beyond when the time seemed appropriate to move on to another plane of existence. Most of us were worker-philosophers, but there were lots of artists, too, and a cadre of professional scientists and engineers who kept the necessary machinery in order.

I was one of those, until the Restless Time began.

It's not easy for me to explain our Restless Time to a simple-minded person like yourself, accustomed to life in a relatively harsh pre-industrial culture. (Don't look at me like that! You're nothing but a barbarian – an intelligent primitive . . . Oh, very well. I apologize for insulting you. But it's still true.)

To you, the world we lived in then would have seemed like paradise: No one was hungry, sick, ignorant, or oppressed. Crime was almost unheard of. Everyone had a fulfilling job to do, as well as plenty of leisure time for other pursuits. Nevertheless, after years of tranquillity, a strange new discontent seemed to appear out of nowhere. All of a sudden, people began to question the old customs and beliefs and systems of values. We argued passionately about things such as the nature of the universe and our own place in it, about the profundities of life and mind and love and free will.

At first the debates were civilized and rational, but as time went on the opposing philosophical groups became more and more intolerant and fanatical. Disputes began to end in physical violence. That should have warned us of what lay ahead, but it didn't. We'd been at peace for so long that we had no true weapons. The rowdiness seemed part of the fun and excitement that were sweeping the world.

Not everything that happened during the Restless Time was bad. Scientific inventions proliferated – including the wonderful viaducts that were

117

capable of carrying a person anywhere in the world within an eye-blink. New forms of entertainment and new schools of art sprang up. The Three Moons were built, originally as holiday colonies and pleasure parks for those who found themselves unsatisfied with traditional modes of amusement. Novelty piled upon novelty, squabble upon diverting squabble. It was a thrilling time and it was scary, too, for the wisest among us suspected that our once-peaceful society would never be the same again.

None of our historians was ever sure who first resurrected the ancient human craft that some people call magic . . . but there it was, all of a sudden, seeming to appear out of nowhere. Fascinating, eh?

Magic was more than just another passing fad. The practitioners learned to manipulate both the inner resources of the human mind and also those mysterious wellsprings of the natural order that the mind is able to influence. Genuine magicians are always avid for more and more power – especially the ability to control other human beings. We worked away at it, and interestingly enough, those of us who had been scientists (like myself) turned out to be the best enchanters. Not everyone could perform magic, of course. Those who couldn't do it began to fear and envy and hate those who could.

As the magicians became more influential, they split into two opposing factions – the magi, who were very self-righteous about using their occult skills for the so-called good of humanity, and the sorcerers, who tended to look down on non-adept persons and think that they had a God-given right to dominate society.

A woman named Nerenyi Daral was the spark that finally set our precarious social tinder alight. Her sort of charm and personal magnetism hadn't existed among us for uncounted ages. She was supremely beautiful and appealing – not by dint of mere physical perfection, but because of her brilliant intellect, the strength of her will, and her ability to compel loyalty and the deepest kind of devotion.

She founded the organization of sorcerers called the Star Guild and the best of the sorcerers flocked to follow her. The express purpose of the Guild was the forcible improvement of the world through magical science, and the restoration of travel through the firmament. The most powerful of the magi belonged to an opposition group called the Archimagical College, dedicated to a more conservative view of society, where no one would ever be oppressed by magic – not even in the name of the common good. I was the head of the College, and no one envied me the position.

The conflict between our two factions grew into a war that raged for over two hundred years. It was fought with the most ingenious weapons and magic that we could produce. Over four-fifths of our populace died, and in the end the very planet itself seemed finally to wash its hands of us – although we magi knew that humankind was to blame for upsetting nature's balance.

From the start of the war of enchantment, devastating earthquakes shook the regions where the worst of the fighting was going on. Volcanos spawned by magic gone awry sprang up where none had existed before, filling the sky with smoke and turning day into night. Plants and animals perished from mysterious murrains. Wildfire engendered by occult conflicts swept the forests and grasslands. When the Three Moons did shine, they were a dreadful colour like clotted blood, a seeming portent of the great disaster to come.

Then the climate began to change.

Don't think that the worldwide temperature abruptly plunged below freezing. Not at all! The winters did become more severe, but what actually doomed us was a speeding up of the natural precipitation cycle. It had something to do with the dust in the air produced by the new volcanos, and the smoke from the burning woods and plains. In the lowlands, the rain almost never stopped, and in the mountains and the interior highlands snow fell in massive amounts and didn't melt. Instead it piled higher and higher, turning to ice as it was compressed by its own weight. By the end of the two hundred years of magical strife, the Sempiternal Icecap was established and a true Glacial Age had begun.

Even then, when most people came to their senses at last, the Star Guild refused to abandon its original goal or halt its hostilities. Not even the sindona, those marvellous mechanical servants of ours, were able to conquer the Star. In desperation, the surviving members of the Archimagical College created the threefold device called the Sceptre of Power, which was designed to counter the awful sorcery of the Star Guild and restore the world to its previous natural balance.

The Sceptre was entrusted to the three principal Archimagi, one of them being me. We set about to destroy the headquarters of the Guild, which was located in the Ohogan Mountains in the western part of the world. Each Archimage wielded a separate part of the Sceptre – those devices that you Petals of the Living Trillium have called your talismans. But we prayed heaven that we would never be forced to put the three pieces together and call upon the Sceptre's full potential.

We were afraid of it, you see.

When the talismans were used separately, they were formidable channels of occult power. That we had already demonstrated. But the unified Sceptre would theoretically command totipotent magic. It was able to tap the vitality of the entire planet and all of the living things dwelling upon it, capable not only of conquering the Star but also of reversing the ecological insult that had brought about the Ice Age.

There was also a danger that the Threefold Sceptre's power might cause the unbalanced world to be torn to bits.

In the end we could not bring ourselves to use the device, not even to end the war that had destroyed our civilization. Instead, each of us three Archimagi carried a separate piece of the Sceptre in the final assault upon the Star Guild's stronghold. We were supported by an army of those sindona called the Sentinels of the Mortal Dictum, who are empowered to kill.

My two colleagues fought valiantly against the sorcerers, but they perished in the far-ranging battle. I myself, using the Three-Lobed Burning Eye, defeated the Star Men in a climactic contest of magic against magic. Afterwards, I gave the three pieces of the Sceptre to the sindona, commanding that they be hidden where no one would ever find them.

A handful of surviving sorcerers fled and hid away in the glacier-bound highlands near the centre of the world-continent. Nerenyi Daral was among the Star Guild members captured and imprisoned by us in the Chasm of Durance. Most of my colleagues demanded that she be put to death, but I would not allow it, for as soon as I saw the Star Lady in person, I loved her with all my heart and soul. I still do, heaven help me.

When the great war of enchantment was finally over, our beautiful World of the Three Moons lay in ruins.

Less than a million people remained alive. The monstrous icecap persisted, in spite of the combined science and magic exerted by the Archimagical College, and it seemed certain to continue growing until it engulfed all dry land excepting the coastal margin and the fringing islands. In such a world, human life could exist only on the most desperate, primitive level. Not even our undersea colonies, dependent for food upon a relatively warm ocean, would be able to survive when the icebergs ruled the waters.

We knew what must be done. We would have to Vanish – abandon the world and attempt to find another home beyond the Outer Firmament. Most people began to prepare for the emigration, while we Archimagi undertook a different task. Since we shared responsibility for the war, we made a collective vow to ameliorate some of the terrible damage humanity had inflicted upon the planet. Our own race could no longer survive here, but it was possible that another, more hardy species might. Then, after aeons of time passed and the glaciers melted, perhaps the World of the Three Moons would be repopulated once again by thinking beings.

Our College created a new race, combining the heritage of humanity and of the savage Skritek – the only sentient aboriginals, who still lived in the swampy Ruwendian Plateau where the climate was not yet too severe. Our laboratories were in the subterranean Place of Knowledge, also situated in the Mazy Mire, where our greatest university had been. The newborn race we eventually created was that of the Vispi – handsome, intelligent beings having a modest ability to utilize magic in their daily lives. We also bred a species of companion-helpers for them, giant telepathic birds that you call lammergeiers or voors, who would assist the Vispi to travel between their scattered settlements amidst the ice and snow.

Meanwhile, the time came for humanity to go off in search of a new home.

Six immense transport vessels had been constructed and were waiting near the Three Moons. Since the voyage was expected to last for uncounted years, everyone on board was to be put into an enchanted sleep, from which they would be awakened automatically at a suitable destination. One of the Moons was modified into a holding area for the passengers, since it took some time to prepare them for sleep and enclose them in special containers.

The first five vessels were loaded with sleepers and successfully launched into the firmament. Then it was time for the sixth to depart.

As you know, my dear Haramis, at the last minute numbers of human beings elected to stay behind. Some of them were stubborn diehards who refused to abandon their old homes, but others had more serious motives for remaining.

You see, a new disaster had occurred.

Nerenyi Daral and several other ranking members of the Star Guild had escaped from the Chasm of Durance. We had thought the prison was impregnable, knowing nothing of the Star Men's magical safety device called the Cynosure. This contrivance – the same that twice rescued Orogastus from certain death – had been carried away from the scene of the last great battle by the sorcerers who avoided capture. Those fugitives eventually found a place of sanctuary in the Inaccessible Kimilon, where they activated the Cynosure and snatched Nerenyi and a few of her chief lieutenants away from us.

We of the Archimagical College were unsuccessful in our attempts to track the escaped Star Men down. When the time came for us to board the last sky ship we hesitated, fearing that the powerful sorcerers of the Star might find some way to enslave the naive Vispi and frustrate the noble scheme we had worked so hard upon.

121

Hoping to prevent this, we Archimagi also decided to stay behind.

The last group of emigrants, already unconscious inside their womb-bubbles, waited in one of the Moons to be transported to the ship through a viaduct. The world below was locked in winter and ghastly storms roared over the land and sea. With great difficulty, we had de-activated all of the landside viaducts that were not already buried in ice so that the escaped Star Men would not be able to use them. None of us suspected that a single viaduct located in the Kimilon had been melted free by the original small group of fugitives.

We were in the midst of manoeuvring the vessel into its proper position before putting the passengers on board when it happened.

Nerenyi Daral and her cohort came through that viaduct onto the ship and attempted to seize control. There was a brief but fierce affray. Nineteen of the twenty-eight surviving Star Guild members and most of our College were killed. Only six Archimagi remained unhurt, while eleven survived with serious injuries. I captured Nerenyi Daral, but the eight sorcerers who still lived escaped back to the surface of the world through the reprogrammed viaduct and once again disappeared.

We sent our wounded back to the Place of Knowledge for the sindona consolers to nurse, while the rest of us attempted to resume our urgent work loading the sky ship. But a fresh disaster had occurred: the great vessel was mortally damaged by the artificial lightning of the Star Men's weaponry. Being semi-sentient, the ship bespoke us a warning of its inevitable destruction within two days, showing us also how we might send it speeding away from the Three Moons so that they would not be harmed when the vessel burst into fragments.

We moved the ship to the other side of the planet, where it was consumed in a fireball brighter than the sun.

My fellow Archimagi retired to the Place of Knowledge to mourn. I remained in the Moon that now bears my name as custodian of the Ones Unable to Vanish, together with Nerenyi Daral, the Lady of the Star whose dead body you have seen. It was my intent to convert her through my love, but instead she contrived the ultimate escape, leaving me alone with those poor sleepers who would never open their eyes upon a new world.

I have remained here close by them, meditating upon ways to better their sad fate and that of the world, ever since.

Over eleven thousand years passed. The Glacial Age seemed to wane. The tiny pockets of human settlement endured a difficult, primitive existence, but they survived. So did descendants of the escaped sorcerers of the Star

Guild, who concealed their powers and attempted to blend in with ordinary humanity.

The Vispi had a better life, thanks to the remaining members of the Archimagical College and their sindona assistants, who were their benevolent guardians. But our cherished new creatures did not multiply as quickly as we had hoped. Because the Vispi are beautiful, the stay-behind humans sometimes mated with them. The offspring (who proved more fertile) frequently did not resemble the parents. Some of these Oddling children were cruelly abandoned by human parents in infancy, while others voluntarily left human or Vispi society to live with their own kind as they matured. Over the ages the Oddling tribes became true races – Nyssomu and Uisgu and Dorok and Lercomi and Cadoon, the people of mire and mere and mountain and jungle. The ferocious Skritek also persisted, and inevitably their blood merged with that of the Folk, giving rise to taller aborigines of less human appearance – the Wyvilo, the Glismak, and the Aliansa.

But the most prolific race of all was the paradoxical remnant of humanity! They managed to thrive in spite of the ice, and after thousands of years had passed they greatly outnumbered the Folk and took over the most desirable lands. A new human civilization was born, much simpler than that of the Vanished Ones, and the ancient history of the World of the Three Moons was almost completely forgotten.

We Archimagi were less successful in propagating ourselves. The surviving original members of the College were longlived, but in time all passed beyond . . . except me. Our adopted successors eventually left the Place of Knowledge and took up residence in different parts of the world, where they served as caretakers and fonts of wisdom.

Now only three of us remain.

So does the Star.

And the world, which had seemed to be regaining its lost balance, totters once again on the brink. Nine hundreds ago, I witnessed the dire retrogression's beginning, and so did Iriane and your predecessor, the Archimage Binah. I caused the birth of Orogastus – last of the true Star Men – and Iriane and Binah contrived the birth of you triplets in the hope of counteracting him. As the Blue Lady and White Lady had hoped, you and your sisters Anigel and Kadiya found the lost pieces of the Sceptre of Power.

You Three and the Star Master have endured many vicissitudes since then. My vision of your joint destiny and the future of the world is clouded and flawed. I'm so old, so worn, so tired . . . and very likely I am no longer even sane.

123

Be that as it may, I do know that there are two possible ways of restoring the great balance, both dependent upon the Sceptre of Power and both exceedingly perilous. Orogastus is certainly capable of performing the restoration. If he becomes ruler of the world, he can do what must be done by brute force and the dark sorcery of the Star.

The Flower – and you Three, who are its human embodiment – might also restore the balance, and your victory would certainly be a more propitious and elegant one than that of the Star. But I do not understand the Black Trillium. It is part of the original magical heritage of this world, more ancient than either the College or the Star, and for this reason I do not trust it. All logic says that you Three Petals of the Living Trillium will surely fail.

But I could be mistaken . . .

That's why you're here, my dear Haramis! Perhaps we can work out the elegant solution together, and perhaps not.

But I won't let you leave my Moon and interfere with Orogastus. I saw the pair of you together, when you were ready to kill him in spite of your love and your holy oath. Fool! He is the true hope of the world – not you and your futile sisters.

No, don't you dare argue with me, Archimage of the Land! Here you are, and here you'll stay, until Orogastus conquers the world and uses the Sceptre to save it.

Or destroy it once and for all.

CHAPTER 13

Following the orders of the Lady of the Eyes, Captain Wikit-Aa brought the flatboat to the confluence of the River Oda. With the Wyvilo crew manning the sweeps, the vessel moved upstream a short distance and was moored in a backwater where there was easy access to the left bank. It lacked an hour until sundown and the rain had stopped.

'Now I ask that you send scouts ashore,' Kadiya said to Wikit, 'and determine whether or not there is a passable trail that parallels the Oda. Meanwhile, I will confer with my people.'

She retired to the sternhouse, where the Oathed Companions, Lummomu-Ko, Jagun, Prince Tolivar, and Ralabun waited. The cabin had been somewhat tidied up after the fight with the factor's men; but one of the two windows was boarded over, making lamplight necessary, and the odour of poisoned karuwok stew and spilled salka still pervaded the air.

'I have revised my plans once more,' Kadiya said, after the others were gathered around her, seated upon bunks, stools, and baggage chests. 'This new scheme depends upon Wikit's scouts finding a clear trail up the River Oda, but he thinks they will succeed.'

'You plan to march on land, Lady?' The youthful knight Edinar was full of astonishment. 'But why?'

She explained patiently. 'As most of you now know, the wretched Turmalai Yonz was incited to attack us by the Star Guild. I was the principal target. A huge reward was offered for my person, dead or alive. It was to be collected if I were delivered to a certain site on this very River Oda, near the so-called Double Cascade some twenty-three leagues upstream from our present moorage.' She paused and let her eyes rove over the group. 'The place of reward coincides with the site of a viaduct.'

'Zoto's Sacred Earlobes!' cried Sir Bafrik. He was the new leader of the knights, a stalwart blackbeard thirty years of age, now the eldest of the Companions. 'Can we then assume that the magical passageway leads to the place where the Star Men dwell?'

'Such was my own deduction,' Kadiya said. The others began to exclaim eagerly, but she held up her hand for silence. 'Companions, you have anticipated my next statement. I intend to enter the viaduct, using it as a shortcut to the realm of our enemies. Jagun has already agreed to accompany me, and it is my fervent wish that you five will also join us.'

'I speak for all,' Bafrik said. 'We will go gladly.' The others shouted their agreement.

'And I also,' said the Wyvilo Lummomu-Ko, 'if you think I can be useful.'

Kadiya made a gesture of regret. 'My friend, the situation remains as it was before. Your inhuman appearance and great height would make disguise too difficult when we move among the enemy. I beg you to take charge of Prince Tolivar and Ralabun during the remainder of the voyage down the Great Mutar, and see them safely off to Derorguila according to our original intent.'

The aborigine nodded. 'I will guard them with my life.'

Kadiya turned then to the Prince. 'Tolo, my dear, there are grave tidings I must convey to you, that have largely influenced my change of plan.' And she told him how Queen Anigel had probably been kidnapped through another viaduct back in the Mazy Mire, and how the Archimage had discovered that other rulers had also been abducted.

'Can the White Lady do nothing to save my poor mother?' the boy asked in desperation.

Kadiya said, 'She has told me that she cannot even descry the place where the Queen and the others are being held. Her talisman is mute on the subject. Both of us believe that the captives must be in the hands of the Star Men, shielded from overview by dark magic.' She turned from Tolivar to address the men. 'There is only one way to find out whether the headquarters of the Guild lies in Sobrania, as we have conjectured. We must pass through the viaduct at the Double Cascade.'

The knights murmured among themselves, and then Sir Kalepo addressed Kadiya. 'Lady, you have said that the enchanted passageways are imperceptible to the naked eye and able to be used only through the application of wizardry. Since you no longer have your talisman, the Three-Lobed Burning Eye, how shall we find the opening?'

'The viaducts can be opened by anyone who pronounces certain words of power,' Kadiya said. 'It is true that the things are normally invisible, but there are sure to be clues in the vicinity of the waterfalls that will point out where the reward for me was to be paid. The viaduct will not be far away.'

'If we fail to find it,' Jagun pointed out, 'we will have wasted at least four days.'

Lummomu added, 'This part of the forest is inhabited by a particularly savage band of Glismak. They still practise cannibalism, in defiance of the White Lady's edict. Would it not be better if Wikit's crew and I accompany you to this twin cataract?'

'I will not have innocent Wyvilo Folk endanger themselves further on our account,' Kadiya said. 'It will suffice if you and the skipper wait here on board the flatboat for five days. If we have not returned by then, you may assume that we found the viaduct and are embarked upon our new mission.'

'Or else you have suffered some fatal misfortune,' Lummomu muttered, 'and passed beyond.'

'You will have to pray for a happy outcome,' Kadiya said. 'But be assured that my Companions and I will not be taken by surprise twice. We will go well armed and wary.'

'Lady.' The most stolid and burly of the young knights, Sir Sainlat, spoke up with reluctance. 'Please do not think that I hesitate to follow your command. But how shall we know what might be awaiting us at the other end of the magical passageway? We could encounter the vile sorcerer Orogastus himself, or some overwhelming force of his Star Guild –'

'Don't think that I intend to pop through the viaduct like some impetuous shangar plunging headlong into a hunter's snare,' Kadiya replied. 'I have devised a prudent course of action – which I will not discuss at this time – that will enable me to spy out conditions at the viaduct's destination in advance.'

Melpotis chimed in. 'You will consult the White Lady!'

'I think not,' Kadiya said evasively. 'My sister Haramis is deeply involved in her own affairs. If we succeed in reaching the country of the Star Men, there will be time enough to take counsel with her.'

Jagun said, 'What if you ascertain that we would face hopeless odds upon entering the viaduct?'

'If this should be the case, we will abandon the endeavour, return to the flatboat, and fall back upon our original plan to travel to Sobrania by sea.'

'That would be a great pity,' Sir Bafrik growled. 'The thought that we might soon encounter the villains who abducted our Queen fires my heart with ardour!'

The others agreed. Kadiya gave a few instructions, ordering them to assemble their gear for a departure the next day at dawn, and then took leave so that she could discuss the arrangements with Wikit-Aa. But no sooner had she opened the cabin door and gone out onto the rainy deck than Prince Tolivar came hurrying after her, an expression of great agitation on his pale features.

127

'Aunt Kadi, I beseech you to reconsider. Let me go with you and assist in the rescue of my mother. I – I know that I am not strong, but there are many ways that I could help you.'

Kadiya regarded him with impatience. 'I cannot think how. Nay – you would be naught but a useless burden, Tolo. And if you had the wit God gave a qubar you would know it already and desist from wasting my time. If I dare not risk having a stalwart warrior like Lummomu-Ko accompany my party, why ever should I think of taking a child of twelve?'

'Because . . . because . . .' But he could not bring himself to speak the words.

Kadiya pushed past the boy, striding forward to the other cabin. Tolivar stood alone at the flatboat rail for some time, pretending to look inland at the dense forest even though his vision was blurred. When Ralabun finally came outside to join him, the Prince spoke rudely, ordering him to go away.

But the old Nyssomu had already seen his angry tears.

The nightmare came again to the Prince on the threshold of the most important adventure in his life. This time it was exceptionally vivid and lacking in the fictitious details that had previously distorted his memory.

He was four years younger, decked out in a tawdry miniaturized imitation of the royal regalia of Laboruwenda. A tiny sword hung at his waist and he wore a crown with paste jewels on his head. An army from Tuzamen and the pirate kingdom of Raktum had invaded the northern capital of the Two Thrones, and the city was near to capitulation.

In the dream the Purple Voice, that foul henchman of Orogastus, and a squad of six Tuzameni guardsmen were leading Tolivar through the tumult and carnage of embattled Derorguila. The boy had discovered that Orogastus only pretended to be his friend, lying when he promised that the little Prince would become his adopted son and the heir to his magic. Instead, the terrified boy had learned that when Laboruwenda finally fell, he was to be set up as its puppet ruler. Even worse, he was destined to be an unwilling accomplice in the murder of his father, his mother, and his older brother and sister.

All of them would have to die before Prince Tolivar could inherit the Two Thrones.

Dreaming, he wept with rage and shame as he was dragged helplessly through the devastated streets of the capital. The exceptionally severe winter signalling the imbalance of the world had Derorguila in icy thrall. Dead and wounded soldiers and civilians lay everywhere, their blood staining the snow. Smoke from burning buildings and the ghastly smells

128

of death made the boy cough and gag. The ice-glazed cobblestones were too slippery for him to walk upon and he fell again and again.

Complaining bitterly at being delayed, the Purple Voice finally hauled the faltering Prince up onto his back, making him hold onto the sorcerer's precious star-box. The Voice was taking it to his master, who was leading the attack against the palace.

They forged onward, past small knots of defenders engaged in final, hopeless combat. Screaming mobs of Raktumian pirates and Tuzameni clansmen were everywhere, laden with loot stolen from the burning mansions.

And then the earthquake struck.

A great wall of masonry crashed down upon the Purple Voice and the six guards, killing them instantly. By a miracle, Tolivar was thrown clear, scratched and bruised but otherwise not hurt.

The star-box was also unharmed.

The Prince acted swiftly, for all that he was nearly out of his mind with fright. He had only his little sword to defend himself and knew that he would soon freeze to death or suffer a worse fate at the hands of the invaders if he tried to hide in the ruins of the city. After leaving the toy crown and some of his garments among the rubble so that Orogastus would think him dead if he searched by magical means, the boy hastened to the palace through back alleys and twisting lanes near the frozen Guila River. Eventually he was able to enter the royal stable block through a secret door in the fortress wall once shown him by his friend Ralabun.

A climactic battle was being fought around Zotopanion Keep, the last resort of the outnumbered Laboruwendians. Thousands of Raktumian and Tuzameni attackers surged about the palace compound. Orogastus himself bombarded the stronghold doors with balls of lightning flung from the Three-Lobed Burning Eye.

Slipping through the dark corridors of the stables on his way to Rala-bun's chamber, where he hoped to find refuge, the little Prince came upon a terrible sight. The body of a pirate with a pitchfork in his throat lay in a pool of gore outside the grooms' quarters. Sprawled atop him, still gripping the fork's handle, was Ralabun . . . with a Raktumian dagger in his back.

'Oh, no!' the Prince cried, bending over his friend.

The Nyssomu gave a faint groan. One bleary yellow eye opened. 'Go quickly to my room, Tolo. Hide there until I come for you.' The eye then closed and Ralabun spoke no more.

As it happened, Ralabun was not dead, only badly wounded and in a swoon; but in the dream, as in life, Tolivar felt himself bereft of his last hope. Hearing someone coming, the Prince fled into the Nyssomu stablemaster's cosy little chamber, where he concealed himself beneath a discarded cloak in a corner.

A man, moving furtively and breathing in painful gasps—as though he, too, had been fleeing for his life – entered the room and closed the door behind him. The Prince's hand tightened upon his little sword. Meagre firelight from Ralabun's hearth showed that the intruder was clad in a dirty golden robe. It was the acolyte whom Orogastus called his Yellow Voice, sent by the sorcerer to act as an aide to young King Ledavardis of Raktum during the invasion.

A silvery gleam shone from beneath the Voice's hood and Tolivar nearly cried out in astonishment. The man was wearing the talismanic coronet called the Three-Headed Monster! Orogastus had lent it to his minion so that the Voice could transmit to his master news of the battle action going on around him.

It was obvious to Tolivar that the cowardly Yellow Voice had run away, abandoning his duty when the fighting grew too furious.

In his dream, the Prince's heart swelled with brave resolution. (In reality, he had acted almost without thought.) Except for the area next to the hearth, where the Voice now stood, helping himself to Ralabun's abandoned supper, the room was in deep shadow. Tolivar crept up behind the acolyte as he began to ladle hot stew from a pot on the fire into a bowl. The boy pressed the sharp point of his little sword to the nape of the man's neck, cutting through his hood.

'Stand still!' the Prince hissed. 'Drop those things.'

'I meant no harm,' the Voice quavered, but Tolivar pricked the acolyte with the blade until he let fall the bowl and ladle. 'I am only an unarmed townsman, caught up by mistake in the fighting –'

'Silence – or you die! And do not move.'

'I will stand quite still,' the Yellow Voice whimpered. 'I would not dream of moving.' The sword withdrew from his neck, and faster than lightning it whisked off his hood and flipped the magical coronet from his shaven head. The Three-Headed Monster spun away through the air, striking the floor with a clang and rolling out of sight in the dimness.

'Dark Powers – not the talisman!' the acolyte shrieked. '*Master! Help me –*'

The true foolhardiness of his action now came home to Prince Tolivar, for the Yellow Voice whirled about and fell over him, uttering a great howl and bearing both of them heavily to the floor. The boy was able to wriggle free, but he had somehow lost the sword. The acolyte struggled to his knees, swaying and clutching at his breast where a dark stain was spreading. His eyes had become brilliant white stars and Tolivar knew beyond doubt that Orogastus himself now looked out through them.

As the Yellow Voice writhed in his last agony, trying vainly to pluck forth the small blade that had by chance lodged in his heart, his head slowly turned. For a brief instant his brilliant eyes, like two small beacons in the darkness, illumined Prince Tolivar. The boy crouched in the corner, his mouth wide open in voiceless horror.

Then the shining orbs winked out and the Yellow Voice fell dead on the floor.

In his dream, the little Prince arose and pulled his sword from the body, wiping it clean on the acolyte's robe. Then he went calmly to Ralabun's bed, fished under it with the blade, and drew forth the magical coronet. He stared at the Three-Headed Monster for some time in silence, knowing by the Star emblem inset beneath the central face that it was still bonded to Orogastus and would kill him if he touched it with his bare flesh. The silvery circlet that formed one part of the mighty Sceptre of Power had belonged to his mother the Queen before she surrendered it to Orogastus as ransom for her husband King Antar . . . and for her youngest son Tolivar as well.

But the Prince had refused to leave the sorcerer then, blinded by the great delusion that Orogastus loved him and some day would pass on to him his power.

'You lied to me,' the boy whispered, strangely excited. 'But I shall have power nevertheless.'

He fetched the star-box, knowing full well its operation, and opened it. Inside the shallow container was a bed of metal mesh, and at one corner a group of small, flattened jewels.

Using his sword, Tolivar dropped the coronet into the box. A bright flash seemed to indicate that it had unbonded from Orogastus. One by one, the Prince pressed the coloured gemstones in consecutive order, and each one lit. Finally he pressed the white jewel. There was a musical sound, and all of the tiny lights went out. The boy stared at the Three-Headed Monster, hesitating. Had the star-box done its work? Was the talisman now bonded to him? If it was not, it would very likely kill him if he touched it.

At that same moment there came rough shouts and crashing sounds from outside the door. The pirates were coming!

His hand shook as he reached into the star-box. The metal of the coronet was warm as he took it up. It did not slay him. Beneath the central carven monstrosity, where there had once been a many-rayed emblem of the Star Guild, now shone a tiny replica of Tolivar's princely escutcheon.

'You *are* mine!' he marvelled, and set the talisman upon his head. The loud voices were now right outside the chamber. 'Make me invisible, talisman, and the star-box, too,' he commanded.

It must have happened, for the door was flung open and three rogues with bloodied swords peered in, made scornful note of the dead Yellow Voice, and betook themselves elsewhere. The Prince felt a wonderful swell of confidence fill his heart.

'I will be an even greater sorcerer than you, Orogastus!' he proclaimed to the empty air. 'And I'll make you sorry you deceived me.'

At that point the dream ended and the Prince's waking nightmare began.

Tolivar! Tolivar, Prince of Laboruwenda! Do you hear me?

'No . . . go away.' Still half-asleep, the boy pulled the rough pillow over his head and burrowed deeper into the covers of the bunk-bed.

I will not go away, Tolo. Not until you agree to be my ally.

'No!' Tolivar whispered. 'I'm only imagining you, Orogastus. You aren't really speaking to me. You don't even know where I am.'

That is not true. You lie abed in a Wyvilo flatboat. The boat is tied up for the night in the River Oda, not far from its confluence with the Great Mutar.

You can't know that, the boy said to the voice in his mind.

But I do. And do you know why, Tolo? Because deep in your secret heart you want me to! If you did not, your two talismans would shield you from me.

No. You're only a dream. It's my bad conscience conjuring you up. I feel guilty because – because I once chose you over my parents. When I hated them . . .

You were too young to understand what you were doing. Your hatred was not genuine. Your father and mother know that. You have long since atoned for those juvenile sins. They are of no account now, when you have very nearly reached manhood's estate. At any rate, none of that infantile naughtiness has anything to do with my solemn pledge to you . . . which I am now prepared to fulfil.

I'm not interested in your lies. Let me alone!

Of course you are interested. How could you not be, since you are so very intelligent? More than anything in the world, you long to taste the full power hidden within those marvellous things you own.

Go away. Leave me in peace. Get out of my dreams. I despise you! One day I will kill you myself to expiate my sins.

Nonsense. Be honest with yourself, Tolo! You know that only I can teach you the full use of the talismans. You will never learn all by yourself. Come to me in Sobrania, dear boy. Only step through the viaduct –

132

Never! You're trying to trick me.

No one can possibly harm the owner of the Three-Headed Monster and the Three-Lobed Burning Eye. You know that.

I don't have them.

Yes, you do. I saw you in the stable as my Yellow Voice died. You are the only one who could have taken the coronet and the star-box. And who but their owner could have made away with the Burning Eye?

Not me. Not me . . .

Dear Tolo, you know what your Aunt Kadiya plans to do on the morrow. Follow her! When you step through the viaduct and arrive in Sobrania, warriors of my company will be waiting to conduct you to me. There will be a joyous celebration to welcome home my long-lost adopted son and heir. You will be initiated at once into the Guild, just as I promised four years ago.

I – I don't trust you.

You must. I am the only one who can help you fulfil your destiny.

No!

Tolo! Come to me!

No no no!

You know you must come to me! Tolo . . . Tolo . . . Tolo . . .

The Prince moaned aloud, and he felt a hand shake his shoulder. 'No! Get away from me –'

'Tolo! Wake up, lad. It's Aunt Kadi. You're having a bad dream.'

The Prince crept out from under the covers. His aunt was kneeling beside him in the darkness, her face faintly lit by the glowing drop of trillium-amber that hung about her neck. It was still deep night. Rain tapped on the cabin roof and the heavy breathing of the slumbering Oathed Companions, Jagun, and Ralabun vied with the noise made by the forest creatures outside.

'I'm sorry,' Tolivar whispered miserably. 'The dream seemed so very real.'

Kadiya kissed his forehead. 'It's gone now. Try to sleep again.'

He turned away, facing the cabin wall. 'I will try.'

She gave him a final pat of reassurance and then went back to her own pallet. The Prince lay very still until he was certain that she slept. Then he let one hand drop down from the bunk, feeling for the locked iron strongbox shoved beneath it. It was there, with his treasures still safe within.

Eyes wide open, Prince Tolivar waited for the dawn.

CHAPTER 14

After bidding Tolivar and Ralabun farewell, Kadiya put on her hoodcloak and came out onto the deck of the flatboat into the early morning air.

It was cold and very quiet. Thick fog enveloped the water and the land, but at least the rain held off. Lummomu-Ko and Wikit-Aa were near the gangplank, assisting the five Oathed Companions to don packboards that bore sacks containing spare weapons, clothing, a few necessities, and food. Jagun had already gone ashore to confer with the Wyvilo scouting party.

'We are nearly ready, Lady Kadiya,' said Sir Bafrik. 'The skipper says we must keep a keen lookout for man-eating goblet trees and poisonous suni-bugs on the way to the viaduct.'

Sir Edinar spoke up with morbid zest. 'And because of the fog, there is a special danger from ravening namps, horrible creatures native only to these parts. They lurk at the bottom of cleverly concealed pits, waiting for unsuspecting prey to tumble in.'

'I have heard of these namps, Edi. They are formidable, but no match for a well-armed champion such as yourself.' She addressed Wikit-Aa. 'How does the trail look? Do your scouts think we will be able to reach the cascades and the viaduct by mid-day tomorrow?'

'The way is partially inundated here in the lowlands,' the flatboat captain reported. 'My men have marked a short alternate route. As the land rises to the west, the original trail will soon become clear. Barring misadventure, you should easily traverse the distance in a day and a half. But I am still worried about the possible presence of cannibal Glismak.'

Kadiya touched the heraldic Eyed Trillium device emblazoned upon her milingal-scale cuirass. 'Even here in the southern wilderness of Var, the Forest Folk will have heard of the Lady of the Eyes.'

'I fear,' said Wikit-Aa with portentous softness, 'that they will *also* have heard of the thousand crowns offered by the Star Men for your capture.'

Kadiya only laughed. 'I shall claim from those villains a reward of my own choosing once we have successfully passed through the viaduct.'

'We will wait the five days,' the skipper promised. 'Lady, farewell.'

She nodded to him, gave a brief embrace to Lummomu, then turned to the knights, who were waiting with ill-concealed restlessness. They wore steel helmets and full coats of mail beneath their leathern raincloaks. 'Companions,' she said. 'It is time for us to disembark.'

As they filed down the gangplank, Jagun handed out freshly cut walking-staves to everyone. He led the way into the misty jungle thicket with the men close behind. Kadiya brought up the rear, giving a final wave to Prince Tolivar, who watched from an open window of the boat's sternhouse. In a few moments the party was lost to sight.

'Cousin, I like this not.' Lummomu followed Wikit-Aa as the skipper made a tour of inspection, personally checking the bindings that held the massive log raft together. It had begun to drizzle. 'My nose has itched fiercely ever since we left the Mutar and entered this tributary stream. I should have insisted on accompanying the expedition – at least as far as the Double Cascade. I cannot escape the feeling that some great calamity impends. But whether it will strike us or the Lady of the Eyes I cannot say.'

Wikit-Aa shrugged, rolling his large eyes. 'Cousin, my nose itches also, but I can think of only one misfortune that threatens us at the moment, and that is losing our mooring. This left bank is too low-lying for comfort. Soon the rain will begin again, and as the Oda rises this shore will flood. Unless we want to risk being swept back downstream into the Great Mutar, we are going to have to move the boat across the river into yonder cove and tie her up to stouter trees. If you truly desire to fend off disaster, go up to the bow and get ready to wield a bargepole.'

It took over three hours of hard labour to get the awkward craft into a more secure position. When the job was done, Lummomu-Ko joined the skipper and the rest of the crew in the forward deckhouse, where the cook served an enormous meal. After that, with the drizzle turned to a steady downpour, all of the Wyvilo settled down for a welcome nap. The Speaker had forgotten his earlier apprehensions.

He woke late in the afternoon with his nose itching worse than ever. Something prompted him to investigate the sternhouse, where Prince Tolivar and Ralabun had remained in seclusion since the departure of Kadiya's party. To his horror, Lummomu discovered that the boy and his Nyssomu crony had both disappeared, leaving behind an open and empty iron strongbox beneath the Prince's bunk.

'I must go after them!' the dismayed Speaker of Let said to the skipper, who had followed him aft. Both Wyvilo stood on deck in the pouring rain, staring across the channel. The expanse of swift-flowing brown water was at least fifty ells wide. 'We must move the boat back to the opposite shore at once!'

But Wikit-Aa was more practical. 'Cousin, the crew is exhausted. We could not manage it before nightfall. And once we put you ashore, we would have no choice but to let the current carry us down to the Great Mutar, for there is no safe moorage over there now that the river has risen.'

'I promised to guard Tolivar with my life! If you will not carry me across, I will swim!'

Wikit-Aa laid restraining hands on the Speaker's shoulders. 'Cousin, only stop and think! The Prince and Ralabun must have managed to slip off the boat before we cast off from the left bank. This means that they left us over six hours ago, not long after the Lady of the Eyes herself departed. In my opinion, the boy impulsively decided to accompany his aunt. It was a rash thing to do, certainly, but when the Lady's party halts for the night the Prince will certainly catch up. You could not reach him yourself before then.'

Lummomu smote his scaly brow in a fury of frustration. 'Damn the boy's foolishness! Damn that Ralabun for conniving with him instead of acting sensibly! Ah, if only I were able to bespeak Jagun and alert him!' But the Wyvilo, unlike the small Folk of the Mazy Mire, were unable to use the speech without words across any appreciable distance.

'It is futile for you to follow after,' Wikit-Aa insisted.

'My honour demands that I go!'

'Logic demands that you stay.'

Lummomu-Ko lifted his taloned hands to heaven and gave a great roar of fury and humiliation. But the skipper only folded his arms, shook his head, and waited for his cousin's usual good sense to prevail. When that finally happened, the two aborigines went together into the deckhouse and helped themselves to mugs of salka from the big wicker-covered jug Turmalai Yonz had provided. The crew had long since determined that it was not poisoned.

Kadiya's troop halted at mid-day beneath a huge sheltering bruddock for a brief lunch of cheese and journey-bread, finding seats on rocks that were dry once their shroud of krip-moss was peeled away. Jagun attempted to make a fire for tea, but the air was so laden with moisture that even his skill failed to kindle a flame. They made do with cold water. A measure of good cheer was restored when the little Nyssomu spied a bush with pendant clusters of white berries.

'These are sifani,' Jagun said with enthusiasm. 'They are delicious and thirst-quenching and will be a fine dessert, even if the rest of our rations are modest.'

'I like dessert best,' said Sir Edinar. The boyish knight began devouring the succulent fruit with no more ado, and broke off bunches to toss to the others.

The rain had abated a little but visibility was still very poor. They had passed out of the densely vegetated bottomlands into a more elevated region where the going was somewhat easier, if more steep. In a few places landslides had obliterated the trail, but detours were readily accomplished and they had kept up a good pace. They noticed stands of deadly goblet trees from time to time – deceptively handsome things having fleshy trunks and a cup-shaped crown of coloured leaves that concealed tentacles capable of hauling a man to his doom – but the party had encountered no venomous snakes or large predatory animals.

'I reckon that we have come nearly eight leagues,' Jagun said, munching bread. 'We can safely continue for another three or four hours, but then we must find a safe stopping place well off the trail, where night-prowling Glismak will not easily find us. The big rocks down along the riverside may provide shelter from the rain. Unfortunately, we dare not light a fire after dark.'

'A pity,' sighed Melpotis. He and Kalepo, brothers of the murdered Lord Zondain, were long-faced men having yellow beards and snapping dark eyes. 'Fire would help keep wild beasts at bay.'

'Our main concern must be the Glismak,' Kadiya said, 'and possibly marauding Star Men venturing through the viaduct. My trillium-amber will give warning if my life is in danger, so we must stay close together after dark and keep our weapons handy.'

'Do you think,' said Sir Bafrik uneasily, 'that we will find the Double Cascade viaduct guarded by a troop of sorcerers?'

Kadiya said, 'The villain Turmalai Yonz stated that the reward for me would be payable at dawn. It seems likely that the Star Men would appear only at that time each day to see whether my precious carcass was on offer. If we arrive at the viaduct site around noon, as I have planned, we may very well find it deserted. Certainly we will do a careful reconnoitre before approaching.'

'Surely,' said Bafrik, 'we would be wise to wait until dark before actually entering the viaduct.'

'If the passage leads straight into the den of Orogastus,' said big Sainlat dourly, 'it will not matter whether we pass through in daylight or night. We will be forced to fight for our lives.'

'I'm ready for anything!' young Edinar declared, wiping sifani juice from his mouth. Kalepo and Melpotis also expressed their eagerness for combat.

But Kadiya said, 'I must dash your bloodthirsty hopes, Companions, at least for the short term. When we reach the viaduct, I will go through first, and alone.'

Immediately the men began to exclaim, 'Nay!' But she forged on.

'My amber amulet will conceal me from hostile eyes. If all is well on the other side of the magical gate and it affords a safe way into the sorcerer's domain, I will immediately return to fetch the rest of you.'

Jagun made protest. 'And what if you emerge from the viaduct into some deadly locale, Farseer?'

'My trillium-amber has saved my life many times, as you know very well. It will not fail me in the present instance.'

The five knights sat without speaking for some minutes, each one mulling over Kadiya's words, having grave misgivings about her plan but being unwilling to speak against it and be thought disloyal.

At last Jagun said, 'And what shall we do, Farseer, if you enter the viaduct and do not return?'

'Then you will bespeak news of my fate to the White Lady,' she told him, 'and follow her commands.'

'Would it not be more prudent to consult her beforehand?'

'No,' Kadiya said firmly.

Jagun bowed his head in silent reproach.

Kadiya rose and picked up her backpack. 'We have tarried here long enough. Let us be on our way.'

The Oda tribe of Glismak had only a single settlement of less than forty souls, lying three days' journey above the Double Cascade. Most of their race eked out an austere living by simple hunting and gathering. Those who dwelt further north, near Wyvilo territory, occasionally did rough manual labour for their aboriginal kinfolk or even for humanity. The Oda tribe, luckier than most, had been taught by factor Turmalai Yonz to trap, skin, and cure the fur of the coveted blue diksu. Thus introduced to commerce, they were more ambitious than other members of their kind, having become accustomed to certain luxuries such as strong drink, pearl ornaments from Zinora, and steel knives. Factor Turmalai purchased their furs at the start of each Wet Time, and the Glismak had seen him very recently. A fur bale as tall as the Oda village headman's hut, which had taken the tribe nearly half a year to accumulate, had brought them a single golden Varonian crown.

The Folk of the Oda had been astounded when Turmalai Yonz told them about the fabulous reward offered by the Star Men for the capture of the Lady of the Eyes. The sum of a thousand platinum crowns was far beyond Glismak comprehension. (Having only three digits on each hand, they had never learned to count higher than six; still, they knew that a thousand must be considerably more than that.) Mendaciously promising to share the reward with Turmalai if they found the Lady, the Oda Glismak returned to their wilderness traplines.

As they worked, they kept their big red eyes peeled for the valuable human prey. Yesterday, they had found her.

The Wyvilo flatboat had come into the lower reaches of the Oda just before dusk. It had been misty, but lurkers on shore had clearly seen a smallish human female with braided russet hair standing at the rail as the boat tied up for the night. The Glismak had not dared to attack then. The Wyvilo boatmen, their close racial kin, were too formidable a foe to mess with. The watchers could only wait and yearn, beseeching their three-headed god to cause the Lady of the Eyes to come ashore without her aboriginal companions.

In time, their prayers were answered.

The Glismak of the River Oda were a primitive race of Folk, but they were by no means stupid. They decided to wait until the prey and the armed men accompanying her had reached the Magic Door before attacking, so that they would not have to carry her dead body very far.

On the next morning the weather was much better. The rain and fog had disappeared completely, and by the time Kadiya and her party returned to the trail from their bivouac by the river the sun was out. They hiked for four hours, seeing nothing unusual and hearing only the noise of the river tumbling over boulders, a rare trill of birdsong, and the occasional cry of some distant beast.

'The Double Cascade cannot be far now,' Jagun said, when the sun was nearly overhead.

'A good thing,' Sir Sainlat replied, 'for I am well nigh worn out climbing this rocky trail. I would sell my soul for a saddled fronial.'

The others laughed and began to tease him, but in truth they were all very tired, not being used to going afoot armoured while carrying heavy loads on their backs.

Kadiya, still bringing up the rear as she had done throughout most of their march, paused and looked back the way that they had come. The valley of the Oda had narrowed and the character of the forest had changed. They had passed out of the humid Tassaleyo lowlands and into the foothills of the southern Ohogan Range. Something scarlet high in the tree-canopy above the trail caught her eye. It was a huge gauze-wing, wider than her two hands, fluttering in search of nectar. Kadiya smiled at the sight of the lovely creature, then turned to resume her march. The others had already gained the top of the steep ridge that she now ascended.

She saw Jagun beckoning to her and froze, her hand automatically going to her sword hilt. But he did not seem to be alarmed, and so she made haste climbing and in a moment stood beside him and the others. Ahead was their goal – two narrow streams of water glistening as they fell for nearly eighty ells down the face of the mountainside. At the base of the Double Cascade was a pool, foaming white where the cataracts impacted and limpid blue-green in its outer reaches. The glade round about it seemed completely deserted.

They made a stealthy approach, encountering no one, and at length stood at the foot of the twin waterfalls in a dense grove of peculiar trees. These had trunks with vertical openings over an ell high that constantly opened and closed, revealing a maw lined with shiny green spikes like enormous fangs. Here and there a tree had its 'mouth' closed, and blood and other nameless fluids seeped from its wooden lips.

'These trees are called lopa by the Wyvilo,' Kadiya remarked to the Companions, who had gathered around one specimen and were staring at it with apprehension. 'They appear repulsive, but they are not dangerous to human beings unless one is so foolish as to reach into the toothed opening. When my sister Anigel undertook her original quest for her talisman, the Three-Headed Monster, she found the coronet concealed within a gigantic lopa tree and only retrieved it by dint of great courage and ingenuity.'

Jagun had left the group in order to explore the area near the pool. He now called out, 'Farseer! I think I have found the site of the viaduct.'

The others ran to him. There, between two exceptionally large lopas growing at the water's edge, was a flat slab of rock oddly free of moss or other forest growth. A perfectly straight groove was incised in it, and spiked to one of the adjacent tree trunks was a board with a many-pointed star painted upon it.

'We will soon see if you are right,' Kadiya said to Jagun. Cautioning the others to stand back, she commanded, 'Viaduct system activate!'

A tall black disk seeming to have no thickness sprang into being to the sound of a deep bell-chime, whereupon the knights gave cries of amazement. Kadiya nodded in satisfaction and cast off the straps of her pack. Before any of the others could say a word, she drew forth from her jerkin the shining amber droplet that hung on a cord around her neck and held it tightly in her left hand. Her right rested upon the hilt of her sword.

'Black Trillium,' she said, 'I pray you shield me from the sight of hostile persons and keep me otherwise safe from harm.' She stepped into the viaduct's ominous dark surface and disappeared.

There followed an instant of utter silence. Then came a heart-stopping bellow of frustrated rage from many throats.

Jagun and the knights whirled about. Over a score of huge aboriginal warriors, tusks bared and eyes flaming, came bounding down the wooded rocky slope with steel-tipped spears held at the ready.

'Glismak!' Jagun cried. No sooner had he spoken than the creatures flung their weapons. The spears, aimed at the Lady of the Eyes, went toward the viaduct; but the black disk winked out of existence and most of the blades soared harmlessly across the cascade pool. One spear caught Sir Bafrik in his unarmoured throat. He staggered backward, blood pouring onto his chest, and fell from the riverbank into the water, which turned scarlet.

The crowd of cannibals halted momentarily, bellowing in disappointment at the unexpected loss of their prey. Then some drew Varonian short-swords while their comrades hefted flint maces and other weapons. They advanced upon Jagun and the four surviving knights, intending to make short work of them.

After that, they would prepare a consolation feast.

CHAPTER 15

Going invisible has its problems.

When Prince Tolivar and Ralabun left the flatboat and began to follow Kadiya and the others through the river bottomland in thick fog, they soon discovered that the vapours did not penetrate the space occupied by their unseen bodies. If one looked carefully, a human form might be perceived, outlined by swirling mist. The Prince was baffled. No command that he could think to give the talismans would alleviate the predicament. In the end, he and Ralabun simply kept far behind the others, hoping that they would remain unnoticed.

When the worst of the fog finally dissipated and the pair became truly invisible again, another difficulty presented itself. Neither the Prince nor Ralabun knew where the other was at any given moment. Once, when the boy paused to answer a call of nature, the Nyssomu continued on oblivious – only to panic as he realized that his own footsteps were the only ones to be heard. Ralabun then dashed back along the trail, frantically crying out the Prince's name.

Tolivar tongue-lashed the old stablemaster roundly. 'You blockhead! What good is it to be invisible if you betray our presence with your big mouth? I should never have brought you with me!'

'Then, Hiddenheart, you would have had to carry the star-box yourself,' Ralabun retorted with injured dignity, 'as well as our food and other supplies. Besides, without my knowledge of wilderness ways, a young lad like you would surely become lost or suffer some mortal misadventure before travelling half a league.'

But that was not true. The Prince had learned a good deal from his clandestine excursions into the Mazy Mire, while Ralabun had for over forty years spent most of his days in the royal stables, enjoying civilized human comforts, and had forgotten most of the mirecraft learned in his youth. In truth, he was worse than useless as a guide.

He made a great fuss warning the Prince not to touch goblet-trees or tanglefoot or other obviously hazardous flora, while neglecting to point out more subtle dangers such as the deadly suni-bugs that dangled on a thread of slime among the bushes, or the snafi, which resembled fallen leaves but were actually small animals that crept along on multitudinous fringe-like feet, capable of injecting poison if they got into the clothing and touched one's bare skin. Ralabun also vexed Tolivar by stopping again and again to survey the forest, swivelling his long upstanding ears, sniffing the rainy air, and cautioning against the stealthy approach of ravening beasts that never actually appeared.

Eventually the Prince became quite out of patience and took the lead himself, after which they made more steady progress. From then on, if a stream had to be forded, it was the boy who chose the place where they would wade or hop across on stones. Tolivar also decided how they would negotiate washed-out places on the trail, picking the way with care so that their passage would not set the unstable earth moving again. And when the path now and again seemed to vanish amidst downed trees or dripping underbrush, Tolivar was the one who would find the route again, even though Ralabun would bluster and profess to have known the way all the time.

Pressing on through the rain, they reached the spot where Kadiya and the Oathed Companions had eaten their mid-day meal, and there they found a nasty surprise. The Prince pointed out numbers of large, three-clawed tracks in the soupy mud.

'These were not made by animals,' he said, trying to keep his voice from trembling. 'They must be Glismak. See how the prints overlie the ones made by Aunt Kadi and her companions? The brutes are following them.'

'Oh, Holy Flower forfend!' Ralabun moaned. 'We must find some way to warn the Lady's party of the cannibals' presence!'

'Perhaps I can whisper in her ear, and she will think that her Black Trillium amulet speaks. Or even one of the Lords of the Air.' The Prince laughed nervously, rather liking the idea of being mistaken for a heavenly guardian. He pressed his fingers to the sides of the coronet, closed his eyes, and bade it give him Sight of Kadiya. This was a kind of magic he had often practised, becoming fairly proficient.

'Do you see the Lady?' Ralabun whispered anxiously.

'Yes.' In Tolivar's mind was a clear picture of her and the others, tramping along the steepening trail with tendrils of mist swirling around them.

He heard Ralabun's voice say, 'Tell her of the danger, Hiddenheart. Quickly!'

'Aunt! Can you hear me?' But Kadiya moved on heedlessly, even though Tolivar called out again and again, keeping his eyes shut to maintain the

143

Sight. 'It's useless,' the boy said at last. 'There must be a knack to bespeaking that I do not yet grasp.'

'Very likely. You'd better find out what the cannibals are up to.'

Tolivar commanded the coronet to show him the Glismak. It promptly complied, and the Prince beheld a vision of very tall, fearsome aborigines trotting single-file along a narrow path choked with tall ferns and other undergrowth.

'Where are the Glismak in relation to me?' the boy whispered to the talisman.

They are approximately a league south of the river trail, moving away from you.

'Are they pursuing my Aunt Kadiya?'

They are moving away from her also. It is impossible to ascertain their intentions, since they do not speak of it and are beings with free will.

Tolivar told Ralabun what the talisman had said, and the Nyssomu was much encouraged. 'Perhaps the cannibals have decided that the Lady's party is too formidable to attack. After all, they are only simple-minded savages. You must check up on the brutes from time to time with your talisman, to be certain that they don't return. But now we had better move on. It would be unwise for us to fall too far behind the Lady of the Eyes if we hope to pass through the viaduct immediately after her.'

They set off again at as rapid a pace as they could manage, but neither of them had long legs. To make matters worse, the trail now trended mostly uphill and they were often forced to halt, gasping for breath and with stitches in their sides.

Then it began to get dark.

Tolivar turned them visible once more, fearing that they might be accidentally separated in the deepening gloom. 'It's time that we thought about stopping for the night, anyway. Shall I ask the Three-Headed Monster to find a dry cave or hollow tree? Or shall I try to use the Burning Eye's magic to cut down wood for a lean-to shelter?'

'I care not.' The old Nyssomu was now very down-hearted. 'I would settle here and now for a pair of dry boots – and relief for the blister on my right heel.'

'Let me try to help you,' Tolivar said. He pulled the dark pointless sword from his belt and held it by the blade, as he had seen Orogastus do. 'Three-Lobed Burning Eye! I command you to restore Ralabun's feet to health, and render his boots dry.' At the same time that he spoke, the Prince visualized what he wished to accomplish.

The lobes forming the sword pommel split open, and three magical Eyes stared at Ralabun's feet.

'Oh! Oh! It's hot! It's hot!' Clouds of steam suddenly poured from the boots and Ralabun danced about in a frenzy, yammering aboriginal oaths.

The Prince made haste to apologize. 'Forgive me! I didn't realize that would happen. Perhaps I should have used the coronet instead. I had forgotten that Aunt Kadi's talismanic sword is more of a weapon than a magical wand. Um . . . is your blister healed?'

'How can I tell,' the old man wailed piteously, 'with my feet afire? Next time, let me at least take the boots off before you experiment. Better yet, practise your amateur sorcery on someone else – like the Glismak cannibals!'

'I hope that I will not have to,' the boy said in a low voice, 'and you would do well to hope so, too.'

Ralabun sighed. His feet had cooled rapidly and the blister was indeed healed. 'I'm sorry, Hiddenheart. I know you only wanted to help. But I am so very weary and wet . . .'

Tolivar pressed his fingers to the coronet. 'Talisman – can you lead us to a dry place where we might safely spend the night?'

Yes. There is a sizeable niche among the rocks on the hillside to your right. Follow the green spark.

A tiny emerald light sprang forth from the open mouth of the middle head on the coronet and began to drift slowly off the trail. Tolivar took Ralabun's hand.

'Come. It's time for us to rest and eat. With luck, I will find a way to dry the rest of our clothes with magic. But have no fear, old friend. This time I will practice first on myself.'

They awoke refreshed in the morning, and Tolivar quickly ascertained that Kadiya and her party were less than a quarter of a league ahead of them, eating breakfast down by the River Oda.

'And are the Glismak following them or us?' the boy asked his coronet.

No.

Well satisfied and confident that his bold plan was succeeding so splendidly, the Prince rendered himself and Ralabun invisible once again. They set off at the same time that Kadiya and her companions did and hiked for several hours, growing more and more weary as the sun climbed but managing to stay fairly close behind the others.

And then they discovered fresh Glismak tracks crossing the trail to the right.

Tolivar halted and studied the ominous evidence with consternation.

Ralabun said, 'This is strange. I thought your coronet said that the cannibals were not following.'

145

The awful truth came to the Prince in a flash. 'No – they were circling around us to prepare an ambush! I was too stupid to ask the talisman about that possibility, and it always answers questions literally. Quick! We must try to give warning!' He set off at a run, sometimes falling and scrambling ahead on all fours, for the trail at that point was extremely steep.

'I cannot keep up with you, Hiddenheart,' the stablemaster gasped. 'Go ahead without me and –'

There was a sudden volley of bestial cries in the distance, followed by the agonized scream of a man.

Stricken with terror, the invisible friends crept to the top of a rocky ridge. Below lay a small clearing near the paired waterfalls, hedged about by monstrous trees. It seemed crowded with enormous beings who leapt and flailed about with swords, stone-headed maces, and rusty Varonian axes, yelling hideously all the while. They wore no clothing, having plates of shining skin armouring their backs, shoulders, and upper arms. Their bodies were otherwise covered with auburn hair, which grew longer on their heads, forming manes. They possessed muzzled faces like those of their Wyvilo kin, but instead of yellow eyes they had orbs of glaring red. Great white teeth shone in their mouths and both their hands and feet were beclawed.

The mob of Glismak were engaged in a pitched battle with four vastly outnumbered Oathed Companions. There was no sign of the fifth knight, nor of Jagun, nor of the Lady of the Eyes.

'What are we to do?' old Ralabun wailed. 'Look! One of the Companions has gone down. Oh, no! The savages are hacking him to pieces!'

'You must do exactly as I say.' The Prince was all at once full of stern resolution. 'Go off the trail to the left, creep downhill, and make your way to the crag near the waterfalls. Get up on it, then begin flinging rocks down on the Glismak with all your strength. Screech as though you were a phantom from the Thorny Hell. It will distract the fiends and perhaps help frighten them away. Meanwhile, I will do what I can with the talismans.'

'But –'

'Hasten!' the Prince hissed. He set off slipping and sliding down the trail, drawing the Three-Lobed Burning Eye. When he reached the clearing and could see the battle participants distinctly, he halted, dropping to one knee. Holding the talisman by its blunt-edged blade, he pointed the hilt at the tallest of the three Glismak assailing the fallen knight.

In his mind, the boy saw this heinous creature burnt to ashes. He said: 'Burning Eye, slay him.'

146

The three orbs forming the sword's pommel split open, revealing eyes that stared at the giant Glismak. From the human eye shot a golden beam, and from the Folk eye a ray of green, and from the silvery eye of the Vanished Ones a beam of searing white. The body of the savage warrior was enveloped in tricoloured radiance. In an instant his flesh was consumed, and then the glowing bones also vanished, leaving only a splash of grey resembling wet ashes on the muddy ground. The other attackers drew back, stunned. Their intended victim still lived, for the knight hauled himself to a sitting position, unrecognizable for the gore that covered him, and regarded the ashes with wonderment.

The Prince was also amazed that the new talisman had so readily obeyed him. A fierce jubilation welled up in his heart. He pointed the Burning Eye at the other two Glismak, who still stood near the downed Companion as though paralysed, and incinerated them also with magical lightning.

The rest of the cannibals set up a furious clamour, shouting one to the other in their guttural language. They began to flee, and inside of a few moments all were gone into the forest. Tolivar, standing invisible at the edge of the clearing, could not help but utter a shout of triumph.

'Who's there?' cried Sir Edinar. He and the brothers Kalepo and Melpotis were the only Companions left on their feet. The three of them had many wounds, but none were mortal.

'It is some sorcerer come to our aid,' said the knight hunched on the ground, who then groaned in agony and fell limp. By his voice the Prince identified Sir Sainlat, bleeding in a dozen places. One of his feet had been hacked from his leg by a Glismak axe, and blood spurted forth like a small scarlet fountain.

Tolivar hurried to him. Touching the coronet on his head with two fingers, he closed his eyes and saw Sainlat in his imagination, tall and strong as he had been that morning setting off from the flatboat. 'Talisman,' he whispered, 'let him be so.'

Sainlat's body was enveloped in soft green light. The burly knight stirred and sat up. His face was unbloodied and stupefaction caused his mouth to sag, for all traces of his injuries had vanished. Even his armour and garments were clean and undamaged.

'Sacred Flower!' Edinar cried. He ran to his restored Companion, followed by Melpotis and Kalepo, and the three of them pulled Sainlat to his feet and began to laugh and pound him on the back. As this went on, the Prince commanded the Three-Headed Monster to heal the others. A triple pulse of emerald light announced the accomplishment of the magic, leaving the transformed knights numb with shock and delight.

'O Wizard, come forth and accept our thanks!' Kalepo managed to say.

147

Tolivar spoke in a disguised croak. 'Where are the others? Where is the Lady of the Eyes?'

'Did you hear?' Sainlat exclaimed. 'He's somewhere close by!'

The Companions began to gabble all at once until Tolivar cried out, 'Edinar, answer me!'

The young knight controlled himself. 'Unseen Wizard, the Lady of the Eyes has passed through a viaduct – we hope into the land of the Star Men – and promised to return to us anon. Sir Bafrik fell gravely wounded into yon pool and I fear he is dead. As to the Nyssomu Jagun, I know not where he may be. I have not laid eyes on him since the Glismak savages sprang upon us. But who are you? Are you one of the Vispi servants of the White Lady? The invisible Eyes in the Mist?'

The Prince silently asked the coronet: Is Bafrik alive?

No, said the voice in his head. *He has passed safely beyond and his body has floated some distance downstream.*

Where is Jagun?

At this moment he stands at the brink of a namp's pit, halfway up the hill to your left, wondering who it is that the beast has just now devoured.

'A namp!' the Prince wailed aloud. 'No! Oh, no!' And he dashed away, crashing through undergrowth and tripping over concealed rocks. The four knights saw the disturbance he made in the vegetation and followed after, giving voice to their mystification.

Within a few minutes Tolivar caught sight of Jagun, who was staring sombrely into a ragged-edged cavity in the ground that measured some two ells in diameter. Obviously, it had once been roofed over with thin saplings, dead leaves, and other trash from the forest floor to mask its presence. Something – or someone – had broken through the flimsy covering and tumbled in.

'Burning Eye, bring him out safely!' the Prince shrieked. 'Oh, please! Rescue Ralabun!'

The request is impertinent.

The invisible boy fell to his knees at the brink of the hole opposite Jagun and looked down. The pit was full of shadows; but there, half buried in soil and duff, was a gigantic shape that almost filled the bottom. It resembled a bloated bald head, having two saucer-sized bright blue eyes that looked up from between wrinkled lids. The namp shifted and seemed to smile, revealing a huge mouth that stretched from one side of its head to the other. Very short limbs with twiglike digits sprang from the place where the creature's ears might have been.

'Did – did this vile beast take Ralabun?' the Prince inquired of the talisman in a quavering voice.

148

Yes.

Tolivar burst into tears. 'Oh, no! My poor old friend! If only you had been more proficient in wilderness ways . . . if only I had not sent you off the trail! Now you are gone and no magic can bring you back.'

Jagun was frowning, his gaze fixed on the place where the unseen lad's weight had compressed the forest detritus. The Oathed Companions had come up and were casting horrified glances into the pit. The namp licked its purplish lips at the sight of them and scratched at the dirt with its tiny hands.

'Prince Tolo?' the old Nyssomu hunter said. 'Is that you?'

Just then the namp gave a grotesque hiccough, shuddered, and blinked its eyes rapidly. Tolivar, Jagun, and the knights made haste to move back from the edge of the hole as the creature hiccoughed again, showing row after row of stained, pointed teeth. The namp's shuddering turned into violent spasms, punctuated by gagging sounds. Suddenly its maw gaped wide like the opening of a titanic, fang-fringed sack, and there was a thunderous eructation.

A slender silvery container flew through the air, accompanied by a quantity of phlegm, and landed at Jagun's feet. Thus relieved, the namp sighed, shook itself, and burrowed down until only its half-closed eyes remained above ground, glowing faintly in the dimness of the pit.

There was a crackling sound in the underbrush and Kadiya emerged.

'You have returned safely!' Jagun exclaimed. 'Praise be to the Triune!'

'Indeed,' she replied, 'and I have met with some success. But before I speak of it, let me introduce you to a certain wizard.' Swiftly, she circled the namp's hole to where the two footprints indented the ground and seized something that seemed naught but thin air. 'You may as well turn yourself visible, Tolo.'

The Prince appeared, crowned with the Three-Headed Monster and having the Three-Lobed Burning Eye still in one grubby hand. His cheeks were streaked with tears. Kadiya had hold of him by the back of his jerkin, and even though they two were nearly of a size, Tolivar seemed helpless in her grip, like the newly captured prey of a lothok, numbly resigned to its fate.

'*This* is the wizard who saved our lives?' Sir Edinar gasped.

'Impossible!' said Sainlat.

'He wears the magical coronet,' Melpotis pointed out, 'and carries the talisman stolen from the Lady of the Eyes.'

'But he is only a child,' Kalepo scoffed.

'I slew the Glismak and healed your wounds,' Tolivar said in a dull voice. 'I *am* a sorcerer, and your contempt will not make it otherwise.'

149

'You are also a thief,' Kadiya said calmly, 'but that is by the bye.' Firmly, she guided the Prince to the slime-covered star-box. 'Open it!'

As though overcome with an immense fatigue, Tolivar obeyed. When she commanded him to place the Three-Lobed Burning Eye within, he obeyed without speaking a word. Then the Lady of the Eyes made finger play upon the gemstones within the box. There was a blaze of light and a musical sound. A moment later Kadiya took up the magic sword with a triumphant smile, holding it in both hands by the dull-edged blade with the hilt upright.

'Talisman,' she asked, 'are you once again mine own? Is your power restored?'

Nestled amongst the conjoined knobs on the sword's pommel was Kadiya's trillium-amber, shining like a tiny flame in the deepening twilight. The dark lobes seemed to split open, and three gleaming Eyes that mirrored those on her golden-scaled cuirass gazed at her.

I am bonded to you, Lady, and fully potentiated.

'Good,' she said. 'Now I command you to shield me and my companions from the Sight of Orogastus and all his Star Guild.'

It is done.

The Eyes closed and Kadiya thrust the sword into her belt and addressed the others. 'Jagun, please take charge of the star-box.'

'Certainly, Farseer.'

'We cannot tarry here any longer,' she said. 'The sun is descending and we must pass through the viaduct. Someone waits for us at the other end who has promised to help us reach the city of Brandoba, where the Emperor Denombo resides, but he will not wait long.'

Edinar exclaimed, 'So the passageway does lead to the land of Sobrania?'

'Yes.'

'And the Star Men?' Melpotis inquired. 'Have they conquered the country?'

'Not yet,' Kadiya said. She turned to Prince Tolivar. 'Before we move on, I want you to give me the Three-Headed Monster for safekeeping. Jagun! Open the star-box.'

The boy took a step backwards. The life had come back into his face. Eyes wide with dread, he lifted his hands to hold the coronet tight to his head. His voice was a broken whisper. 'No! I – I will never give up my talisman. Not while I live!'

'It is not yours,' Kadiya said. 'It belongs to your mother, just as the Three-Winged Circle belongs to the Archimage Haramis, and this Three-Lobed Burning Eye belongs to me.'

'Mother gave the talisman freely to Orogastus,' the Prince said stubbornly.

'To ransom you and your Royal Father!' Kadiya exclaimed in a terrible voice. She snatched the star-box from Jagun and advanced upon Tolivar, holding it open. 'Place the coronet inside the box.'

'No,' the boy whispered.

She drew the black, pointless sword from her belt and lifted it to Tolivar's forehead, holding it less than a finger's width from the coronet's rim. The three Eyes opened. 'Tolo, do as I say. Give up the talisman.'

'Do not touch it!' he warned, desperation in his eyes. 'You know it will kill you if you try to take it from its bonded owner. I was only able to secure it myself because Orogastus had lent it to his Yellow Voice, who was not so protected.'

For several heart-beats she glared at him, but his willpower was too strong. 'Keep it then, for what good it may do you.' Kadiya whirled the sword away and slammed it into her belt. The three-lobed pommel once again seemed only black metal. 'Sainlat, Melpotis – take Tolo back to the riverboat.'

'No!' the Prince cried. 'I have vowed to rescue Mother! If you try to send me away, I will use magic to thwart you.'

'Farseer,' Jagun spoke urgently to Kadiya. 'Perhaps it would be best if the Prince did accompany us. He may be able to assist in the rescue of Queen Anigel, since it is evident that he has some expertise in commanding his talisman.'

'His invisibility trick was actually rather impressive,' Sir Edinar remarked.

'And his healing of us,' Sainlat added encouragingly, 'was even more so. I was myself at the point of death, and now I am not only restored but quite invigorated.'

The other knights murmured agreement.

Kadiya regarded the boy with a thoughtful scowl.

Jagun continued. 'When his mother is safe with us, he can then give the talisman to her.' The little old Nyssomu said to the Prince: 'Will you do that, Hiddenheart?'

At the sound of his mire-name, given him by the dead Ralabun, the Prince flinched, but he made no reply.

More patiently, Kadiya said: 'Tolo, if I allow you to go with us, will you promise to submit to my leadership, and desist from wreaking any magic through the coronet without my express permission?'

The Prince hesitated, his mouth tightening. But he finally said, 'I do promise.'

Kadiya was about to demand that he also promise to return his talisman to Anigel; but she feared that the boy might continue to balk, and perhaps even attempt to flee, invisible, if she pressed the point. Besides, he was much more likely to give up the coronet at the request of the Queen herself.

She sighed. 'Very well. Now let us prepare to pass through the viaduct. There are no Star Men or other villains on the other side, but the person who does wait, a man of the Folk who has consented to guide us, is of a nervous and fearful temperament and may go off without us if we do not hasten.'

'Wait!' cried the Prince. He went to the edge of the namp's pit. 'Aunt, this miserable creature murdered my poor friend, Ralabun. I do not know if my magical coronet will kill it, but I ask you to let me make the attempt.'

'But the namp did not commit murder,' the Lady of the Eyes said. 'It is only a wild animal, not having the faculty of reason. It sought food in its customary fashion, without malice. It would be unjust to slay it now, in cold blood. Don't you understand that, Tolo?'

'No.' The boy would not look at Kadiya.

Her voice hardened. 'Then let the creature live because I command you to.' She turned her back on him and set off down the hill with Jagun and the knights following.

'But I must kill it!' the Prince cried in desperation. 'I must!'

Kadiya glanced at him briefly over her shoulder. 'You will not and *must* not, because the namp is not to blame for Ralabun's death. Someone else is, as you know already deep within your heart.'

The colour drained from Tolivar's face. He said not another word, but came down the hill after the others.

CHAPTER 16

The tiny sound made by the door opening caused the Queen to regain her senses fully at last, but she kept her eyes closed. Footsteps approached her bed. A woman's voice, vibrant and imperious, spoke.

'She should be fully restored by now, Star Master.'

A man gave a grunt of agreement.

'There was no way we could take the Black Trillium from her, however. Not even the power of the Star sufficed. When touched, both amulet and chain seemed to become white-hot. They did not burn *her* flesh, but only that of the person trying to grasp them. We even used tongs and other instruments, but these either burst into flame, or else became too hot to hold.'

'Never mind. I don't think the amber can harm us. It only protects her. Now give me the diagnostic contrivance.'

'Yes, Master.'

'Queen Anigel!' The man's voice was all too familiar. 'Wake up.'

She opened her eyes.

Two people dressed in the black-and-silver robes of the Star Guild stood looking down at her. One was a tall woman, the very spit and image of the beautiful redheaded she-warrior of the feather tapestry on the bedchamber wall behind her.

At her side was Orogastus.

'Now I understand everything!' Anigel said to him with icy anger. 'When your scheme to drown me failed, you kidnapped me through that damned viaduct.'

'Good afternoon, Majesty,' the sorcerer said politely. He was holding a small metallic device, which he held momentarily against her forehead. It squeaked faintly, whereupon he gave a nod of satisfaction and pressed the thing to her covered belly. She uttered an angry protest, to which he paid no attention, only tucking the little machine away into his robe and smiling.

'You will be happy to know that you are quite recovered from your recent injuries. Your unborn sons are likewise in good health. As to your drowning, that was not my plan at all, and the cack-handed fool who so clumsily engineered it has been reprimanded.'

'Where is my Nyssomu nurse, Immu?' Anigel demanded. 'She was swept away into the flood with me. Do you hold her captive as well?'

The sorcerer shook his head. 'I know naught of her. There was only a single Ruwendian knight and some men-at-arms there in the Mazy Mire, who attacked my servants as they were carrying you through the viaduct.'

'Sir Olevik! What happened to him?'

Orogastus shrugged. 'He and his men were killed in the affray, blasted to ashes by our invincible weapons.'

The sorcerer's offhandedness filled the Queen with renewed indignation. 'Free me!' she cried, straining at her bonds. 'How dare you tie me to the bed like some base criminal?'

Orogastus said, 'The restraints were only to keep you from squirming during the six days that you healed, unconscious. We could not have your valued bones mend crooked.'

'Why have you abducted me? I give you fair warning – neither my Royal Husband nor the Archimage Haramis will submit to you in order to spare my life and those of the babes I carry. I am no longer the coward who supinely handed you her talisman four years ago! Now I am prepared to die if your evil schemes are thereby defeated.'

Orogastus smiled and pushed back his long white hair with one slender hand. 'I would much prefer that you live, Queen Anigel, but the decision is entirely up to you. We shall discuss the matter later.' He turned to the female of the Star Guild. 'Naelore – loose the Queen and help her to dress, then conduct her to the secure hall. I will be waiting with the others.' He left the room, closing the door behind him.

Not bothering to disguise her contempt, the Star Woman flipped the coverlet from Anigel's body. 'I shall serve as your tiring-maid this once, Queen. But if it had been up to me, you would have done your recovery in the dungeons, together with your haughty fellow-rulers.'

'What? You hold other monarchs captive as well? Who?'

Naelore bent to Anigel's ankles, releasing them, then unfastened the padded cuffs at her wrists. 'You'll find out about that soon enough.' None too gently, the Star Woman helped the Queen to sit up.

Anigel discovered that she was swaddled about the loins like an infant, otherwise naked except for her Black Trillium amulet. Peculiar yellowish material, delicate and shrivelled as the skin of a boiled yarkil, fell away in shreds from her right shin, her left forearm, and the left side of her ribcage

when she swung her feet slowly to the floor. Another great patch of the
stuff dropped from her left shoulder, disintegrating into fine flakes as it
fell among the bedclothes.

'What is this?' Anigel asked, brushing it from her body.

'Bone-mender,' the redheaded woman said shortly. 'Part of the Master's
miraculous paraphernalia.' She rummaged in a cupboard and set out
underlinen, then opened a chest and shook out a curiously styled gown
of grass-green brocade. It was very light in weight, having a myriad of
tiny yellow feather rosettes affixed to it with embroidery.

Anigel stretched, running her fingers through her unbound blonde hair.
It seemed quite clean. 'I suppose my other garments were ruined.'

'As was your regal body, until the Master worked his healing enchantment upon it.' Naelore's lips twisted in a fastidious grimace. 'There is a
basin and a ewer for washing in that alcove, and a necessarium behind
the small door. Don't dawdle about.'

Anigel did not condescend to reply, but made her toilette as quickly as
she could. She donned the undergarments and the dress, then coiled her
hair at the nape of her neck and fastened it with two gilded wooden pins.
Naelore had laid out a yellow-and-green featherwork girdle for her waist
and a cloak of ochre wool. Soft shoes of brown leather with emerald feather
puffs completed the outfit.

Anigel surveyed herself with pleased satisfaction, arranging the amber
amulet with its fossil Black Trillium so that it lay on her breast. 'Thank
you for providing me with suitable attire, Naelore.'

'It was not I,' the Star Woman replied brusquely, 'but our Master who
selected your clothes. And here is one last ornament for you to put on.'
She held out a pair of golden wrist-gyves connected by a chain. In silence,
Anigel allowed herself to be shackled.

'Now come along,' Naelore commanded. 'They will be waiting for us.'
She headed for the door.

'One question,' Anigel said, pausing before the feather tapestry showing
the female warrior among the fiery fountains. 'Is this a depiction of you
yourself?'

'No,' said the Star Woman. For the first time a smile untinged by
discourtesy touched her lips. 'It is my ancestress, for whom I was named,
and who built this castle. She also was unjustly deprived of her empire.
But she regained it – as I shall, very soon.'

Anigel followed Naelore through stone corridors, looking about with keen
interest. Could this place possibly be the headquarters of the Star Guild
that Haramis had thus far sought in vain? If this was truly Sobrania, and

155

not one of its benighted subkingdoms, she might be able to escape with the help of her Black Trillium and throw herself upon the mercy of Emperor Denombo. He made alliances with no nation, but he was fiercely chivalrous and would surely give her sanctuary until Haramis or some other rescuer arrived . . .

'In here,' Naelore said, gesturing to an open door. Within was a small hall, a kind of withdrawing room with only narrow slits for windows. Silver oil-lamps hanging along the walls gave additional illumination. Still, it took some minutes before Anigel was able to determine who the other occupants of the chamber were.

Nine chairs were ranged about a large round table in the centre of the room. Orogastus sat in one seat and another beside him was empty, presumably awaiting her. The other places were occupied by five men and two women, all shackled as Anigel was with gilded handcuffs. Behind each prisoner stood a man of the Star Guild armed with one of the peculiar weapons of the Vanished Ones.

'Welcome, Queen of Laboruwenda,' said Orogastus, inclining his head in an urbane gesture of respect. 'You know everyone else at the table, I think.'

And so she did. Appalled at the recognition, Anigel let her eyes rove over her fellow-captives, who wore expressions ranging from sullen anger to debonair unconcern.

At the right hand of the sorcerer sat an insouciant elderly couple dressed in old-fashioned court finery: the Eternal Prince Widd and the Eternal Princess Raviya of the Isles of Engi. The three soberly attired men across the table were President Hakit Botal of Okamis, and the Duumviri Prigo and Ga-Bondies, who jointly governed the Imlit Republic. The crimson-gowned matronly woman with the wry smile was Queen Jiri of Galanar. Between her and the chair intended for Anigel, slouched down in his seat and glowering like a caged gradolik, sat Ledavardis of Raktum, a man twenty years of age, whose malformed stocky body and unattractive countenance had earned him the nickname of the Goblin Kinglet.

Anigel had last seen him three months earlier, when he had come to Ruwenda Citadel to ask for the hand of her daughter Janeel in marriage. King Antar had turned him away, asserting that no princess of Laboruwenda would ever wed a pirate – even one who professed to be reformed. Janeel had been heartbroken. She professed to adore Ledavardis, who had been kind to her when she was held prisoner on a Raktumian ship. Anigel herself, against her better judgement, also rather liked the Goblin Kinglet. Although his body was ill-favoured, he was physically strong and had an imposing presence and elegant manners. Ledavardis had vowed to Janeel that he would change Antar's opinion of him some-how, and claim her in time as his bride.

The splendidly garbed young monarch who had come as a suitor to Ruwenda Citadel was hardly to be recognized now. The raiment of King Ledavardis was torn and filthy, as though his capture had not been easily accomplished. A stained bandage covered his left eye, while the right one was bloodshot and the skin around it bruised. The chains of his handcuffs were twice as thick as those of the others.

'Oh, my poor friends,' Anigel murmured. 'What a sad meeting!'

'Sorry to see they nabbed you too, sweeting,' the Eternal Princess Raviya piped. 'Fine kettle of fish, isn't it?'

The Eternal Prince Widd grinned with perfect good humour. 'Seven days ago we were playing knockers on the esplanade green with our great-grandchildren, when a couple of starry blokes popped out of nowhere at the blue wicket and hauled us away. The scoundrels warned the young folks that we'd be killed if anything was said about the kidnapping.'

'The Star Men threatened to maim all of my precious daughters if word of my abduction got out,' said Queen Jiri.

The elected officials of Okamis and Imlit nodded in unison. They had all made marriages with the royal house of Galanar, wedding three of Jiri's brood of nine princesses. President Botal said, 'Every one of us was snatched through those weird magical trapdoors – or whatever you call 'em.'

'We call them viaducts,' said Orogastus courteously. 'Please be seated, Queen Anigel, and we will begin our conference.'

Naelore led Anigel to the empty chair. Then the Star Woman drew up the hood of her silvery robe to cover her flaming hair, took a small object from an inner pocket of her garment, and stationed herself at the Queen's back.

'Lowborn conjurer!' cried King Ledavardis, starting up from his chair and lifting his chained fists threateningly. 'It will do you no good to hold me captive. Do you think the sovereign nation of Raktum will ever accept you as its overlord? Not until the Three Moons turn to spiny melons!'

He would have continued his tirade, but Orogastus frowned and made an impatient gesture. Naelore abruptly stepped away from her position behind Anigel's chair, lifted the slender metallic device she held, and tapped the King's shoulder with it.

Ledavardis' scream shook the rafters. The other prisoners started with shock, then hurled exclamations of outrage at the calm-faced Star Woman. The young King dropped back into his chair, gasping.

'Whether or not Raktum will accept me as its liege lord is not a point

157

we will debate now,' Orogastus said, when the disturbance diminished. 'It suffices that its ruler and all the rest of you are now my prisoners. You will remain here in Castle Conflagrant, hostages to the good behaviour of your nations, until a certain plan of mine matures.'

'What plan is that?' Queen Jiri inquired innocently.

Orogastus said, 'We will discuss its details in due course, Majesty, when we are all better acquainted.'

'Hmph,' snorted the Duumvir Prigo. He was a spare individual with crafty brown eyes and the prim manner of a scholar. 'How long do you intend to hold us here, wizard?'

'It may be for some time, Excellency,' Orogastus admitted.

'Until the leaders of the other countries are also captured?' Hakit Botal persisted. 'And the government of the world dissolves into chaos?'

The smile on the face of Orogastus vanished. 'The Archimage Haramis has unfortunately given warning concerning the viaduct locations. I think those rulers who are still at liberty will be more wary of abduction from now on. But no matter. I have the most important of you in my power.'

Yes, Anigel thought. Except for one: my own husband, Antar! The other rulers who remain free are either weaklings, like old King Fiomadek of Var – or else, like Yondrimel of Zinora and Emiling of Tuzamen, already inclined to ally with the sorcerer . . .

The pale eyes of Orogastus held a fearsome, implacable gleam. 'You will all remain here as hostages, insuring that your subjects do not hinder my activities, until the Sky Trillium announces my great victory to the whole world.'

The captives stared at him in silence. Finally the Eternal Prince Widd shook a bony finger at the sorcerer. 'Look here, young man! I can put up with life in a clammy dungeon myself, and I daresay the other men can, too. But my poor wife Raviya has been a martyr to sciatica in that damp cell of hers. If you've any decency at all, you've got to give the women better quarters.'

'That can be arranged,' Orogastus said equably. 'Up until today, the detention of all of you save Queen Anigel, who was recovering from injuries, has been made deliberately arduous so that you would recognize the seriousness of your situation. But from now on – provided that you assent to certain simple conditions – you will all be given more pleasant rooms and treated as honoured guests rather than ordinary prisoners. It is up to you to choose whether you will spend your stay here in attractive apartments befitting your rank, or dwell in windowless cells, in the company of common criminals.'

The heads of state murmured tentatively among themselves. Ledavardis hauled himself upright once more, saying nothing.

'If you agree to the terms of parole,' the sorcerer said, 'you will have the freedom of Castle Conflagrant. But believe me when I tell you that it is not only escapeproof, but also impossible to storm. No power beneath the Three Moons can rescue you.'

Anigel took hold of her amber pendant on its fine golden chain. It was warm, and seemed to give comfort. 'What would you have us promise?'

'Swear that you will harm no one in this place, and that you will comport yourself in a dignified manner so long as you remain here.'

'Very well.' Anigel's words were scarcely audible. 'I do swear, on this sacred Black Trillium.'

Orogastus put the question to each of the others in turn. All of them gave their solemn word except the Pirate King, who lifted his ravaged face and spat at the impassive sorcerer.

The Star Woman brought forth from her robe another magical implement different from the torture device and this time thrust it at the neck of Ledavardis. He gave a profound sigh and collapsed senseless across the table.

'Leave him for the gaolers to remove,' Orogastus said, rising. 'Naelore, please show our other guests to their new accommodations. The rest of you Guildsmen come with me to the observatory.'

'Yes, Master,' chorused the seven Star Men. Still bearing their odd weapons, they followed the sorcerer as he left the room.

'This way,' Naelore commanded, and so great was the force of her personality that the shackled rulers paraded meekly after her without a word. They proceeded to an upper floor of the central keep, where handsomely furnished suites opened off a central corridor lit by window-wells. As each prisoner was shown to an apartment (Widd and Raviya shared the largest one), Naelore removed their golden chains.

'Servants will be assigned to you,' she said ungraciously, 'and you will be instructed about our domestic routine. You may go anywhere in Castle Conflagrant save those regions where the guards forbid you. At night, you will be locked in your rooms. If you attempt to escape or violate your parole in any way, you will be confined forthwith to the dungeons.'

Anigel was the last to be given rooms. As her cuffs were unfastened she spoke in a gentle and offhand manner. 'You have said that you were deprived of your empire. How did this injustice come about?'

Naelore gave grudging answer. 'I was the eldest, but our late father, Emperor Agalibo, declared my next younger brother Denombo heir to his dominion, with my second brother Gyorgibo to succeed him if Deno died

159

without issue. Father did this despite the fact that I am wiser and of higher spirit, saying that the vassal kings of Sobrania would never accept me because I am female.'

'I see. But in certain nations, this is the immutable custom.'

'It was not always so here!' the Star Woman cried with great rancour. 'More than two hundreds ago Sobrania had an empress – that same Naelore the Mighty for whom I was named – and her reign was a time of unequalled prosperity. Sobrania's hegemony then extended throughout the entire Southern Sea! Galanar was naught but a province of ours, and the spineless chieftains of Imlit and Okamis knelt at the Empress Naelore's footstool. Even proud Zinora paid us a yearly tribute of a shipload of their finest pearls.'

'So you hope that Orogastus and the Star Guild will help you to unseat your brother Denombo?'

Naelore's eyes were burning. 'I do not hope for it, I *expect* it – and within three short days!' Without another word she spun about and departed, slamming the door.

The Queen stood still for a moment, deep in thought. Then, rubbing her wrists absently, she wandered about the suite, finally standing at the open window of the tiny sitting room and looking out at the strange countryside. The sun had just descended, leaving a louring sky covered with grey clouds that were touched with crimson beneath.

The view was stupendous. The castle of the Star Guild was perched on a steep-sided hill over four hundred ells high that reared up in the midst of a vast bowl-shaped depression. Tall crags formed the basin's distant, jagged perimeter. Its floor was nearly level, having large outcroppings of black rock and sickly greenish areas that seemed to be bogs. A forest clothed the flanks of the central eminence crowned by the castle, but it seemed as though wildfire had swept through its lower reaches, leaving scorched snags and burnt vegetation in its wake. A tortuously winding trail stretched from the base of the hill through the depression, apparently continuing on to the rocky rampart several leagues away.

'How desolate!' Anigel said to herself. She took hold of the trillium-amber amulet at her neck and found herself shivering. 'Lords of the Air – grant that I will not have to bear my triplet sons in this awful place! Help me find a way to gain my freedom.'

She heard a sound behind her and turned to see Queen Jiri of Galanar standing in the open door. 'Poor sweeting,' murmured the kindly monarch. 'I'm afraid there is scant chance of that. The sorcerer chose the locale of his stronghold too well.'

'Is this castle truly guarded by dark magic, then?'

160

Jiri came and stood by the window with Anigel. 'Oh, there is sorcery enough in the domain of the Star Guild . . . but none is needed to insure the impregnability of Castle Conflagrant. When I was in the dungeons, my Sobranian guard – his name was Vann – was willing enough to tell me all about the place in exchange for my rings and other baubles.' She held up one plump forefinger. 'See? I have only this ruby left. I also learnt much from a chap called Gyor in the cell beside mine.'

'Gyor? You say his name was Gyor? What manner of man was he?'

'I could not see his face, since he was immediately next door, nor did he speak of himself and why he had been imprisoned. But he did entertain me with many a spooky tale about the ghosts that inhabit this old castle, and he also possessed considerable knowledge of the way in which Orogastus had got hold of it two years ago.'

'But how is the castle escapeproof,' Anigel asked, 'if no sorcery is involved?'

'Look carefully at the region below. Do you see or hear any living creature?'

Anigel studied the landscape carefully. It was utterly silent. None of the famous birds of Sobrania sang, no voors, looru or other flying predators took to the air, no insects or beasts announced the fading of the day. The only moving thing was a very thin mist that hovered over the bogs, expanding slowly until it crept up through the region of blasted skeletal trees on the lower slope, halting at the point on the hill where the forest remained healthy.

'I perceive no animal life at all,' Anigel said.

'Because nothing can live down there,' Jiri said. 'Seeping up from underground is a poisonous miasma. Not the mist, which is harmless, but an invisible vapour with only a faint smell. It blankets the floor of the basin just below the burnt trees. Strong winds may blow it away from time to time, but it always returns, unseen and deadly.'

'But there is a road,' Anigel protested. 'And I myself remember being brought here in some kind of wagon –'

'Do you also remember fire?' Jiri asked.

Anigel frowned. 'Why, yes.'

'That is the only way in which the poisonous atmospheres may be foiled. They are flammable, you see. When the Star Master or his henchmen would cross the basin, they ignite the exhalations. Flaming geysers appear, and after they have burned for a few minutes sweet air takes the place of the noxious. One can then travel the road in safety. But it is important to move speedily, for heaven help anyone who has not yet reached the castle's hill or the outer ring of crags when the flaming geysers

161

die! The flow of subterranean gas is irregular and may dwindle to nothing at any moment, whereupon the fires go out and the invisible lethal seepage resumes, filling the basin anew. Heavy rain can also extinguish the fires. The common people are mortally afraid of Castle Conflagrant, which was once the secret retreat of a long-dead Sobranian Empress. No one dares to come here save the minions of Orogastus. Aside from the very real peril of the geysers, legends say that the place is haunted by the phantoms of persons this Empress caused to be burnt alive.'

'Look down there,' Anigel said. 'They are opening the main gate of the castle! Someone must be venturing out.'

'Then let us watch,' said Jiri.

Side by side, the two queens stood at the open window. The dusk thickened, filling the misty basin with impenetrable shadows, and the clouds turned violet in the west. Because of the angle of the castle's curtainwall and the intervening groves of healthy trees, they could not clearly see the progress of the party descending.

It was a stunning surprise when the gas ignited.

A flattened globe of dull vermilion light suddenly appeared at the base of the hill. An instant later the women heard a sharp detonation, then a prolonged fizzing, as of fireworks. The initial fireball sent out blue horizontal tentacles that split into myriad branches, racing in all directions and staying rather low to the ground. A second explosion rang out, then others both great and small, crackling and thundering while the blue fire-net brightened and grew into a sheet of golden radiance covering the entire basin floor. No sooner had the incandescence swelled than it vanished. In its place were hundreds of flaming geysers, surging red-gold fountains that danced and spurted around the hill of Castle Conflagrant like living things, silhouetting the skeletal burnt trees and reflecting in the darkling bog waters.

'There they go,' Queen Jiri said, pointing. 'Great Goddess – it's a small army!'

'And Orogastus and the Star Woman Naelore are leading it,' Anigel stated with conviction.

Fast-moving fiery dots, torches carried by a train of riders urging their beasts to a full gallop, threaded an intricate path among the stationary blazes of the geysers. Anigel watched enthralled until the host vanished in the distance. There seemed to have been several hundred mounted riders and a number of wagons as well.

'Now you see,' Queen Jiri said, 'why escape is impossible. Even if it were possible for us to get out of the castle, we could never cross that basin. We would either suffocate, or signal our escape to our captors by

162

igniting the flammable gas. It's hopeless, as my cellmate Gyor assured me.'

'Perhaps not.' Anigel spoke so quietly that her voice was barely audible. She took hold of her trillium-amber, the glow of which brightened as her fingers touched it. 'Do you see this amulet? It is a magical thing that may help set us free.'

'Then why did Orogastus allow you to keep it?' the older Queen asked bluntly.

'For one thing, his people were unable to take it from me. But more important, he does not understand its power, which is not at all like his own sort of enchantment. From the time we were newborn infants, my triplet sisters Haramis and Kadiya and I have worn these drops of amber, which contain a fossil flower of the holy Black Trillium. Our amulets are symbolic of our destiny and also protective of our persons. They guide us on our life-path and show the way if we become lost. If our lives are endangered by magic, the amber finds a way to save us. I myself have gone invisible with its help, and it will also open any lock if it is but touched to it.'

'No!' whispered the delighted Queen of Galanar.

'Yes,' Anigel said. 'Of the Three of us who wear the trillium-amber, I am the least courageous. But I will do my best, and if the Lords of the Air permit, my magic will effect our escape from this captivity.'

'Never mind asking permission of the angels,' Jiri said. 'We should discuss the matter with our fellow hostages.'

'Assuredly. And we must do so soon, for I think we have a unique opportunity to escape while so many of the Star Guild's force are absent from the castle.'

Jiri made up her mind in a trice. 'We'll have a conference during dinner. I'll go right now and begin passing the word, so that all will be present.'

'Say nothing of your speech with that prisoner in the dungeon cell next to yours. Am I right in assuming that the others did not know his name?'

'Quite right.' Jiri's face was both puzzled and expectant. 'They were all too occupied with their own troubles to care about him.'

'I think I know who this man might be, and why he was imprisoned. It is possible that he may be of great help to us.'

Anigel explained. Then she outlined the escape plan that seemed to have come to her in a single burst of inspiration, while Jiri listened with narrowed eyes.

'Magic,' the Queen of Galanar muttered when Anigel was done. 'And uncertain magic, at that! . . . Well, sweeting, I'm game to try. But we may have our work cut out for us convincing the others.'

163

Anigel continued to stand at the window long after Queen Jiri departed, watching until the fires began to gutter and shrink. One by one the flaming geysers winked out, and finally only a single tall blue-gold plume remained, swaying in the night wind like a spectral dancer. By the time a servant came rapping at Queen Anigel's door to tell her that the evening meal was ready, the last geyser had also faded and died, and the region surrounding the castle's hill had become a sink of poisonous darkness.

CHAPTER 17

'But why must we make the attempt tonight?' President Hakit Botal of Okamis complained. 'Why, we're barely recovered from our stint in the dungeons! We haven't even had time to reconnoitre the castle and find the best escape route.'

'There's only one way out, son-in-law,' snapped Queen Jiri. 'The way we came in, through the main gate.'

Anigel added, 'And the reason we must try tonight is because now is the time our captors will least expect it: When you are newly released from your cells, and I have just awakened out of my enchanted sleep . . . and Orogastus and his force are lately departed to make war upon Emperor Denombo.'

The seven hostage rulers strolled in a casual manner from the dining hall where they had just eaten the evening meal. Each one carried a pewter cup and a full bottle of the strong, flinty wine they had been served at table. Following the plan Anigel had outlined to them while they ate, they pretended to drink and laugh tipsily as they made a show of examining the feathered hangings and the pieces of exotic statuary that stood in wall recesses flanked by blazing cressets. All the while, they moved along a wide corridor toward the great staircase that led to the lower reaches of the castle. Only a handful of guards lounged at their posts in a lax manner, paying no special attention to the wandering captives. Few other servants of the Star Guild were abroad. Most of the diners had remained in the hall to drink and revel.

'I don't know if I'm up to this adventure,' Ga-Bondies whispered. 'You lot may have to go on without me.' The Duumvir, who shared the highest elected office of Imlit with his associate Prigo, looked extremely pale. He was a man in late middle age, portly and with thinning sandy hair and a querulous manner.

'Buck up, old fellow,' Prigo urged. Maintaining the pretence, he uttered a shrill laugh and affected to drink directly from his wine bottle. 'If an expectant mother like Queen Anigel can make it, so can you.'

'That wretched meal!' Ga-Bondies moaned. 'Greasy sausage, nauseating

165

boiled greens, bread so gritty it set one's teeth on edge, suet pudding, and only this atrocious plonk to drink! At least the adop and water we were served in the dungeons was fairly easy on the digestive tract. Right now, I feel so dyspeptic that I may puke at any moment.'

'Oh, poor chap.' Old Princess Raviya's eyes twinkled mischievously as she toasted the sufferer with her empty cup. 'Perhaps you shouldn't have taken that third helping of sausage.'

Somebody snickered. Ga-Bondies pulled out a handkerchief and patted his sweat-beaded brow. 'Madam, I was starving after six days of vile incarceration. One might have thought that a sorcerer intent upon conquering the world would at least set a decent table. But no! We're fobbed off with a repast fit only for peasants.'

'"While the cook's away, the scullions play,"' Queen Jiri quoted. 'I'll wager the whole place has gone slack since Oro and the army went off. Did you notice that the only two Star Men at supper were very young?'

'Apprentices left to hold the fort with the senior servants,' Raviya judged, 'and barely three dozen warriors. The hall could have held ten times as many people.'

Jiri said, 'Anigel and I saw around that number leaving the castle.'

'I wonder how the wizard expects to conquer, using such a small force?' said Widd.

'He's going up against a mob of superstitious barbarians,' Prigo retorted darkly. 'The odds may be just about right.'

'The army probably took the best food along with them,' Duumvir Ga-Bondies muttered bitterly, his mind still on his disordered innards. 'Keep the morale of the fighters high and damn the stay-behinds.'

'I suspect that old Oro has the very devil of a time keeping this establishment in victuals,' Prince Widd observed shrewdly. 'You can't force superior provisioners to make daily deliveries through a miasmic inferno, you know.'

'Doubtless the sorcerer obtains his supplies by black magic,' President Hakit Botal said, 'in the same way that he snatched us away from our homelands.'

'When Ga-Bondies and I were kidnapped,' Prigo remarked, 'we and our captors came out of the enchanted portal in the midst of a dense forest. Men-at-arms from a camp immediately adjacent were waiting to conduct us to the castle. It took us a day and a night to reach here, and nowhere along the way did I see a village nor even so much as a trapper's hut. The trail we followed was narrow and much overgrown, as though it were seldom used. Certainly no regular supply trains came along that way.'

166

The others, excepting Anigel, related similar experiences. In spite of the differing venues of abduction, it was apparent that they had all emerged at the same location, from thence being taken to Castle Conflagrant. None save Anigel knew anything of the viaduct's working, nor did the others seem aware that more than one might exist.

'There is a crucially important matter that we neglected to discuss at dinner,' Hakit said. He had paused, feigning interest in a tapestry depicting a beautiful seaside villa of the Zinoran style favoured by wealthy Sobranians, all golden rooftiles and shining white walls. 'Supposing that we do manage to escape the castle and cross the basin of flaming geysers. Where then shall we go?'

'To Brandoba, the Sobranian capital,' Anigel said. 'We will ask sanctuary from our fellow-sovereign, Emperor Denombo – or, failing that, convince some ship's captain to give us safe passage to Galanar, where Queen Jiri's warriors will defend us.'

'But how shall we find the way through this unknown territory?' Hakit Botal persisted. 'By following Orogastus?'

Anigel nodded. 'My trillium-amber's magic will also guide us – and we may perhaps have help from another source as well.'

'We do not even know how far away the Sobranian capital is!'

'It is approximately four hundred leagues,' Queen Jiri said, 'if my talkative prison guards told me the truth in exchange for my jewellery.'

President Hakit's mouth dropped open. 'Four *hundred*?'

'Oh, dear,' Princess Raviya quavered. 'So far?'

Prince Widd said, 'Is there no place of refuge nearer?'

'None where we would be truly safe,' said Jiri. 'Apparently, the Star Guild has the local chieftains thoroughly intimidated.'

Duumvir Prigo did not disguise his dismay. 'But that's appalling! Why were we not told this before, as we were discussing the plan at table? I assumed –'

'It will take over a month to ride that distance,' Ga-Bondies broke in. 'I can't possibly do it. I am not a well man.'

Hakit glared at Anigel. 'Queen, you have been less than straightforward with us. None of us has experience in wilderness travel. It is madness to think we could reach Emperor Denombo's court if it is so far away. Pursuers from the castle would certainly recapture us.'

'Not if my magic assists us, as I pray it will,' Anigel bestowed a kindly glance upon the ashen-faced Ga-Bondies. 'Nor will you have to endure an arduous journey, Duumvir. A few days at most.'

'Surely you cannot think to re-enter the infernal magic hole that brought us here!' Hakit exclaimed.

'No,' Anigel said. 'That viaduct might still be guarded, and we have no way of knowing where it would take us. I have been told that adept persons are able to change the destination of certain viaducts. The one used to abduct us is obviously one of the changeable sort. Not being sorcerers ourselves, we cannot hope to command it.'

'Then what are we to do?' Hakit demanded. 'Explain yourself, Queen – else I, for one, will decline to follow you.'

The President of Okamis was a man of imposing stature, clean-shaven and with a jutting jaw that he delighted in thrusting forward to emphasize his words. He was accustomed to wielding almost dictatorial powers in his prosperous homeland. Earlier, when Anigel described the initial phase of her escape proposal at dinner, Hakit Botal had at first demurred, chuckling with patronizing disdain at the very notion of entrusting their fate to the alleged power of an amber amulet. Then, seeing that the others saw nothing wrong with pitting benevolent magic against the dark sorcery of Orogastus, Hakit had demanded that he himself be designated leader of the escape, rather than leaving the undertaking in charge of 'a delicately reared dame such as Her Majesty, who would have scant experience in such parlous adventures'.

Queen Anigel had smiled sweetly at the Okamisi President, saying that he was certainly free to propose an alternative scheme of his own, and head it up if the others elected to follow him. However, since Hakit actually had nothing concrete to offer at all, he finally submitted with ill grace when everyone else pledged support to Anigel.

She now said to him, 'I know you are anxious, but I have a good reason to keep the second part of my plan secret for now. It is for our own protection, in the melancholy event that one of us should . . . be taken by the enemy in the course of our escape.'

There was an uncomfortable silence as the captives mulled over her words – for there was more than one implication. Unlike the royals, who had all demonstrated their personal enmity for Orogastus during dinner, the three leaders of the republics had hinted more than once at a willingness to accommodate the sorcerer and his Star Guild if it should be to their national advantage.

They walked on, avoiding one another's eyes.

Finally Prigo, speaking with elaborate casualness, changed the subject. 'It seems obvious that the Star Men must have some magical means of transport if they intend to attack Denombo within three days, as the woman Naelore said to Queen Anigel.'

'I believe this to be true,' Anigel agreed. 'And I hope that we may ultimately reach the Sobranian capital by using that same means.'

168

'But *how?*'

Anigel said, 'There is one who may be able to tell us that, Duumvir, along with other valuable information. Queen Jiri and I will go down to the dungeons and fetch this person shortly, so that he may accompany us in our escape attempt.'

'Not that firebrand Ledavardis!' Ga-Bondies exclaimed, full of indignation. 'Not the Pirate King!'

'We cannot leave him to languish here,' said Anigel evasively.

Prigo gave a sniff. 'It's Ledo's own fault that he's not free on parole with the rest of us.'

'You intend to release him,' Prince Widd inquired, 'using that amber amulet of yours to open the locks?'

'Yes,' said Anigel. 'That is exactly what I hope to do.'

'Do you also expect this enchanted geegaw of yours to whisk us to Brandoba in the wink of an eye?' asked Hakit, speaking with arch scepticism.

She made a mild reply. 'My trillium-amber is unfortunately not capable of such a miracle. But with the grace of the Triune its powers may yet suffice to gain our freedom.'

Hakit scowled. '*May?* This plan of yours *may* be the death of us!'

'Nothing is certain,' the Queen said serenely, 'save that some day we will all pass safely beyond. But I for one am not ready to die yet . . . nor am I willing to surrender my country and my authority to a base sorcerer, as certain other rulers may be. My two sisters and I know Orogastus of old, and the magic of our Black Trillium has saved us from him many a time. If the Lords of the Air smile upon us, we may be aided once again by the Flower.'

'This escapade sounds more and more dubious,' Hakit said, with a sour grimace. 'I'm having serious second thoughts, especially since you refuse to demonstrate your magic to us.'

Anigel nodded, as if to concede the point. 'It was not possible earlier, since the amulet works only to save me from peril, or guide me in dangerous circumstances. Opening the dungeon doors for the rescue of Ledavardis will therefore serve as a crucial test of my plan. If the amber fails in that task, we will know that Orogastus has laid some overwhelming enchantment upon Castle Conflagrant that the Black Trillium is helpless to counter.'

'Then what?' Prince Widd inquired.

'If the dungeon doors do not open, I will return chastened to my rooms, where I will pray for our eventual rescue or ransom and go straight to bed . . . I advise those of you who have no confidence in me to follow that course of action now! I do not intend to waste any more time in talking. Whoever is with me, resume the charade of drunken merrymaking, for we are near to the stairs and I spy a pair of guards on station there.'

After a moment's hesitation, the others all came along after her. Widd and Raviya linked arms and began to sing an Engian ballad about a lass who loved a sailorman. Prigo did a little dance around them and Hakit pretended to swig from his bottle, while keeping his thumb thrust into the neck. Ga-Bondies merely staggered along, looking more and more queasy.

At the head of the staircase, Queen Anigel bade a giggly good evening to the two guards, who gave amused salutes. 'Good men, we are on our way to escape,' she told them slyly. 'Sound the alarm! Call out Orogastus and his crew of conjurers!'

The bored guards made no move to hinder the distinguished hostages, who proceeded down the stairs amid tipsy laughter and song.

On the keep's ground floor was a large vaulted lobby having a well, water troughs, and hitching rails. Fronial droppings, a broken sack of grain, and other debris left by the sorcerer's small army lay on the pavement. A single broad passageway led straight from the foot of the staircase toward the barbican and gatehouse, while other corridors to the left and right gave onto the inner ward surrounding the keep, where there were presumably barracks and stables, kitchens, a bakery, and other domestic offices of a well-found castle. Except for the passage to the barbican, the area was dark and full of confusing shadows, only dimly lit by hanging fire-baskets. The only men-at-arms to be seen were over forty ells away, near the gate.

Anigel went and sat on the wide coping of the great washing trough, where she cupped her hands, took water, and pretended to lave her face. 'Now, if you please,' she whispered, 'gather closely around me, and we will review what we are to do.'

'I still don't feel well,' Ga-Bondies whimpered.

The Queen only smiled at him. 'You, Princess Raviya, Hakit, and Prigo will go down to the barbican. There you must discover exactly how many guards are on duty in the vicinity, and the manner of their patrolling. Prigo must look carefully at the sally-port in the gate, through which we will have to make our exit, and take careful note of the position of any bolts, locks, or bars that will have to be undone.'

'The guards may become suspicious if we linger long,' Hakit said.

'Maintain the pretence of boisterous intoxication,' Anigel told him. 'Tell any persons you encounter how happy you are to be out of the dungeons and free to walk about the castle – even though you find the place very eerie. Remember our plan! Ask the guards if the corridors are haunted.

Say you saw something ghostly as you were carousing about. Ask if they are certain that the Star Master has banished all demons and harmful spirits from the place. When you have made the guards thoroughly uneasy, return here to the well, where Widd will be waiting for you. Accompany him and follow his lead from then on.'

'It will all be done,' said Princess Raviya firmly.

Anigel turned to the elderly Eternal Prince, whose pouched eyes were sparkling with excitement. 'Dear friend, you recall that your job is to find the stable, which is doubtless in one of the enclosure buildings of the inner ward. Jolly up the grooms and hostlers you find on duty there. Ply them with drink.' She handed over her own winebottle to him, and Queen Jiri's also. 'Contrive to examine whatever mounts are left in the stalls. Check out the tack room if you can, and try to find us some stormproof riding cloaks. We will require nine swift and sturdy fronials for our escape.'

'Nine?' Widd said in surprise. 'But there are only eight of us, including young King Ledavardis.'

'Nine,' said Anigel firmly. 'When you have finished your investigations, excuse yourself to the grooms, saying that you are enjoying their company so much that you will find more drink for them. Return here, collect the others, and take them back to the stable with you, as if to admire the animals and meet the lads you have befriended. Give out the remaining bottles of wine. When the stablehands have their back teeth afloat, over-power them as quietly as possible, bind them, and gag them. But remember that we have all given our oaths not to harm any persons within the castle! Harness the mounts and fill saddlebags with whatever food and drink you can find. We will also need pitch-torches and a tinderbox. Each person must have a large hooded cloak of some sort, even if it is only a steed-blanket. You must all remain hiding in the stable until Jiri and I return.'

'I'll see to everything,' the Eternal Prince assured her.

'It would be better,' Hakit broke in officiously, 'if I were the one to undertake the tasks in the stables. I am more able-bodied than Widd, and if there should be trouble I would be better able to defend myself.'

'But the Eternal Prince is so much more harmless in appearance,' Anigel pointed out reasonably. 'And so he is the perfect one to gain the confidence of the hostlers. Until their wits are slowed by drink, they might be wary of a stalwart man such as yourself.'

Hakit gave a dubious grunt, but he said no more.

Anigel studied her trillium-amber. 'Now I shall ask my amulet in which direction the stables lie.' She held the droplet out on its chain so that the Eternal Prince and the others could examine it, and whispered her request.

Within the softly glowing pendant a tiny line of light appeared; its blinking tip pointed to the righthand corridor.

'Mercy!' said the awestricken Raviya. 'It really is magic!'

'So it would seem,' said Prigo. His gaunt face creased in a pedantic smile of approval.

'And now, Black Trillium,' Anigel said, holding the amber steady and staring at the tiny fossil Flower within, 'I pray you show me the way to the dungeons.'

The glowing streak swivelled about and the spark migrated to its opposite end, indicating the area behind the great staircase, where a single cresset burned.

'That's it, all right,' Jiri said. 'The rest of us know the way only too well. Well, come along, lass. Let's be off to rescue that Goblin Kinglet.'

'First, we must see if my amber unlocks the upper dungeon door.'

'The test!' breathed Prigo.

They all went quietly into the area behind the stairs. The portal was of heavy gondawood massively reinforced with iron, and it had a single keyhole as high as a man's index finger. Anigel gripped the amber, which shone like a miniature lantern in the gloom, and touched the lock-plate.

The dungeon door swung open on greased hinges. Beyond was a steep staircase illuminated by guttering flambeaux set in widely spaced wall brackets.

'It worked!' Prigo whispered. 'The magic really worked! There'll be no turning back now.'

Ga–Bondies gave a tiny, fearful moan.

'May good luck attend all of our endeavours,' the Eternal Princess Raviya said in a soft voice. 'Come along, boys.' She set off in the direction of the gatehouse with the three officials trailing after.

Old Prince Widd kissed Anigel lightly on the cheek and also ambled away, singing a sea chantey of the Engi Isles while the winebottles in his arms clinked an accompaniment.

'Ready?' Jiri said to Anigel.

'Take my hand,' the younger queen commanded. With the other, she held tight to the amulet, speaking aloud to it. 'Black Trillium, do again as you did in my youth, when you saved me from doom. Conceal me from the sight of all persons.'

The Queen of Galanar gave a great start. Suddenly it seemed that she stood alone in the tall doorway.

Except there was a warm hand in hers.

'Now it really begins,' said a voice from the air. Jiri felt herself drawn forward, and began to descend the dungeon stairs.

CHAPTER 18

'You were wise,' said Jiri to her invisible companion, as they moved down into the bowels of the castle, 'not to trust Hakit Botal or the Duumviri too far. My three sons-in-law are competent rulers, but they are also thoroughgoing pragmatists who would ally with the Frost Demons of the Sempiternal Icecap if they thought they could preserve the commercial prosperity of Imlit and Okamis by so doing.'

'I know,' said Anigel. 'That's why I had Raviya accompany them in spying out the gate: to minimize the temptation for a last-minute betrayal.'

'Oh, they want to escape as badly as we do, sweeting. But they're afraid for their skins. We royals are beloved by the people of our countries. I know that my own subjects would stop at nothing to get me back alive and in one piece, and I'm sure that your people feel the same. But elected officials command no such devotion. Poor things! They are quite replaceable, as one griss egg may be substituted in a cake recipe for another accidentally broken. In the case of Hakit Botal, many citizens of his country would dance in the streets if they knew he had been kidnapped.'

'Surely not! National pride, if nothing else, would deter them.'

'Well, perhaps.' Jiri's eyes had a gleam of insidious humour. 'Still, a pompous woth like Hakit must be galled to the tripes at having to rely for rescue upon a woman. Even one so intrepid as yourself.'

There was a low laugh. 'He should meet my two sisters! I am the least formidable Petal of the Living Trillium, and by no means as bold as I may seem. I will need to lean heavily upon you in this venture, Jiri. You are the one having a truly valiant character.'

'Tosh,' scoffed the Queen of Galanar.

The voice coming out of the air was heavy with portent. 'My magic may get us through the castle gate, but it is still a long way to Brandoba – as dear old Raviya pointed out. While we are bound to harm no person while we are within the castle, the oath does not hold true once we are outside and fleeing for our lives. Once, long ago, I killed a man. Nevertheless, I know I could not now bring myself to inflict grievous harm upon

173

a human being, even if we are attacked by pursuers. And yet there may be no alternative to fighting if this escape attempt of ours is to succeed.'

Jiri squeezed her companion's unseen hand. 'Leave all that to me and the others.'

Moving swiftly and silently, the two women came to the foot of the steps, where there was a kind of vestibule. On one side was a rusty portal labelled *ARMOURY*, and on the other a gate of iron bars that shut off the passageway leading to the prison cells and the gaolers' watchroom.

'Let's take a peek inside the armoury,' Jiri suggested. 'There may be some weapons we can use later.'

At the touch of Anigel's amber, the door swung inward upon a pitch-black interior. The queens hastened through and shut the door behind them. Immediately Anigel became visible, with the amulet around her neck shining so brightly that the place was lit up as clearly as in daylight. There was not much to be seen within the dank stone chamber, which was festooned in its upper reaches with dusty lingit webs. The army of Orogastus had obviously taken the best of the swords, halberds, and maces, leaving behind dulled and notched blades, overly heavy poleaxes, and spears with crooked shafts. Numbers of open wooden chests contained a few smaller implements of battle, as well as dented helmets and shirts and vests of tattered chainmail. There were none of the wondrous ancient weapons of the Vanished Ones that Haramis had mentioned.

Anigel said, 'Do you see anything that you or the others might make use of?'

Queen Jiri was delving in one of the chests. 'Well, I'm no warrior. My dear late husband, Collo, took care of that sort of thing when Sobranian tribal kings made occasional forays against the western marches of Galanar. But this might eventually come in handy, and I can tuck it away easily enough.'

She held up a simple instrument that consisted of a wooden handle, attached by a chain to a short, thick rod of steel.

'A war-flail. When I was a girl, I'd often help with the threshing at the royal farmstead where we took our holidays and grew special delicacies for the high table. I used a thing similar to this, but much less lethal, to beat the grain from the chaff.' She smiled grimly. 'I could swat a stinging bot on the wing in those days, or flick a single petal from a meadowsweet. Mayhap I haven't lost the knack.'

Anigel repressed a shiver. 'Remember our oath to do no harm within the castle.'

'An oath extracted under duress is nonbinding. Any hedge-lawyer knows as much.' She tucked the flail into a pocket of her gown.

'Please! We must perform this feat without violence! I cannot forswear my Black Trillium!'

Jiri sighed. 'Oh, very well.'

'I will need your help now to dress,' Anigel said. 'I have decided not to use our veils in the deception after all, but rather some of this gear instead. It will be more effective.'

Jiri chuckled. 'Yes. I think you are right. Are there any other changes of plan?'

Anigel shook her head. 'Just put on a good performance when you reach the guardroom, laying the groundwork for my grand entrance.'

The three gaolers sat at a rough table, finishing their supper of bread, cheese, and beer. The occupants of the cells were quiet for the nonce as they consumed their more meagre fare. Only a small number of prisoners remained, now that most of the exalted hostages had been set free.

'I almost miss them,' said the burly sergeant, whose name was Vann. 'It's going to be damned dull down here without them.'

'You'll miss that fat Queen of Galanar, for sure,' sneered one of the guards, a wiry man with a grotesquely scarred face, who was missing one ear.

'Shut your trap, Ulo,' the sergeant growled, 'if you know what's good for you.'

'The whole watch knows you were cosying up to her,' the third guard said, wiping beer suds from his moustache. He was at least sixty years old, but still fairly sturdy. 'And not just because she was a vision of beauty, eh?' He sniggered and his mate joined in.

Vann slammed his fist down onto the table. 'Belt up, damn you!'

'Or what?' Ulo inquired insolently. 'You'll punch our noses? Kobit's right: You were taking bribes from Queen Jiri. Telling her Matuta knows what secrets, in exchange for her jewels. That's treason, that is. Lay a finger on either of us and we'll have a word with the two Star Men upstairs.'

'You can't prove a thing,' Vann blustered. 'And if you try –'

'Hsst!' The guard named Kobit started up from his stool, eyes wide. 'You hear that?'

Vann rose and stumped to the door of the guardroom. One of his legs was gone just below the hip, replaced by a carven peg. 'Merciful Mother Matuta!' he exclaimed, then fell back in astonishment. 'It's herself!'

Queen Jiri of Galanar, magnificent in purple velvet, a white silk veil, and a diadem of enamelled leaves and flowers, came into the chamber smiling. 'Good evening, men.'

The gaolers mumbled a response, touching their foreheads. Vann addressed the royal visitor with some anxiety. 'Madam, you aren't supposed to be down here.'

'No?' Queen Jiri seemed surprised. 'But the doors were all open and unguarded, and so I thought to –'

'The doors open?' Vann exclaimed. 'But that's impossible!'

'The duty roster's thin,' Ulo observed with a smirk. 'Most of the ablebodied marched off with the Master and his wizard crew.'

'I only wish to say a few words of comfort to King Ledavardis,' Jiri said in a soothing tone. 'He was treated most brutally this afternoon by the Star Woman Naelore. Surely, sergeant, there is no harm in that.' She feigned an adjustment of her veil, and the ruby ring on her finger gleamed in the torchlight.

'Well . . .'

The Queen touched Vann's arm. 'Do come with me, if you wish. I must say that the shadows seem especially ominous this night. My courage nearly failed me as I descended the dungeon stairs. As I rounded each turn of the spiral, it seemed as though some half-visible phantasm preceded me.' She gave a trill of nervous laughter. 'Perhaps it was one of the ghosts said to haunt this great pile.' She went off down the corridor leading to the windowless cells, and Vann followed.

'See that ruby?' Ulo remarked sourly. 'What'll you wager that –'

Kobit cocked his head. 'Listen.' His voice was urgent. Both men stood at the watchroom door, looking in the opposite direction from that taken by Vann and the Queen.

The torches lining the long corridor to the stairs were winking out, one by one, beginning with those farthest away. From the darkened area came a sound of hoarse breathing mingled with moans of pain.

Ulo's hand went to his sword. 'What the hell?'

A spectral wail echoed from the stone walls just as the last flambeau was extinguished. Then all was silence. The only illumination came from the flickering cresset in the watchroom and another hanging at the entry to the cellblock fifteen ells away.

'Matuta's Tears!' Kobit croaked. 'Look there.'

Standing in the black shadows was an improbable figure. It wore a ragged, short-sleeved mail hauberk, an old-fashioned pot helmet, armoured gauntlets, and shin-greaves. But these appeared unsupported by human flesh or bone, and were visible only because of the dim golden glow coming from within the mail shirt, where a heart would have been. The apparition held high an ancient rusty sword.

'Woe!' it cried in a shrill, raspy voice. 'Woe to those who dwell in this accursed castle! For they shall soon be as dead as I am.'

176

The ghost doffed its helm, and there was no head beneath. It began to stride toward the frozen guards.

Ulo and Kobit howled in unison and fled toward the dungeon cells, their own weapons forgotten.

Once he had the ruby ring stowed safely in his belt pouch, Sergeant Vann took his ease at the far end of the murky cellblock, where a lantern hung above a stone bench. Queen Jiri had purchased complete privacy for her conversation with the hunchbacked young King of the Pirates.

'Ledo, dear,' she whispered urgently. 'Prepare yourself. We have come to set you free. When your door opens, come out at once. There are three guards, and we may need your help to push them into the empty cells.'

King Ledavardis, his good eye agleam and the other still hid beneath a stained bandage, mouthed a joyous oath. No sooner had Jiri given the same message to the man in the next cell than the shouts of the terrified guards were heard. Vann surged up and limped to the prison entry, only to be met by Ulo and Kobit, who rushed in, nearly trampling the sergeant.

'A ghost! A ghost!' Kobit screamed.

'Bar the cellblock door!' cried Ulo. But Queen Jiri had moved quickly among them, and her bulk was a considerable obstruction.

'Cheeseheaded fools,' Vann bellowed to the men. 'And you, Madam! Stand aside so that I may see –'

'*Woe! Woe to all in this accursed place! Woe!*'

The headless warrior, sword awave and helm tucked into its armpit, appeared in the doorway and gave a gruesome shriek. Vann staggered backward, caught his pegleg in a crack in the floor, and fell sprawling and helpless. The artificial limb parted from the stump as its straps gave way, and the sergeant cried out in pain. The other two guards fled down the line of cells, whose occupants clung to the bars and watched gape-jawed.

The ghost flung away its helmet and stripped off its awkward gauntlets. Something that shone like a small yellow star and floated through the air like a fire-beetle touched the lock of Ledavardis' cell. The barred gate swung open. Swift as an attacking rimorik, the King darted out, seized the fallen Vann by the shoulders, and hauled him into the vacated cell. The ghost touched the lock again and it clicked shut.

'This is Gyor,' Queen Jiri said, indicating a filthy wretch with matted coppery hair and a long beard who inhabited the cell next to the pirate's.

The ghost's soft voice was now clearly that of a woman. 'Come out, friend, for you are also escaping with us.' His lock opened.

'But who are you?' the dumfounded prisoner said. '*What* are you?'

The ghost, which now resembled an animated mail shirt and a pair of greaves strapped to invisible legs, did not deign to answer. Instead it turned and started toward Kobit and Ulo, who cowered in a far corner of the cellblock.

'Woe! Prepare to die!' the spectre keened, its rusty sword slicing great arcs of air. The other inmates of the dungeon were so filled with fear that they set up a great hubbub.

Queen Jiri shouted, 'You guards! Save yourselves from the avenging demon! Get into a cell and close the door. Phantoms cannot pass through iron bars.'

As the headless ghost approached, Kobit and Ulo dived into one of the empty cells and slammed the door to. The apparition paused and the two men gasped, for a body began to solidify within the floating coat of mail. It was a lovely woman with eyes as bright as sapphires and dishevelled blonde hair. Beneath the torn hauberk she wore a green gown kilted up above her knees. She lowered the sword and let it fall to the floor.

Queen Anigel held her trillium-amber in her other hand. She touched it to the lock of the cell that held the two guards, producing a loud click, then returned to Jiri and the men she had rescued. Whispers and incredulous mutters came from the other cagelings.

'My amulet not only unlocks, but also locks.' She smiled at King Ledavardis. 'Will you be so kind as to help me take off this heavy chainmail? We will need to take it with us, and the other armour and the sword as well.'

The Raktumian monarch burst out laughing. 'So the ghost was you, my intended mother-in-law! Marvellous!' He assisted her to remove the hauberk, then unstrapped the greaves from her legs. Jiri was already gathering up the discarded gauntlets and the helmet.

The redheaded prisoner who called himself Gyor dropped to his knee before Anigel and kissed her hand. 'Madam, I am in your debt. Although I do not know who you are, or why you have chosen to rescue me.'

Anigel introduced herself, then said, 'Is your true name not Gyorgibo? And are you not the younger brother of Denombo and the Star Woman Naelore?'

'I am Gyorgibo, Archduke of Nambit,' he said, bewilderment upon his features, 'and I am indeed the Emperor's brother. But you have still not answered my question –'

'Oy!' shouted one of the men still imprisoned. 'What about us, eh? You gonna just leave us here in chokey?'

'What manner of men are they?' Anigel asked Gyorgibo in a low voice.

'Thieves, brawlers, and three who mutinied and refused to accompany

178

the army of Orogastus when it set out earlier today on its nefarious mission.'

'Do you know any details of that mission?' Queen Jiri asked in great excitement.

'Certainly, Majesty. My evil sister came down to taunt me, ere she and the sorcerer departed. In three days it will be the Emperor's birthday, which is always celebrated in the capital in conjunction with the great Festival of the Birds. Naelore and Orogastus intend to attack Brandoba while the inhabitants are distracted by the festival. They will storm the palace, using miraculous weapons of the Vanished Ones, and kill Denombo. Then, with me presumed dead, my sister will by law assume the throne. In exchange for the Star Guild's assistance, Naelore has vowed to use every resource of our empire to help Orogastus conquer the world.'

Anigel came close to the Emperor's brother. He was a tall and comely man beneath the accumulation of dirt and the bush of bedraggled fiery beard and unkempt hair. 'And does Orogastus plan,' she asked, her face intent, 'to fly four hundred leagues to Brandoba with his army before beginning this war?'

'Of course not. There is a magical passage called the Great Viaduct less than two hours' ride from Castle Conflagrant, beyond the geyser basin. It leads to a forest in the mountains above the capital.'

'A second viaduct!' Jiri said. 'Of course. There had to be one to supply the castle.' She pointed a finger at Anigel. 'You suspected as much –'

Anigel held up a silencing hand to her friend. 'There are many viaducts, scattered throughout the world, and no doubt numbers of them in Sobrania. I had a map of their location once, but I have forgotten its details.' She said to Gyorgibo, 'Tell me quickly what you know of this magical passage. Are guards stationed at it?'

'No. They are not deemed necessary. The Great Viaduct is of enormous aperture, capable of accommodating entire covered wagons and even men mounted upon fronials. I myself was taken through it as a prisoner after being seized by Naelore and her henchmen during a hunting trip in the Collum Range eight moons ago. I have since learned that the Great Viaduct serves not only for the delivery of provisions to the castle but also as a regular route for spies of the Star Guild who have long infiltrated Brandoba.'

'How near to the capital does it debouch?' Anigel inquired.

'I am not certain. It lies deep within the Forest of Lirda, an extensive imperial hunting preserve in the Collum foothills forbidden to ordinary folk. A small army could conceal itself in those woods easily, then advance upon Brandoba by night, taking advantage of the celebration.'

179

'That's old Oro's style,' drawled Ledavardis. 'Crashing the Emperor's birthday party! Remember how he broke up Yondrimel's coronation?'

'No one,' Anigel said grimly, 'remembers it more vividly than I. For it was then that you conspired with Orogastus to seize my husband and children.'

The Pirate King looked abashed. 'It was not me, but my evil grandmother – may God rot her. And I have already begged your forgiveness for my inadvertent complicity, future mother-in-law.'

Anigel said nothing.

Gyorgibo spoke with impatience. 'How will we command the Great Viaduct to open for us? When I was kidnapped, the gateway was invisible until Naelore spoke some magic charm that caused it to appear. But I could not hear what she said.'

'I know the words,' Anigel assured them. 'Now we must leave this place, taking with us a few weapons from the armoury for our friends.'

'And the rest of the prisoners?' Jiri murmured.

Shaking her head, Anigel motioned for the others to precede her. The gate of bars at the prison entry, left open when the sergeant escorted the Queen of Galanar on her visit, slammed shut and locked when Anigel touched it with her amulet. The prisoners left behind immediately began raging and cursing.

As she turned to go, Anigel caught Sergeant Vann's eye. He sat on the floor of the first cell, helpless to rise without his wooden leg, a sardonic smile on his face. 'Smartly done, madam,' said he. 'Very smartly done, indeed. But watch out for the she-devil Naelore. Her Imperial Highness doesn't believe in ghosts.'

The Queen nodded. 'Thank you for the warning, sergeant. And I hope *you* will enjoy your ruby.'

CHAPTER 19

They came down the wide corridor toward the barbican at a clattering gallop, with the headless ghost in the lead. The other eight riders wore long cloaks with hoods that concealed their faces. They brandished lighted torches and wailed like damned souls as they drew up before the tall main gate in the barbican, wheeling their antlered steeds about and making as much commotion as possible. When the bewildered men-at-arms came dashing out of the guardhouse they fell back at the sight of the ghost, which had jumped down from its fronial's back. The disembodied armour glowed from within like some human-shaped lantern. It waved a decrepit sword, capered and howled and threatened doom and destruction, while its mounted companions rampaged about the forecourt, scattering sparks from their torches.

Before the watch captain could collect himself and give a coherent order, the dancing spectre reached the sally port, a small door in the gate's left side through which a single rider might pass at a time. A spark of light whisked over the iron locks and the two beams of timber that barred the port, and it flew wide open. The apparition gave a shriek of triumph. Cloaks flying, the fire-bearing troop thundered through the port.

'Doom!' screamed the ghost, catching the reins of its own steed and swinging into the saddle. 'Flaming doom to those who follow us!' Then it was off, and the sally port slammed shut by some enchantment and barred itself once again. Nothing the guards could do would force it open, nor could they open the main gate itself.

'Sound the alarm!' cried the watch captain. 'Summon the Star Men!' He still had no clear idea of what had happened, but he was a veteran officer and intended to do the proper thing: pass responsibility on to a higher authority.

The people in the castle dithered for some time at the inexplicably impassable gate. Both of the Star Men, along with the castellan, the seneschal, and the other senior servants summoned from the great hall, were fuddled by hours of drinking. Axes were brought to bear, but it was plain that it would take hours to hew through the thick wood. Then the trussed-up hostlers in the stables were discovered (although no one yet thought to inspect the dungeon) and the identity of the ghostly riders became clear.

The calamity served to sober one young Star Man, who finally thought to fetch his own wondrous weapon of the Vanished Ones. It emitted a thin beam of scarlet light capable of melting metal or stone, and sliced through the sally port like a rapier through curds. By then the escapees had gained a precious quarter-hour's head start.

'Shall – shall we use our Stars to inform the Master?' The sorcerer whose brain was still befogged by liquor spoke privately to his more alert colleague.

'Better wait until we've recaptured the hostages,' said the second Guildsman, after a moment's thought. 'We wouldn't want to worry him needlessly, would we?'

They assembled a party of thirty mounted warriors and set off in pursuit.

The wind smelled of approaching rain and needletree resin, the clouds had thickened, and without a torch Anigel could scarcely see the steep trail zigzagging down the castle hill.

'Holy Flower, give me more light!'

The amulet on its neck-chain shone brighter, and she urged her fronial along in the wake of her torch-bearing companions. As she rode she tore off the old helmet and discarded the steel-studded leather gauntlets that had helped to sustain her ghostly disguise. There was no way, short of stopping and dismounting, that she could free herself of the onerous mail shirt or release the buckles of the greaves that chafed her legs; but a halt now was out of the question. She must ride flat out as the others were doing, in spite of the growing discomfort, and pray that the amber's magic had rendered the castle gate impossible to open.

I'm free! she said to herself.

Oddly enough, no exultation warmed her heart. Now that the initial elation of the escape had waned, she found herself becoming dazed and lethargic. Her self-confidence faltered, and the trust in the Black Trillium that had sustained her until now seemed to trickle out of her soul like water draining from a shore pool at ebb tide.

Anigel half-lay on the fronial's broad neck, her hands clutching the reins and the horrible weight of the hauberk's iron meshes bruising her shoulders through the thin fabric of her gown. The beast jolted and skidded down the rocky track, but its splayed hoofs did not lose their purchase. Around her, the needletree forest covering the slope was a blur

182

of trunks with spindly branches far overhead. She felt chilled and exhausted, and it was no wonder. She had, after all, only awakened that morning from an enchanted sleep of six days – healed, in truth, but nonetheless deficient in bodily strength.

It began to drizzle.

Anigel clicked her tongue at the fronial, telling it to go faster, but the creature's instincts countermanded her order and it would proceed only at a wary trot. The trail had become too steep for speed, switching constantly back and forth and forcing sharp turns.

The drizzle intensified, becoming a light but steady rain. In minutes Anigel was soaked, for she did not think to put on the military cloak lashed to the saddle behind her. Jouncing, battered, and thoroughly miserable, she gave her mount its head.

Suddenly the fronial squealed and came to a halt. She discovered that she was in the midst of her fellow escapees, several of whom had dismounted and were conferring anxiously. They had paused in the area of burnt snags near the foot of the hill, just above the deadly gas-filled bowl.

Hakit Botal, who was among those standing, spoke in a grating voice to Gyorgibo. 'What do you mean, there is a possibility it won't ignite properly in the rain?'

'I can only tell you what I learned during my months in the dungeon,' the Archduke said. 'There have been occasions when rain caused the flammable exhalations to explode, rather than catch fire. The trees would then burst into flame and people were sometimes struck dead by the great concussion, even though they stood well back from the brink.'

'But there's no other way out!' Ga-Bondies moaned.

'I only wanted you to know the risk,' the Sobranian said.

'I have not come this far only to surrender and return to the dungeon!' Hakit snarled at Gyorgibo. 'Are you too cowardly to make the attempt? Then give me the torch!'

'Jumped-up clerk!' Gyorgibo sneered. 'You know nothing of the geysers' peril!'

Jiri of Galanar said, 'Cease your wrangling, for the love of the Goddess! Here is our leader, and she will say what we are to do. Help the poor lass to dismount and shed that armour. She is drenched to the skin.'

Jiri and King Ledavardis assisted Anigel, putting on her a thick woollen robe and a hooded cloak. When she was warmly attired they all regarded her expectantly.

She said in a dull voice, 'Gyorgibo, are you willing to light the gas, even though there is danger?'

'Yes,' he said simply. 'All of you mount and make ready.'

The Sobranian drew a short-sword he had taken from the armoury, hewed down a scorched sapling, and chopped off its limbs. The resulting pole was twice a man's height. Gyorgibo then lashed one of the pitch-torches to the end of the pole and set off down the trail on foot, holding the flaming brand before him. 'Follow me and bring my steed,' he called, 'but stay at least a stone's throw back.'

The air was still, with only a faint miasmic scent, and the only sounds were the plopping of fronial hooves, the rattle of pebbles, and the whisper of the gentle rain. At length they came to a space that was open and level, devoid of any vegetation. It fell away to the valley floor in a glacis about twenty ells high.

Cautioning the others not to approach, Gyorgibo crept to the rim of the basin on his hands and knees, then dipped the torch-pole downward.

A deafening crackle shook the ground, followed by a slow, sonorous *whoomph*.

The first ignition was a blue-white flare. This bloomed into a flattened, glowing ball of dazzling orange-red that expanded just below the drop-off. As the Archduke scuttled back to the others, who were keeping control of their panicked mounts with difficulty, a loud hissing commenced, punctuated by many smaller explosions. Narrow veins of azure fire like branched lightning raced out across the basin in all directions, travelling at a height of about five ells. The fiery network thickened and turned to a sheet of golden luminescence that entirely filled the depression. A moment later countless flaming geysers erupted into life, and the incandescent mist faded away.

The Eternal Prince and Eternal Princess burst into applause.

'Wait for a few minutes,' Gyorgibo commanded, grinning in relieved satisfaction, 'until sweet air replaces the noxious effluvium. Then we can descend via that ramp.'

The fronials calmed, as did their riders. Anigel murmured shaky thanks to King Ledavardis for having held the head of her mount when it threatened to bolt. He said, 'With your permission, future mother-in-law, I will ride beside you and see to your safety as we cross this inferno.'

Anigel said, 'I welcome your help, for I confess I am tired unto death.' She did not speak of her pregnancy, but wondered anxiously how the three babes fared. She had not felt their movement since long before dinner.

'Forward!' shouted Gyorgibo. He and his steed plunged down the ramp into the basin of fiery fountains. He had lost his torch and Anigel had none; but the others held their brands high and set off after him. When they reached the flat, cindery floor of the depression they were able to move at a rapid trot.

The Queen entrusted herself to the Pirate King's care, clinging to the horn of her saddle while he held her reins. On either hand the pillars of fire rose among outcropping rocks, their flames reflected in the rain-dotted bog pools. It was a scene of appalling beauty. The geysers were both large and small, ranging in size from barely knee-high to over ten ells tall. All of them pulsated in an irregular manner, erupting with showers of sparks, then falling again to burn more quietly. Now and again one would be entirely deprived of its gaseous flow and dwindle to extinction; but shortly there would be a small explosion as it was relit by a stray spark, and the geyser would flame anew.

Because Anigel did not have to concentrate on guiding a skittish fronial, she thought to look over her shoulder after they had gone a half-league or so. Hakit Botal was riding behind her. In back of the President of Okamis loomed the forested eminence and Castle Conflagrant itself, painted luridly by the fires.

Moving swiftly down the hillside trail was a line of twinkling orange sparks.

'Look, oh, look!' the Queen cried. 'They are coming after us!'

King Ledavardis growled a piratical oath.

Hakit said, 'Whip up your steeds!'

But this was not so easily accomplished. In daylight, they would have seen the winding trail easily; but at night, with deceptive shadows everywhere and the fountains of flame bedazzling their eyes, they came near to losing the way several times, and the fronials were always crashing into one another as the confused riders sawed on the reins.

Gyorgibo finally shouted, 'It's no good! We must slow down, at least until we are out of this damned basin.'

The train of pursuers, who were presumably familiar with the trail, closed in steadily. Then it began to rain much harder, and all around them, the flaming geysers began to diminish and die.

'What shall we do?' Duumvir Ga-Bondies shrieked. 'The vapours will suffocate us!'

Gyorgibo called out, 'They are heavier than air. We can continue in safety for a while, so long as the heads of our fronials and ourselves are above it. Extinguish all torches! We dare not take a chance of re-igniting the gas. Queen Anigel, ride in front with me and let the glow of your magical amber serve as a guide . . . Now, press on!'

They splashed along as best they could, keeping their eyes riveted upon the single small light at the head of the file. The pounding rain and a mist that began to materialize above the bog pools soon made it impossible to discern the pursuers. The contours of the basin grew more and more indistinct as the flaming geysers continued to die. At last only two yellow-ish-blue fires remained, glowing exiguously among the tall rocks in the swirling mist. When these blinked out the fleeing hostages were in dark-ness, save for the small, steady gleam of Queen Anigel's amulet.

As if heaven itself were teasing them, the rain promptly ceased.

Her mount was being towed along by Archduke Gyorgibo but Anigel was past caring whether she lived or died. Her heart was too downcast and her mind too spent and desolate for her to pray a miracle. They were going to be caught. She knew that the failure was her fault, and the deaths of her companions would burden her soul as she passed beyond. Then a whiff of tarry odour came to her, bringing a sudden hint of nausea. The poison vapours! Making a great effort, she drew upright in the saddle and opened her eyes. The amber's glow shone on a blanket of thick fog reaching to the chests of their steeds. It would not be long now . . .

'They're nearly upon us!' Hakit Botal cried.

Anigel heard pounding hooves but there was nothing to be seen. The pursuers from the castle had also doused their torches. She whispered, 'Lords of the Air, receive us.'

'We're almost to the opposite side,' Ledavardis said. 'I see the scarp. Faster! Kick the ribs of your animals! We must get up the embankment before the foemen reach us.'

'He's right,' Gyorgibo shouted. 'There is still a chance!'

Anigel felt her mount's gait quicken. Then they were stumbling up a muddy slope, emerging from the lethal miasma as if from a lake. The crags of the basin's rim rose against a sky full of broken clouds. One of the Moons peeped out, silvering the uncanny landscape.

Gyorgibo was no longer in the lead. He came galloping back down the rocky trail, screaming at the others to hasten for their lives. As he passed he gave each fronial a sharp blow on the flank with the flat of his sword. The beasts squealed, shook their racks of antlers, and lurched forward, scrambling up onto the area of sooty rim-rock forming the safe zone above the gases.

The pursuers were now clearly visible, armoured troopers ploughing through the mist on animals that seemed legless, resembling bizarre boats rather than war-fronials. Two Star Men on white chargers came abreast in the vanguard. One of them gave an indistinct shout and lifted to his shoulder the weapon that had cut through the castle gate.

Gyorgibo wheeled his mount about and beat his way frantically up the ramp. 'Beware! Get back!' he cried to the other hostages. Reaching the

186

rim he reined in abruptly, causing his fronial to rear high, and flung his sword into the basin.

The rusty steel blade circled end over end as it fell, ringing out as it hit the rocks below.

Nothing happened, and the Sobranian uttered a curse of despair. 'I thought it would spark and ignite the vapours, but now –'

Anigel clearly heard the laughter of the Star Man who held the weapon. He and his mount, leading the others, had not quite reached the base of the ramp when he triggered the beam of magical red fire.

A shattering blast nearly tore the hostage rulers from their saddles.

For a moment Anigel was deafened and she came near to fainting. Her fronial staggered, then recovered from its first shock and began to buck and caracole from pain and terror. She clung to the beast's headstall with a death-grip and managed to stay on its back until she recovered. Below the ledge a vast gold-and-blue conflagration blazed, and mingled with its bonfire crackle were agonized human screams. After a brief time the voices ceased, the all-encompassing glare diminished, and the basin was once again filled with flaming geysers.

For many minutes the fugitives from Castle Conflagrant could do nothing except work at calming their hysterical mounts. Miraculously, no one had been thrown, and at length all nine of them were able to draw together in a group at the top of the ramp and gaze down upon the basin floor.

Along the lower track lay shapeless black mounds. Thin plumes of smoke rose from them, tinged red by the flickering geysers.

'Great Goddess have mercy,' Queen Jiri whispered, staring at the scene transfixed. 'They did it to themselves.'

No one else spoke. After a few minutes they turned their mounts and slowly rode away.

CHAPTER 20

Kadiya came last of all through the viaduct and quickly deactivated it. After the stillness of the River Oda woodland, the ear-numbing cacophony of the Sobranian jungle struck her like a blow. Her comrades who had preceded her were gathered in an incredulous huddle beneath one of the great spreading nest-trees, shocked by the raucous shrieks, hoots, squawks, and dissonant trills and whistles assaulting their ears.

'Zoto's Anklebones!' cried Sir Edinar. 'What manner of loudmouthed beasts dwell here in Sobrania?'

'I was told it is only the famous birds,' Kadiya said. 'I expect we'll get used to the noise.'

Sir Melpotis looked about warily, gripping his sword. 'Did you find any trace of the Star Men hereabouts?'

Kadiya shook her head. 'Only their emblem, nailed to yonder tree. If they were here at dawn, they are certainly gone now. But I suspect that the reward offer was only a ruse. If the Glismak had tried to claim it, they would probably have been slain for their pains.' She also cast her gaze around, then said, 'Ah. There is our guide, waiting for us as he promised.'

Because of the dense foliage overhead, even Kadiya's exceptionally keen vision had been hard pressed to locate the person standing close against the base of a tree trunk not ten ells away. He was tall and slender and his long-sleeved tunic and breeches were covered with interwoven feathers, mottled grey like bark. The pointed hat atop his grizzled head had a short brim at the front, from which hung a coarse-meshed veil that masked the upper part of his face. His lower features had been daubed with some darkish substance that obscured their lineaments. He did not move as Kadiya approached and gave greeting, speaking loudly to be heard over the clamour of the birds.

'Thank you for waiting, Critch. These are the friends I spoke of, who are also sworn to oppose the evil Star Men.'

Critch came away from the tree and lifted his veil, revealing features that were as regular as those of any human being, for all that they were pinched with suspicion. Only his eyes, huge and golden, and his three-digit hands, which clutched a sharp bill-hook with a long haft, revealed that he was of the Folk.

Kadiya introduced the others, finishing with Prince Tolivar, who had no qualms about asking the question the others were too diffident to bring up: 'To what race do you belong, Critch? I would say you were of the Vispi, except that your eyes are not green.'

'I am a Cadoon,' the aborigine told the boy grudgingly. 'The Vispi are our close kin, but since we have a greater admixture of human blood, we lack their supernatural talents and must earn our living in more humble ways.' He eyed the Prince with a scowl and turned to Kadiya. 'Tell me why a young lad is part of a heavily armed spying party—and why both you yourself and this boy wear devices capable of wreaking tremendous magic.'

'I am surprised that you recognize that,' Kadiya said.

'My people are not so skilled in perceiving enchantment as are the Vispi,' Critch retorted, 'but neither are we as purblind in such matters as some others . . . Lady of the Eyes, when I pledged to help you I believed that you were an ordinary human. But if you are an enchantress –'

'I am not much of one,' she said with a rueful shrug, 'and my nephew, Tolo, is even less adept than I.'

'I will not assist sorcerers – even incompetent ones!' Critch pointed to the board bearing a painted Star. 'Those villains have oppressed my people for nearly two years. They have even killed innocent Cadoon feather-hunters who dared come to this place, which used to be one of our prime gathering-spots until the Star Men decided to claim it less than a moon ago. I am only here today because I chanced to see the Guild warriors who usually guard the site riding hastily away.'

'Excellent!' said Sir Melpotis. 'Do you know where they went?'

'Nay.' The aborigine picked up a large knapsack from behind the tree and took a step backwards.

'Were they true Guildsmen that you saw,' Kadiya asked him, 'wearing Star medallions, or were they only henchmen?'

'Ask me no more questions! I want nothing to do with you.'

Kadiya held out both hands in a placating manner. 'Friend, I am exactly as I told you earlier: a King's Daughter of Laboruwenda, a nation far to the east, come searching for my sister Queen Anigel. She was abducted by the Star Men and may be held captive in this country. If you will take us to the capital, Brandoba –'

'I did not tell you I would do that.' The Cadoon spoke truculently. 'I said I *might* show you the trail, which is a long and arduous one.'

189

'You also said there was a shorter way, by sail in your own boat.'

'Even if you were not sorcerers, I would hesitate to go to the capital. For weeks there have been rumours among the Folk that something terrible will happen in Brandoba during this year's Festival of the Birds, which begins two days from now at nightfall.'

'What kind of rumours?' Kadiya demanded, greatly excited. 'Do they have something to do with the Star Guild? Is the Emperor in danger?'

But Critch would not answer.

'Please reconsider,' she implored him. 'Other rulers besides my poor sister were abducted by the Star Men. There is a strong possibility that the sorcerers plan to kidnap or even kill Emperor Denombo himself. We hope to warn him, as well as enlist his aid in rescuing my sister Anigel.'

'The Cadoon Folk are no great friends of the Emperor. Sobranian humans despise us, for all that they covet the feathers that we gather and sell to them. No . . . You will have to find your own way to Brandoba.'

As Critch began again to edge away into the undergrowth, Jagun stepped forward. 'Wait!' he shouted over the uproar of the birds. 'Do not be hasty. This Lady is no sorcerer and we are not villains. Please let me explain!'

Critch paused, but he still kept a firm grip upon his bill-hook.

Jagun said to him, 'As you see, I am of the Folk, like yourself. The Lady of the Eyes, who is also called Farseer and Daughter of the Threefold and Princess Kadiya, has been my dearest friend since she was a small child. In our land, Kadiya is the Great Advocate and Champion of All Folk. For long years she has faithfully defended the Nyssomu, the Uisgu, the Dorok, the Wyvilo, the peaceable Glismak, and even the Skritek of the Mazy Mire in their disputes with humanity. Only a year ago the Lady made peace between the fierce Aliansa Folk of the Windlorn Isles and the human traders of Zinora. The Vispi of the Ohogan Mountains visit her abode as honoured guests. The talisman that Lady Kadiya carries is not an instrument of dark enchantment but rather a symbol of her noble office. Even now it protects us from the Sight of the evil Star Men.'

'Can you prove the truth of this?' Critch said.

Kadiya made a wry face. 'Given a place of peace and quiet, where we could hear ourselves think, I might call upon my other sister, who is the Archimage of the Land, using the speech without words. She would gladly ask her Vispi friends to vouch for me.'

The Cadoon pointed a finger at Prince Tolivar, whose coronet gleamed in the green shadows. 'What about him?'

190

Kadiya sighed. 'He's a problem. But I swear that he will do you no harm.' She addressed her nephew. 'Tolo, tell him so.'

'I swear it,' the Prince said. 'Please help us. I would give my life to save my mother, Queen Anigel.'

Critch considered for some time and finally said, 'I have finished gleaning the feathers here and I am ready to start back to my home on the seashore. You may accompany me if you stay out of my way and do not impede my hunting.'

'How far away is your home?' Kadiya inquired.

Critch shrugged. 'A fair distance. When we reach the cliffs above the sea, you will have your chance to prove that you are truly friends of our kinfolk, the Vispi. Do that, and I may think again about helping you reach the Sobranian capital.'

They followed him through the noisy forest for many tedious hours, pausing from time to time while he gathered fallen plumage from beneath the great nest-trees and stuffed it into his knapsack. He did not pause when night fell, but continued on. Like all aborigines, Critch could see well in the dark, as could Jagun; but the weary humans were glad when the Three Moons rose, giving faint illumination to the narrow path.

It was in the dreary time before dawn that they left the jungle at last and ascended into a more open region of large-leafed bushes where the bird calls were fainter and more musical. Suddenly the Cadoon cautioned them to stand still and wait. He went forward, knelt, and took from his belt a net no larger than a handkerchief, weighted at the edges with tiny stones. He cast this skilfully beneath one of the shrubs, just above the surface of the ground, and a high-pitched, furious chittering ensued. With great care Critch retrieved his prey, a tiny bird with a single long tail-feather that sparkled in the waning moonlight as though it were sprinkled with infinitesimal diamonds.

'How beautiful!' Kadiya said.

'The vitt is the rarest creature in Sobrania,' Critch told her happily. 'I have never known one in this region before. Usually they frequent the hot springs in the high mountain thickets, but it is true that deep snow has lingered there unseasonably of late.'

Using a pair of small shears, he clipped the sparkling plume and then set the bird free. It darted at his hand viciously, drawing blood with its needle-sharp beak before vanishing. The hunter only laughed, holding up his prize. 'The feather-merchants of Brandoba will pay me enough for this to feed my family for half a year. You seem to have brought me great good luck tonight – or do I have your magic to thank?'

191

'Only your own skill,' Kadiya admitted. 'Is the little bird harmed by the loss of its ornament?'

'Nay, only its pride suffers. Both Sobranian law and our own Cadoon religion insure that we feather-hunters do no injury to the birds. Most of the time, we gather plumage that is naturally shed. Only when we encounter great rarities such as the vitt do we make use of nets or sticky bird-lime.'

They continued on, and as the heavens began to lighten, they came out onto a rocky moorland. Finally, when Kadiya and her flagging companions felt they could go no farther without dropping in their tracks, they reached a rugged bluff overlooking a wide expanse of lead-grey water. On the far shore rolling hills were dimly visible, and beyond that jagged mountains rose in silhouette against the dawn-tinted eastern sky. A cold breeze blew from the sea and they heard the murmur of surf below.

'This is the greatest estuary indenting the Sobranian coast,' Critch said, 'and on the other side lies Brandoba.'

'How many hours' sail is it to cross over?' Sir Melpotis asked.

'At least ten,' Critch said. 'Unfortunately, the winds at this time of year are light and unfavourable.'

'We are totally exhausted and we must sleep first,' Kadiya said, 'but there is plenty of time. If trouble is likely in the capital, it would be safest for us to enter after dark, when the bird festival is actually in progress and the citizens are less likely to take note of strangers.'

The aborigine had long since stowed his bill-hook in a sheath on his back, but his body now tautened in defensive wariness. 'I will take you nowhere, Lady of the Eyes, until you prove yourself to me. Do as you promised and call forth the Vispi, using the speech without words, else I will leave you here. The trail to Brandoba lies to your left, beyond the ravine. It will require at least twelve days for you to reach the city on foot, skirting the estuary, and you will come under the scrutiny of Sobranian officials when you cross the toll bridges at the Isles of Zandel.'

She ignored his hostile tone. 'May my companions sit down to rest? I will then bespeak the White Lady, my sister, who will summon one of her Vispi friends to satisfy you.'

Critch inclined his head and muttered gruff assent. Kadiya and her party gratefully shed their heavy backpacks. The knights and Jagun flopped down onto the grass amid sheltering rocks while Prince Tolivar stood by, watching his aunt with both curiosity and well-concealed fear. He knew she was certain to tell the Archimage that he possessed the Three-Headed Monster and had stolen the Three-Lobed Burning Eye.

Kadiya took the magical sword from her belt and held it by the dull-edged blade. 'Talisman,' she intoned with confidence, 'show me and all

192

persons here present a vision of Haramis, Archimage of the Land.'

One of the conjoined dark spheres at the pommel of the dark sword split open, revealing a gleaming brown eye. Immediately the tall figure of the White Lady, clad in her shimmering pearly cloak and with arms outstretched, materialized in the air between Kadiya and the Cadoon. Critch uttered a cry of amazement.

'Sister, greetings!' Kadiya said. 'We have come safely to the land of Sobrania, and I would make a request of you.'

The Archimage remained motionless and silent.

'Hara? Speak to me!'

The request is impertinent.

Before the chagrined Kadiya could react, Prince Tolivar said to her in a superior tone, 'That is not really the Archimage, but only a lifeless image of her. You have made the same mistake that I often do and worded your request to the talisman wrongly.'

'Then,' she snapped in exasperation, 'why don't you use your own Three-Headed Monster and pose the question correctly?'

Tolivar's expression changed to one of mortification. 'I – I cannot do the bespeaking at all. It is a function of the talisman that has thus far eluded me. I'm sorry, Aunt. It was rude of me to correct you.'

Kadiya sighed. 'Use a less snide tone next time, and I will welcome any help you can give me using these cursed things. I have not had my talisman in working order for four years, and I am badly out of practice . . . Burning Eye! I would speak to the White Lady across the leagues. Let me do so, and let us also have Sight of her.'

The simulacrum winked out and the talisman again spoke aloud: *This is not possible.*

'Why not?'

She is not in this world.

Kadiya felt her blood freeze. 'What! Do you mean to say that my sister Haramis is dead?'

She is not dead.

'Where is she, then?' Kadiya cried in desperation.

The question is impertinent.

The Cadoon regarded her with stony scepticism, and Jagun and the Oathed Companions were aghast. Fighting to keep control of her dismay, Kadiya forced a smile.

'Well, I warned you that I was no true sorcerer. This magical talisman of mine was oft-times balky and uncooperative even when I was well accustomed to its usage.'

'You might try to bespeak Magira,' Tolivar suggested.

'Hmm. That should be easy enough, since she is of the Folk and able to use the speech without words.' Kadiya took a deep breath. 'Talisman! I would Speak and have clear Sight of Magira, the chatelaine of the White Lady's Tower. Let her also be seen and heard by my companions.'

Instantly the Vispi woman seemed to be there, standing before Kadiya with a startled expression upon her beautiful face. She wore her usual filmy scarlet gown and jewelled collar. Her pale hair, with the graceful upstanding ears peeking through it, seemed to stir in the sea breeze.

'Lady of the Eyes,' Magira said. 'How may I serve you?'

'Tell this person' – Kadiya gestured at the Cadoon – 'who I am, and that I am no sorcerous ally of the wicked Star Men but a reputable leader come with my people in search of Queen Anigel.'

Obediently, the Vispi woman gave a brief description of Kadiya's exalted position in Laboruwenda, and also confirmed the abduction of the human rulers. As Magira spoke, the feather-hunter relaxed visibly.

So did the relieved knights and Jagun.

'I have tried unsuccessfully to bespeak the Archimage through my talisman,' Kadiya said to Magira, after the chatelaine had finished her reassurances. 'Do you have any notion of what has become of her?'

'This is melancholy news indeed, Lady of the Eyes! Two days ago the White Lady passed through the viaduct that had swallowed Queen Anigel, thinking that it would lead her to the lair of Orogastus and his Guild. We have not heard from her since.'

'Haramis is not here in Sobrania,' Kadiya said impatiently, 'else the talisman would have told me.'

'If she has been captured by Star Men, she may be detained in the same enchanted place as the Queen and the other kidnapped rulers. The Archimage's own talisman refused to give her Sight of the missing ones, and she concluded that they were shielded by some terrible dark magic.'

'I suppose that might explain her silence. But why did my talisman say: "She is not in this world"?'

Magira cried out in horror. 'Ah, no! Tell me it did not speak thus!'

'Haramis is certainly not dead,' Kadiya made quick to say. 'The Burning Eye assured me of that. But what could its words have meant?'

The chatelaine spoke with great reluctance. 'Perhaps I should not tell you this . . . The sorcerer Orogastus came to my Lady in her Tower. She – she loves him in spite of herself.'

'I know,' Kadiya said tersely. 'What of it?'

'She had thought him dead when he seemed to perish down in the Chasm of Durance, because her Three-Winged Circle said he was "not in this world". In actuality, Orogastus was rescued by the Archimage of

194

the Firmament and held captive in the Dark Man's Moon, which is assuredly beyond our reach and ken – *out of the world*. Might it be that the White Lady is there?'

'Holy Flower,' Kadiya whispered. 'I think it is quite possible. The viaducts may have their point of destination changed by those who are adept in their use. But Haramis would never have gone to such a place on purpose without telling us! And why would the Man in the Moon take her against her will? He is supposed to be indifferent to human affairs.'

'Who can fathom the deeds of Archimages?' Magira said desolately.

'Thank you for your help,' Kadiya said. She dismissed the Vispi and turned to her friends. 'Here's another pretty mess! And my talisman is apparently helpless to tell me anything about it.'

Tolivar said, 'Perhaps both of our talismans, working together, can do what a single one cannot.'

Kadiya's eyes lit. 'Let's try it. Take my free hand, and with your other grasp the Burning Eye with me.' But the Prince held back, fearing to touch the sword now that it was bonded to her, and she said, 'I give you permission! It will not harm you.'

He reached out, and all of those watching gasped in awe, for both the woman and the boy were suddenly haloed with rainbow radiance. The Burning Eye was no longer dull black but shining like molten silver, with rays of gold, green, and white streaming from its three Eyes. The coronet on Tolivar's head also glowed brightly, with similar coloured beams coming from the open mouths of the Three Monsters carved thereon.

'Now!' Kadiya cried. 'Ask the question with me, Tolo: Where is Haramis?' They spoke the words together, and the answer came.

She dwells with the Archimage of the Firmament.

'Again, lad! Request that she speak with us.'

But this time they received the old, frustrating reply: *The command is impertinent.*

'When will she return?'

The question is impertinent.

Jagun and the Oathed Companions groaned in disappointment.

Kadiya and the Prince attempted to discover other things about Haramis, but the talismans refused to answer. 'Well, so much for that,' said the Lady of the Eyes. 'At least we have learned more than we knew before.'

'What of my Royal Mother?' Tolivar asked anxiously. 'Perhaps we can discover where she is imprisoned.'

'Smart boy!' Kadiya said. 'Why didn't I think of that?' Again working together, they bade their talismans tell the whereabouts of Queen Anigel.

She rides in the Forest of Lirda.

195

'Zoto's Sacred Shinbones!' Sainlat exclaimed. 'Is the Queen then free?'

'Tolo,' Kadiya said, 'we must ask for a private Sight of her, at first without her knowledge, so that she will not inadvertently betray us to any enemy who may be near her. Do you know how this is done?'

'Perhaps better than you, Aunt,' he retorted. 'Let us close our eyes and give the command.'

They did, and into their minds sprang an astounding vision: a line of fronials plodding very slowly through a sinister woodland at sunrise, and the Queen with her head lolling in slumber. Her mount was being led by none other than the King of the Pirates, and the other riders were clearly recognizable as the kidnapped rulers of Galanar, Imlit, Okamis, and Engi. Some dozed in the saddle like Anigel while others were awake but appeared haggard and fatigued. The column was headed by an unfamiliar man of disreputable appearance who had hair and beard of a coppery red.

'Help me call out to your mother!' Kadiya urged her nephew. 'Say her name within your mind, using all your strength of will.'

But even though they both tried to bespeak Anigel, she took no notice of them, but continued her stuporous sleep, unable to respond to the magical summons. Kadiya then asked the talismans if her sister and the others were safe from danger.

No.

'Can you tell us how we may aid them?'

No.

'Where are they going?'

To Brandoba.

'Good God!' Kadiya exclaimed. 'Can it be true?'

The question is impertinent.

She laughed. 'Yes, of course it is . . . Tell us if the Star Men plan some villainy during the festival in Brandoba.'

The question is impertinent.

'Tell us where Orogastus is.'

The question is impertinent.

Kadiya and Tolivar opened their eyes and exchanged rueful glances. 'I think our talismans will say nothing of the foul sorcerer and his minions because the Star protects them,' she said. 'But when your mother awakes we can try again to bespeak her, and mayhap succeed.' Their hands separated and the occult radiance was extinguished.

'Lady,' Sir Edinar said, 'how did our dear Queen and her companions seem? Are they truly uninjured?'

Kadiya described the vision to the others. As she spoke of the frowsy leader of the riders, Critch broke in:

'This ragged redheaded man you saw may be Archduke Gyorgibo, the Emperor's younger brother. He disappeared many moons ago while hunting in the Forest of Lirda.'

'Where is the place?' Kadiya asked.

The Cadoon pointed toward the mountainous skyline across the bay. 'It is an imperial preserve, the haunt of fierce beasts and carnivorous birds such as the terrible nyar, and lies deep in the eastern highlands on the other side of Brandoba. It has long been forbidden to human commoners and to all Folk. Only the Sobranian nobility hunt there – and not even many of them, for within the past two years the Lirda has become notorious as a haunt of sorcerers. When the Archduke disappeared, all but one of his party were found slain. The surviving huntsman was mortally wounded, but before he died he said that Star Men led by the outlaw Archduchess Naelore had seized Gyorgibo. Since then, no one has dared to enter the preserve except the renegade lords who support Naelore's claim to the throne. If your Queen travels through the Forest of Lirda, she may be in great peril.'

'The riders with my mother did not seem to be fearful or in flight for their lives,' Prince Tolivar said. 'Indeed, they seemed only exceedingly weary, and their mounts near worn out.'

Kadiya shook her head slowly. 'I can think of no way we might help them. But there is another person we must bespeak now: King Antar. You must help me again, Tolo, since I have never been able to bespeak ordinary humans, as your Aunt Haramis can.'

They called out, and behind their closed eyes appeared a clear vision of Antar roused suddenly out of sleep in his chambers at Ruwenda Citadel. The King was astounded that Kadiya had her stolen Burning Eye back and that it was once more in working order.

Kadiya brushed all this aside. 'Dear brother-in-law, I have some encouraging news.' And she went on to tell the King what the talismans had revealed about Anigel.

Antar's joy was only slightly dampened when he learned what had befallen Haramis. 'Perhaps,' he said, 'the White Lady has gone to the Three Moons in order to enlist the help of the Sky Archimage. Perhaps he knows a way to destroy that wretched Orogastus once and for all.'

'I suppose it is possible. After all, Denby did help us before . . . But now I must tell you that there are rumours of impending trouble in the Sobranian capital. Orogastus and his Star Men may be on the verge of making their move.'

'Is there anything I can do?' Antar said. 'I feel helpless, being so far away.'

Kadiya thought hard for a moment. 'I think you should have a Nyssomu friend summon numbers of the Vispi to you, using the speech without words.'

'Immu can do it. We rescued her from the swamp.'

'Excellent. If we do manage to rescue Ani and the other kidnapped rulers and take ship out of Sobrania, the Vispi Folk can fly on their lammergeiers and spread the tidings to the other governments.' She paused. 'If we fail, or if Orogastus mounts a successful coup and topples Denombo from his throne, that information must also be transmitted.'

'No matter what happens,' the King said, 'all of the Peninsular nations will have to make immediate preparations for war. There is no time to waste holding conference, as Haramis hoped to do.'

'I fear you are right.'

'Most of the court turned back with me to the Citadel because of the severed road,' Antar said. 'But General Gorkain and Marshal Lakanilo pressed on to Derorguila with a small band of stalwarts, and they will rally our lowland subjects while I raise a smaller army here to defend the Mazy Mire. Even so, there will be little we can do to counter sorcery without the assistance of the White Lady. We must pray for her swift return – and hope that you are wrong about Orogastus going to war.'

'If he conquers Sobrania, he will certainly use the great fleet of imperial galleys to invade the eastern nations. I intend to do my utmost to forewarn Emperor Denombo, and give him what help I can with my talisman once Ani and the other hostage rulers are out of danger.'

'May the Lords of the Air assist you,' Antar said.

They discussed strategic matters for a few more minutes, and then said farewell. Kadiya and the Prince opened their eyes.

'You did not tell Father that I had the magical coronet,' Tolivar said in a low voice.

'No. Let him learn of your foolishness after you have freely returned the talisman to your mother. It will mitigate his sorrow and anger.' She then bade Tolivar join hands with her a final time. 'We will now try to inform the Sobranian Emperor of his peril.'

They commanded their talismans, and a vision of the ruler came to them. Denombo was sound asleep, alone in his sumptuous chamber except for a pet snithe curled up on a rug at the foot of his bed. His dearly beloved wife Rekae had died six years earlier, together with the stillborn baby boy who would have been the imperial heir. In spite of the urgent pleas of his counsellors and the subkings of the loosely knit barbarian empire, Denombo had not remarried.

Kadiya bespoke him softly: 'Emperor! Emperor of Sobrania, awake.'

The sleeper stirred beneath a great mound of down quilts. He was wearing a gold embroidered nightcap and his face was half-buried in the bed linen. When Kadiya called him again, a single bleary eye opened slowly.

'Who is there?' Denombo mumbled, through unkempt brick-red whiskers.

'I am Kadiya of the Mazy Mire, sister to Queen Anigel of Laboruwenda. I speak to you by magical means.'

The Emperor sat bolt upright, instantly awake, and his gaze swept the room. No one was there.

'Avaunt, dream-demon!' he croaked. The startled snlthe, splne-scales erect with anxiety, got up and trotted to the side of its master, uttering muted howls.

Kadiya tried to reassure the ruler. 'I am no demon, Emperor, but your friend, come to give you an important message. Do not be afraid.'

Denombo's eyes bulged and his face turned purple with anger. 'Sobranians are afraid of nothing! Show yourself, damn you!'

But Kadiya, although slightly more expert in the use of her talisman than Prince Tolivar, had never been able to Send an image, nor could she do it now with the two talismans working together. When she tried to explain this to the Emperor, the barbarian whisked a large dagger from beneath the pillows, flung back the bedclothes, and bounded onto the floor with the weapon ready.

'I know who you are!' he bellowed. 'You are an evil wizard – one of those damned Star-bearing lackeys of my traitorous sister! Guards! To me! Guards!'

'Emperor, the sorcerer Orogastus may be planning to attack you! Listen to me –'

But Denombo only continued shouting. The door of the bedchamber banged open and a dozen warriors armed with swords and battle-axes charged inside. A great altercation broke out, with the Emperor giving incoherent orders to his men (for he was actually terrified by the disembodied voice), and the warriors yelling and stomping about, overturning chests and chairs and tables, slicing up the wall hangings in search of lurking villains, and even skewering the pillows and heaped-up quilts of the imperial bed in case Star Men were hiding among them.

The Lady of the Eyes sighed and said: 'Talismans, enough . . .'

The tumultuous scene vanished.

She let go of Tolivar's hand and thrust the Burning Eye back into her belt. 'It's no use. The Emperor is too frightened of the Star Men to pay heed to any message that smacks of magic. I shall have to deliver the

199

warning in person.' She turned to Critch. 'My friend, are you satisfied now that we mean you no harm? Will you carry us to the Sobranian capital in your boat? Of course we will pay you well.'

'I will take you to Brandoba without payment,' the Cadoon said, 'now that I am certain you are an enemy of the Star Men. But there is something in my hut that you might gladly buy – trade goods that I held back from market this season because of the disquieting rumours.'

Sir Edinar gave a scornful guffaw. 'Feathers? Hah! Surely you are joking! What use would they be to us?'

'My home is in a cove not far from here,' Critch said. 'Come and look at what I have for sale, and then we will see who laughs.'

CHAPTER 21

Dawn had come to the Forest of Lirda.

Having finished his light repast in the imperial suite of the great hunting lodge, Orogastus strode to the windowed door leading onto the balcony, flung it open, and went outside. The lodge was perched at the edge of a dramatic bluff, and in the canyon below were rapids where the oddly chalk-coloured waters of the River Dob raged and rumbled over enormous boulders.

The morning chill struck through the padded linen undergarments the sorcerer wore in preparation to donning his armour, but he paid it no heed, moving around a corner so that he was able to look down on an open section of the lodge grounds, bordered by enormous trees. There his small army had encamped for the night. The warriors moved slowly in the morning mist, dismantling their tents and packing their gear with sloppy carelessness, coughing and spitting and grumbling and snarling at the sergeants who tried to hurry them along. The quartermaster, Star Captain Praxinus of Tuzamen, was shouting furiously at the fronial wranglers over some botch-up concerning the supply wagons. There were going to be delays before the force moved on to the final staging area for the invasion of Brandoba.

Not for the first time, Orogastus rolled his eyes heavenward and asked the spirit of Nerenyi Daral why she had sent him to Sobrania, of all places, to reinstitute the Guild's great work. The people were intelligent enough, but they were also stubborn and wilful and prone to dispute the simplest commands. And if these, his own elite fighters, were so lacking in discipline, then how could he hope to keep control of the larger partisan force being mobilized in the capital by the secret followers of the Archduchess Naelore? Once that gang of bravos got their hands on weapons of the Vanished Ones, they might go berserk in the heat of battle. Even the power of the Star might not suffice to restrain thousands of rampaging barbarians who had suddenly discovered the lethal potential of high technology. It was vital that he secure a talisman in order to insure that the assault on Denombo adhered to his own meticulously drawn plan.

201

It was time to exert the ultimate pressure upon the boy.

Orogastus left the balcony, returning to the pseudo-rustic imperial sitting room with its carved rafters, polished log walls, gem-bedizened candle-sconces, and feather rugs. He sat down again at the table where he had earlier eaten a frugal meal of ferol porridge and fruit, and spent some time gathering his thoughts. Then he took hold of his Star medallion and observed Prince Tolivar at some length.

It was not yet a propitious time to bespeak him, but the time would soon come. Orogastus turned to the more difficult task of communicating with Haramis. Unlike Tolo, whose ambivalent feelings left a chink in his talismanic barricade, both the White Lady and her sister Kadiya were fully shielded from both his oversight and mental speech; but there was a long chance that Haramis' love might render her receptive to his Call.

He took up his Star again.

My love! I know that you can hear me if you want to. Answer! It is your last chance to avert war. Say you will come to me. Together we can restore the lost balance of the world and prevent its destruction. Answer me, I beg of you!

But he heard nothing, save the distant roaring of a nyar or some other forest predator, and the squeals of the army's fronials as they submitted unwillingly to saddling. Haramis was aloof and silent, as she had also been yesterday, when he had called out to her before leaving Castle Conflagrant.

Haramis! You must believe that I underwent a change of heart during my sojourn on the Dark Man's Moon. My ambition is no longer to rule the world, but to save it! I will accomplish this by force only if the restoration can be done no other way . . . You can compel your sister Kadiya and your nephew Tolivar to give you their talismans. You and I will then assemble the Threefold Sceptre, and together we will use it to heal the wounded land and banish the Conquering Ice forever. Haramis! Speak to me!

He had risen from his seat and approached the windows above the encampment. Whips were cracking and wagoners shouting to their teams. The slow-moving supply train and its mounted escort would depart first and the main body of warriors would follow shortly. He and his Guildsmen would leave the lodge last of all after holding a brief council of war.

Haramis . . . I will even agree to let you yourself wield the Threefold Sceptre against the planetary imbalance. Only come to me, beloved! Let me tell you what I learned from Denby's archives of the Vanished Ones – dire intelligence that the Dark Man seems indifferent to.

He paused, his brow furrowing with anger as he recalled the old man's apathetic reaction to his discoveries, his senile laughter and the contemptuous way he had dismissed the fate of the world, saying: 'Let it be, lad.

No sense in messing about, trying to interfere with the direction that the cosmos wheels. You might manage to deflect the inevitable for a little while, but in the long run things will happen as they were supposed to happen . . .'

If Denby does know that disaster impends, he refuses in his madness to do anything about it. Speak to me, my love! Say you will come and I will turn my army back at once and withdraw to the castle. Otherwise this war must commence according to my plan, and I will have no way of halting it. My dearest Haramis, answer!

His eyes closed, he saw her in yearning memory, tried with all his soul to project his love, his willingness to turn aside from violence if she would only join with him. But there was no reply. His shoulders sagged and his fingers, which had clamped painfully around the Star, relaxed. He opened his eyes, and within the dark pupils glowed two cold points of light.

Very well. Let it be as the Dark Powers of the Star Guild command.

As if in reply, he felt the lodge tremble slightly. It was only one of the harmless small earthquakes that were commonplace in the region, called by the locals the 'Sighs of Matuta' and alleged to signify the forbearance of the goddess before the manifest sins of mankind. When Orogastus first came to Sobrania the tremors had alarmed him; but Naelore declared that never in the history of the nation had the earth movements caused any damage, nor had the great mountain range above Brandoba ever shown signs of noteworthy seismic or volcanic activity.

The sorcerer touched his Star. 'Dark Powers – are these underground disturbances a symptom of the greater imbalance of the world? Do they portend the disaster to come?'

He closed his eyes and stood utterly still, letting all thought drain from his mind so that it might be more receptive to a response. But the Powers had never bespoken him directly through his Star, nor did they give a clear answer now. A second tremor, so minuscule that he would never have noticed it under ordinary circumstances, caused the lodge floor to vibrate beneath his feet.

It might have been only a coincidence, or perhaps the Dark Powers had replied as best they could. He sighed, knowing that the whole truth would not be known until he asked the question of the Three-Headed Monster. Then he put on all of his armour save the glittering helmet with its halo of pointed rays, which he carried under one arm, and went downstairs to confer with the other sorcerers.

There were thirty fully adept members of the Star Guild, but two had been left at the castle to supervise the royal hostages, and Praxinus had his hands full coping with the balky army. The others were gathered in the main lounge of the hunting lodge, a chamber with a monstrous fireplace (now harbouring only a meagre fire), and grotesque furniture fashioned from bones of the imperial hunters' quarry. The walls were crowded with dusty trophy heads of animals and formidable birds, together with cracked leathern shields and displays of primitive weaponry.

Gathering the Guildsmen in an informal group before the hearth, Orogastus reviewed with each one his upcoming role in the assault, speaking last of all to the Archduchess Naelore.

'The ship bearing the magical armament will reach Brandoba late tomorrow,' he said. 'Can we be certain that no busybody port official will board it?'

The Star Woman uttered a cynical laugh. 'The wharfingers and excise agents will all have gone home to prepare for the Festival of the Birds, abandoning their duty. Even though the festivities do not properly commence until the fireworks display at midnight, the entire city begins roistering as soon as the sun sets. Have no fear, Master. My faithful friend Dasinzin will unload our cargo without hindrance.'

'The only thing I fear,' he said coldly, 'is that incompetence among your loyalists might cost us the element of surprise.'

She was immediately contrite. 'Forgive me if I spoke disrespectfully. All will go well – I swear it! The lords who support my bid to overthrow the usurper are a rough and ready lot, but they are not stupid. They realize fully that their only chance to seat me upon the throne depends on your magic. They would die for me, but they would prefer to live and regain their lost power.'

'And our disguises? My Star has as yet shown no sign of your people transporting anything to the staging point in the forest.'

'The carts will slip out of the city in late afternoon tomorrow, as revellers begin to converge from the surrounding countryside in anticipation of the celebration. We will have the costumes in plenty of time – entirely black, as you commanded. And the loyalist forces will wear scarlet, so that we may readily identify them.'

The sorcerer nodded his approval. When there were no more questions, he said to the assembled Guildsmen, 'All that remains is for me to bespeak our fellows at Castle Conflagrant, notifying them that all is well. You may prepare now for departure.'

The sorcerers dispersed except for Naelore, who stood quietly by as Orogastus used his Star to call to the two young Star Men who had remained behind to guard the hostages. Unaccountably, communication with them proved to be impossible. The sorcerer then used his magic to oversee and overhear the ordinary persons within the castle, and almost at once he discovered the escape of the prisoners and the grisly fate of their pursuers.

'Dark Powers have mercy!' he whispered, stricken with horror.

Naelore approached. 'Master, what is it?'

'There has been an appalling disaster!' Speaking in an undertone, he told her what had happened. 'This means that we shall have to postpone – or even abandon – our campaign.'

'Surely not! You had intended to use the hostage rulers only after the conquest of Sobrania. We can easily recapture them in time.'

'But I had also counted upon Queen Anigel being a key bargaining piece in regaining the Three-Headed Monster from Prince Tolivar. Without his talisman, my overall strategy may collapse.'

The Archduchess would have spoken again, but he motioned for her to desist and took up his Star again to search for the escapees. 'There they are,' he muttered, 'travelling along the trail not far from the Great Viaduct. I cannot see Anigel, but she must be there, shielded by her trillium-amber.' He cursed under his breath. 'They are at least six hours' ride from the lodge! If I send a troop of Guildsmen to recapture them, the army will be deprived of vital leadership during the invasion . . . but I could never entrust ordinary warriors with the task. Their loyalty to the Star is shaky at best, and the hostage rulers would doubtless offer irresistible bribes.' He drove one silver-gloved fist into the other in helpless rage. 'There is no alternative. We shall have to call off the invasion until the escapees are retaken. It means a delay of at least a day, and losing the advantage of striking during the Imperial Handsel, when the Emperor is most vulnerable.' He caught up his helmet and started after the Star Men who had already left the lodge.

'Master, wait!' Naelore called out in a low, excited voice. 'I have an idea how we might salvage the situation.'

'What?' He spun about.

'The scheme is a desperate one,' she admitted, 'but I believe it is well worth trying.' And she explained.

Incredulous at first, Orogastus realized that there was no practical alternative. 'Very well,' he said at last. 'If you are willing to risk your throne in this lunatic ploy, I will not stop you. But remember that the army will have to leave the staging area no later than an hour after sunset tomorrow in order to be in position before the fireworks start.'

'My old comrade Tazor and I can do it,' she said, her face shining. 'I will bring you Queen Anigel, and he will make certain that the other hostages remain secure here in the lodge until after Brandoba falls.'

The sorcerer smiled at the Star Woman. 'I can see more clearly now why your people deem you fit to be Empress.' He took her hand. 'May the Dark Powers support you.'

'And you,' she said, bowing her head so he would not see the fervid emotion that suffused her features. Then she clapped on her rayed helm and dashed off to find Tazor.

CHAPTER 22

The Archduchess Naelore studied the two tall flightless birds, tethered by neck-straps to trees outside the imperial hunting lodge, and scowled to conceal the fear rising within her. 'My friend, if this mission were not so crucial to our fortunes, nothing would compel me to touch these hideous brutes of yours.'

The feathered carnivores stood over two ells high at the shoulder and their plumage gleamed steel-blue in the sunlight. The birds had been temporarily paralysed by enchantment while Tazor worked on them, but their fierce red eyes glowered at the two sorcerers, evidence that while the nyars' bodies might be under constraint of magic, their spirits were not.

'So long as we wear our Stars and command the creatures with unwavering confidence,' Tazor said, 'they will obey us and harm neither ourselves nor any human prey we pursue.' He was putting bridles on the birds while Naelore watched, both repelled and fascinated. Orogastus and the other Guildsmen had ridden off after the army an hour earlier. It had taken Tazor that long to summon the nyars from the depths of the forest, even with the aid of his Star.

'You are absolutely certain that the monsters will not turn on us?' Naelore said.

'No, Imperial Highness. There is still some risk. But one well worth taking, as I told the Star Master.' He slipped a bridle cautiously over a terrible toothed beak.

'Nyars! Only a crazy man such as you would make pets of such horrible predators, much less train them for riding. What possessed you to undertake such a bizarre project?'

'I looked upon the task as a challenge to my Star,' he admitted, patting one bird's neck. It was as thick as one of the logs making up the walls of the building. 'This mated pair frequented the vicinity of the lodge because I often fed them salt-chuck. When their ferocity diminished I conceived the notion of taming them, and I confess that I was surprised that the sorcery eventually worked and rendered the nyars docile. It was a way of passing the time while I languished in this forsaken spot six moons ago, deprived of the glory of your imperial presence during my tour of duty as warden of supply for the castle.'

'Tchah!' said Naelore, dismissing the flattery. But she smiled at him, for they were very old friends indeed. Before the coming of Orogastus had changed their lives forever, Tazor had been chief steward of the Archduchess' villa just outside Brandoba. Now they were fellow Guildsmen and theoretically equals; but both of them knew better.

'Should the Dark Powers smile upon us,' Tazor said, 'the birds will enable us to undo the damage done by those negligent fools at the castle. Nyars are as fleet as the winter monsoon. Not even a polled racing fronial can compare with them. We should reach the hostages within three hours.'

'If I miss the battle of Brandoba because of this mission,' Naelore said through lips drawn tight, 'I shall roast the liver of whichever hostage engineered their escape!'

'I think both of us know who it must have been: the only one the Master could never descry with his magic, because she is protected by her trillium-amber.'

'Damn that witch-queen! I knew we should have taken the pendant away from her somehow . . . or else kept her senseless until she was no longer needed and it was safe to kill her. But Orogastus would not listen to me. Now we can only conjecture that Anigel accompanies the other hostages.'

'Where else would she go? We'll find her, Imperial Highness. Don't fret. You won't miss the battle, nor will you be deprived of your triumph over Denombo.'

'Ah, what a long way we have come in two short years, my old friend! Who would ever have thought, when you opened my villa door to a peremptory midnight knock, that you would admit a sorcerer? And one who would turn our disorganized little band of political outcasts into a cohort capable of toppling an empire.'

'I knew Orogastus was a dangerous man as soon as I clapped eyes on him,' Tazor said dryly. 'And so did you.'

'That was the principal reason I decided to trust him.'

'And is that also why you have fallen in love with him?'

'Insolent bastard,' she said, laughing again. But her eyes had lost their good humour, and he fell silent and hastened to buckle on the second bird's saddle.

Tazor was a well built man, even taller than the statuesque Archduchess and possessed of considerable physical strength. His knowing eyes were close-set above a broad nose. Like so many other members of the Star Guild – with the notable exception of flame-tressed Naelore herself – he had hair turned prematurely white from the rigours of his initiation into the magic of the Dark Powers.

'Tazor.' She spoke in a tone unusually hesitant. 'Do you really think Orogastus will fulfil his promises to me?'

'I believe that he will make you Empress of Sobrania,' the former steward said. 'I am much less sanguine about his grandiose plans to conquer the world by means of sorcery and set you up as his coadjutor. The Star is a wondrous thing, but the world is a very large place . . . and recent events have reminded us that other magicians exist in it besides Orogastus and our Star Guild.'

'I admit that I was deeply troubled when the Master told us that the young Prince had given up one of the talismans to the swamp-witch Kadiya. But by permitting both the boy and the enchantress to pass through the viaduct into Sobrania, Orogastus has cleverly brought both pieces of the Sceptre within easy reach.'

'Easy?' Tazor shook his head. 'No more than unseating Denombo will be easy.'

'Just let me get him within reach of a sword-cut! . . . At any rate, we can speed both eventualities by recapturing Queen Anigel and the others. Let us be off.'

They mounted the wingless birds, which stood like statues in the fore-court of the lodge. Naelore lifted her Star medallion and touched it to the neck of her feathered steed. The nyar's toothed beak opened wide and it gave a thunderous roar. When she spoke a command it sped off like a meteor down the trail leading to the Great Viaduct, leaving her comrade coughing in a cloud of dust.

Cursing, Tazor followed after.

It was only by great good fortune that the Eternal Prince Widd caught the Eternal Princess as she began to slip from the saddle during the fording of the muddy river. 'Help!' he cried desperately. 'Something is wrong with Raviya!'

President Hakit Botal whirled his fronial about, re-entered the water, and took hold of the elderly Princess in his strong left arm. She was listless as a bundle of rags. Her senses had left her, and her lined features were grey. Together with Prince Widd, the President brought the elderly woman safe to the river's opposite bank, where all except Gyorgibo immediately dismounted and gathered about. Queen Anigel and Queen Jiri of Galanar gently lay the Princess down on the ground.

'Triune pity her!' Widd began to weep. 'Oh, my poor Raviya. The rigours of the escape have been too much for her.'

'She breathes,' said Jiri, after loosening Raviya's bodice, 'and her heart-beat seems regular. Doubtless she is only overcome with exhaustion and stress.'

Duumvir Ga-Bondies snorted. 'As we all are! It's madness to ride further. Our fronials are still spent from their overexertion and breathing of the noxious vapours yesterday. They will certainly founder if we do not let them rest – and so will I. Every bone in my body screams with pain and I am dying from hunger.'

'Then die silently,' said the King of the Pirates heartlessly. The sturdy hunchbacked monarch took off his own cape and covered Princess Raviya. Her eyelids fluttered and she moaned.

Prince Widd sighed. 'If she could only have a morsel to eat and some truly restful sleep.'

The small amount of food and drink they had managed to take from the stablehands at the castle had been consumed the previous night when they had rested precariously, nearly frightened out of their wits by the appalling sounds made by the Lirda Forest creatures around them. Since then they had had only water and a few insipid wild fruits that Gyorgibo had assured them were wholesome.

'It would be dangerous to stop and rest now,' the Archduke said. 'There is small risk from fierce beasts and birds during daylight, but if the Star Men have learned of our escape, they might come looking for us.'

'I almost wish they would,' Ga-Bondies growled.

'We are moving steadily westward, out of the highlands,' Gyorgibo continued. 'Before long, we will surely come upon landmarks that I am familiar with and we can leave this trail. There are shortcuts to Brandoba in the Lirda's lower reaches that we can use to elude pursuit.'

'Not if Orogastus uses magic to hunt us,' Prigo pointed out.

Hakit Botal spoke in testy resignation. 'If the Star Men come, there is no way we can defend ourselves against them. But I suspect that the sorcerer and his force have other business to occupy them. They may already be in the capital city, storming Denombo's palace.'

'Why should we continue this killing pace?' Prigo demanded. 'It is manifestly impossible for us to give warning to the Emperor. We must consider our own needs . . . as well as the needs of our respective countries, thrown into confusion by our abduction. What matter our having escaped the sorcerer, if we perish miserably in this howling wilderness?'

Last night, after crossing the basin of flaming geysers, they had ridden another two hours before reaching the place where the Great Viaduct was,

210

clearly identifiable because of the peculiar appearance of the trampled ground around it. Anigel spoke the magic spell, and their passage through the black gateway was without incident. They spent an uneasy night in the clearing adjacent to the viaduct's exit, then pressed on slowly at first light.

The wide trail was easy to follow – too easy. The Archduke and King Ledavardis, the best riders in the group, had taken turns scouting ahead, making sure that they did not inadvertently overtake the sorcerer's force. The others had plodded painfully along, lulled by the singing of countless birds. From time to time they were roused from their stupor by the bellow of some unseen beast, but otherwise they had dozed in the saddle until Raviya's misfortune.

The Eternal Princess now roused herself and spoke in a weak voice. 'I'm quite all right. Just put me back on the fronial. I can ride well enough.'

'No, dear,' Anigel said emphatically. 'You cannot. Prigo is right. We've gone far enough and we must rest.'

Ledavardis said, 'If this forest is an imperial preserve, there should be some sort of shelters. How about it, Gyor?'

The Sobranian Archduke lifted his hands in a helpless gesture. 'There is indeed a great lodge beside the River Dob, as well as huts and comfortable hunting blinds and permanent campsites galore. Unfortunately, nothing along this particular trail looks familiar. The Star Men must have cut it to serve traffic to the Great Viaduct. This river – it might be the upper Dob, but its waters are so thick with white mud that I doubt it. The Dob flows crystal clear from the Collum Range and is the main water source for Brandoba. It has never been muddy, not even during the heaviest rains.'

'Perhaps,' Anigel said, 'my trillium-amber will point the way for us.' She took hold of the pendant and studied it with eyes strained by fatigue. 'Holy Flower, in which direction may we find a safe refuge?'

The amber continued to glow, but no magical directing spark appeared within it. 'It's not working. Perhaps my life is not sufficiently endangered.'

'Or perhaps,' Jiri said softly, 'there is no safe place for us hereabouts. Ask your amulet if we should stop or continue on.'

Anigel did so, only to cry out in dismay when the amulet flared to a blinding brightness, then as suddenly went dull. 'There's something wrong –'

All around them, the singing of the forest birds became a discordant screech. Gyorgibo, the only one still in the saddle, rose in his stirrups with a rusty sword drawn, peering anxiously down the trail that bordered the river. But the attack, when it came, was from a different direction. A cloud of innumerable tiny feathered creatures, bright blue and green and yellow, exploded out of the thick undergrowth and began to whirl crazily about the heads of the shocked rulers, darting into their faces and battering their bodies with buzzing wings. Raviya gave a thin scream and several of the men howled curses. The terrified fronials reared and slashed the air with their hooves. Then those without riders fled back across the river while Gyorgibo used all his strength to keep from being thrown. Everyone tried to shield exposed flesh from the sharp beaks, pulling cloaks over heads and waving arms in a futile attempt to drive the small birds off.

'Enough!' a stentorian voice commanded.

The storm of flyers disappeared as quickly as it had come.

Anigel peered out from beneath her cloak and saw two ghastly apparitions a scant stone's throw away down the trail. They were enormous long-necked birds with massive scaled legs, bigger than any voors she had ever seen. Their bodies were dark blue, their toothed beaks gaped wide, and their eyes blazed like hot coals. Seated on their backs were sorcerers attired in silver-and-black Star Guild regalia, steel cuirasses, and impressive helmets with starry diadems.

One of the riders came forward, drawing from a scabbard a weapon of the Vanished Ones. 'Gyorgibo of Nambit! Dismount and yield to me!'

Anigel recognized the voice, and also the red hair streaming from beneath the sorceress' helm. It was Naelore.

The Archduke's grimy features contorted with hatred. Instead of surrendering to the Star Woman he spurred his fronial and charged her at a gallop, sword poised to strike. She lifted her weapon and there was a sudden golden flash and a peculiar loud chirping sound. Gyorgibo's mount screamed and crashed onto the trail, legs sprawling and antlers broken, and lay there keening piteously. He himself was flung from the saddle, rolling head over heels and fetching up in an unconscious heap at the base of a great nest-tree.

'Would anyone else care to fight?' Tazor brought his nyar up to Naelore's and pointed his own strange weapon at the wounded fronial. A scarlet beam shone forth, striking the animal between the eyes and killing it instantly.

'We submit!' President Hakit Botal cried, raising his hands. 'Spare us!'

Ga-Bondies fell to his knees, whimpering, also with hands up. Prigo stood wide-eyed, still partially shrouded in his cape. Prince Widd, King Ledavardis, and Queen Jiri, who had tried to protect the Eternal Princess from the onslaught of the frenzied little birds, crouched beside Raviya's supine form and glared at the sorcerers. Anigel ignored the nyars and their formidable riders, went to Gyorgibo, and bent over his body in concern.

'Leave him!' Naelore commanded. She swung down from her bird's back, leaving it motionless, and strode toward the Queen.

'Your brother has struck his head,' Anigel said calmly, 'but he seems to be recovering his wits. Let me –'

'Silence! Come here.'

Anigel rose with dignity and approached the Star Woman, who pointed the ancient weapon at her.

'That's far enough,' Naelore commanded. 'Remove your amber amulet and place it on the ground between us.'

'No,' said Anigel. 'Though you slay me where I stand, I shall not take off my Black Trillium.'

'Then prepare to die, stupid slut!'

'Imperial Highness!' Tazor dismounted and approached. His nyar also stood frozen in place. 'I have a suggestion.'

'Speak,' the sorceress said.

'We hold two Duumviri of Imlit in our power, but only one hostage is needed to ensure that nation's compliance.' Tazor hoisted his weapon and took hold of Ga-Bondies by the collar. 'Perhaps if I slice an arm from the elderly one –'

'No!' shrieked the cowering Duumvir. 'Have mercy!'

'– Queen Anigel would reconsider her disobedience.'

'Do it,' said Naelore.

Ga-Bondies burst into hysterical tears. Anigel immediately lifted the amber on its chain from around her neck and lay it in the mud of the riverbank. The Star Woman now wore a smile of poisonous satisfaction. She aimed her weapon at the amber, and there was a blaze of yellow light; but the amulet remained unharmed.

Naelore spat out a curse of vexation, 'Tazor! See if you can destroy this thing.'

His deadly scarlet beam was no more effective than the golden blast had been. 'Highness, the Black Trillium's magic renders it invulnerable. But I have another idea.' He took the old sword that Gyorgibo had dropped and used it to pick up the amulet by its chain. Although the sword at once grew hot, he was able to fling the amber overhand into the dense woods. Tazor dropped the smoking sword and grinned. 'Let the wild beasts puzzle over the magical amulet on dark nights.'

Naelore threw back her head and laughed. She seized Anigel painfully by her shoulder and pushed her toward a nyar. 'Tazor, help her up onto

213

my bird. She will ride pillion as I hasten to the staging area, while you deal with these worthies.'

'The foul sorcerer will kill us all!' Ga-Bondies wailed.

Naelore regarded the stout Duumvir with distaste. 'We have other plans for you, quiver-guts. Only this witch-queen is needed by the Star Master, to ensure that her son surrenders his talisman.'

Anigel stiffened in the arms of the former steward. Her breath caught in her throat. 'My son? Which son are you talking about?'

'Your son Tolivar, of course,' said the Archduchess. 'The one who wears the Three-Headed Monster. He had the star-box and the second talisman as well – the Burning Eye – but your sister Kadiya forced him to give those back to her.'

'Tolo . . . my talisman . . . This is impossible! The boy is in Var, thousands of leagues from here, and so is Kadi. And Tolo does not have the coronet.'

Again Naelore laughed. 'What mother truly knows her own child? He has possessed it – and used it – for at least four years, unbeknownst to all save the Star Master, who speaks to the boy in his dreams. Now your precious son and his aunt and their surviving henchmen are here in Sobrania, just as you are. I doubt not that you will meet the lot of them before long, to your mutual sorrow.'

Tazor hoisted the Queen, who had gone flaccid with shock, onto the rear of the Archduchess' saddle. He then bound Anigel's hands and wrapped her well in a cloak. 'I will deal with the others and catch up with you, Imperial Highness,' he said to Naelore. 'But do not let the Master delay the invasion on my account.'

Naelore nodded curtly and mounted. Lifting her silver-gloved hand in farewell to Tazor, she sent her nyar speeding away.

'Will you take us back to Castle Conflagrant, then?' Ledavardis of Raktum asked the Star Man. Ledavardis and Queen Jiri were now on their feet, while old Widd knelt with his arms about Raviya, both of them pale but serene of countenance.

'No,' Tazor said, peering down at Gyorgibo, who had begun to groan and stir from promptings of the Guildsman's boot. 'I am going to shut the lot of you up in the imperial hunting lodge, where our army spent the night. It lies about eighty leagues downriver from here, a six- or seven-hour ride. The ferocious denizens of the Lirda will keep you secure for a few days until we complete our business in Brandoba and retrieve you.'

He addressed Hakit Botal. 'Sir President, you and the Goblin Kinglet wade across the river and catch your wandering fronials. Make haste, or

214

I will burn the ears off one of these ladies with my fire-squirter.' Resting his weapon on one shoulder, he turned to Duumvir Prigo. 'You! Take up that old sword and cut two long poles and several lengths of stout vine. We will have to make a drag-litter for Princess Raviya.' And to Ga-Bondies: 'Remove the harness and blanket from that dead steed, then unbuckle the leathers and make them into separate straps.'

As the ablebodied male hostages went to their chores, Tazor ambled over to Jiri, Raviya, and Widd, who had been whispering among themselves. 'How fares the old dame?' he asked, not unkindly.

'The Eternal Princess is suffering mostly from exhaustion,' said the Queen of Galanar. 'The litter is an excellent idea. Will you also make one for the poor Archduke?'

The Star Man gave a nasty chuckle. 'Let him travel trussed and flung over my saddle, like a dead nunchik. It matters not. Unlike the rest of you, he will not long survive his sister's ascent to the imperial throne.'

'I don't suppose,' Jiri said in a wheedling manner, 'that you have wine you might spare for Princess Raviya? It would give her strength.'

'Take the bottleskin from my saddlebag.'

Jiri eyed the tall nyar askance. 'Oh my! I would not dare approach that dreadful bird —'

'I have enchanted it with my Star. It will not move nor harm you unless I give the command.'

Jiri went to the great creature and began rummaging in one of the saddlebags, which was so high as to be nearly above her head. 'Perhaps the bottle is on the other side,' she said, and went around the bird out of Tazor's sight. A moment later she called out, 'I still can't seem to find it.'

Grumbling, the Star Man went to assist her. The plump, middle-aged Queen stood back, smiling apologetically with both hands thrust up her ample sleeves. Holding his weapon in one hand, Tazor turned away from her and groped inside the feather-trimmed leather pouch with the other.

Jiri stepped up behind him. The space between the bottom edge of the sorcerer's starburst helmet and the upper part of his cuirass was narrow, only about two fingers wide. The Queen whipped a war-flail out of her sleeve, whirled its chain overhead, and sent the heavy iron swingle at the chain's end squarely into the aperture of the armour. There was a ghastly snap. His neck broken, Tazor dropped in his tracks without uttering a sound.

The nyar came abruptly to life, roaring, and gave a short hop backward. It scraped one huge clawed foot in the mud in challenge, lowered its head, and tensed to spring at the Queen.

215

From the bushes came a figure scuttling on hands and knees. It was the Archduke Gyorgibo, who scooped up the weapon of the Vanished Ones which Tazor had let fall and fired it directly into the wide-open fanged beak of the monster that menaced Jiri. The nyar's head vanished in a burst of red fire and the colossal body thudded onto the ground.

'Heldo's Tentacles!' cried King Ledavardis. He and Hakit Botal were standing on the opposite bank of the small river, awestruck at what the Queen and Gyorgibo had done.

'I am truly sorry about Tazor,' Jiri said. 'He was by no means as deep-dyed a reprobate as Naelore.' A tear gleamed in her eye and the Archduke put a comforting arm about her.

The two Duumviri now sidled up and gaped at the dead Star Man and the headless carnivore.

'Mother-in-law,' Prigo said shakily, 'I am overwhelmed. I salute your warrior prowess.'

'What in God's name did you hit the fellow with?' Ga-Bondies asked.

'An old war-flail that I picked up in the castle dungeon.' She shook loose of Gyorgibo's embrace. 'I must go to Raviya. All this violence must have been a great shock to her.'

But the Eternal Princess was sitting up, calmly rearranging her mussed snowy hair, while Widd squatted beside her. 'I don't suppose you ever found that wine,' Raviya said to Jiri.

The Queen smiled. 'It was in the first saddlebag I examined. Fortunately, the nyar did not fall on top of it. There is food, too.'

'We can all share it,' Raviya declared, 'and then we really ought to be riding on. I'll be fit once I get a little something into my stomach.' She cocked her head at her husband. 'What are you waiting for, old man? Go fetch the victuals from that dead brute and set them out for us.'

King Ledavardis, who had re-crossed the water and returned to the group, took Queen Jiri aside. 'Do you think Raviya is really well enough to travel?'

Jiri considered. 'She feels better for the moment, but she cannot last long. It would be best if we carried her in a litter. By following the distinctive tracks of the nyars, we should reach the imperial hunting lodge where the dead Star Man intended to take us. There we will surely find decent food and beds, if it was intended to be our prison.'

'We might discover that the lodge is inhabited by minions of Orogastus.'

'Then we will simply have to subdue them,' Jiri said gently.

The King of the Pirates winked at her with his good eye. 'Right! I don't think we have to worry about Naelore coming back for some time.

Not with Queen Anigel to guard and the sorcerer instigating a brawl in the Sobranian capital.'

'Anigel . . .' The kindly Queen's face crumpled in regret. 'Poor child. I fear that we shall have to leave her fate to the Lords of the Air.'

'There may be something I can do.' King Ledavardis' unlovely countenance brightened as an idea came to him. 'If you will attend to our preparations here, I will try to find the lost amber amulet. I doubt it would harm one who is a friend and would-be son-in-law to its royal mistress. Who knows? The Black Trillium might condescend to aid a certain pirate in coming to Queen Anigel's rescue.'

'You would go after her?' Jiri's eyes widened.

'The late Star Man's sword and miraculous antique weapon would help to even the odds between me and the Queen's captors.'

'Ledo, you are a brave young man,' said Jiri.

The King lifted her hand and kissed it. 'From you, that is the greatest of compliments.'

CHAPTER 23

In spite of his intense fatigue, Prince Tolivar tossed restlessly in the hut of Critch the Cadoon, lying on a sack of soft down. They had gone to bed in daylight, but the upper level of the dwelling was dim and cool, with only two tiny latticed windows, one at each end up under the eaves of the thatched roof. From the bare beams hung scores of string bags, each holding feathers of a different hue. The snores of the four Oathed Companions sleeping at the other end of the loft mingled with the faint rumble of surf on the pebble beach outside and the mewing and squeals of griss and pothi and other sea-birds.

Kadiya and Jagun had said they would rest downstairs, but Tolivar heard them conversing for a long time with the aborigine and his family. The Prince's promise to his aunt deterred him from using the coronet to eavesdrop – not that he really cared what kind of mysterious merchandise the Lady of the Eyes was purchasing for her foray into Brandoba on the morrow. Kadiya had made it clear that *he* would have to remain on the boat with Jagun and Critch, while she and the knights went off into the city, to warn the Emperor that the Star Men were planning some sort of skulduggery and beg for help in rescuing Queen Anigel and the other hostages.

Tolivar had removed the magical coronet from his head and tucked it into his shirtfront where it would be safe. He had commanded it to wake him instantly if anybody came near him. As he lay there dozing, his fingers gripped the talisman through the cloth.

You are mine, he told it again and again.

And the Three-Headed Monster always replied: *Yes.*

Although he desired his mother's safe return with all his heart, the knowledge that the adults would surely try to coerce him into giving her the coronet gnawed at his entrails.

It was so unfair!

The Queen had surrendered the talisman to Orogastus – under duress, it was true, but still of her own free will – and Tolivar had taken it in turn from the sorcerer's minion. Was his mother's claim to the Three-Headed

Monster any more valid than that of Orogastus? Even when she had possessed the coronet she merely kept it hidden away, almost never making use of its magical power except to bespeak her two sisters from afar.

The talisman is mine, Tolivar said to himself, rightfully mine – no matter what the others may think or say.

But only for a little while longer.

Who –? You are not my talisman speaking!

No. I am the Star Master. Your master, Tolo.

No! Never! Begone from my dreams!

You are not dreaming. And I have already told you that I would not be able to bespeak you if you did not wish it.

That's a lie –

It is the truth, as you know full well. You still admire me and yearn to share my power as my adopted son and heir. It is ignoble of you to deny it . . . just as it is ignoble of you to deny that you brought about the death of Ralabun the Nyssomu.

Ralabun! My poor old friend. I didn't mean for him to die. It was an accident, even though Aunt Kadiya says –

Responsibility is not necessarily guilt. Listen to me, Tolo: If you had not commanded Ralabun to accompany you on the Oda River trail, he would still be alive. Accept that burden, as every commander must! But do not torture yourself with feelings of blame. The cruel Lady of the Eyes seeks to control you by imputing that you are morally culpable in the matter of your friend's death. But you are not.

. . . Truly?

Do you think Ralabun would have stayed behind while you undertook a dangerous journey alone?

No. Even if I had not commanded him, he would have come with me.

And did you know that a namp was lurking nearby when you sent Ralabun off the trail?

Of course not!

Therefore he did perish by simple misadventure, and not through any fault or negligence of yours. Do you understand?

Yes. I – I thank you for explaining, Orogastus.

Tolo, we have been separated for many years, and much of the blame lies on me. But it is now time for our estrangement to be mended. Come away from those coldhearted, neglectful people who fail to appreciate your true worth. Once you loved me as your adopted father. Come back to me now and resume your position at my side. My Guildsmen and I were prevented from meeting you at the viaduct by other, vitally important matters. But I can meet you elsewhere.

No!

Tomorrow you will sail to Brandoba with the others. I shall also be there in the city. Use your talisman to elude Kadiya and come to me, bringing the star-box. We can meet at –

No! Orogastus, you tricked me once when I was a silly, spiteful child. It will not happen again. All you want is to take my talisman away from me.

I cannot take it. You know that. What I want you to do is return the talisman to me freely, as you gave back the Three-Lobed Burning Eye you took from your aunt.

That . . . was different.

You do not know how to use the coronet's awful magic properly. It is a tool for restoring the balance of the world, not for petty conjuring. I know that you have been unable to master the talisman – that you have merely toyed with it in that secret grass shack of yours out in the Mazy Mire.

I understand the talisman better than you think!

Tolo, there is only one way you can become a competent sorcerer: by giving the coronet back to me and joining my Star Guild. Come to me, dear boy. I will forgive your disloyalty and reinstate you as my adopted son and heir. And when I die, the Three-Headed Monster will be yours once more – only this time you will truly be its master . . . and master of the world as well.

Orogastus, you used me once as a puppet. But never again.

Deep in your heart, Tolo, you still yearn to be my son.

Perhaps. But the wish is only a childish fantasy. It is a temptation hidden away inside of me that emerges only when I sleep. When I am wide awake and in control of my wits, I reject you. I reject you now!

I had hoped you would come to me of your own free will – but so be it. Let me pose another question to you: Do you care whether your mother, Queen Anigel, lives or dies?

Certainly I do!

Then use the coronet to have Sight of her. Her fate is now entirely in your hands, in a way that poor old Ralabun's never was.

What are you saying?

The Queen is the prisoner of my ally, the Archduchess Naelore, a dangerous and implacable woman.

That is not true! I have already had Sight of Mother. She is free in a forest somewhere above Brandoba, accompanied by the other rulers you kidnapped.

Queen Anigel did escape from my castle with the others, but she has been recaptured. Your coronet will show her to you, a wretched prisoner in Naelore's

220

power. Rouse yourself and command the Three-Headed Monster to verify what I have said.

I – I have given my word to Aunt Kadıya not to use the talisman's magic without her permission.

What? Ask permission? Are you a puling schoolboy who must beg leave of his nursemaid to use the garderobe – or are you the owner of one part of the great Threefold Sceptre of Power? You owe your aunt no fealty. She took advantage of your grief to extort that promise. It is worthless. Use the talisman to confirm your mother's captivity. Do it now!

I . . . will take your word for it.

Foolish boy. Do you dare to play games with me?

Why should I do such a thing?

Perhaps because you still entertain maudlin hopes of rescuing your mother yourself! Tolo, I have heard enough of your childish prattle. Queen Anigel and the three unborn babes she carries will die horribly under Naelore's sword unless you come to the Sobranian capital with all haste and give over to me both the Three-Headed Monster and the star-box.

I don't believe you –

In the centre of Brandoba is the imperial palace, and before it lies a vast pleasance, an open area where citizens celebrating the Festival of the Birds will gather at midnight to watch the display of fireworks. Be there, near the Golden Griss Fountain! I will find you, and give your mother free and harmless into your safekeeping just as soon as you hand over to me the talisman and the box.

The coronet is rightfully mine!

And your mother's life belongs to me . . . Make no mistake, boy! If you fail to obey me, you will find her disembowelled body lying beside the fountain.

Holy Flower – no!

And this time the death-guilt will be yours irrevocably. You will suffer from it as long as you live.

No no no . . .

The Prince seemed to see his mother's face, tears pouring from her eyes. She called his name again and again, pleading for him to surrender the coronet to the sorcerer so that her life and the lives of the babies in her womb would be spared. But Tolivar had been unaccountably struck dumb. He could not answer her. No matter how hard he tried, he could not pronounce the single word 'yes' that would free his mother.

Could not give up his talisman.

No! Never!

He woke with a start, rising up on his elbows, and looked frantically around the feather-loft. It was much later in the day. A beam of afternoon

221

sunlight illumined dancing dust-motes. The four knights had apparently awakened and gone downstairs. Only his own mind's ear still perceived the echo of Queen Anigel's heartbroken appeal and his own shameful refusal.

Unless it had been a dream after all.

He would have to discover the truth of it. The promise he had made to his aunt now did seem naught but the words of a gullible, frightened child. What right had the Lady of the Eyes to demand that he eschew magic, especially when his mother's life might depend upon his use of it?

'Talisman,' he whispered, tightening his grip on the hidden metal circlet. 'Show me Queen Anigel.' He closed his eyes, and into his mind sprang a vision, as though he were one of the Sobranian birds soaring down from a height and coming to rest upon a tree branch a few ells above the ground.

In a sizeable forest clearing, several hundred heavily armed warriors took their ease. Some of them were Star Men, wearing steel breastplates over their wizard garb, and helmets with pointed metal spikes. In the midst of the army was an open-sided cloth pavilion. Orogastus sat beneath it, drinking wine from a golden cup. Just outside the shelter stood Naelore, clad in gleaming black-and-silver armour and smiling triumphantly as the army cheered her. She held a longsword.

Tied to a small tree before the sorceress was Queen Anigel.

The prisoner's robe was stained and torn, her blonde hair straggled in disarray, and her wrists and ankles were bruised and bloody from the rawhide thongs that bound her. As Tolivar watched in horror, Naelore's sword descended until the sharp point rested between his mother's breasts. Very lightly, the blade moved down her belly, inscribing a short vertical cut in the robe's coarse cloth.

As always, his talisman's vision was silent. The Archduchess appeared to be plying the Queen with questions, but Anigel remained serenely indifferent, her gaze unfocused. The throng of soldiers and Star Men were laughing derisively.

'Mother!' Tolivar moaned softly. 'Oh, Mother.'

Queen Anigel could not hear her son – but evidently Orogastus could. His head turned and he seemed to look directly at the Prince. The Star Master's helmet had rays longer and more ornate than those of the other Guild members. A visor masked the upper part of his face, but his sardonic silvery eyes were clearly visible. Even though the sorcerer's lips did not move, Tolivar heard his voice speak distinctly:

Tell no one what you have seen, or else the Queen and your brothers in her womb will be executed here and now. Remember: Meet me at midnight at the fountain near the palace. I will be in disguise, but you will know me. Bring both the coronet and the star-box. Do you understand?

Tolivar was finally able to say the word.

'Yes,' he whispered. 'I will do as you say.'

The vision vanished, and the Prince saw only a reddish void behind his closed eyelids. Bitter tears forced their way out and slid slowly down his face. He paid them no heed, lying still as a stone with the talisman clutched in his hands until his helpless rage melted into numb misery. After a long time, his Aunt Kadiya called his name and told him to descend for the evening meal.

'Coming,' he said, and tucked the Three-Headed Monster back into his shirt with its sharp cusps turned inward, so that they pricked his bare skin.

It was an hour past sunset on the next day when the Cadoon sailing craft, manned by Critch alone, came slowly into the harbour of Brandoba. Behind it, across the estuary to the west, were towering clouds tinted with sullen purple – a sure portent of rain before morning. The light wind that had slowed their passage now also swung around to the west, helping the aboriginal skipper to guide his small boat through waters crowded with galleys, lofty-masted merchantmen, and a myriad of lesser craft anchored in the roadstead. The rigging of most of the vessels twinkled with coloured glass oil-lamps, in honour of the Festival of the Birds.

Inland, the Sobranian capital city was ablaze with light. Fire-baskets on tall pylons lined the boulevards and main streets, and festoons of lanterns hung from every building. The waterfront esplanade was thronged with costumed people who danced and cavorted and even swung from the ornamental balustrades along the quays. Several brass bands on the wide esplanade stairs were apparently having a musical contest, seeing which could drown out the others.

Critch's passengers stayed belowdecks when his boat neared the shore, since it would have been suspicious if humans were seen on an aboriginal vessel. Kadiya and the others peered out from the boat's portholes, watching the spectacle, until Critch tied up at a quay used only by Cadoon traders, situated some distance from the central harbour area.

The feather-hunter went briefly onto the dock to speak to the local Folk, then reboarded and called down into the cabin. 'It is safe for you to come up and disembark.'

Jagun and the Prince climbed the companionway ladder first, followed by those who were going ashore. Kadiya and the Oathed Companions wore costumes purchased from Critch that would enable them to pass unnoticed among the festival celebrants. But because the cabin had been so dark and cramped, this coming on deck was the first opportunity for them to see each other clearly in the fancy dress they had donned with the help of Jagun and Tolivar.

The Lady of the Eyes wore a cape and under-robe of gorgeous iridescent purple plumage. Atop her matching hood was a tall yellow crest, and a golden beak above her brow shaded her face. Her talisman in its scabbard was concealed beneath her cloak.

'You look splendid, Farseer,' Jagun said, and she made a mocking bow.

The brothers Kalepo and Melpotis were both dressed in dark blue costumes intended to represent nyars. Their large, enveloping headpieces had wide-open befanged beaks, through which they were able to see. Edinar's plumage was bright red, with a peculiar flat bill attached to his hood. When Melpotis snickered at the young knight's droll appearance, Edinar found the built-in noisemaker in his headpiece and blew a raucous quack that sent the two nyars into gales of laughter.

The final costumed figure to emerge was Sir Sainlat. Because of his heroic physique, only one avian disguise had been found to fit him – that of a marine pothi-bird. It was fashioned of bright pink feathers and had a ludicrous wide-spreading rose-and-black fantail mounted at the rear. The feathered hood left Sainlat's face exposed except for his nose, which was concealed behind a big cone-shaped black beak.

'I feel like a perfect idiot,' the big knight said cheerfully.

'You look even worse,' Edinar assured him.

'I congratulate your family's skill,' Kadiya said to Critch. 'The costumes are excellently made. They do not restrict one's motion overmuch, and our armour and weapons hidden beneath are quite unnoticeable.'

The Cadoon opened a large wicker hamper that stood on deck and took out a net bag filled with rounded coloured objects. 'Perhaps you would like to take some of these. They are griss eggs, blown dry, filled with confetti and sneeze-spores and sealed with wax. It is an old carnival custom to smash them and scatter the contents on other revellers. The eggs may prove useful if you are impeded by the crowds.'

'Thank you,' Kadiya said to him, 'but my magic will suffice for us. I do not wish us to be further encumbered. Now then: If we have not returned by dawn tomorrow, or if serious trouble breaks out in the city, put out to sea with Jagun and Prince Tolivar. I will bespeak Jagun through my talisman in due time, and he will transmit to you new instructions.'

She nodded to the knights, and the men made their way down the gangplank and awaited her on the dock. In contrast to the mob scene further along the waterfront, the area used by the aboriginal vessels was nearly deserted except for a few sailors from the handful of small boats similar to Critch's that rocked gently in the dark water. The Cadoon Folk paid no attention to the outlandishly dressed humans.

Before departing herself, Kadiya went to Prince Tolivar, who had gone to sit in the bow, and spoke a few words of admonition to him. He responded meekly. Then she returned to the waist of the boat where Jagun and Critch were standing.

'Watch the boy carefully,' she told them in a low voice. 'Never leave him alone for an instant. He seems very downcast and I do not think he will attempt any rash action. But if he does, bespeak me at once.'

'We will take care of him, Farseer,' the old Nyssomu assured her.

She would have gone then, but Critch bade her stay. 'Lady, I have some strange tidings I must impart before you leave, told me by a certain wherryman of my race whom I encountered while securing our lines.' He pointed toward the murky outer reaches of the harbour. 'Do you see that great ship out there, with but a single red light at the stern?'

Kadiya nodded.

'It flies the ensign of Zinora and arrived only this afternoon. My friend has assured me that it is not an ordinary coastal trader but a three-masted trireme galley, one of the speediest vessels afloat. Its crew are not Zinorans but Sobranians, and the owner is a nobleman named Dasinzin, known to be a sympathizer of the rebel Archduchess Naelore.'

Kadiya muttered an imprecation and drew forth her talisman. Aiming the sword at the mysterious ship, which was little more than a black silhouette against the fading evening sky, she said: 'Burning Eye, tell me if this vessel belongs to the Star Men.'

The question is impertinent.

'Give me Sight of its cargo hold.'

The command is impertinent.

Her face grim, Kadiya sheathed the magic sword.

'I think,' Jagun said, 'that your talisman has answered your query by not answering.'

'Star Men – or I'm second cousin to a cross-eyed togar!' She addressed Critch: 'Do you know if the Emperor's port officials have gone on board this ship?'

'Nay. Because of the impending festivities, all inspections have been postponed. Cadoon wherrymen such as my friend have brought fresh food and other supplies out to the galley, and the crew were careless in their speech around them – as humans often are when dealing with my people, thinking us dull-witted and inferior. The wherrymen learned that the vessel came not from the east, where Zinora and the other human nations

225

lie, but from the distant northwestern latitudes, beyond the country of the lawless tribes, where none dwell save the tiny Mere Folk.'

Kadiya's eyes narrowed. 'Do you mean those aquatic aborigines who have Iriane, Archimage of the Sea, as their guardian?'

'Even so. But it has been said that the Blue Lady is now dead, and her Folk subjugated by the Star Guild.'

Kadiya and Jagun exchanged glances. Both of them knew of Iriane's immuration in the enchanted ice, and of the probability that Orogastus had compelled the Mere Folk to gather armament of the Vanished Ones from beneath the sea. If the trireme did belong to the Star Men and carried such arcane weaponry, it might well be the precursor of an invasion.

'Thank you for this important information,' Kadiya said to Critch. 'I urge you to warn the local Cadoon Folk to give that ship a wide berth. Whoever it belongs to, it is here in Brandoba for no good purpose.'

'I will do as you say.'

'At present,' Kadiya went on, 'I dare not make any attempt to investigate the galley in person. I must first tell Emperor Denombo how the Star Guild abducted the other rulers, and warn him that his nation and his own life may also be in imminent danger. I will inform the Emperor of the trireme's presence and let him deal with it.'

Jagun said, 'We will watch the mysterious ship, Farseer. If the crew attempt to bring any suspicious cargo ashore, or if they act as blatant invaders, I will bespeak you.'

'Pray that the Lords of the Air will be with us tonight.' Kadiya commanded her talisman again to shield her and the knights from the magical Sight of the Star Men. Then she ran down the plank onto the dock, where the four Oathed Companions waited impatiently. Inside of a few minutes the costumed infiltrators had vanished among the warehouses, leaving Jagun and Critch staring after them.

'They will not find it easy to reach the Emperor tonight,' the Cadoon observed. 'He will first be occupied with ceremonial duties on behalf of the Goddess Matuta, and then he must preside over the great fireworks display. There will be an enormous crowd round about the palace precincts, and sometimes there are riots. The guardsmen will be on the alert. But the crowds are usually peaceful during the first night, especially if the fireworks show is a good one and the Imperial Handsel that follows is generous.'

'What is a handsel?' Jagun asked him.

'A lucky gift, distributed by the Emperor to the common people in honour of the festival. Tiny packages are thrown to the crowd by maidens riding in a parade of decorated wagons. Most of the handsels contain a slip of paper with a wise or humorous saying wrapped about a candy or some other sweetmeat, but a few hold silver or gold coins – and there is always a single platinum piece to be found by the luckiest human of all.'

The noise of the merry-making crowds became louder. In addition to the music of the roving brass bands, there were now rhythmic blasts of sound from massed bird-whistles as the people formed into impromptu parades and marched through the streets. Critch the Cadoon turned away from the colourful extravaganza on shore and stared glumly at the anchored trireme.

'The wind tonight carries upon it a scent of cold rain out of season and of some great evil.' Critch pointed overboard to the harbour waters. 'And do you see how strangely discoloured the sea is hereabouts? It is grey as baby-gruel, and I have never seen such a thing before, nor heard of it. I wish with all my heart that I had not agreed to bring you to Brandoba, Friend Jagun.'

'By doing so, you may enable my Lady to save many lives.'

Critch muttered, '*Human* lives! . . . How can you serve a mistress belonging to the race of our oppressors?'

'In our Mazy Mire country,' Jagun said, 'certain of my Folk have been the close allies of humankind for many hundreds, earning their respect and even their love. And in recent times, thanks to the three women known as the Petals of the Living Trillium, of whom my Lady is one, the ancient antagonism between humans and Folk has been much alleviated. We know now that the same blood flows in the veins of both our races, and so we strive to be true brothers and sisters even though we differ in appearance.'

'The Sobranians think differently,' Critch said, 'and so do the Cadoon Folk. Why, then, are you so sure your beliefs are true?'

Jagun spent some time telling him the history of the Vanished Ones, and the great war between the Archimages and the Star Guild, and the near-destruction of the world that had resulted, and how the survivors had fared for twelve times ten hundreds until the present. When Jagun finished, Critch the Cadoon marvelled at the tale – although he took a gloomy satisfaction in knowing that the world was mysteriously out of kilter, since this confirmed his own formless anxieties. Then the two aborigines stood together at the boat's rail in silence, until Prince Tolivar came away from the bow, where he had stood alone out of earshot, and addressed them.

'I slept poorly last night,' the boy said. 'I think I will go below now and turn in. It is not very amusing to watch a festival from so far away.'

'I will go with you,' Jagun said.

The Prince smiled. 'There is no need.'

'All the same,' the old huntsman persisted, 'we'll go together.' He waited until the boy began to descend the companionway ladder, then followed closely behind.

Tolivar helped Jagun clear up the discarded clothing and other litter from the costuming, then climbed into one of the sailboat's narrow forward bunks and pretended to go to sleep. The Nyssomu sat for over an hour in the boat's tiny galley, then quietly crept back up on deck, just as the Prince had hoped he would.

None of the boat's portholes was more than two handspans wide and the after deck-hatch was dogged shut, so the only way topside was up the ladder. Tolivar was quite certain that Jagun or Critch would guard the companionway all through the night, and he was also sure that neither of them seriously expected him to attempt an escape. They thought he was still in mourning for Ralabun, and that he would keep his word not to use magic. Since they also believed that Queen Anigel was still at liberty, they would think he had no motive to go off seeking her.

Wrong, the Prince said bleakly to himself, on every count.

Sliding out of the bunk, he put on his boots, then drew the coronet out of his shirt and settled it onto his head.

Talisman, he commanded silently, tell me where Jagun has hidden the star-box.

It is within the central locker in the galley.

Tolivar then commanded the talisman to render him invisible. He secured the box, which he put into one of the bags that had held a costume, and then tied the long bundle to his back. When both bag and star-box were also made invisible, he addressed a fresh request to the coronet:

Tell me how I may put Jagun and Critch into an enchanted sleep.

Simply see them so in your mind, and order it done.

Will – will the spell harm them?

They will eventually perish of thirst and hunger unless you release them betimes, or else modify the spell.

Can I order them to sleep only until sunup?

Assuredly.

Prince Tolivar closed his eyes and imagined the two Folk lying down and drifting peacefully into unconsciousness. Then he visualized them awakening at dawn, commanded the magic, and opened his eyes.

Are they asleep?

Yes.

Venting a sigh of relief, the boy went up the ladder and onto the deck. The aborigines were curled up, one on either side of the wicker hamper

228

filled with coloured eggs. Tolivar dragged little Jagun over beside Critch and covered both of them with a tarpaulin against the chill and the possibility of rain. He looked thoughtfully at the hamper, and then took from it a net bag of the missiles, which he fastened to his belt and made invisible.

'Talisman! Tell me where my mother is now.'

The request is impertinent.

The Prince felt his heart plummet. 'Is she concealed by the power of the evil Star?'

The question is impertinent.

But the Prince knew that it was so. Before, when Orogastus had wanted him to know of his mother's jeopardy, the Sight of her was clear enough. 'Well, I know how to find her,' Tolivar said to himself.

He looked up into the sky. A veil of high clouds had drawn ghostly haloes around the Three Moons, and a rising wind whined in the sailboat's rigging, making an eerie countermelody to the distant braying of the brass bands. He had no idea how many hours there were until midnight, when he would have to meet Orogastus.

Tolivar had yet a single question to ask of his talisman – one upon which his last faint hope hung.

'Will Orogastus be able to see me, even though I am invisible?'

Yes, for you still waver in your rejection of him.

The Prince had suspected as much.

Still invisible, he went down the gangplank and onto the quay, not bothering to look out at the ships in the harbour. One of them, a very large trireme lacking the festive lighting of the other vessels, seemed to be dragging its anchor in the pallid waters and slowly drifting closer to shore.

CHAPTER 24

The army of Orogastus rode stealthily into Brandoba early in the evening, entering a few at a time through the little-used Hunters Gate at the northeastern edge of the sprawling city. Following the Star Master's orders, the warriors and Guildsmen melted away unobtrusively into the crowds of festival celebrants. At a designated time they were to rendezvous with the partisans of the Archduchess Naelore at the central pleasance, where – if all went well – the massed invaders would receive the command to storm the palace.

Every follower of the Star was identically costumed in a voluminous cape of glossy black plumage and an avian hood-mask with distinctive golden eyes. The single exception among the dark flock was a rather small person riding pillion behind one of the blackbirds, who wore the modest grey and white feathers of a sea-griss over a simple woollen robe.

'Stop wriggling,' Naelore said to her passenger, 'or I will command my Star to sprinkle you with pain.'

'If you would just unfasten the bonds on my wrists,' Queen Anigel replied, 'I could cling to the saddle skirts and would not constantly be in danger of losing my balance. It doesn't help that the headpiece of this wretched bird costume keeps slipping over my eyes.'

The Archduchess laughed. 'Release you? Not likely, witch-queen! Even deprived of your loathly Flower, you are doubtless capable of dire magic.'

'I am no witch,' Anigel said mildly, 'and the Black Trillium you seem to fear so much only protects my life and cannot harm anyone.'

'Hah! Tell that to the Guildsmen who tried to remove it from your neck while you lay senseless in Castle Conflagrant. Their fingers were scorched to the bone by magical fire when they touched that cursed amulet.'

'Indeed? I did not know that my trillium-amber was capable of such a thing. I would not willingly have caused your people injury.'

'I suppose,' Naelore said in a scathing voice, 'that you likewise intended no hurt to those you burnt alive during your escape across the basin of flaming geysers!'

'I regret the death of our pursuers,' Anigel said, 'but they fired upon us with an ancient weapon, endangering the lives of me and my companions. It was that selfsame weapon that ignited the flammable vapours.'

'So *you* say,' Naelore retorted. And when Anigel would have made further expostulation, the Star Woman ordered her to be silent.

Orogastus, who had entered the city gate last of all, had been riding immediately behind the Archduchess and her prisoner. He now spurred his mount and came up beside them. His pale eyes glimmered beneath the black beak of his bird headpiece.

'I will go on ahead a short distance,' he told Naelore, 'so that I may scan the throng more readily for our enemies. It is unlikely that the Star will give me Sight of Kadiya, since she is almost certainly shielded by her talisman. But I might descry others of her party if they should stray from her immediate vicinity. Keep alert, and beware any woman bearing a pointless dark sword.'

The sorcerer urged his steed forward through the growing crowd, and Naelore and Anigel followed. They were soon caught up in a great river of costumed people, some on fronialback but most afoot, making their way toward the city centre in advance of the fireworks display at the pleasance. Groups of musicians, moving with the mob or ensconced on balconies overlooking the streets, laboured to play above the cadenced din of birdwhistles, noisemakers, and drunken singing. From time to time roisterers would smash eggs filled with glittering confetti and fungus spores, and there would be sneezes and shrieks and good-humoured curses until the airborne nuisance dissipated. Orogastus and Naelore used their Star magic to fend off the nose-tickling dust, as well as to impel obstructive festival-goers out of the way.

At length, having come within a few blocks of the imperial palace, the two sorcerers and their prisoner turned off the packed, noisy avenue onto a much quieter side street. It was lined with stately mansions all decked with bird effigies and feathered banners. Twinkling lanterns of green and gold, the heraldic colours of Sobrania, hung in the tree-branches and stood atop the high outer walls of mortared stone that enclosed most of the houses. There were numbers of costumed people loitering about, but they seemed strangely subdued in demeanour, clustering in silent groups beneath the trees or sitting on the kerbstone side by side. Even in the uncertain light, Anigel could see that every one of them was dressed in red feathers.

Naelore rode stiffly, holding tight to the reins and never turning to look at Anigel. It was plain that she was holding back her beast in order to keep well behind Orogastus.

231

Suddenly, she said: 'Tell me about your sister Haramis!'

The surprised Queen began to recite the duties of the Archimage of the Land, but this was not what the Star Woman wanted to know.

'Is your sister beautiful? Describe her to me.'

'Haramis is much taller than I,' Anigel said. 'She has black flowing hair and silvery-blue eyes with wide pupils, in the depths of which lie minute flecks of golden fire. She is certainly beautiful, but one is more likely to take note of her commanding aspect and the aura of preternatural power that seems to enshroud her.'

'Does – does she love *him*, as he loves her?'

Taken aback, Anigel nonetheless knew instinctively what the other woman meant, as well as the motive behind the question. 'I think Haramis wishes with all her heart and soul that she did not love Orogastus. His life-goals are utterly at odds with her own. She cannot help loving him, but she has long since renounced any hope of consummating that love.'

The Star Woman's posture softened, as though she had been relieved of some burden. When she resumed her questioning her manner was less surly. 'I know that your sister Haramis possesses the third piece of the Threefold Sceptre of Power. What does this marvellous instrument look like?'

'The Three-Winged Circle is a short wand with a kind of hoop on its end. The wings themselves are tiny, perched at the top of the hoop and enclosing a piece of trillium-amber identical to my own. Haramis wears the wand on a chain around her neck.'

'Is she able to make full use of this Circle's magic – or is she only minimally competent with her talisman, as are the witch Kadiya and your prodigal son with theirs?'

Anigel paused momentarily before answering, wondering why the Star Woman had not put the query to Orogastus, then thinking that perhaps she *had* . . . Still, there seemed no good reason not to give reply.

'I doubt that anyone now alive truly understands the working of the Sceptre of Power. It is an artifact of the Vanished Ones, supposedly so formidable that those who invented it were ultimately afraid to use it. Taken apart, the three pieces of the Sceptre that are called talismans are much less powerful. Haramis is certainly more adept at wielding hers than is Kadiya, but her greatest magical skills are quite independent of the Winged Circle, deriving rather from her sacred and beneficent office.'

'Beneficent? But she is a tyrant, as are the Archimages of the Sea and the Sky! The Star Master says that the three of them have manipulated both humanity and the Oddling Folk from time immemorial. They oppose

232

all scientific and social progress because it would threaten their positions of power.'

'Nonsense,' said Anigel. 'I cannot speak about the Dark Man in the Moon, but both my sister Haramis and Iriane, the Archimage of the Sea, are kindly guardians who would not dream of oppressing the peoples of this world. They have made solemn vows never to use magic to harm a living soul.'

'And yet,' Naelore said, 'Haramis once assembled the Sceptre and attempted to kill the Star Master with it!'

'No,' Anigel corrected her. 'Haramis, Kadiya, and I used the Sceptre to turn the sorcery of Orogastus back upon him when he would have destroyed us Three and conquered our little kingdom.'

'That is not what the Master says!'

'Orogastus often bends the truth to suit his purposes.'

'He has never lied to me, nor to others of the Star Guild.'

Anigel sighed. 'And has he promised that your Guild will rule the world with him if you assist him in his vainglorious schemes? I must tell you that he once tempted Haramis with the same ridiculous proposal –'

The Sobranian woman whirled about in the saddle and regarded Anigel with blazing anger. 'You silly fool!' she hissed. 'What do you know of the Master's grand and noble intentions? Rule –? So he will! But not to satisfy some overarching private ambition. Rather he seeks to save the world from the hideous cataclysm toward which it hurtles, all unknowing!'

'What cataclysm? What are you talking about?'

'Unless Orogastus saves us, we are doomed. This world of ours totters on the brink of destruction, racked by mysterious internal maladies set in motion long aeons ago. The Star Master learned details of the awful peril while he was imprisoned by the Archimage of the Sky. And only the Master knows the method by which we can be saved.'

'Then why,' Anigel inquired with sweet reasonableness, 'doesn't he simply get on with this exalted work of his? Instead, he has sent out secret agents to foment sedition and discord all across the continent. He kidnapped and held hostage the legitimate rulers of six countries. And, unless I miss my guess, he is here in Brandoba tonight hoping to engineer the overthrow of Emperor Denombo, so that you can seize the Sobranian throne! If the true intent of Orogastus is the salvation of the world, why is he embarking upon a war of conquest?'

'The necessary remedy for healing the world is a drastic one,' Naelore said earnestly, 'requiring much sacrifice from the population as well as the exertion of ineffable magic. Left to your own devices, you proud, ignorant rulers would never be able to control your people during the

233

days of rebalancing. You are too cowardly, too undisciplined and selfish to do what must be done. It is necessary for an all-powerful leader to compel you.'

Anigel would have remonstrated indignantly, but Naelore swept on, speaking like one entranced. 'I myself am no more than the willing servant of the Star Master. When I become Empress of Sobrania, I will do whatever he asks in order to forward his grand strategy. Later, when the work is done and the Sky Trillium shines above our land – after the Sempiternal Ice is banished forever and the Vanished Ones walk among us again – then I will share in the Master's triumph. And perhaps I will even win his love, if the Dark Powers will it.'

Anigel was reduced to speechlessness.

The great continental ice cap somehow melted? The Vanished Ones returning? It was absurd!

But the world *was* out of balance in some fundamental way. Haramis had been convinced of it, citing the severe earthquakes, the widespread volcanic eruptions, and the disastrous weather that had afflicted so many parts of the continent during recent years. However, the Archimage had never hinted that these events might be portents of planetary doom.

Or had she?

Involuntarily, the Queen's bound hands lifted to her throat, seeking the comfort of her Black Trillium amulet. But the Flower was gone, just as Haramis was gone, and there was no one to answer her questions except herself . . .

Orogastus now drew up his steed at a residence with a sturdy iron gate, where the groups of red-garbed celebrants were especially numerous. He lifted his Star and a gatekeeper unlocked the portal. Beckoning Naelore to follow, he rode his fronial inside. The two animals moved down a short gravel track flanked by gardens, coming at last to the lighted entrance of the dwelling. Nine Sobranian men in ornate armour and blood-red feathered cloaks waited at attention beneath the portico, plumed casques tucked under their arms.

Several liveried lackeys stood apart. Orogastus dismounted and gave his fronial over to one of them, then took off his hood and cape and gave them to another. The Sobranian noblemen gasped at the sight of his exotic Star Guild armour. Waving off a third footman, the sorcerer himself assisted Naelore to alight, leaving Anigel perched on the pillion.

With a single movement, the Archduchess removed her own dark bird disguise and let it fall to the ground. She also wore the silver-and-black war regalia of the guild of sorcerers, except for the rayed helmet, but each piece of her plate armour was adorned with golden chasing and brilliants.

234

The Star of Nerenyi Daral hung from a jewelled chain around her neck. Her flaming tresses were partially hidden by a crown of platinum and gold in the form of a bird with downswept wings, having a single gigantic emerald for a head and studded with hundreds of sparkling white and yellow diamonds. She gave her arm to the Star Master, who bowed his head respectfully and brought her forward to the waiting men.

'My Lords,' Orogastus intoned, 'I present your Empress.'

The nine nobles whipped out their two-pronged swords and held them high in a salute of fealty. 'Naelore!' they cried. 'Long life to Her Imperial Majesty the Empress Naelore!' One by one they came forward, holding up their blades for the benison of her touch. Then the two most imposing among them brought a gorgeous feather cloak, shading from vivid scarlet at the hood and shoulders to deepest garnet colour at the hem, and vested Naelore in it. When the little ceremony was over, she spoke.

'Beloved vassals and liegemen! We thank you for joining us on this night of destiny, which will never be forgotten so long as our nation endures. At long last it is time for the great injustice to be righted. With your help, and that of the forces you have assembled, we will pull down our usurping brother Denombo and take our rightful place upon the imperial throne of Sobrania. Later, after we have savoured this first victory, we will personally lead our imperial armada into the Southern Seas, for the purpose of restoring to the empire those other lands once ruled by our ancestor, the first Naelore of glorious memory.'

'Hail, victorious Empress Naelore!' The nine lords smote their steel gauntlets against their breastplates. 'Hail, Naelore the Mighty! Hail, Naelore the Conqueror!'

They would have kept up the cheers and martial shouts, except that Orogastus suddenly lifted his hand, whereupon every voice was abruptly stilled. The barbarian lords were like men turned to stone, unable to move a muscle.

'The celebration can come later,' said the sorcerer dryly. 'Which one of you owns the great trireme lying in the harbour?'

Another gesture by Orogastus restored the Sobranians to normal mobility. They were both discomfited and frightened by the sorcerer's casual exertion of power, but none dared to complain. Naelore herself seemed unconcerned. She rested her hand on the forearm of a man who wore a great curled moustache and armour decorated with blue enamel, one of those who had held her red-feathered cape.

'Star Master,' said she, 'this is the Sealord Dasinzin, our loyal ally and dear friend of our youth. It is his vessel that has brought us the matériel so vital to our great enterprise.'

Dasinzin cleared his throat and glowered. His fingers strayed to the hilt of his sheathed sword. 'So you are the great wizard who has promised to restore our Empress.'

Orogastus only smiled.

'Will you condescend to discuss your strategy with us?' Dasinzin inquired with dangerous civility. 'Or do you intend for us to follow your corps of conjurers on blind faith?'

Orogastus seemed not to have heard the insult. 'Sealord, did you order your galley's crew to bring the sealed crates ashore?'

'We should have them here at my house within the hour. I was told by your advance men that the cargo must be unloaded and transported surreptitiously, a few boxes at a time.'

'And your chieftains and their lieutenants?' the sorcerer went on. 'Are they also close at hand?'

'They are assembled in the back garden, awaiting their orders.'

The sorcerer nodded in satisfaction. 'Very well. I will confer with them anon. I have seen the warriors waiting out on the streets. How large a fighting force were you able to raise?'

'Over four thousand. All of them wear similar disguises, as Her Imperial Majesty commanded, and all are well armed. Even so, we cannot hope to overcome the Imperial Guard unless –'

'Unless powerful magic assists us,' Orogastus said softly. 'And it will.'

Another nobleman, tall and florid in countenance, spoke out. 'We have done all that was asked of us, even though we knew nothing of the battle–plan, because of our devotion to the Empress. But the time has now come for you to confide in us, wizard. Before we proceed further, you must outline your strategy and demonstrate to us the offensive capability of your Star Guild weapons.'

Naelore herself answered him. 'Do not be troubled, Lucaibo. Just as soon as the cargo from Dasinzin's ship is delivered here, you will see with your own eyes what manner of wondrous armament we have assembled. What is more, you will wield a magic weapon yourself – and so will the rest of you lords, and as many of our troops as we can equip.'

The Sobranian men all began to talk excitedly, but subsided when Naelore lifted her hand. 'Friends,' she said, 'hold your peace for just a few moments longer. Let us go into Dasinzin's house and the Star Master will tell you everything.'

There was a rumble of approval from the nobles. Dasinzin bowed to the Archduchess, then offered his arm to lead the way inside.

Anigel still sat demurely on Naelore's fronial, eyes lowered and cross-bound wrists resting on the saddle's cantle. The lackey who held the beast addressed the sorcerer diffidently:

'My Lord, what of this prisoner?'

Orogastus studied Anigel for a moment. Then he commanded that she be taken to the lady of the house and given bodily ease and refreshment. 'Tell your mistress that the Star Master commands her to guard this woman as though her very life depended upon it. For in truth, it does.'

As he came closer and closer to the Brandoba pleasance, Prince Tolivar discovered that invisibility was a futile ploy in a dense crowd, just as it had been out in the foggy river forest. Unable, perhaps because of the distracting pandemonium, to move people harmlessly aside by means of magic, he had to resort to pushing and shoving just like everyone else. The 'empty' space occupied by his unseen but substantial form was perilously conspicuous, so he climbed up into one of the decorated trees that lined the street, and when he was concealed from the surging throng below by the foliage, he became visible once again.

'Talisman,' he said, 'I need a bird costume. Nothing fancy. Get me one like that fellow over there is wearing.' He pointed to an adolescent garbed in a simple cape and beaked hood of brown feathers, and simultaneously imagined himself wearing the outfit.

And he was. The bag containing the star-box was still tied to his back, but his talismanic coronet was hidden beneath the costume's headpiece. Well satisfied, he climbed down from the tree and resumed his journey.

He had not expected Brandoba to be so big, or so rich. The people were barbarians, after all, having a fierce suspicion of outsiders and an invincible belief in their own superiority and self-sufficiency. Sobrania and its allied tribes had no universities, no literature, no traditions of fine art or classical music. They kept human slaves, oppressed the local Folk, and indulged in loathsome blood sports. Only their feather crafts were unique enough to be traded abroad; the rest of their commerce with the more civilized nations to the east was based upon the sale of raw materials and certain spices. Sobranian 'culture' was sneered at by their civilized neighbours as being a hodge-podge of borrowings: music and drama from Var, arts and architecture from Galanar and the republics, extravagant couture and jewellery-making from Zinora. The empire had imitated the shipbuilding technology of Raktum and Engi, and appropriated weapon-making and other military science from Labornok.

On the other hand, Prince Tolivar thought, looking at the shining buildings and the mostly well-dressed citizenry around him, the Sobranians of Brandoba, at least, hadn't done badly for themselves at all. Neither had Orogastus, in choosing the prosperous barbarian capital for his initial exploit in the conquest of the world.

And the sorcerer had offered to share it with him . . .

Tolivar wondered if he had been a fool to reject it. Was there a chance that Orogastus would permit him to change his mind? He touched the hidden coronet and thought for a moment of posing the question; but then the memory of his mother flashed into his mind, standing calm and indomitable before Naelore's sword, and he lowered his treacherous hand and pressed on toward the city centre.

When he reached the pleasance at long last, it lacked only a half hour until midnight. Once again the Prince climbed up into a tall tree, this time in order to get the lay of the land. Below stretched a sea of people filling an immense rectangular space dotted here and there with patches of ornamental trees. The area was encompassed on three sides by boulevards, which were kept open for the carriages and mounts of nobility and other privileged citizens by cordons of imperial warriors armed with stout wooden quarterstaves. The boulevards were backed by rows of elaborately decorated public buildings and large dwellings, protected from the churning throng by walls of stone.

At the eastern end of the pleasance lay the imperial palace. It was a sprawling structure, illuminated externally by countless fire-pots, its architecture a blend of efficient fortification and eye-popping vulgarity. The main façade was of white marble and scarlet jasper, with lofty spiralled columns of green malachite. Piled around the colonnaded central structure were crenellated towers and innumerable wings, all connected by arcades and buttresses. Every angle of the vast roof dripped with gargoyles and they, like the roof tiles, were gilded, as was the great rotunda of the inner keep. Thrusting up from the gleaming dome was a red jasper pinnacle topped by a golden bird with wings outspread. The entire confection was tricked out with multicoloured enamelled shields, painted friezes, fancifully carved mouldings, and niches holding statues. There were hundreds of casement windows with gilded frames, all blazing with candlelight.

The palace grounds were enclosed by a thick wall seven ells high, topped with ornamental spikes, fire-baskets, and flagpoles flying festive banners of green and gold. Gilded iron gates, locked and patrolled by warriors in handsome parade armour, fronted the grand staircase leading to the palace's vestibule of entrance. Flanking the gate were twin stone guardhouses adorned with bunting, and before it stretched a broad forecourt hemmed by more troops.

At the pleasance's far western end, where Tolivar perched in his tree, stood a bandshell (from which the Imperial Brass boomed out rousing

Okamisi and Varonian pop tunes), a glass conservatory housing rare birds, and a shrine to the national goddess, Matuta. The curved section of the Western Boulevard fronting the holy building, roped off and surrounded by guards with pikes and naked swords, held the pyrotechnic materials that would soon be ignited for the fireworks display.

Tolivar touched his coronet and whispered, 'Show me the Golden Griss Fountain, where I am to meet Orogastus.'

A voice in his mind said: *There.* And at the same time his mind's eye perceived something glowing amidst the crowd near the far end of the vast open area, situated between two of the miniature parks. It was a tall jet of water rising from the middle of an ornamental basin. Gold-leafed statues of waterbirds spouting lesser streams of water surrounded it, and the rising wind scattered the fountain's spray in a manner that kept most of the crowd away from its farther side, which was adjacent to the palace forecourt. Unusual numbers of those who braved the wet area wore black-bird costumes.

'That is where the sorcerer will be,' the Prince said to himself. He dismissed the vision, climbed down from the tree, and began moving as quickly as he could out into the pleasance. He took advantage of his small stature to worm through the mob, ignoring cries and curses as he cleared the way with outthrust elbows, stepped ruthlessly on people's feet, and kicked their shins.

'Ow!' an infuriated male voice sang out. 'You damned brat! I'll teach you!' Strong hands seized Tolivar's shoulders and shook him until his teeth rattled. In a panic, he was about to appeal to his talisman when he chanced to get a clear look at the face of his stocky captor, who had lost his costume headpiece in the tumult.

The face was broad, supremely ugly, and had one eye bandaged and the other alight with fury. Its owner was well known to Prince Tolivar, who stopped squirming from astonishment and exclaimed, 'What are *you* doing here?'

'Probably the same thing you are,' retorted King Ledavardis.

CHAPTER 25

Earlier, the King and Archduke Gyorgibo had found themselves trapped by the mob in one of the great commercial plazas a quarter league or so north of the pleasance. The elegant shops were closed with steel shutters, but food and liquor stalls and purveyors of festival novelties were open and doing a roaring business. In the centre of the marketplace was a platform where an ensemble of musicians played rollicking airs on horns, doodlesacks, fipple-flutes, and drums. Because of the constricted space, people who wanted to dance were limited to jumping up and down and flapping the wings of their costumes. An illuminated clockface mounted on the façade of a great banking establishment showed an hour and a half until midnight.

'This is no good, Ledo,' said the Archduke to the Pirate King. 'The crowd is getting so dense we can scarcely move.'

'But the spark inside the amulet points in that direction! God only knows why the villains have taken the Queen into the city's centre, but they have certainly done so. See for yourself, Gyor.'

The Sobranian eyed the trillium-amber pendant thrust beneath his nose. 'Yes, yes, I know. But look – the avenue on the opposite side of the market is packed solidly with people heading toward the pleasance. It's impossible for us to go that way. We'll have to find another route.'

Gyorgibo and Ledavardis had left the other rulers at the imperial hunting lodge, to which Queen Anigel's recovered trillium-amber had obligingly led them on the previous day. The escaped hostages had found the place deserted, and for a few precious hours, the King and the Archduke had slept like dead men. Awakening shortly before dawn, they shared a hearty meal that Queen Jiri and Duumvir Ga-Bondies scratched up from the lodge's larder. Gyorgibo was almost unrecognizable after he had shorn his vart's-nest of tangled hair, shaved, and dressed in clean garments. The two young men then bade their companions farewell, cautioning them not to stray away from the lodge, and rode off toward Brandoba via a round-about trail familiar to Gyorgibo. The journey took them all day and part

240

of the evening. All unknowing, they had barely avoided catching up with the rear guard of the Star Guild.

Before entering the Hunters Gate the pair abandoned their fronials for fear of attracting unwanted attention. Once inside Brandoba they bought a couple of cheap bird costumes, using money from the late Tazor's effects, and slowly tracked Queen Anigel by means of the guiding spark within the heart of the trillium-amber until further progress through the crowd seemed to be impossible.

'How can we find another way,' Ledavardis complained, 'unless the magical Flower turns us into true birds, and we fly?'

'Follow me,' the Archduke commanded. He unhooked a small gate shutting off a narrow space between two buildings, then slipped into an arrow-straight alley so constricted that it would accommodate only a single person at a time. It was very dark, having a deep gutter in the middle and trending rather steeply downhill. A noxious stench revealed the gutter to be an open sewer that collected effluent from cess-pipes of the structures on either side.

'Phew!' Ledavardis cried. 'Where the devil are we going? This is the exact opposite direction from that indicated by the trillium-amber!'

But the Sobranian hurried on without explanation, and after a time they came to an inky little canal clotted with floating detritus. Windowless walls with widely spaced doors fronted a narrow walk beside the sinister waterway.

'This is one of several small canals that flush municipal waste down to the lower River Dob and into the sea,' Gyorgibo said. 'Each dawn, garbage-barges drift along them and public scavengers empty the litterbins set out on the embankment.' He pointed upstream, where the sky was brightest. 'If we go that way, we are bound to come to one of the great sewers serving the palace. When Denombo and I were lads, we used the tunnels to escape our tutors and prowl the city incognito.'

The Archduke moved swiftly along the slippery paved walk, coming at length to a massive wall. At water level was a semicircular opening twice his height, barred by a stout metal grate. 'The wall is part of the palace's northern perimeter. The grate of the sewer-pipe is locked, of course. Deno and I once had keys – but you have something even better!'

King Ledavardis nodded and touched the grate's lock-plate with the drop of trillium-amber. There was a click, the bars opened, and Gyorgibo led the way into fetid blackness. Anigel's amulet obligingly brightened like a tiny lantern.

'There's a ledge just above the effluent. Keep close behind me, and for the love of heaven don't fall into the muck. We don't have too far to go.

241

There's a branch ahead that serves as a drain to the bosquets and fountains of the pleasance.'

They shuffled along and finally turned right into a narrower tunnel. Fortunately, the liquid flowing through it was fairly clean water, only a bit greyish in colour, for here there were no ledges and they had to wade along ankle-deep. To the surprise of the Pirate King, this pipe was faintly lit by widely spaced overhead grilled shafts. When they had gone a few hundred ells it became evident that they were beneath the pleasance itself. The noise of the crowd penetrated underground like rolling thunder.

'I think we'll climb out here,' Gyorgibo said, indicating iron rungs that led up one of the shafts. 'It should lead to one of the bosquets.' He ascended hand over hand and lifted the grille at the top. When Ledavardis emerged behind him he saw that they were within a small planting of trees and bushes, one of many miniature parks dotting the great square, set off from the open areas of the pleasance by iron fencing. The crowd stood shoulder-to-shoulder round about it, waiting for the fireworks display to begin. The din was deafening.

The Pirate King took out the trillium-amber and inspected it. Seeing that the directing line of light in its heart was now exceedingly bright, he spoke to the amulet. 'Is your mistress nearby?'

The spark at the line's tip began to blink rapidly. Ledavardis gave a cry of triumph and bellowed into the Archduke's ear. 'Queen Anigel is somewhere over in that direction, near that big fountain!'

Gyorgibo shook his head in puzzlement. 'Incredible! I cannot fathom why the Star Men would bring her there, of all places.'

'Never mind. Let's go!'

The two men penetrated the press of costumed people only by main strength, making their way with glacial slowness. A clock on one of the public buildings indicated that it was nearly midnight.

And then a costumed urchin heading in the same direction trod sharply upon the toes of Ledavardis and elbowed him in the stomach and kicked his shins for good measure, whereupon the King took hold of the boy and tussled with him, shouting, 'You damned brat! I'll teach you!'

The bird-hoods of both of them fell away as they tumbled to the torn turf. The child's eyes widened in recognition and he ceased his struggles, and Ledavardis saw that he was chastising none other than Tolivar, Prince of Laboruwenda. What was more, the boy had a peculiar silvery coronet clamped to his brow that had to be the fabled Three-Headed Monster talisman of Queen Anigel.

'What are *you* doing here?' Tolivar exclaimed.

'Probably the same thing you are,' the King retorted. He and the boy were on hands and knees down on the flattened lawn, a forest of legs surrounding them. No member of the crowd paid them any attention.

'My Royal Mother –' the Prince began.

'Is here in the pleasance somewhere,' snapped the King, 'and you had best leave her rescue to me.'

'You don't understand,' the boy wailed. 'Orogastus and the evil Star Woman Naelore have Mother and they have promised to slay her unless I surrender to them this talisman. I was commanded to meet the sorcerer near that fountain during the fireworks.'

'Did he tell you exactly where?' the King asked.

'Nay, he said he would find me. Once I have given him the ransom, he will turn Mother over to me.'

Ledavardis thought quickly. 'I doubt that! More likely, the wizard intends to take both of you prisoner. Queen Anigel is too valuable a hostage to be set free. What do you think, Gyor?'

The Archduke squatted beside the two of them and said, 'I think the same as you.'

'Why can't you use your coronet's magic to rescue the Queen?' the King asked Tolivar.

'I'm not a good enough sorcerer,' the boy said miserably. 'I hoped to go invisible and save her, but the talisman said that Orogastus would be able to descry me regardless.' Desperation brought tears to the Prince's eyes. 'Oh, please, King Ledo! Do not interfere. I am the only one who can save Mother. Even if the Star Men do capture both of us, at least she will be alive.'

A loud flourish of trumpets sounded from the bandshell, and it was echoed immediately by another fanfare coming from the palace at the opposite end of the pleasance. A collective roar went up from the crowd.

'It is the Emperor,' Gyorgibo said, 'coming out to signal the start of the aerial display.'

The three of them climbed to their feet. A twin file of torchbearers was visible, filing out of the palace's grand entrance and down the stairs. They were accompanied by lackeys bearing a portable throne and many golden stools, imperial guardsmen in ornate armour, and a procession of courtiers wearing magnificent bird-robes. The Emperor appeared last of all, attired in shining vestments of iridescent white vitt feathers and a platinum crown-helm with a beaked visor entirely covered by diamonds.

The trumpets blared again, and the mob responded by chanting Denombo's name. So lofty was the palace staircase that the members of the imperial court were clearly visible above the gates. They marched down to a kind of terrace that divided the steps into two sections. The throne was emplaced there, flanked by stools for the high nobles. The Emperor lifted his arms and the sleeves of his robe seemed transformed into great sparkling wings. Instantly, silence fell.

He declaimed: 'Let the heavens proclaim the glory of the Goddess Matuta – and that of her loyal servant, Denombo!'

A thundering detonation rang out. Six skyrockets took off from the space in front of the temple, soaring into the cloudy sky trailing sparks. When they reached the top of their trajectory they exploded into an overarching canopy of gold and green stars. The assembled throng broke into a riot of cheering. Then the trumpets and flugelhorns in the bandshell began to play sprightly melodies and everyone settled down to watch the show.

'I have an idea.' The Archduke leaned close to Ledavardis and began speaking into his ear. The two men conversed for a few minutes in words inaudible to the Prince.

Finally the King of the Pirates said: 'Tolo, do you see the small bosquet – that enclosed park to the left of the fountain?'

The boy nodded, and Ledavardis explained his plan – and what he, Tolivar, must do to abet it.

Blood drained from the Prince's face. 'If we fail, Mother might be killed after all!'

'The sorcerer needs Queen Anigel alive,' Ledavardis told him curtly. 'He never intended to slay her, only to frighten you into handing over your talisman. Look here!' The King pulled the trillium-amber from its place of concealment and explained how it had guided him and Gyorgibo in their search. 'The Holy Flower will continue to protect your mother as it has done since her birth. You must believe that, Tolo. Now go. But before you do, give me that.'

And the King pointed to a mesh sack hanging from the Prince's belt.

Queen Jiri came into the grand salon of the hunting lodge, where Widd, Hakit Botal, Prigo, and Ga-Bondies sat sipping mulled wine before the blazing hearth.

'My friends, we have a problem. After I helped Princess Raviya to retire upstairs, I stepped outside onto the balcony for a breath of air and saw something that worries me greatly.'

President Hakit Botal gave a gusty sigh of annoyance. 'Not another pack of forest monsters sniffing around the fronial stables! I assure you, Majesty, there is no way the creatures can break in and devour the mounts, any more than they can harm us here in the lodge. The buildings are very sturdy.'

'I am not concerned about wild beasts eating us or the fronials,' the Queen said with asperity. 'Come and see for yourselves what is going on, then draw your own conclusions.' She whirled about and climbed the open rustic staircase to the upper level. The four men followed reluctantly.

At the end of the hallway she unfastened the window-doors leading to the balcony. The others came out into the dark after her. It was a raw evening with intermittent moonlight piercing the dark clouds. 'What do you make of that?' Jiri pointed to a gap in the trees, where the sawtoothed Collum Range loomed black against a widespread rosy glow in the sky.

'It is a most sombre sunset,' Prince Widd began tentatively.

But Jiri cut him off. 'The mountains lie to the *east*.'

'It cannot be a freak of moonrise,' Duumvir Prigo said thoughtfully, 'since all three orbs are high in the sky, albeit partially masked by clouds. Do you suppose it is a forest fire?'

'There is no smoke,' said the Queen. 'I thought at first that a mighty storm was approaching, and that the glow might be distant thunderbolts. But the wind blows from the other way, and while the redness does vary somewhat in intensity, it is too steady to be lightning.'

'D-do you think it might be m-magic?' Ga-Bondies stuttered fearfully. 'Orogastus beleaguering the Sobranian capital city with eldritch f-fire?'

'Imbecile,' Hakit Botal snapped. 'Brandoba also lies to the west, in the opposite direction.'

'The glow might still be magical,' said Prince Widd. 'I can understand why Jiri is uneasy.'

'There is something else,' said the redoubtable Queen. 'Listen!'

They cocked their ears momentarily. Then Prigo announced, 'I hear naught but the sound of the great river, and it seems to flow more quietly than usual.'

'The forest creatures are silent,' the Queen told them, 'and that is hardly normal.'

'Hmm. No cries of beasts or birds at all,' the President said, concern entering his voice for the first time. 'Yes – that is queer. Something must have frightened them.'

'But what?' Ga-Bondies whispered.

'I don't know,' Jiri admitted. 'But there is another, even more ominous development I would call to your attention. It is best seen from further along the balcony.'

The men shuffled along after her, coming to a place where the sound of the River Dob in its canyon was louder. The Queen bade them look down, but they could see almost nothing because the Three Moons were

245

temporarily hidden; but after a few minutes the clouds parted and the rulers beheld a startling scene lit by silvery light.

The canyon of the Dob was no longer two hundred ells deep, as they had seen it that morning. A gleaming expanse of pale liquid filled it halfway to the rim, and in it floated countless huge uprooted trees. The debris moved downstream with extraordinary slowness, and it took the men some time to realize that the water had thickened almost to the consistency of batter.

'It's mud!' Prince Widd marvelled. 'A stupendous flow of grey mud, coming down from those mountains. What in the world does it mean?'

'In my opinion,' said Queen Jiri, 'it means that we must ride out of here as though all the demons of the ten hells were at our heels.'

CHAPTER 26

Once the fireworks display was in progress and the people standing still, occupied in looking skyward, it was much easier to slip through the crowd. Tolivar came to the Golden Griss Fountain, where many were standing. Then, following the instructions given him by Ledavardis, he began moving very slowly around the wide ornamental basin to the northeastern side, where flying spray from the fountain jets had discouraged large numbers of spectators from gathering.

Black Trillium! the boy prayed. Do not let Orogastus or Naelore find me yet!

The area of wet cobbles was some twenty ells in width. The nearest fire-basket lampposts were further east at the guardhouses flanking the palace gates, another thirty ells distant, and the only useful light came from the fireworks. To the north was the fenced bosquet, densely planted with trees and flowering shrubs. Tolivar skirted the sprayfall, his eyes darting back and forth as he apprehensively searched the thinning crowd for Star Men. But all he saw were people in costumes: elaborate ones, modest ones, comical ones, frightening ones. The human birds went *Oooh!* and *Ahhh!* as each skyrocket exploded, and there were cheers and applause and whistles and quacks for particularly noteworthy displays. A large proportion of the crowd seemed to be well-supplied with liquor; the pavement was littered with discarded jugs and crocks, and here and there a drunken reveller lay insensible on the cobbles.

When he reached the park fence the Prince gave a great sigh of relief. His greatest fear had been that he would be intercepted too early. Only a thin crowd of costumed citizens was close by, braving the occasional wave of spray. On the palace stairs, Emperor Denombo and his glittering court enjoyed the show while the band played on and the citizenry grew more boisterous in their enthusiasm.

Now the Prince became increasingly aware of the weight of the star-box on his back and the tightness of the coronet on his brow. His body reacted also to the physical effort he had expended making his way from the harbour to the city centre and he slumped down on the damp pavement, sitting with his back against the low wrought-iron fence. He closed his eyes.

'Oh, talisman!' he whispered desolately. 'Are you still mine?'

Yes.

'Is there no way that I can keep you and still save poor Mother?'

The question is impertinent.

'I know. But I had to ask.'

Someone called: 'Tolo!'

He opened his eyes. Standing before him, silhouetted against the blazing sky, was a tall figure dressed as a blackbird. Before the Prince could speak, the costumed man pulled back his hood, revealing the awesome rayed helmet of the Star Guild. His eyes were twin white beacons.

'Get up,' said Orogastus. 'The time has come.'

Moving as slowly as he dared, Tolivar climbed to his feet and confronted the sorcerer.

To Queen Anigel, the brief journey afoot from Dasinzin's mansion to the Golden Griss Fountain was a time of peculiar detachment, beyond sorrow and despair, with the fireworks a kaleidoscope of fiery beauty overhead. Her wrists had been untied, but her arms were firmly pinioned by two taciturn Star Men named Zanagra and Gavinno, whose black capes concealed deadly antique weapons hanging from their belts. They hustled her along behind Orogastus, who cleared the way with his magic, and the cheering mob seemed not even to notice their passing.

Within a few minutes they would reach the fountain, and there poor foolish Tolivar would hand over both the coronet and the crucially important star-box to the sorcerer, thinking thereby to gain her freedom. But she was certain now that Orogastus would never let her go, any more than he would release the other hostage rulers that the Guildsman Tazor held captive somewhere in the Forest of Lirda. The truth had come to Queen Anigel as she sat numbly in Dasinzin's kitchen, an ignominious prisoner waited upon by terrified Sobranian women.

She and the other heads of state had not been abducted in order to insure some nebulous 'cooperation' by their nations with the sorcerer. From the beginning, Orogastus had had only one objective: to exert irresistible pressure upon *Haramis*, forcing the Archimage to give up her talisman in exchange for their lives.

And the same dreadful choice would now face Kadiya as well.

Threefold God of the Flower, she prayed, give my sisters the strength to hold fast and let us die . . .

They reached the fountain and she felt its spray on her face, mingling

248

with her slow tears. The tall central jet was swaying oddly from side to side independent of the wind's direction, and the waters cascading over the gilded stone ornaments into the basin were clouded, as though admixed with milk.

Orogastus touched his Star, nodded in satisfaction, and said, 'There's the boy. Sitting at the railing of that little park on the left. Hold the Queen here, amongst the crowd, until I summon you.'

Anigel would have cried a warning, but Zanagra's gloved hand clapped over her mouth and she felt a dagger prick her abdomen. 'Stand quietly,' the Star Man hissed, 'or your babies will perish, even though the Master's magic permits you to survive.'

She ceased struggling. If only they had not taken her trillium-amber! But without the amulet and its Holy Flower, she was bereft of all energy. She saw Tolivar rise and confront Orogastus. Their words could not be heard over the explosions of the pyrotechnical display. Then the sorcerer beckoned. Still wearing her griss costume of grey and white, she was led forward to the small clump of ornamental greenery where her son waited. He had removed the hood of his drab costume so that the Three-Headed Monster was clearly visible, seeming to shine amidst his fair hair with a faint silvery light of its own.

'Mother,' he said in a strained voice. 'Have they harmed you?'

'In truth, no,' she said. 'Only my heart is wounded ... by the sad discovery that you have possessed my talisman in secret for four long years –'

But Orogastus cut her off. 'Queen, enough!' And to the Prince: 'Tolo, give me the star-box.'

The sky was filled with enormous blossoms of violet, blue, and green light, criss-crossed by soaring flares tracing lines of white and gold. The music reached a grand finale of flourishes and the Emperor on the palace steps some fifty ells away rose from his throne and stood with his arms outstretched. The crowd began to chant: 'Denombo! Denombo! Denombo!'

Prince Tolivar unfastened the cord that had bound the sack to his back and drew forth the long narrow box with the Star emblazoned on its lid.

'Open it,' the sorcerer said, 'and place the coronet inside.'

The boy's jaw tightened. 'Not until you free my mother!'

Orogastus lifted his hand in a brief gesture. Six men dressed in black feathers, having weapons of the Vanished Ones protruding from the openings of their cloaks, emerged from the oblivious mob. They flanked the two Star Men in charge of the Queen and formed a close semicircle about Tolivar and the sorcerer. For the first time the Prince noticed how many celebrants in the area of the pleasance nearest to the palace were wearing black costumes. Of course! They had to be the henchmen of Orogastus.

The boy lifted his fingers to touch the sides of his coronet. 'I command you to free the Queen!'

For a moment, nothing happened. Then Orogastus smiled contemptuously and waved one hand. The two Star Men released weeping Anigel, who held out her arms to Tolivar. He rushed into her embrace and they stood locked together until a voice of thunder said: 'The talisman! Now!'

Orogastus and his Guildsmen stood shoulder to shoulder, and the eyes of all three blazed with malignant power. Anigel tottered and sagged to her knees, moaning and pressing her hands to her belly.

'You must not do it, Tolo!' she cried. 'He will use the talisman to conquer the world! Resist him, dear son! Never mind me. He cannot take the coronet from you by force – *aah!*'

At the Queen's cry of pain, the boy screamed, 'Let her alone!' He tore off the talisman and dropped it into the open box. There was a small flash, lost in the colourful bombardment of the fireworks.

Anigel murmured, 'No! Oh, no.'

'At last!' Orogastus swooped down to seize the container. The Prince pulled the Queen to her feet and drew her back against the fence, where there was a dense thicket of dripping shrubbery. The Star Master removed his rayed headpiece and handed it to Gavinno, leaving his head bare and his long white hair flying in the wet wind. Then he began to press the jewelled studs within the box, bonding the talismanic coronet to himself.

All at once no less than a dozen rounded small objects flew out of the bushes and smashed on the cobblestones, releasing a cloud of sparkling confetti and fungus spores that was hardly hindered at all by the mist. Orogastus's bellow of rage was cut off by a mighty sneeze.

Queen Anigel felt herself hauled backwards over the low fence. Branches scratched her face and she wailed in astonishment, struggling to free herself. 'Nay!' someone said in a harsh voice. 'We are friends. Hold your breath!' She heard violent sneezing and curses from the Star Men and the warriors in black, and then her shoulders were painfully compressed as her saviour thrust her head-first down an opening in the ground that was rimmed with iron. Other hands took hold of her, pulling her into some sort of vertical conduit. She was flung over a second man's back and the two of them slid into darkness and landed in shallow water with a loud splash. Faint illumination came from overhead and she saw Tolivar scuttle down iron rungs affixed to a lofty shaft. The man still holding her called out, 'Hurry! Blast the drain closed before the Star Men recover!'

'Get back out of the way!' shouted the person above. He came hurtling down the ladder. Anigel was dragged through water into total darkness, hearing her son mouth reassurances from somewhere nearby. Then a dazzling burst of ruby light silhouetted a stocky misshapen figure cradling something in its arms. She heard a rumble of collapsing masonry. Some of the stones were red hot, sizzling as they hit the water, and the tunnel was filled with roiling dust.

'Keep moving!' yelled the hunchbacked shadow. He lifted the thing he held and produced another explosion, dancing away from the fresh avalanche of stones.

Instinctively, the Queen pulled her soaking wet costume hood over her head to assist her breathing and scrambled along on hands and knees through water and slimy sediment. Incredulous excitement replaced the deadly languor that had numbed her wits. She had recognized the burly malformed body of the young King of Raktum.

'Ledo? . . . It's you? Oh, thanks be to the Lords of the Air!'

'Aye, Mother-in-Law-Elect. And thanks also to the Archduke Gyor, here, who remembered this warren of sewer tunnels, and to your Black Trillium amulet that led us straight to you, and even to young Tolo – who brought along the sneeze-eggs.'

She was suddenly hoisted to her feet. A golden glow, visible through the open weave of the hood's feathered fabric, dispelled the darkness. The air had cleared miraculously. Anigel discarded her soaked griss costume and saw that she was in a vaulted tunnel with water running through it. Tolivar and two men in sodden clothes stood there, grinning at her. She gave a cry of joy as King Ledavardis stowed his antique weapon, lifted the shining droplet of trillium-amber from around his neck, and transferred it to her own.

Gyorgibo said, 'We dare not stay here. The Star Men will soon discover that there are other drains in the pleasance leading to this tunnel. They will be after us. We shall have to block the passage behind us as we flee, and hope they do not cut us off.'

'But where shall we go?' Prince Tolivar asked, his glee changed abruptly to panic.

Anigel gripped her amber. 'Oh, Black Trillium, protect us now! Show us which way to go.'

The pendant began to blink rapidly, and in its heart the Flower was bisected by a line with a bright tip.

'It points in the direction of my brother's palace,' Gyorgibo said, 'the only possible place for us to find refuge. Run!'

*　　*　　*

Encumbered as he was with the star-box and its precious contents, which he instinctively held to his breast, Orogastus could at first think only of protecting the Three-Headed Monster. It had bonded to him at the instant the diabolical eggs smashed, and even as he doubled over in a helpless paroxysm he managed to pull out the coronet and clap it safely onto his brow. A miniature of the Star at his breast now shone beneath the central head of the Monster.

'Talisman!' he gasped. 'Banish the damned spores! Cure me and my men of the sneezing! Do you hear me?'

Yes. It is done.

His eyes and sinuses cleared and he darted to the bosquet fence and parted the bushes, revealing a large hole amidst the trees with a displaced iron grating beside it. Before he could command the Guildsmen he heard hollow voices issue from underground: '. . . blast the shaft . . . out of the way . . .'

'Beware!' the sorcerer cried, falling back against one of his warriors. He still held the star-box tightly. 'They have magic weapons!' An instant later a flash of red light came from the hole, along with a thunderous noise and a plume of dust. A second blast followed. Cursing, Orogastus cleared the air again with the talisman, only to find the opening in the ground sealed with rubble.

'Talisman, clear this debris from the tunnel!'

The request is impertinent.

'Why?' he raged.

To do so would endanger Queen Anigel, and she is shielded from magical hurt by the Black Trillium.

The sorcerer groaned. 'It cannot be! Unless —' He broke off and requested Sight of Prince Tolivar; but the boy was shielded also by the proximity of his mother, as were Anigel's rescuers. 'Then show me the layout of the drainage system beneath this pleasance, and the site of this blocked shaft.'

This time the coronet obeyed, and into his mind sprang a lucid diagram of the tunnels, with a blinking spark showing where the Queen and Prince had gone to ground. 'Show me the drain openings nearest this one!' Two additional lights began to flash, and hope sprang into his heart as he realized that one of them lay behind him, near to the fountain, and another was not twenty ells beyond the bosquet, across the cordoned-off boulevard that skirted the pleasance.

But before he could order his men into position there was a third red flare, dimly visible through the crowd lining the thoroughfare as it shone up through a storm-drain. The fugitives were sealing the access points as they moved away. But he could trap them easily if he could but study the sewer diagram for a few more moments –

'Master! The main gates of the palace are opening. The Imperial Hand-sel procession is beginning!'

Again Orogastus groaned. He heard trumpets and drums. There was no time left to spare. The army was poised to advance, and Naelore and her group of nobles awaited a successful outcome to the attack. He grasped his Star and bespoke the Guildsmen in charge of the partisan warriors:

'Prepare to storm the palace when I give the command.'

CHAPTER 27

'What the devil was that?' Sainlat shouted. 'I could have sworn I felt the pavement move – but with this accursed throng making such a hullabaloo, I cannot be certain.'

'It is only the fireworks exploding,' Melpotis yelled at him.

Edinar laughed. 'Or your own big feet crushing the cobblestones.' The four Oathed Companions moved forward through the close-packed celebrants on the southern side of the pleasance, with Kadiya in the midst of them wielding her talisman to part the crowd. She had removed her headpiece to see better and Sainlat had lost the pointed beak worn on his nose, but otherwise their disguises were still intact: Kadiya in purple feathers, Edinar in red, Melpotis and Kalepo wearing steel-blue, and Sainlat voluminously swathed in pothi-pink.

The talisman, with Kadiya's trillium-amber embedded in the hilt, had guided them from the waterfront directly to the audience portal at the far southern wing of the palace, through which visitors were usually admitted to the presence chamber of the Emperor. But there they were stymied by the imperial porter, who refused them entry, backed by a squad of guardsmen. The man was adamant: Denombo would see no one this night, not even an emissary from the King and Queen of Laboruwenda. Kadiya was told to return in the morning.

But morning would be too late.

She had tried to coerce him, but her talisman balked; somehow, she lacked the expertise to overcome his willpower without harming him – and this would have alarmed the guards and caused a furore. In the end, Kadiya and the knights were forced to turn away. 'Come,' she told them. 'We will try again at the main gate.'

They moved through the mob with increasing difficulty. With so many people now impeding their way, it had become nearly impossible for her to clear a path by magical prodding, as she had done earlier.

'The crowd thins out near that fountain with the golden birds,' Kalepo pointed out. 'Once we reach it, we should be able to approach the front of the palace more easily. But I don't see how we can hope to have better luck at the main gate than at the visitors' portal. It's plain that the Emperor and his court don't want to be disturbed during the big show.'

'You should have smitten that insolent palace flunky and his guards with your talisman's magical fire when they denied us entry,' Sainlat grumbled. 'Or blasted a hole through the palace wall.'

'No,' said Kadiya. 'I told you that the success of our venture depends upon Denombo's good will. He would hardly receive us graciously and give credence to our warning if we broke into his palace by force or harmed his servants. He is obviously a man terrified of magic. If I could only think of a stratagem that '

'Aagh!' Suddenly, Sainlat found himself unable to budge. 'This bloody costume! The tail has snagged again on something. Help me!'

'Help *me!*' squealed an indignant stout woman who had become attached to Sainlat's hindquarters and was being dragged along behind him. 'This oaf is ruining my lovely outfit!'

Snickering, the other Companions disentangled their pink-clad comrade from the lady, whose orange feathers were adorned with fussy furbelows of gold netting spangled with oversized sharp-pointed sequin stars. The big knight's awkward fantail had been a nuisance all evening, and when he was free Sainlat demanded that it be cut off immediately and discarded. They had to wait until they were nearer the fountain to find enough room to work in, for people kept jostling them in spite of Kadiya's fending magic. Presently, when they reached a nook formed by the elaborate basin's gilded coping, Melpotis took his dagger and began slicing away the appendage from Sainlat's cloak. Veils of fine spray rained down on them, the music of the Imperial Brass soared to a crescendo, and the climax of the fireworks display filled the sky with traceries of coloured flame.

The tail had been well anchored and it was going to take a few minutes to accomplish the amputation without destroying the costume. Kadiya decided to contact her Nyssomu friend back on the Cadoon boat and inquire about the mysterious trireme.

'Talisman, I would have mental speech with Jagun.'

He cannot bespeak you, for he lies in an enchanted sleep.

'What?' she exclaimed in astonishment. 'Release him at once!'

The request is impertinent.

'Why?' she demanded.

I cannot undo the spell laid by another talisman.

Kadiya smote her brow in exasperated comprehension. 'Tolo! Oh, the miserable brat!' Ignoring the bewildered queries of the men, who were unable to hear the talisman's speech, she bade it show her every part of

255

the aboriginal vessel. It obeyed, rather than balking as it would have done had Tolivar with his shielding magical coronet been aboard. The Prince was gone, and there was no way she could find him with her own talisman. A suspicious canvas-covered lump that lay on deck amidships proved to be Jagun and Critch, snoring peacefully. When she expanded her magical oversight to survey the harbour, she saw that the trireme was now moored at one of the large commercial docks. There was no sign of any unusual activity aboard the vessel or nearby.

'Has that ship's cargo been unloaded?' she asked the talisman.

Yes.

'What was it?'

The question is impertinent . . .

While Kadiya put other urgent questions to the Burning Eye (and received few useful answers), Kalepo and Melpotis tended to Sainlat and young Edinar moved around the fountain to avoid the worst of the falling water and get a better view of Emperor Denombo. It was obvious that the pyrotechnic display was just about over, and something curious seemed to be going on just inside the main gates of the palace. To the left of the great flight of stairs, teams of volumnials had appeared, hauling large four-wheeled carts surmounted by some kind of gaudy structures. A wagonmaster was forming the floats into a parade . . .

And guardsmen were slowly swinging wide the great golden portals before the grand staircase of the palace!

Edinar trotted over to a knot of a dozen revellers who were dressed, as he was, in red costumes. 'Hello! What's next?' he called eagerly to them, as a brazen fanfare rang out and drums began to roll.

Only one man took note of him, and as he turned about, the young Oathed Companion caught the gleam of armour beneath his scarlet feathered cloak. 'Get back to your station, fool!' the fellow growled. 'It is the Imperial Handsel, and the command to strike will be given at any moment.'

Edinar dashed back through the curtain of spray, his heart thudding and an icy lump expanding in the pit of his stomach. Until this moment of dread revelation, he had not noticed how many other red-costumed men had gathered around the fountain. He realized now that they were everywhere – scores of them, maybe hundreds! – standing in tense groups among the ordinary celebrants with their eyes fixed on Denombo and his courtiers. Mingled with the redbirds were others garbed in black, skulking about purposefully.

'Lady Kadiya!' Edinar bleated, and made haste to tell her of his discovery. She and the others had already taken note of the open gates, and were eagerly discussing the possibility of going through them invisible.

256

At the same time the Emperor delivered some bombastic proclamation, the drums settled into a stirring *rat-a-tat-BOOM* beat, and the volumnial-drawn carts began to roll out of the open gates, turning right onto the upper stretch of the boulevard that encircled the pleasance. Whistles and thunderous cheering arose from the crowd. Each float, flanked by drummers and trumpeters, bore a huge wicker effigy of a different fantastic bird, adorned with plumes, glistening tinsel, and glass 'jewels'. At the rear of every wagon stood four young women in scanty attire holding golden baskets, from which they flung showers of tiny gifts to the people on either side.

Emperor Denombo and his courtiers were now being served refreshments by genuflecting servants, while the scattered groups of redbirds, marshalled by those in black costumes, were coming together. Upon receiving Edinar's news, Kadiya looked around her, seized with uncertainty. The ordinary folk were being shoved roughly aside as more and more men wearing black or scarlet gathered on the pavement between the fountain and the open palace gates.

A gust of wind blew one redbird's cloak aside, and Kadiya saw that he was carrying an odd-shaped instrument. The others, with their hands concealed beneath their cloaks, also seemed to be burdened.

'Triune God!' she exclaimed, finally understanding. 'They have weapons of the Vanished Ones! It is an attack upon the palace, just as I feared.'

'Smite the foemen with your talisman's magical fire!' Sainlat cried.

'There are too many of them,' she groaned, 'and they are swarming through the throng of innocent people. I dare not risk it —'

'We must do *something*,' Edinar said desperately.

Kadiya stood paralysed by indecision. Denombo was too far away for them to reach. At any moment a pitched battle was going to break out . . . and somewhere in the mob was young Prince Tolivar, wearing the precious Three-Headed Monster.

The parade of handsel floats had completed its traverse in front of the palace and turned now onto the boulevard bordering the north side of the pleasance. The musicians accompanying it played on and the gift-giving maidens continued strewing imperial largesse. Only a small portion of the vast throng yet realized that anything unusual was happening; the others, oblivious, flocked to the cordons at the boulevards hoping to catch a gift when the parade passed by.

'Look at the fountain jet!' Kalepo cried in wonder. The tall plume of water above them was waving eerily from side to side, while at the same time a distinct rolling vibration seemed to stir the ground underfoot.

'It is only a small earthquake,' Kadiya said, still distracted, 'and of no importance –'

'Naelore!' came a shout from voices on either side of them, and the cry was taken up by more and more throats until the name echoed from one end of the pleasance to the other, drowning out the music. 'Naelore! Naelore!'

The assault began.

The costumed warriors nearest the gates surged forward in a tight formation and overwhelmed the imperial guards fronting the grand staircase. Another force of invaders burst from the main body of celebrants and charged toward the palace, splitting into two columns as they streamed around the great fountain and joined the advance force. These were armed with two-pronged swords, and cut down anyone who impeded them. Kadiya and her four knights huddled in their small island of safety as the army of Orogastus raced past them, pouring through the palace gates like a tide of black-streaked blood. Bursts of multi-coloured light, resembling fireworks set off too low, began to explode all along the palace façade. Those attackers who were equipped with weapons of the Vanished Ones were using them. Another fusillade at the middle of the steps signalled the clash between the sorcerer's men and the imperial warriors who had rallied to surround the Emperor and his court.

It took a few minutes more before the confused throng realized that something had gone terribly wrong with their festival. Then all they could think of was running away. The cordon of imperial troops along the northern boulevard wavered and fragmented and the panicked mob flowed out onto the thoroughfare, blocking the parade of floats. Like some mindless, shrieking beast the crowd attempted to escape from the pleasance, trampling one another and fighting as they fled into the side-streets.

Sainlat said, 'Our mission has failed! We are but five against thousands . . .'

Kadiya stood unmoving, with eyes glazed, gripping her talisman. *Tolo!* she called. *Tolo! For the love of God, tell me where you are!*

'The wizard's men have overrun Denombo and his defenders!' Melpotis exclaimed. 'Lords of the Air have mercy on them.'

'And on us,' Edinar appended grimly. 'We've got to get out of here!'

But Kadiya ignored the tumult and her Companions as well. Her magical Sight had already shown her the Emperor seized by Star Men, and she now posed agonized questions to herself and to the Three-Lobed Burning Eye: *Where can the boy be? Why did he violate his solemn promise to me and use his talisman's magic? I cannot believe Tolo enchanted Jagun and Critch simply in order to indulge in a childish escapade. He is thoughtless, but not so basely disobedient as that. Holy Flower – could there have been some other reason for him to leave the boat?*

But the magical sword, no mind-reader, always replied: *The question is impertinent.*

Then it came to her – whether from talisman or Black Trillium or from her own instinct, she did not know. But she was suddenly certain that Prince Tolivar had come ashore hoping to rescue his mother.

Kadiya addressed her talisman aloud. 'Burning Eye, is my sister Anigel in Brandoba?'

Yes.

'Where?'

She is in a drainage tunnel beneath the pleasance.

Kadiya stifled a cry of elation. 'What is she doing in such a place? Is – is she imprisoned?'

She flees from Orogastus. She is not imprisoned.

'Does the sorcerer pursue her underground? Is she in danger of capture?'

Orogastus does not pursue her. At present, she is not in danger of capture. The situation may change.

'This is unbelievable! Where is Anigel going?'

She goes to the palace of Emperor Denombo.

Kadiya blurted out to the knights what the talisman had said. They became very agitated, speaking all at once, begging her to bespeak the Queen and urge her to turn away from the imminent danger. The vanguard of the invasion now poured into the main entrance of the palace, while in the pleasance a deadly panic had broken out among the frenzied populace. But Kadiya was concerned now only with the safety of her sister.

'Gather closely around me,' she ordered the Oathed Companions. 'I shall have to bespeak Queen Anigel. She is doubtless fearful and distraught, and it will be very difficult to catch her attention without the aid of a second talisman.' She crouched low while the four knights spread their feathered capes over her in meagre shelter, then stared into the open brown Eye of the pointless dark sword. 'Talisman, let me descry my sister Anigel,' she prayed, 'and let me bespeak her also, so that I may save her life. I ask this in the name of the Triune and the Black Trillium.'

For a moment she thought she had failed. Then the noise and confusion around her was cut off as if some door had slammed. She beheld a tunnel lit by the golden glow of trillium-amber, a place of hewn granite blocks dripping with glistening mould, where a rivulet of greyish water flowed underfoot and the air was oddly filled with drifting dust. Standing stock still with his mouth wide open in shock was King Ledavardis of Raktum, bearing Anigel in his powerful arms. Another man, having coppery hair

259

and looking equally stunned, stood behind the King. At his side was Prince Tolivar.

'Lady of the Eyes!' the pirate croaked. 'What are you doing here?'

Anigel smiled tremulously. 'Dear Kadi! Have you come to join us in our tour of the Brandoba sewers? . . . Put me down, Ledo.'

Kadiya realized then that she had succeeded beyond her wildest hope. Not only did she descry and bespeak the Queen and her companions, but they in turn saw her image as well, in a magical Sending.

'How did you get down here?' Kadiya asked her sister. 'Are you hurt?'

'Ledo and his friend snatched me from the very clutches of Orogastus,' Anigel said. 'I am unharmed, save for an ankle sprained during my rescue that makes it hard for me to walk.'

The Pirate King said, 'You are a welcome sight, Lady Kadiya – and your mighty talisman even more so.'

'I am not with you in the flesh,' Kadiya said with regret. 'This is only a simulacrum of my true body, which actually remains above ground near the golden fountain. I have come with awful tidings. Orogastus and his army have stormed the imperial palace. You must turn back at once –'

'We cannot,' said the redheaded man calmly. He carried a weapon of the Vanished Ones, which he rested on one shoulder. 'In order to foil any pursuit, we have from time to time blasted the tunnel behind us with this useful implement's magical lightning. It is impossible for us to turn back.'

'In a few short minutes the palace will belong to the sorcerer's warriors and Star Men,' Kadiya said. 'The Emperor is already taken prisoner.'

'I was unable to warn him of the attack, and my talisman seems useless to halt the invasion. I am too incompetent at magic to wield it in the necessary manner.'

'Poor Denombo!' The man bowed his head. 'My sister will surely slay him. May Matuta grant him eternal peace.'

'This is Gyor, the Emperor's younger brother,' Anigel explained to Kadiya. 'The two of them played in the sewer system as boys. Coming this way, we had hoped to give Denombo warning of the sorcerer's plot.' Ledavardis added, 'The sister of whom Gyor speaks is the Archduchess Naelore, a member of the Star Guild and a thoroughgoing she-devil, who has conspired with Orogastus to seize the throne.'

'Is there no other way out of the sewer,' Kadiya asked, 'save through the palace?'

The Archduke raised a woeful countenance. 'This is a storm drain, not a true sewer. The shafts ahead of us serve the hanging gardens and the downspouts of the palace roofs. But once we get below the north wing of the palace, we can enter another sewage conduit. It is a vile and noisome tunnel that I never explored, but I know that it eventually debouches into a canal emptying into the River Dob. Unfortunately, there is no egress from the tunnel aside from those within the palace until one reaches the canal, nearly half a league away from the fortified wall.'

'You will have to continue on to the canal,' Kadiya decided. 'My men and I will find a way to enter the sewer system ourselves. My talisman is at least able to guide me. Eventually we will meet you. Find a safe spot and wait for us. Together we will find a way to travel down the river to the sea. Only God knows what will happen then. My Companions and I had an aboriginal boat at our disposal, but its skipper was put into an enchanted sleep –'

They had all forgotten Prince Tolivar, who broke in, saying, 'Jagun and Critch will awaken from my spell at dawn, Aunt Kadi. You can summon their boat then, and we can all sail away to safety.'

The vision of Kadiya stared at the boy in silence for a moment. Then she asked, 'Tolo, where is your talisman?'

Queen Anigel suddenly spoke in a ringing voice. 'My dear son gave it in ransom for my life, and the lives of his unborn brothers! Orogastus has the Three-Headed Monster now, but it will do us no good to bemoan the fact. We will speak no more of the matter.'

'Very well,' the Lady of the Eyes said through clenched teeth. 'I dare not stay with you any longer. May the Holy Flower protect you and guide you true until we meet again.'

The Sending vanished.

Kadiya told the Oathed Companions what had transpired in the tunnel. They rejoiced that both Queen Anigel and Prince Tolivar were safe, and declared that they were willing to fight their way out of the pleasance at Kadiya's side if she would but use the Three-Lobed Burning Eye against their enemies.

'It is the poor citizens of Brandoba,' she chided them, 'rather than the henchmen of Orogastus who hinder our escape. Look about you: Almost all of those wearing the red or black disguises have joined the assault on the palace. The rampaging mob surrounding us is made up of ordinary people. Shall I destroy them in order to save our own skins?'

She crouched low again, holding her talisman. All around them, the night was filled with screaming and a horrible rumbling sound; the crowd were trampling one another in their efforts to escape. 'We must go into the sewer system as Anigel and her party did, and move underground towards a certain canal that flows into the River Dob. It is there that

Anigel and the others will meet us. Let me ask the Burning Eye how to manage it.'

The knights waited grimly while Kadiya muttered her queries and listened to replies inaudible to ordinary men. But when she lifted her head again her face was bleak. 'The sections of tunnel closest to us have been deliberately collapsed by my sister's rescuers in order to prevent pursuit by the Star Men. To circumvent the obstacles, we shall have to make our way to the North Boulevard yonder and proceed along it for two city blocks. We can gain access to the drain shaft by pulling up a grating in the front garden of one of the mansions.'

'That means penetrating the very heart of the riot,' Melpotis warned. 'It may not be possible to shunt people aside gently, as you did before. There will be no place for them to go.'

'If only I were a more experienced sorcerer,' Kadiya lamented. 'But I never learned the subtle points of my talisman's operation, as did my sister Haramis.'

'Lady,' Melpotis said implacably, 'you will have to blast a path with your talisman's fire. There is no other way we can penetrate that crazed mêleé.'

'I cannot incinerate blameless people!' she cried.

Sainlat uttered a despairing curse and tore off his ridiculous pink costume, stamping it with malicious satisfaction. Then he drew his sword. 'We cannot remain here dithering! I for one am ready to cut our way to the tunnel entrance.'

'And I,' said Melpotis, also removing his disguise and donning his helmet.

'I have it!' Edinar's beardless young face brightened. 'Lady, beseech your talisman to put the people hindering us into an enchanted sleep, just as Prince Tolivar did to Jagun and the Cadoon! They will fall, and we can leap over them.'

Kadiya was sceptical. 'I have never done such a thing, but let me try.'

Once again, as during the unexpected Sending, Kadiya used all her strength to summon a calmer frame of mind. She winced when a loud blast came from the direction of the palace and flames shot forth from several upper windows, causing a great roar of fear to arise from the mob. But then she steeled herself, concentrating on a single pathetic reveller clad in tattered feathers who sat weeping and gibbering at the fountain's edge a few ells away.

Sleep, and wake only at dawn, she told him, holding the talisman high and at the same time closing her eyes to visualize him in peaceful slumber.

When she opened her eyes the man lay prone in a shallow puddle of grey water, a faint smile on his lips.

'I've done it!' she exulted. She tried again, singling out a pair of brawlers belabouring each other in pointless ferocity. Keeping her eyes open this time, she imagined them both sinking to the spray-washed cobbles unconscious and again pronounced the spell. The pair folded as gently as children drifting off to dreamland.

'Companions,' Kadiya said, drawing a deep breath, 'we are ready to venture forth.'

She removed her own costume, revealing her scale-mail cuirass emblazoned with the Eyed Trefoil, and donned the helm she had carried in a bag at her waist. Then she lifted the talisman. The droplet of trillium-amber inset among the lobes shone warmly.

'Stay close to me,' she ordered the knights. 'I will try to make a broad enough swath so that we need not tread upon the sleepers.'

They set off through the falling water toward the same small bosquet where Anigel and Tolivar had gone to ground, at first penetrating the fringes of the throng with relative ease. Kadiya swept the talisman back and forth, back and forth, her gaze pausing only for a split second upon each obstructing person. Rioters who had been screaming hysterically or flailing about in demented rage began to topple. Those who remained upright, untouched by magic, drew back in terror as others dropped around them. Someone shouted, 'A sorcerer!' A great wailing arose, punctuated by more cries of 'Sorcery! Beware!' The crowd shrank back on all sides of Kadiya, struggling madly to get away, believing that the felled ones had been slain by enchantment.

Kadiya and the Companions marched on, stepping over bodies. She used every whit of her concentration to bring on the magical sleep, trusting in the knights to keep her moving in the right direction. After passing the small grove of trees they headed for the boulevard, where the mob was packed thicker and in an uglier mood. The handsel floats had been overturned, sending the draught-beasts into foaming fits of terror. Looters had seized the coffers containing the imperial gifts and now battled over possession of the boxes, scattering coloured favours everywhere as they pummelled each other. One of the giftgiving maidens lay unmoving, covered in blood, where a maddened volumnial had stamped her. Other injured and dead people were everywhere on the pavement now, but Kadiya and her knights could only continue slowly down the seething boulevard, leaving unconscious bodies in their wake and fending off the occasional deranged attacker.

The mansion that was their goal now lay less than thirty ells away, just beyond a side street jammed with a howling rabble. Paradoxically, those on the lesser thoroughfare were striving to return to the pleasance rather than to flee it. At first, there was no clue to the anomalous movement.

As Kadiya and the Companions attempted to breast this mass of humanity their thus-far-successful manoeuvre began to falter because of the sheer numbers surrounding them. No matter how many people fell, others surged forward to take their places. The inexorable pressure of the advancing throng was making it impossible for Kadiya to perform the magic. Her justified fear that the enchanted sleepers would certainly be crushed to death destroyed her mental focus.

Edinar and Sainlat, at her right hand and subject to the strongest onslaught, found that even their swords were useless to fend off the human flood. They could advance no further. Helpless, they were being swept across the boulevard and back toward the pleasance.

To the north, down the jam-packed side street, there came the loud chirping and buzzing sounds of ancient weaponry being fired, bright flashes of coloured light, and the anguished cries of burn victims. Kadiya knew then that a secondary force of invaders was advancing from that direction, herding hysterical people ahead of them, clearing the way of laggards with nefarious efficiency.

'Star Men!' Edinar howled into Kadiya's ear. 'And other villains in red, mounted on fronials! Turn your talisman's deadly lightning upon them —'

The young knight's words slurred to a scream. He was torn away from Kadiya's side and disappeared in a dark welter of bodies. An instant later Sainlat also vanished, and the brothers Kalepo and Melpotis stumbled and were sucked down beneath her feet.

'Talisman!' Kadiya cried in despairing appeal. 'Help!' She held the pointless sword high, but at the same instant felt herself falling. The Three-Lobed Burning Eye slipped from her fingers. She saw a blinding green flare and heard someone shriek. Tossed and buffeted like a leaf in a torrent, she was stunned into insensibility before she struck the cobblestone pavement.

She revived, half suffocated beneath a great weight and unable to move. The maddening din of the rioters had receded and the only sounds coming from nearby were moans, weeping, feeble calls for help, the whickering of fronials, and the grunting and cursing of men exerting themselves mightily.

They were pulling corpses off her.

One of her knees throbbed, but her armour — or the Flower's magic —

seemed to have saved her from worse hurt. She still wore her helmet and lay face down on something. Or someone.

'Companions!' she managed to gasp. 'It is I, Kadiya. How fare you?'

'Your warriors cannot help you now,' said a resonant female voice.

Before Kadiya could utter another sound the last of the bodies was pulled away and gauntleted hands took hold of her and hoisted her roughly upright. Vertigo dimmed her sight, her knee stabbed her with pain, and she would have collapsed had not two Sobranian warriors kept a grip on her.

Slowly she lifted her head. Her vision cleared and she saw that most of the mob had gone from the boulevard, leaving heaps of torn bodies in its wake. A troop of fronials all trapped in bejewelled damask encircled her, wheeling nervously amidst the carnage. The riders were armed head to toe in barbaric splendour and all wore scarlet feathered cloaks. Their leader, gazing down at Kadiya with a fierce smile, was a woman wearing a magnificent bird-shaped crown. Her armour was black-and-silver, and hanging from her neck was a platinum Star. She said: 'Bind the witch, Lucaibo, then secure the talisman. Do exactly as I instructed you, unless you would end up as Kiforo, Tedge, and those other luckless wights.'

One of Kadiya's captors tied her wrists and ankles while the other held her. Then the man named Lucaibo unbuckled her scabbard and lay it on the pavement. Looking down, Kadiya saw that the Three-Lobed Burning Eye lay in an open space on the blood-stained stones. The amber inset in the talisman's hilt was dull. Round about it lay a burly dead man with eyes wide open and five smoking husks that had once been human beings. Hostile persons had obviously tried to pick up the magical sword and had perished for their pains. But the unburnt body . . .

A pang of grief shot through Kadiya as she realized that it was Sainlat. The knight had not died through trampling; a two-pronged Sobranian sword was driven vertically into his throat.

'Go safely beyond, dear Companion,' she whispered, feeling tears spill down her cheeks.

She hardly noticed when Lucaibo used his steel-plated boot to nudge the scabbard over the dull-edged blade of the talisman, sheathing it safely. He then picked up the Burning Eye and strapped it to Kadiya's back, winding many turns of rope around her for good measure and fixing her upper arms immovably to her sides.

'Now put her over your saddle,' said the crowned woman, 'and we will proceed to the palace, where all is in readiness.'

'Where are my other three knights?' Kadiya asked in a low voice. 'And who are you?'

'Your henchmen are dead, witch, crushed by the mob. I am the Empress Naelore. It will be your privilege to see me ascend my throne – after I have turned your talisman over to Orogastus.'

CHAPTER 28

The Archimage of the Firmament had ensconced Haramis in a handsome apartment near his enormous library, urging her to make free use of it. He also introduced her to the several kinds of sindona who would attend to her every need – bearers, messengers, servers, consolers, and sentinels – and showed her fixed viaducts that would enable her to travel from one Moon to another. Then, saying he would return to her when the time was ripe, he hurried away toward his study.

'Ripe for *what?*' Haramis had demanded to know, running down the hall after him. The old man only tittered and slammed the study door in her face.

When she used the trillium-amber on her otherwise useless talisman to gain entrance, Denby was not inside. He had apparently used the study's viaduct to travel to an unknown destination, and this magical portal refused to activate when she spoke to it. Clearly, her amber did not consider the viaduct to be a true door.

Boiling with frustration, Haramis then went to the library and combed it for a clue that would enable her to escape. Three days passed, but she found no pertinent information about the working of the viaducts. However, one ancient reference, together with the schematic diagram of the Sceptre the Dark Man had given her, did seem to bear out what Orogastus had said earlier: The three talismans, put together, were capable of restoring the world to its original nonglaciated state if properly wielded. Unfortunately, the rebalancing would produce such horrendous changes in the climate and the continental landform that civilization would surely collapse – unless someone disciplined the terrified population with a will of iron and invincible magic.

A tyrant . . . like Orogastus.

After the dreadful confirmation, Haramis fled again to the Death Moon, crying out to the Vanished Ones who slept in limbo: 'Is there no other hope? Must it be a choice between the Conquering Ice and the ruthless regime of the Star Guild?'

The beautiful forms floating in their golden bubbles evoked no alterna-

267

tive solution, nor did her heartbroken pleas to the Black Trillium. Her own wisdom and common sense seemed to have deserted her, leaving only a void of despair.

'If I could only return to the land – to the solid ground that nourishes my personal magic! As long as I remain a prisoner here, there is no way I can reshape the awful destiny that Denby has decreed.'

Or was there?

The Dark Lord of the Firmament was an Archimage, after all, and bound by the solemn obligations of that office as she herself was. Neither of them could deliberately do harm to a thinking person . . .

She pondered a certain notion for a long time. Its success would depend upon capturing the madman's attention, and there seemed only one hope of doing that. She went to the Grotto of Memory in the Garden Moon and settled down on the bench in front of the shining world globe, praying in silence. After many hours a sindona consoler appeared, a being having the form of a woman dressed in a golden tunic, with a body as smooth and hard as ivory, yet able in some miraculous way to move as gracefully as a human being. The thing was kind and solicitous, exhorting Haramis to return to her apartment, partake of supper, and go to sleep.

But she refused. 'If you would really console me,' she told the living statue, 'tell Denby to grant me release from these Moons. Let me return to the land so that I may resume my duties, guiding the people who live there. Otherwise I will stay here in this grotto, neither eating nor drinking, until I pass safely beyond. And my death will be Denby's fault for having kept me unjustly imprisoned.'

The sindona bowed its gold-coiffed head. 'I will tell the Archimage of the Firmament what you have said.' It went away through a viaduct at the rear of the small cave, which Haramis had not noticed before.

She maintained her vigil for three days more, growing weaker and weaker from her fast and suffering a burning thirst. At last, lying prone upon the mossy cave floor, she heard the Dark Man call her name reproachfully.

She raised her head and spoke in a frail whisper. 'You are too early, Dark Man. I am not yet dead, and the talisman you covet is still bonded to me.'

'Whatever do you mean, my dear?' Denby's voice quavered with injured innocence.

She hauled herself up to a sitting position. 'Can we not be honest with each other? It is plain that you intend to keep me captive until I turn the Three-Winged Circle over to you – or until I die, and its bonding to my soul dissolves. Why else would you have brought me here?'

His purplish lips twitched into a sly smile. 'Perhaps to get to know you better . . . perhaps to teach you a thing or two about saving the world! It is not easy for a madman to know his own motives.'

She deliberately averted her face, as from a revolting spectacle. 'I do not believe you are mad at all. You are only old and mortally tired, and perversely determined to see the end of the dire game that you and your Archimagical colleagues started so long ago.'

'Why do you say that?'

'I found the account in your library – the one that Orogastus also read. For twelve thousand years you have manipulated the destiny of Folk and humankind as well, attempting vainly to undo the disaster you wrought during the war of enchantment. Perhaps you had the best interests of the world in mind at the beginning. But latterly, I think you became impatient. Your meddling became more reckless and capricious, with the result that the original world imbalance – which had been slowly healing – worsened drastically. And now the planet is doomed to be enveloped entirely in ice, and your arrogant tinkering is responsible.'

He spoke calmly. 'You are correct in all save your last statement.'

With difficulty she climbed to her feet and confronted him. 'Binah and Iriane did not understand that *you* were the reason for the world's fresh deterioration. Those two Archimages were genuinely selfless and benevolent. Under their plan, the Three Petals of the Living Trillium would have resurrected the Sceptre of Power and effected a great healing. They believed that the calamitous natural events that would attend the restoration of the lost balance might be abated by the loving influence of the Flower.'

Denby made an offhand gesture. 'Their scheme seemed worth a try.'

'But you only pretended to agree with them,' Haramis accused. 'You had already engendered a quicker, more drastic solution – and its name was Orogastus! You have embraced the dark philosophy of the Star, that would compel free souls to bow to a despot, supposedly for their own good.'

'If one waits upon the Triune,' the old man said coldly, 'one may wait indefinitely. I have waited twelve thousand years. I can wait no longer.'

Haramis eyed him with sudden understanding. 'You are dying.'

'Yes. And before I go, I will either see the balance restored, or see an ending! You and your precious sisters served my purposes by finding the lost pieces of the Sceptre. Powerful as I am, I was unable to do that. The talismans had been concealed by the sindona, so that no human would ever again use them as tools of aggression. When the Flower's magic led

269

you to them, I was quite surprised . . . But enough of this nattering! Why should I justify myself to a young upstart? You and your sisters are as cowardly as the original College of Archimagi. Their solution to the first world imbalance was to command the people to flee into the outer firmament! Since you are also afraid to use the Sceptre, you are irrelevant. Only Orogastus matters now.'

'My sisters and I did not fully understand the nature of our destiny nor that of the talismans. Given time, we might well have seen that the Sceptre is the world's only hope, and found a way to use it safely.'

'Time!' barked the old man contemptuously. 'There *is* no time! Orogastus now has the Burning Eye and the Three-Headed Monster. He must be given the third piece of the Sceptre at once – and he must use it. The earthquakes that herald the end have already begun. Soon the continental crust will fracture in a thousand places. Newborn volcanos will belch forth their dust and lava, darkening the sun and poisoning the sea for all time. Only the Sempiternal Ice will endure!'

Having made this awful pronouncement, he faltered, seeming to be overcome with a profound weariness. He waved one gnarled hand feebly, and two Sentinels of the Mortal Dictum appeared from the viaduct inside the grotto. The living statues with their crown-helms and belts of shining blue and green scales stood side by side, serene and deadly, with golden skulls tucked beneath their left arms.

'Haramis,' Denby whispered, 'give me the Three-Winged Circle. Command it to rest harmlessly in my hands and I will set you free at once, so that you may rescue your sisters Anigel and Kadiya. Refuse me and they will both meet an atrocious death.'

She rose again to her feet, touching the trillium-amber of her talisman, which hung on its chain at her neck. 'No. I think you are bluffing.'

'Am I? See for yourself.'

He stepped up to the world globe and touched it. The geographical features vanished and the globe became a great scry-sphere filled with pearly vapour. The mist congealed into images, and Haramis saw a dismal chamber containing many instruments of torture. Chained to one wall and sitting in a pile of straw was Kadiya, her face blank with hopelessness. She was watching as a squad of laughing guards headed by a Star Man dragged in four unconscious prisoners. One was a redheaded individual unknown to Haramis, another was King Ledavardis of Raktum, the third was Prince Tolivar, and the last was Anigel herself, whose dirty garments were half torn from her body. The villain wearing the Star dropped the Queen roughly upon the straw and began fastening rusty manacles to her wrists.

Haramis cried out in horror, and the vision within the globe was instantly extinguished.

'They are in Sobrania,' Denby said without emotion, 'captives of the new Empress, Naelore, who seized the throne of that country after personally decapitating her brother Denombo. You should know that tomorrow morning your sisters and their companions will be tortured to death . . . unless Orogastus has your talisman in hand by sunrise.'

'He – he would never do such a thing!' Haramis asserted. 'Not even for the Three-Winged Circle.'

'Perhaps not,' the Archimage of the Firmament conceded. 'But I assure you that the lovely Naelore will do so with enthusiasm, now that a mysterious magical voice has planted the notion in her mind. The Empress is most vexed because Orogastus neither attended her coronation nor otherwise assisted in the consolidation of her power following the coup. Instead, he closeted himself in a room of the imperial palace with the two talismans. His purpose is to re-familiarize himself with their operation . . . so that he may find you.'

'*Me?*'

'You.'

'To – to compel me to surrender my talisman to him?'

'Not even that. The besotted imbecile would merely bespeak you sweetly, to continue his futile attempts to convert you to his point of view through what he thinks of as logic. And love.' Denby gave a snort of derision. 'Faugh – he is a disappointment! A sentimental fool who must be goaded back onto the correct path of action. The Empress Naelore will see to it – with my help.'

'I – I don't understand.'

The old man began to laugh uncontrollably, and only when his mirth trailed away into a coughing spasm did he regain control of himself. 'Oh, it's such a delicious irony. Naelore has an unrequited passion for Orogastus, just as *he* has for *you*, my dear! The Empress has already presented her beloved sorcerer with Kadiya's talisman. Poor woman – she was so crestfallen at his aloof response. She thinks now that if she were able to give him your talisman as well, Orogastus would be more grateful. Especially if such gratitude were a condition of her bestowing the gift . . . as the mysterious voice in her ear suggests.'

'You vile manipulator!' Haramis cried out in loathing. 'Must you treat everyone like a game-piece?'

'Evidently, yes. It's very tedious.' He held out his brown hand. 'The Circle. Give it to me now, or take responsibility for the final conquest of the Ice.'

271

'You arrogant bully!' she cried. 'I don't believe that Orogastus is the world's only hope – and I think that you yourself also have doubts. You are so proud and so consumed with guilt that you refuse to give consideration to any solution but your own!'

'Give me the Circle,' he repeated, 'or I will command the sentinels to take it from you. As you well know, they are able to kill.'

'You would violate your Archimage's oath?' she asked him steadily, already knowing the answer.

He said, 'Don't be silly. I would do whatever is needful.'

Abruptly, Haramis rushed at the old man with arms stiffly outstretched, giving him a sharp push that sent him staggering back into the arms of the sentinels, squeaking with surprise. Before he could act to stop her, she darted into the grotto's interior and said: 'Viaduct system, activate!' She stepped through the black circle and disappeared.

'You shall not defy me!' Denby screamed. 'Not like *she* did!' He limped to the viaduct and entered it, calling out to the two sindona to follow.

He had programmed this magical portal to open into his own study in the Dark Man's Moon. When he emerged he saw Haramis striding toward a round door beside the big observation window. It was the same one he had bade her beware of when they first met, six days earlier. He shouted, 'Stop!'

'My trillium-amber will open any lock,' she said, turning to face him. 'Even this one.' She lifted the wand, and the golden droplet nestled amidst the wings glowed in response.

'Don't!' he wailed, standing frozen between the two sentinels. 'That hatch is a relic of the Days of Vanishing and opens now into the airless void between the Moons. We will both die if you open it, and the talisman will be lost forever!'

'Then so be it,' Haramis said. 'At least your diabolical game will end. Let our world meet whatever fate that the Triune intends – not one that you dictate.'

'Stop her!' Denby shrilled to the sentinels.

Before Haramis could command the door to open, the right arms of the sindona whipped up, their fingers pointing directly at her. She saw two beams of near-invisible light lance out, stop a scant hand's span away, and reflect back as her trillium-amber flared. A stunning explosion rocked the room. Blinded and coughing in a sudden cloud of dust, she fell against the closed hatch, clapping her hands to her face in an instinctive gesture of protection. She expected instant death; the sentinels should have blasted her body to ashes, leaving only her seared cranium intact. But instead she heard a great clatter, as though a devastating hailstorm assaulted the room. Finally there was silence, broken only by a faint bubbling moan.

Lowering her hands, she saw through the dust that the study was in ruins, except for a small area immediately surrounding her. The leather chairs had been shredded, the desk and table and sideboard reduced to kindling, the bookshelves toppled and smashed, the ancient scientific instruments battered into shapeless, twisted metal. On the floor were deep piles of sharp ivory-coloured fragments, mingled with coloured bits of blue and green mosaic. A single undamaged golden skull had rolled to her feet.

He lay half-buried in the rubble, bleeding from a hundred wounds. Haramis went to him and knelt, lifting his head. There were no recognizable features within the mask of dusty gore save for his mouth.

'I will call a consoler,' she began, 'one of the sindona healers –'

'Too late.' The words were barely discernible. 'The Black Trillium . . . I might have known . . . older than the College, older than the Star . . . Three Petals to wield and the Sky Archimage to guide, if you wish it, Haramis . . . love is permissible, devotion is not . . . I only wanted to save it . . . the poor world.'

'I know.' She cradled him in her arms. The droplet of amber was dazzling bright. 'Tell me how I may return.'

'Nerenyi's . . . viaduct.' The two words were forced out with his last breath. Then Denby Varcour, last hero of the Vanished Ones and Archimage of the Firmament, passed safely beyond.

She summoned one of the sindona consolers to effect her own healing from the ordeal of the fasting. It was necessarily incomplete, for what she most needed was restful sleep; but afterwards she was able to eat and drink and don her white tunic and trousers and her cloak of office in preparation for departure. When she left her apartment, she was astonished to find a throng of other living statues waiting in the lobby outside. There were seventeen servers, twelve bearers, five messengers, another consoler, and twenty-two sentinels.

'These servants are ready,' said the consoler who had attended her, 'to obey you without question now that the Archimage of the Firmament is no more.'

'Will you show to me the operation of the viaduct transport system,' Haramis asked, 'so that I may choose my destination upon entering?'

One of the messenger sindona stepped forward. 'I can do that readily, Archimage, provided that you use a viaduct capable of being programmed.

273

Some systems have a fixed routing. It will require some twenty hours of study for you to learn the programming process.'

'So long?' Haramis exclaimed in dismay. 'But I must rescue my poor sisters and the others before the sun rises in the land of Sobrania!'

'The viaduct within the chamber of Nerenyi Daral is one of those that is fixed,' the messenger said. 'It will transport you to the place where you wish to go if you simply step into it. Furthermore, if you take me with you when you travel, I will be able to reprogram other viaducts according to your commands.'

'Thanks be to the Flower!' She gave a great sigh of relief and thought hard for a moment. Then she said, 'All of you save this one messenger wait here until I order you to attend me.' The gently smiling heads nodded in compliance. 'You,' Haramis said to the chosen sindona, 'lead me at once to the viaduct of Nerenyi Daral.'

CHAPTER 29

The magical portal opened into a small grove of trees. When Haramis emerged into the open, followed by the messenger, she found a dirt road paralleling a bluff beside the sea. The Three Moons shone overhead, framed by racing clouds, and a brisk wind blowing in from the water carried a few preliminary drops of rain. There were glimpses of lightning out to sea, and a faint muttering of thunder. The country round about was rocky and desolate, except for a darkened small villa fashioned of white stone situated on a promontory across the road. Below the house on either side were pebble beaches pounded by waves that were oddly luminescent and sluggish.

'Exactly where are we?' Haramis asked her Three-Winged Circle. The sindona messenger had known only that the viaduct opened in Sobrania.

This is the former villa of the Empress Naelore, said the talisman. *It lies three and one-quarter leagues south of the capital city of Brandoba.*

'Does anyone abide here?'

It has been abandoned for two years, since Naelore and her chief steward Tazor joined the Star Guild.

Haramis nodded in satisfaction and said to the sindona at her side, 'Then we will take possession.'

Commanding her talisman to shield the house from the oversight of Orogastus or any other enemy, she unlocked the door and went inside. The place was musty and drear, with a few pieces of simple furniture remaining. The sitting room overlooked the sea, and on one side was a vista of Brandoba up the coast. Fires seemed to be burning in several parts of the city, for the clouds over it were tinged with baleful crimson and orange. There was also a peculiar intermittent red glow in the eastern sky that was too irregular to be the light of dawn.

Haramis studied the scene for a few minutes, sore perplexed, then lifted her talisman. 'Why is Brandoba burning?'

Fires were started during the riots that accompanied the invasion by Orogastus.

She put more questions to the Circle until she had obtained a full picture of the successful coup and the way in which Kadiya, Anigel, and the others had been captured. It now lacked three hours until sunrise. The capital city was under the control of Naelore's loyalists and the Star Guild. Denombo, his nobles, and most of the imperial guard had been slaughtered, and many thousands of ordinary people had died in the rioting, which had now almost completely subsided. There was no organized opposition to the conquerors. The new Empress had been hastily crowned, and subordinate kings and tribal chieftains of Sobrania who had been in the city for the Festival of the Birds were tripping over one another in their eagerness to acclaim her.

The woeful tidings did not surprise Haramis. She made no attempt to view Orogastus, recalling that when he last possessed two talismans, years ago during the siege of Derorguila, he was somehow able to scry her whereabouts whenever she had Sight of him. The time for their confrontation had not yet come.

When she tried to ascertain the exact place where her sisters were being held, Haramis was frustrated by the Star's magic that still blanketed the imperial palace, as it had when she first tried to warn Denombo of the Star Guild's peril. Unfortunately, there was no convenient viaduct anywhere inside the palace wall or even hard by that she might use, and so it would not be possible for the sindona to assist her in the rescue. She would have to transport herself bodily inside in order to save her sisters and their companions. Carrying them away was possible, but it would strain her magic to the utmost; and if Orogastus should discover her, he would undoubtedly be able to frustrate the rescue by using his two talismans.

But there seemed to be no alternative.

Almost as an afterthought, Haramis asked the Three-Winged Circle about the mysterious distant glow in the eastern sky. The reply astounded her.

It is the reflection of molten lava issuing forth from certain craters in the Collum Range, over a hundred leagues away. The peaks are of volcanic origin, with deep layers of ash on their slopes that were formerly covered with snow and ice. The heat of the upwelling lava has melted the ice and created great mudflows, which increase in volume with every passing hour.

'Will – will the flow reach Brandoba?' Haramis whispered.

It follows the beds of local rivers. The River Dob, which bisects the city, is a principal conduit. Mud will eventually fill the basin where Brandoba lies to a depth of over fifty ells.

'How long –?'

Less than four hours.

276

'Good God! Does Orogastus know what is happening?'

No.

'Show me the flow of mud that menaces the city.'

She closed her eyes, and saw a forested valley illumined by moonlight. Many of the trees were tottering and falling into a viscous grey tide swirling about their trunks. One particular tree caught her attention, an enormous thing with lower branches an ell thick. Although its trunk was engulfed, it stood fast while lesser trees on either side of it subsided into the flow.

There were people clinging to its upper parts.

'Holy Flower,' murmured the Archimage, wondering who the flood victims might be. She concentrated her Sight upon them and immediately recognized Princess Raviya and Prince Widd of Engi, Queen Jiri of Galanar, President Hakit Botal of Okamis, and the Imlit Duumviri Prigo and Ga-Bondies. Even as she watched, the great tree that gave them refuge shuddered and tilted. Its roots were being undermined by the mudflow.

Haramis let the talisman fall from her hand and sat staring out the window of the villa. If she used her magic to carry away the imperilled rulers, she might not have enough strength remaining to rescue her sisters. But the tree would fall at any moment, while Ani and Kadi were safe at least until sunrise . . .

Taking a deep breath of resolution, she vanished like the blowing out of a candleflame.

The crystalline vision that signified magical transport darkened and turned into gale-lashed leafy branches. Haramis found herself hovering in mid-air beside the tree. She lifted her arms and her archimagical cloak became like sunlit snow, lucent white with brilliant blue shadings. The trillium-amber in her talisman was a miniature golden star, held on high like a beacon.

'My friends!' The Archimage's voice rang like a great bell. 'I have come to rescue you.'

The heads of state cried out in relief, and all except Ga-Bondies, who began to blubber incoherently, hurled questions at Haramis.

'There is no time to explain,' she said. 'I must take you out of danger, then return to Brandoba and do what I can to avert this impending catastrophe.'

'God help you,' Queen Jiri called out from her perch. 'The mud is heading straight for the city. We tried to veer away from it to the left while we still rode our fronials, but another great channel full of sludge cut us off.'

Old Princess Raviya piped up, 'Will you carry us away through magic, dear?'

'Yes,' said Haramis. 'Two at a time. You and Widd first. Come and stand together so that I may cover you with my cloak.'

The elderly couple scrambled upright on one of the larger branches, a task made doubly perilous as the wind blew keenly and the tree continued to sway and sag closer to the mudflow. Haramis drifted close, embraced the Prince and Princess, and all three disappeared. A few minutes passed, after which the Archimage alone reappeared. Her occult aura had faded and her face was tense with the great effort.

'Now Jiri and Ga-Bondies,' she commanded.

'Where are you taking us?' the stout Duumvir demanded fretfully.

'To a certain villa by the sea, south of Brandoba. It is the best I can do for the time being. Transporting other persons strains my magical powers to the utmost.' She put her arms about the two ample figures and vanished once again.

Her return took much longer this time, and when she reappeared she floated with her head bowed, praying for strength, while the strong wind billowed her cloak and the tree continued to subside. The two remaining men, fearing to move, were side by side on a branch less than an ell above the roiling flood.

Prigo called out, 'Are you sure you can do this, Archimage?'

'No,' she admitted. 'And if I falter in mid-route, there is a chance we will all three perish in some unknown realm of darkness.'

The tree gave a violent lurch as its roots were finally torn loose. It began to revolve and float away, and the grey flux covered the men's feet.

'Take us,' screamed Hakit Botal. 'Any death is preferable to drowning in mud!'

Haramis snatched them up like a voor stooping for its prey. 'Talisman! Transport us to the villa by the sea.'

The chime signalling the start of the magical journey sounded, but it was discordant and off-pitch. Her mind attempted to construct the crystal image of their destination, but the magical depiction shivered, assumed a sinister fluidity, and melted away to formlessness. For many heartbeats Haramis and her passengers hung suspended in a pool of prismatic brilliance. Their lungs could draw no breath and the wild chiming sound intensified to the point of agony. Prigo and Hakit felt the arms of the Archimage weaken. The uncanny vision dimmed. They began slipping away from her, smothering, into an abyss filled with mind-crushing clamour.

Holy Flower, be thou my protection and strength!

Light! A dwelling fashioned from rainbows, standing on land that was an enormous faceted diamond . . . changing slowly, becoming ordinary, becoming real. The two despairing rulers could finally breathe. They smelled seaweed, felt rain on their faces, saw the villa's wet stone walls glimmering in the windy dark. Their boots touched rocky soil and they were safe, supporting each other to keep from collapsing.

The door of the dwelling opened. A lofty figure stood silhouetted within the frame and a flash of lightning revealed it to be inhuman, an exquisitely carved female statue of ivory and gold that nonetheless moved. As Prigo and Hakit Botal quailed in confusion, the thing emerged into the rain, bent down, and picked up the senseless Archimage in its gleaming arms.

'Are you injured?' the consoler asked the officials. They shook their heads mutely. The living statue began to carry its burden into the house, looking back over its shoulder and saying, 'Enter. There is food and drink for you inside, and warm clothing. Do not be afraid. I am a sindona, one of the White Lady's servants.'

'Is – is she going to be all right?' Prigo inquired timidly, following after.

'She will awake betimes and go about her work,' the consoler replied. 'As to the other, I cannot say.'

My love . . . speak to me!

The talismans have told me that you are no longer in the Dark Man's Moon, but they will not reveal your whereabouts except to say that you are in Sobrania. I know that Denby is dead. I know that you retain the Three-Winged Circle. Are you well? Did that madman harm you trying to take away your talisman?

Haramis, say a single word!

Only bespeak and I will See and come to you. We dare not wait any longer. The ground trembles beneath the palace and I am unable to calm it through my magic. I am uncertain whether these small earthquakes portend the start of the final catastrophe. The talismans that I possess refuse to speak of it.

If you know the truth, then tell me!

You know what the ancient spell says: The Wand of the Wings, your own talisman, is the key to the Sceptre and its unifier. Without it, the Burning Eye and the Three-Headed Monster are futile.

I am futile.

Come to me, here in the feathered barbarian's palace – or let me come to you! We must assemble the Sceptre of Power together and use it before it is too late.

Haramis! Haramis, my only love . . . speak.

*   *   *

279

'Dawn . . . Tell me it is not yet dawn!' She struggled up from the improvised pallet. Queen Jiri was kneeling at her side, laving her forehead with a wet cloth. An impassive sindona consoler stood behind her, holding a basin of water. The sky visible through the villa window was full of pallid mauve clouds.

'They will be killed at dawn!' Haramis cried. 'Let me up –'

'Peace, dear!' The Galanari Queen put an arm about her. 'It lacks half an hour to sunrise. This – this odd servant of yours told us the impending fate of your sisters. It also said that you would have to sleep as much as possible to restore your strength, if you were to have any chance of saving them.'

The Archimage relaxed. 'Half an hour. Yes . . . it will suffice.' She sat up slowly, saying to the consoler, 'Bring me my cloak.' When the sindona left the room, Haramis accepted some of the wine that Jiri offered. 'Where are the other rulers?'

'Another kind of statue-person took them away into a viaduct across the road,' the Queen told her, 'explaining that it would bring them safely home to their own countries. I decided to stay with you, even though the nurse–statue tried to prevent me. It said that when the mudflow reaches Brandoba, there will be a great earthquake and a tidal wave will wash away the villa – along with whatever parts of the city are not already buried in mud. Is that true?'

Haramis passed one trembling hand over her brow. 'The dire events will come to pass . . . unless I can prevent it.'

Jiri sat back upon her heels and looked calmly upon the Archimage. 'Can you?'

Shall I tell her? Haramis wondered. Tell her that it is not only Brandoba, but the entire world that is on the verge of destruction?

Her fingers dropped to the talisman hanging about her neck. The Circle's wings were open and the drop of amber with its fossil Black Trillium throbbed with each beat of her heart.

Holy Flower, can you not advise me? If I give Orogastus the third piece of the Sceptre, he might be able to prevent the ultimate unbalancing. He could certainly turn aside the deadly flow of mud. Is it my destiny to surrender to the Star? Black Trillium, is this what I must do?

But the Flower within the amber was silent, as always, and she was afraid to pose the questions to the talisman.

Eyes welling, Haramis turned for comfort to the older woman kneeling at her side. The maternal countenance of the Queen of Galanar wore a melancholy smile that still reflected invincible hope. Seen through the screen of tears, that smile reminded Haramis of another woman long dead, one who had bestowed upon her and her sisters magical amulets, who had sent them on their talisman quests, who had finally given over to Haramis her own precious cloak.

Daughter of the Threefold, do not lose heart.

'Binah?' Haramis whispered incredulously.

The White Lady who had been godmother to the Petals of the Living Trillium said: *Years come and go with speed. That which is lofty may fall, that which is cherished may be lost, that which is hidden must, in time, be revealed. And yet I tell you that all will be well. Believe it, Daughter! Remember the last words of the Archimage of the Firmament. Remember . . .*

Haramis blinked away the tears. Queen Jiri was now gazing at her with an expression of anxiety. The sindona consoler, standing there holding the shimmering white cape in its ivory hands, inquired, 'Archimage, are you well?'

'Yes,' she said. 'Help me to my feet.'

Jiri and the sindona raised her. Haramis put on her cloak, then said to the living statue, 'Return this good woman promptly to her realm of Galanar.' She then kissed Jiri on her cheek. 'Dear friend, whatever happens to me, you can be sure that your own people will soon have great need of your courage and wisdom. Do not fail them. If the Triune wills, I will come soon to assist you. Farewell.'

Clasping her talisman, Haramis disappeared.

'What did she mean?' Jiri asked the sindona. For the first time, she seemed fearful.

'She means that the day of the Sky Trillium has come upon the world,' the living statue said, 'but what its blossoming portends, only the Lords of the Air can say. Come along, Queen. I will take you home to your family and your loyal subjects. That which is hidden will, in time, be revealed.'

CHAPTER 30

Distant clanks and rattles announced that the outer door of the imperial prison block was being unbarred. Queen Anigel stirred, opening her eyes with a soft yawn. 'Ah, dear friends – is it dawn already?'

'I fear so,' King Ledavardis said to her gently. They were all shackled in a row, slumped against the wall in heaps of stinking straw. High up near the torture chamber's ceiling were narrow embrasures, through which they could see dull purple clouds.

Anigel sat up and began to brush off and arrange her torn garments. 'Then we shall have to do our best to die well . . . I only regret that Kadi and I were deprived of our trillium-amber. The Holy Flower might have bolstered my puny sense of valour.'

'To say nothing of unlocking our fetters,' said Kadiya wryly. 'Ah, well. We must take solace from the knowledge that we will not suffer our fate in vain.'

Anigel's blue eyes seemed rapt by some comforting inner vision. 'We must all pass safely beyond sooner or later. But only a fortunate few are allowed to die in defence of a world. May the Lords of the Air come for us swiftly.'

The King and Archduke Gyorgibo murmured their assent, as did Kadiya. But unlike the Queen, who appeared calm almost to the point of entrancement, the others could not keep their eyes from the array of fiendish instruments mounted upon the wall opposite, nor from the stained and pitted granite slab three ells long that stood in the chamber's centre. The slab was inclined, and cuffs for wrists and ankles were affixed to the lower end; just beyond the other end was a large brick structure resembling a forge. A bellows, operated by wooden gearing that Gyorgibo had said was connected to a windmill, had pumped air into the fire-box all night, keeping it glowing, and from time to time a soot-stained minion had shuffled in to add charcoal and stoke it. Two massive chains were attached to something buried in the bed of coals. Forming an inverted V, they joined to a single chain which was in turn suspended from a pulley device on an overhead iron beam. Gyorgibo had stubbornly refused to speak about what the thing hidden in the fire might be.

Voices could now be heard approaching, and a harsh peal of female laughter echoed along the vaulted corridor outside the chamber.

The Archduke said, 'My imperial sister is coming to supervise our final torment. She seems in high spirits.'

'Much good may it do her,' growled Kadiya. 'It is probable that the Archimage Haramis is still held by the Man in the Moon, and knows nothing whatsoever of our own imprisonment. I would give much to see Naelore's face when she discovers she has squandered the lives of crucial hostages for naught.'

King Ledavardis sighed. 'I wouldn't.' He turned to Anigel. 'It seems that I will not be your son-in-law after all, dear Queen. May I at least ask now for your blessing, and your forgiveness for the harm I inflicted upon your family and your kingdom so long ago?'

'I give them willingly. And . . . I have changed my mind about you, Ledo. If our fate had been otherwise, I would gladly have given the hand of my daughter Janeel to you in marriage.'

Prince Tolivar, placed between Anigel and the King by a compassionate jailer, had remained so quiet that the adult captives thought he still slept. He said to Ledavardis, 'I would also have been proud to be your brother. The way that you rescued Mother and me was – was legendary!'

'You stood up to the sorcerer most bravely yourself, Tolo.' The King clenched his right fist except for the little finger, which he extended to the Prince like a hook. 'Join your own last finger with mine, thus! Come, now, don't hesitate. I have a last gift for you . . . Tolivar of Laboruwenda, I dub thee a Corsair of Raktum, and herewith declare that you are both my brother and shipmate on the high seas! . . . There. Now we are sworn.'

Awe and delight spread over the Prince's features as he stared at the linked fingers. 'I am a true *pirate?*'

'As ever was! Only remember that we Raktumians are reformed now, and the title is one of honour.'

'I – I will try to die honourably under the torture,' Tolivar said to him in a voice barely steady. 'But if I make a lot of noise, please do not hold it to my shame.'

'Pirates never suffer in silence! Make all the noise you like, lad – and I shall bellow louder still, because I am the Pirate King.'

The iron-bound door banged open. Four men, bare to the waist and having their heads covered with black leather hoods, marched inside. They were followed by the Empress Naelore, who was dressed in a maroon

283

velvet robe trimmed with silver-blue diksu fur. She wore a simple platinum diadem on her coiled hair, and hanging from her neck was the Star of Nerenyi Daral.

'Good morrow,' she said. When no one responded, she tossed her head, smiling thinly. 'You will learn politeness soon enough! Unless a certain Archimage decides that she values your paltry lives above her talisman.' She nodded to the torturers. 'Make ready.'

The men went efficiently about their business. One took a poker to the fire, two began cranking away at a winch behind the forge, and the fourth checked the restraints on the grisly stone slab.

The Empress struck a dramatic pose, hands on high, and cried out in a loud voice to the thin air. 'Haramis, Archimage of the Land! I know that you are able to hear and see us. I, too, have secret friends in the realm of magic! One of them, speaking covertly in my ear, has told me how to secure the Three-Winged Circle. Come now, Archimage! Abase yourself before me and give up your talisman, and these captives will be spared. Ignore me and they will endure a frightful death.'

The torturers wound away at the winch, hauling something out of the coals. Slowly, a white-hot iron drum emerged, an ell or so long and perhaps two handspans in diameter. Through it ran a horizontal bar, having at its ends rings connecting it to the twin chains. When the cylinder was hoist above the foot of the slab and somewhat cooled, the prisoners were able to see that the thing was a kind of roller. Its incandescent surface was studded with a myriad of sharp spikes.

'Heldo's Holy Haunches!' breathed the awe-struck Ledavardis. The others, save Gyorgibo, who had known well enough what to expect, were too appalled to utter a word.

'Haramis!' Naelore lifted her Star. 'Do not tarry! It is sunrise. The deadline that I posed to you has come.'

Nothing happened.

Kadiya spoke out. 'Empress, does the Star Master know and approve of this torture?'

'Be silent, witch!' Naelore commanded.

But Kadiya persevered. 'I told you last night that my sister Haramis was visiting the Three Moons. She is unable to respond to a magical hail. I myself was unable to bespeak her, even using the two talismans. This ploy of yours is useless.'

'Sister, why do you do this?' Gyorgibo cried in entreaty. 'Kill me, if you must, but these others have done you no harm.'

'*She* has!' the Empress raged. 'The haughty White Lady! And if she lives, she will hear their cries, whether she resides with the Man in the

Moon or hides in the lowest of the ten hells.' And again she called out to Haramis, in tones increasingly furious and frenzied.

The Archduke shook his head. 'Playing at sorcery has unhinged her reason.'

'No,' Anigel said sadly. 'It is another kind of derangement that afflicts her.'

'Be quiet!' Naelore roared. 'Or I will have your tongues torn out!'

The captives fell silent. One of the hooded men said, 'Imperial Majesty, all is ready.'

Drops of perspiration beaded the high brow of the Empress and her face was flushed. She began pacing back and forth in front of the five chained captives, twisting her Star on its chain with a restless hand. 'Which one shall be the first to feel the fiery roller's caress? The ugly and foolhardy Pirate King? . . . Nay, I think not. He is insufficiently beloved by the White Lady. Why should she trade her talisman for the life of a one-eyed, hunchbacked sea-bandit? And for that same reason I will neither choose you, my worthless Baby Brother, even though your agony would give me the greatest pleasure.' She uttered a giddy laugh.

Gyorgibo's face had become a stony mask. He did not deign to speak.

The Empress paused to confront Anigel. 'Shall it be this woebegone and grubby Queen? Poor pathetic creature! Ah – but you sprained your ankle attempting to escape, didn't you, and fainted away from that insignificant pain as my war-lords fetched you here. I fear you would perish with unseemly swiftness under the torture, perhaps before the Archimage even took note of your cries of agony.'

'Try me, Skritek spawn,' hissed Kadiya, straining at her chains.

Naelore pretended to consider the suggestion. 'The brave witch who would have thwarted our invasion and deprived me of my throne! But you wept when I gave your talisman to the Star Master. You bawled like a whipped snithe pup! I think I would like to see you weep again, and beg my clemency' – she stepped forward and seized Prince Tolivar by his hair – 'as this treacherous brat finally pays the penalty for sinning so grievously against you.'

'He is forgiven by us all!' Kadiya shouted.

But Naelore beckoned peremptorily, and two of the torturers came to unfasten the Prince from the wall fetters and drag him unprotesting to the long granite slab. The hooded men fussed about, having trouble adjusting the gyves to accommodate Tolivar's slight body; but finally the boy was immobilized at the low end of the tilted slab.

The Empress came and brushed aside a lock of damp fair hair that had

285

fallen into the Prince's eyes. 'You must be able to see, brave lad,' she cooed. Then she shouted to the ceiling, 'And the Archimage Haramis must also see! Watch his face, White Lady, as the fiery roller burns and crushes him from toe to head.'

She snapped her fingers. Two of the torturers bent again to the winch, this time unwinding it. The other pair hauled away at a thick rope that swung the travelling block and tackle forward, so that the heavy, red-glowing drum came down precisely onto the slab's upper end, less than an ell and a half away from the Prince's feet. The spiked cylinder touched the inclined stone surface and, of itself, began to move with excruciating slowness toward the boy, shrieking hideously on its axle-bar. The men at the winch left off their labours and stood back expectantly, while the others on the rope controlled the roller's progress, lest it do its job too quickly.

'Haramis!' Naelore cried. She stood at the slab's opposite end, just behind Tolivar's head. 'Are you watching?'

The flagstone floor of the torture chamber trembled.

'Earthquake!' Ledavardis shouted, but no one heeded him – least of all the Empress. Her eyes were locked upon the advancing roller and her hands gripped the edge of the stone torture-bed.

The fiery cylinder on its chains was pulled sideways as the room swayed, but Naelore only braced herself, waiting. Spikes grated on the rough stone, flinging sparks in all directions, as all four torturers hauled at the rope and got the smoking roller back on course. It continued toward Prince Tolivar.

There was another tremor more violent than the first.

The torturers howled curses, staggering against one another and dancing about, trying to hang onto the rope while avoiding hot coals that spilled from the ruptured forge in an incandescent welter. A great crack rent the wall opposite the chained prisoners, and instruments of torment that had hung there fell clanging to the floor. From beneath the chamber came a profound rumbling, shot through with creaks and an uncanny moaning sound.

The spiked cylinder accelerated along the slab. The four men abandoned the rope and ran from the room in spite of the angry cries of the Empress. Tolivar felt the heat scorch the soles of his boots and a wail like that of a terrified infant was torn from his lips.

Above him, a dazzling white figure sprang into existence. He saw the Archimage Haramis pointing her talisman. His shackles sprang open and his helpless form levitated, flying sideways as the fiery drum, no longer restrained, sped over the place where he had lain.

At the slab's end it swung out on its chains like a glowing pendulum. The Empress Naelore tried to back away from it, too panic-stricken to call upon the magic of her Star. It struck her full in the face. Tolivar, now shrieking for his mother, felt himself lowered to the floor. Beneath the oscillating red-hot cylinder was a thing that writhed and convulsed and would not be still.

The boy's gorge rose as a vile odour of burnt cloth and seared meat reached his nostrils. He fell to his knees, vomiting, then tried to pull himself together as he heard the Archimage call his name. She had freed the other prisoners and was herding them toward the door.

'Tolo! Hasten!'

When he faltered, compelled irresistibly to look back at the horror he might have suffered himself, Haramis soared to him and seized his hand. Far overhead, something cracked with a thunderous report and the vaulted ceiling of the torture chamber began to collapse. The Prince flew over the flagstones, through the doorway, and into the corridor, dragged along behind the shining white cloak.

When he touched down again the floor was solid beneath his feet. The temblors seemed to have ended and the masonry of the corridor held firm, although the room they had just quit was a mass of rubble. Nearly all of the wall-cressets had fallen from their brackets, but they still flickered in the dust-laden air. Queen Anigel snatched Tolivar up in a joyful hug. The others stood about coughing and exclaiming with relief.

When they had all caught their breaths, Haramis said, 'Sisters, I have something for you.' In each hand she held a glowing droplet of trillium-amber, strung on simple thongs. Anigel and Kadiya took their amulets, kissed them, and hung them about their necks.

There were no sounds at all from the demolished torture chamber, but faint cries came from the other direction.

Ledavardis, who remembered too well the earthquake that had attended the siege of Derorguila, spoke urgently. 'We must get to open ground quickly. If another tremor strikes, it may bring the palace down around our ears.'

Kadiya addressed the Archimage. 'Can you carry us off by magic?'

'I'm sorry. That would require great strength, and mine was depleted earlier when I rescued the other kidnapped rulers from –'

'They are safe?' Anigel exclaimed. 'Oh, Hara! Thank God!'

'Then we have no choice but to run for it,' Kadiya decided.

'That way.' Gyorgibo pointed. 'Up the stairs. We can go through the barracks of the Imperial Guard into the north transept of the great rotunda, and thence escape into one of the garden courtyards.'

Haramis said, 'I can still defend us well enough. It is only the magical transport that is temporarily beyond me.'

'Ani, can you walk?' Kadiya asked the Queen.

'The Holy Flower has healed my petty wound. I am hale again – and so filled with bliss that I can scarce help bursting into tears!'

'Restrain yourself,' muttered the Lady of the Eyes, 'at least until we are safely out of here, when you may weep to your heart's content. I may even join you . . .'

They ran up the narrow stairwell into a barracks anteroom, which showed considerable damage. Several roof-beams had fallen and part of a long wall had tumbled down. They picked their way carefully through the mess. The place was completely deserted save for a lone member of the Imperial Guard, a grizzled fellow in half-armour who sat amidst a heap of building stones, covered in dust and clutching his lower leg.

'They've all run off,' he croaked, as Haramis and Gyorgibo discovered him. 'Yonder wall fell on me. My mates must have thought I was a goner. The torturers who went galloping through a few minutes ago didn't give a damn. So here I sit with my leg broke.'

The Archimage stooped and touched the limb with her talisman. The guard uttered a surprised oath and began poking and prodding at the place where the wound had been. 'Blessed Matuta! You've fixed it, sorceress!' He jumped up, then regarded her with sudden confusion. 'But if you're one of them – where's your Star?'

'She needs none,' said a quiet male voice.

Haramis rose and turned slowly about. Orogastus stood in the far doorway of the ruined anteroom. He wore the silver-and-black vestments of his Guild and its Star medallion, but lacked the forbidding starburst mask. His visage was furrowed with stress, his long white hair hung free, and on his brow was the Three-Headed Monster. A scabbard at the sorcerer's side held the Burning Eye, and his right hand rested upon its triple pommel.

'Leave us!' he commanded the cringing guardsman, who fled.

Haramis said, 'So you have found us, Orogastus. I thought you would.'

'I knew of your presence as soon as you materialized in the torture chamber. I had been seeking you for hours.'

'Then you know that Naelore is dead.'

His well-formed lips tightened in anger. 'The fool! Believe me – I did not know what she planned. I suppose she hoped to coerce you into giving up your talisman.'

'She intended to present it to you,' Haramis told him, 'and thereby win your love.'

288

He made a gesture of exasperation. 'Love? Love *her*? What arrant non-sense! All I thought of, from the time I bonded the two talismans to myself, was finding you.'

'So you could work upon me your own form of coercion? Still . . . I am relieved that you did not approve the torture.'

'The man who would have done such a thing is no more, Haramis. Why can't you believe it?' The sorcerer came toward her, arms outstretched. 'Why can't you understand –'

'I understand you quite well, just as I understood that prideful wretch, Denby Varcour, who created you! You are both manipulators of human emotions and deeds, consumed with arrogance and vainglory.'

His arms dropped again to his sides and his tender expression turned to one of desolation. 'My love for you is honest and I am not afraid to proclaim it. You love me, too – yet all you can do is revile me, giving me no chance to explain myself.'

Kadiya interrupted firmly. 'This tender reunion – and its mutual recriminations – must wait. You two must realize that there could be another great quake at any moment. The city itself might be devastated! You must do something.'

The pale eyes of Orogastus darted sidelong. 'I cannot control the movements of the earth with my talismans. I tried earlier, when the tremors were milder, and had no success.'

'That is because the earthquakes are only a symptom of the world's great imbalance,' Haramis said, 'as is the colossal mudflow hurtling down from the mountains.'

'*What mudflow?*' The sorcerer, Kadiya, Ledavardis, and Gyorgibo spoke all at once. Anigel and Tolivar only stood open-mouthed.

Haramis lifted her talisman. 'Brandoba lies directly in its path. Behold!'

Half of the ruined room seemed to dissolve away, and it seemed that they stood on some towering precipice above the Forest of Lirda. The dawn sky was invisible in low-hanging storm clouds, which obscured the heights of the wooded foothills like a curtain partially lowered. Surging out from under that curtain, filling the Dob River valley as though it were some green trough, was a churning mass that looked from a distance like grey porridge.

'Dark Powers forfend!' whispered Orogastus. 'I had no idea . . . Talismans! How far away from Brandoba is the front of the flow?'

Six leagues.

'It will be here in less than half an hour,' Haramis stated. 'When it comes, it will bury the city.' She brandished her talisman again and the vision disappeared.

Gyorgibo groaned. 'My poor people. My poor country.'

King Ledavardis shot him a glance of comprehension. 'Yes . . . you are the emperor now.'

'Emperor of oblivion!' He stood with hands on hips, glowering at both Orogastus and Haramis. 'What happens now? Will you waft your Guildsmen away from danger, Star Master? Will the Archimage likewise rescue those she loves, leaving Sobrania and its contemptible barbarians to the onslaught of the mud?'

Orogastus said to Haramis, 'Will we?'

The Archimage's gaze swept over her sisters and the others, who waited in silent apprehension. Should they be told the entire truth of the situation? They would have to know soon, but perhaps not yet. Not if there was any inkling of hope, no matter how small.

She said to them, 'Orogastus and I must speak privily of this. Please excuse us.' Then she motioned for the sorcerer to accompany her, and moved out of their earshot — although not out of sight.

'Shall we part forever, then?' he asked her. 'This Sobranian adventure of mine is over. I will have to begin again elsewhere, if such a thing is even possible. You will have your talisman and I will have my two. Separated, they are not invincible — merely extraordinary — especially since I am so inexpert in utilizing mine. I presume that you now have access to the viaducts also?'

She nodded in assent.

'So we may travel through them as we will, so long as their outlets are not blockaded. You need only collect your friends, after which there will be nothing to keep you in this doomed country. My Guildsmen and I can go to my old home in Tuzamen. If you promise not to attack me there, I will tell you how to free the Archimage Iriane from her prison of blue ice. Then we two can await the world's final descent into frozen silence — you in your sanctum and I in mine — with our dependents none the wiser. Until the end. Is this what you want to do, Haramis? Run away?'

'There is nowhere we can flee, even if we would,' she replied.

'What are you talking about?'

'The Archimage of the Sky, the greatest practitioner of magic who ever lived, told me that the great imbalance culminates and commences *now*. This Sobranian catastrophe, dire as it is, only marks the beginning of a myriad of such events that will immediately beset all nations of the world. There is no refuge for us anywhere, Orogastus, no escape. From here on, there is only a swift downhill slide until our world is entombed in the Sempiternal Ice.'

'So! I was not certain —'

'Denby Varcour believed that only a single despot, wielding the Threefold Sceptre of Power, could stave off this planetary doom. He demanded that I give him my talisman, so that it might be turned over to you. I refused.'

'And you still do,' the sorcerer stated.

'Yes.'

'You would see the world destroyed, rather than saved and subjugated by me?'

'I would see it saved . . . otherwise.' She took a deep breath. 'Will you give *me* the two talismans, so that I may assemble the Sceptre and attempt the healing without the enslaving?'

'Never!' he said. 'I know that it would be futile. The healing is itself a horrific process. The simple people of this world and their naive rulers would not know how to survive it. Your gentle persuasion would not move them. They would be insane with terror.'

'I think I have found an answer to that.'

'Then tell me!' He seized her upper arms. But she drew away, shaking her head, and he did not try to restrain her.

'Once,' she reminded him, 'you *did* pledge to let me wield the Sceptre.'

'Only if –' He broke off, unable to say the words.

Haramis said, 'In his last moments, Denby Varcour changed his mind about his tyrannical scheme. Dying, he invoked the Black Trillium, speaking of the Flower with both irony and a strange resignation. Then he said to me: "Love is permissible, devotion is not."'

'That damned enigmatic phrase!' Orogastus cried. 'You quoted it in your Tower as you repudiated me . . . What *is* the difference, then?'

'In the first,' she said, 'the lovers remain true to themselves. They unite without loss, without submission. Neither one is diminished but instead, they grow.' She paused, lowering her eyes: those eyes identical in colour to his own. 'I love you. But the Star demands pre-eminence over its devotees. The Flower does not.'

He stood before her sombre, the long fingers of one hand touching the medallion hanging from his neck. 'I must do what I was born to do. Denby does not matter. He did his part when he let me discover the truth about my own role, allowing me to discard the foolish beliefs of my early years and concentrate upon the one and only reason why I came to exist. I will not surrender my destiny to anyone, to anything. Haramis – my dearest Haramis! – you must understand.'

She smiled remotely. 'I do. But perhaps true understanding has yet to dawn in you. Denby also said to me, "Three Petals to wield and the Sky Archimage to guide" . . . if I wished it.'

291

He was dumbfounded, almost laughing at the audacity of her. 'You? If *you* wish it? What does it mean? Do you believe that the old man was passing to you and your sisters responsibility for the Sceptre of the Vanished Ones?'

'He might have been. Binah and Iriane were convinced we would be able to use it. I have never been certain, and perhaps my hesitancy is the reason why Denby suggested a fourth, who would be our guide.'

'The Archimage of the Sky is dead,' Orogastus declared angrily. 'How could he help in the wielding? Denby Varcour was a madman, and even at the end he was raving.'

'There is another authority that says that the Three Petals of the Living Trillium must use the Sceptre together – an ancient chant that Denby recited:

One, two, three: three in one.
One the Crown of the Misbegotten, wisdom-gift, thought-magnifier.
Two the Sword of the Eyes, dealing justice and mercy.
Three the Wand of the Wings, key and unifier.
Three, two, one: one in three.
Come, Trillium. Come, Almighty.

He was mocking me as he spoke the chant. But I have heard these words before, among the Uisgu Folk of our Mazy Mire. They say that the chant dates back to the foundation of their race.'

Orogastus shook his head. 'It makes no sense. It is mystical twaddle.'

'Since my Three-Winged Circle is the prime element of the Sceptre, the key, I would have to command – not as an archimage, but as one of Three with my sisters. If it were mine to choose, I *would* wish that the Living Trillium be strengthened and guided by a courageous friend – both in the wielding and during the dire aftermath. But we Three could never be guided by a Star Man.'

'You have been toying with me, Haramis.' This time there was no wrath in his voice but only despair. 'Without the Star I am nothing! You and your Flower would diminish me, demanding devotion while refusing to submit yourself.'

She took his hand, drawing it to the Three-Winged Circle on the chain at her breast. He tensed, still fearful and refusing, and she said again, 'I do love you. And I would never harm nor think of diminishing a new Archimage of the Firmament.'

'A new –'

'The office is now mine to bestow. I am the last active member of the

292

College. I am certain that Iriane would concur. And so, I think, would the sleeping Vanished Ones. We are of them, you and I.'

'Haramis . . could such a thing be?'

'It depends, I think, on you. On your love.'

She pressed his fingers to the Flower. He felt the tiny wings on her talisman open, and within was something that set his nerves afire as he touched it. Momentarily deprived of equilibrium, almost falling, he clung to her. 'Of course I love you! Ah, Haramis, I love you more than my own life! More than . . .' His voice trailed off to a soft groan.

He recovered and the nearly frantic embrace eased. It became reverent, lending strength to both of them.

When at length they drew apart, she whispered, 'The coronet!'

Frowning in perplexity, he took it from his head and studied it. The central Monster head, which had been surmounted by a tiny replica of the Star, now had a new escutcheon of three crescent Moons. It was the same with the Three-Lobed Burning Eye.

Its chain broken, the Star lay on the rubble-strewn floor at their feet.

A fresh tremor shook the palace.

Anigel and Kadiya left the others and approached. 'Hara,' said the Queen. 'You must decide at once what we are to do.'

Together, Haramis and Orogastus told them.

CHAPTER 31

Surmounting the palace's golden dome was a lofty pinnacle of red jasper, and within it a narrow spiral staircase leading to the enormous gilded bird effigy mounted at the top. Leaving Tolivar, Gyorgibo, and Ledavardis below, the three sisters and Orogastus climbed to the small platform at the pinnacle's summit. They stood there looking up at the spread-winged image.

'Why, it's a voor!' Kadiya said in surprise. 'The bird created by the Vanished Ones to be a helper and companion to the Vispi. I thought they were extinct in this part of the world.'

'They are,' Orogastus said. 'Which is why they are held sacred.'

'It is appropriate,' Haramis said. Then she asked the sorcerer to lift all four of them to the statue's back. He drew the pointless sword and held it high, giving the command. The three lobes became eyes, and from the open mouths of the monsters on the coronet shone beams of white, green, and golden light.

They wafted through the cloudy air, from which a light rain fell, and landed upon the broad surface of gold-leafed stone.

'Now we must assemble the Sceptre,' Haramis said. She bade her trillium-amber to quit its nest among the wings, attaching it to her neck chain after she removed the wand with its Circle.

Momentarily, the gigantic statue shuddered beneath their feet. They tensed, but did not lose their footing. The bird swayed very slowly from side to side. Down below, parts of the city still burned, and there were many areas where buildings had collapsed; but most of the devastation in Brandoba was veiled from their sight by smoke and mist and they did not look upon it.

Haramis said to Orogastus, 'Tell your talismans that we Three Petals of the Living Trillium may touch them freely.'

He did so, his teeth clenched in a grimace. Then he proffered the coronet in his right hand and the sword in his left. Queen Anigel and Kadiya stood on either side of him. At the Archimage's command, they lay their own hands upon the talismans they had once owned. The amulets at their throats blazed golden, and an answering throb of light came from the amber on the breast of Haramis.

Haramis inserted the wand into a channel on the sword-blade, then guided the Three-Headed Monster inside the Circle, so that it and the coronet formed a meridian and equator. Atop the Circle the wings opened and became large, and at their centre shone a great Black Trillium embedded in glowing amber the size of a fist. Haramis took the completed Sceptre and lifted it, while the others stood closely around her, laying a single hand upon hers.

'Come, Trillium,' said the Archimage of the Land. 'Come, Almighty.'

The Sceptre seemed to ignite with a yellow flame. No longer were the individual parts silver or black; they were shining gold. Kadiya, Anigel, and Orogastus felt a marvellous warmth spread from their fingertips, down their arms, and into their hearts.

'Sceptre!' The voice of Haramis was exultant, and the others knew that she felt the magical heat also. 'Carry us safely into the sky, high above this place. And banish all clouds, so that we may see the ground clearly.'

The gilded bird did not come alive. They saw no flapping wings, felt no sense of motion nor even any wind of passage; nevertheless they suddenly found themselves soaring upward beneath an expanse of limpid blue air. Still standing on the statue's back, they came to a halt. The dawn sun was poised above the Collum Range, which was now ominously smoking. Rivers of mud poured forth from the highlands in multiple courses, snaking through the forest, with the greatest flow of all nearly touching the outskirts of the city at the Dob River Watergate. Far-flung Brandoba itself, lying wounded within its walls, smouldered like a trampled campfire. The great harbour still held many ships, and the waters were turgid grey near the shore and luminous aquamarine in the outer depths of the estuary.

In the west, the Three Moons hung low, ready to set. The smoke in the air had turned them a drab orange colour.

'Now,' said Haramis to the Sceptre, 'we call upon the fullness of your magic. Tap the spirit-rich wellsprings of this world, its plants and animals, and all its people. Turn away the mudflow that threatens Brandoba, calm the unquiet earth beneath it, and if the Triune wills, restore the city's broken parts to wholeness. Let this be done without the loss of a single aboriginal or human life.'

The Sceptre's glow intensified until it became a near-twin to the solar orb in the east. The four people who wielded it flinched from the radiant power that streamed forth, averting and closing their eyes. A terrible noise smote their ears, grinding and wrenching and roaring, but their touch upon the hilt stayed firm, as did their foothold upon the golden bird so miraculously hanging in mid-air. When the noise diminished somewhat, all but Haramis removed their hands from the Sceptre. They dared to look down.

Around the city's landside perimeter, where the enclosing wall had been, a high rampart was rising. Thrust up from underground, soil and rock were creating a dike that diverted the advancing mud northward, where it would reach another river valley and there flow harmlessly into the sea. Other land movements, looking like the subterranean burrowings of some colossal creature, transformed hills into valleys and altered the course of minor streams. The terrain heaved and rolled like a shaken rug, accompanied by a mighty rumbling. And then it was still. Directly below them, the city seemed to shimmer. The smoke shrouding it faded away.

'Show us now a closer vision of Brandoba,' Haramis commanded. They seemed to swoop down, still secure, until they hovered above the pleasance and the palace. The imperial edifice itself and all of the surrounding buildings gleamed whole in the sunlight. Streets and boulevards were no longer blocked with rubble.

But the bodies of those killed and injured in the riots and tremors remained.

'Sceptre,' Haramis whispered. 'Can you not restore the broken people?'

Not the dead. Only those who live may be brought back to health, when touched individually by my parts.

'There is no time for that,' said Orogastus. 'If we fail to mend the greater imbalance, those who have perished will be the lucky ones.'

'He's right,' Kadiya said, with grudging respect.

'We shall help the wounded later,' said Anigel. 'If we can.'

'Very well.' Haramis addressed the Sceptre: 'Let our golden bird take us higher.' And then: 'Higher! . . . Higher still, and keep us safe!'

They rose to such an altitude that the sky became deepest indigo blue. Stars were visible together with the sun and the Moons. Neither chill nor lack of breath afflicted them. The world-continent with its shining white Sempiternal Icecap, beautiful and deadly, lay curved upon an azure sea streaked with clouds. Mysteriously, there were no clouds above the land.

'If the Sceptre tries to right the imbalance and fails,' Orogastus said to Haramis, 'we may die up here as our golden steed tumbles from the sky. But withal, you have chosen a right and proper place to attempt the magic – where we will know at once whether the world is healed and the ice defeated.'

He was standing before her, Anigel and Kadiya being on either side, and she smiled at him. 'Whether we succeed or not,' Haramis said, 'I am glad that at the end the Flower blessed our love.'

296

'I would marry you,' he said. 'I would live and work with you forever, if this were possible.'

'I desire it with all my heart and soul, my dearest, but we dare not think of such things now.'

'Still, I wanted you to know.'

Haramis nodded. Behind Orogastus, the Three Moons hovered at the western horizon in a tight group. She bade the others lay their hands upon her own once again, lifted the Sceptre, and spoke to it.

'Now do the deed for which you were made! Fulfil the hopes of those long dead, of those departed into the Outer Firmament, of those who sleep in limbo, of those who caused us to be born. Fulfil our own hopes as well, now that we come finally to wield thee, and heal our wounded world in God's good time. Defeat the imbalance that would condemn us to the Conquering Ice. Summon all that is magical, beautiful, and true from our hearts and from the land beneath us. Do it now! . . . Come, Trillium! Come, Almighty!'

This time there was no storm of light and noise, only a whisper like a sighing of stars that sounded and then faded to silence. The feeling of magical tension that had pervaded the Sceptre drained away. Its luminescence was extinguished as the three wings closed about the great piece of amber and shrank to their usual small size. The Sceptre became a depleted thing. The three eyes in the pommel closed and the carven monstrous faces were lustreless and inanimate.

At the same time another sort of illumination sprang into being in the deep blue western sky.

Haramis' eyes widened in astonishment, and the other three, seeing her staring, let their hands fall away from the drained Sceptre and turned about to discover what had happened.

The Three Moons in their close conjunction had changed colour from wan ochre to a pure, effulgent silver. Sketched about the orbs were three enormous petals of vibrant rainbow radiance. The central one extended almost to the zenith, while the other two seemed to embrace the horizon.

'Dear God,' whispered Anigel. 'What is it?'

'A Sky Trillium,' said Kadiya.

Orogastus blurted out, 'But is that all?'

'We asked,' Haramis said, 'that the healing take place in God's good time . . . Look down at the ice cap.'

They did, and saw countless tiny puffs of cloud rising everywhere from the gleaming surface. These expanded as they watched, forming a vast cloak of cloud that hid the continental interior from view. The mass elongated, caught by the prevailing winds, and began a slow progress eastward.

297

'What is happening?' Anigel asked.

'I'm not quite sure,' Haramis replied. 'But . . . I think it is beginning to melt.'

She spoke to the Sceptre. 'Are you able to return us safely to the imperial palace in Brandoba?'

Yes. We will fly somewhat more slowly.

They began to descend. The bird-image's back was almost as wide as the floor of a cottage. In their curiosity Orogastus, Anigel, and Kadiya peered down at the world below while Haramis, emotionally spent, sat quietly at the centre.

'Perhaps,' Orogastus said, when they came lower and had a better view of the ice's margins, 'the fires within the world, which would have burst out volcanically under the imbalance, have now focused in a more moderate way beneath the continental glacier. Those plumes of vapour – they will become rainclouds. Even though they dump most of their moisture in the sea, there will still be mighty storms and floods in the eastern lands – especially in my old home, Tuzamen, and in Raktum.'

'Poor old Ledo,' Kadiya said. 'Still, his nation has a plethora of ships. And here in the western part of the world there is much empty land for the pirates to colonize. As for Tuzamen, it is sparsely populated and a marginal place to live at best. I doubt that its people will be too miserable leaving it.'

'Then perhaps the aftermath will not be so bad after all,' Anigel said.

'The sea will rise,' Orogastus said, shaking his head. 'It will slowly encroach upon coastal cities in every nation of the world, as well as drowning the low-lying islands. Vast numbers of humans and Folk will be forced from their homes. The rivers will change their courses, inundating the old farmlands. Enormous lakes will be born again, where they existed before the Conquering Ice. Your Mazy Mire, Queen Anigel, was once such a lake.'

'Oh!' she said. 'Oh . . .'

'New mountains will rise as the interior land is relieved of its glacial burden,' he continued. 'This will alter the pattern of the seasons. It will be a frightening time for the people, perhaps even a Dark Age, even though we explain to them what is happening, and that it is for the good. A universal despotism might have kept the people under control and supervised the rebuilding. Without one . . . who can say?'

'I am sure,' Queen Anigel said stoutly, 'that you, Hara, and Iriane will do your best.'

'We may find our talents thinly spread,' he said, with a sigh.

298

'Other helpers will aid us,' Haramis said suddenly.

They turned to her in surprise. The golden bird was plummeting down above Brandoba; but as before, those who rode it had no sensation of rushing through the air.

Kadiya said, 'What helpers? Do you mean the sindona? But there are not very many of them left.'

'In one of the Three Moons,' said Haramis, 'thousands of persons lie in an enchanted sleep. They are the ones who were unable to Vanish – our ancestors – members of a civilization much more advanced than ours. Denby Varcour could never bring himself to release them. Their numbers and their superior abilities would have disrupted our simple way of living irreparably. He knew it would be both unjust and cruel to revive them in a world such as ours. After all, their war had caused the original imbalance.

'But Denby never lost hope that one day he would be able to undo the damage. He knew that in the aftermath of the Sempiternal Ice – if it ever came to pass – those sleeping geniuses would be able to lend us invaluable assistance in healing the land and sea. And so they will, guided by a new Archimage of the Firmament, an old Archimage of the Sea, and an Archimage of the Land who is presently weary unto death, but expects to feel much better tomorrow.'

'Yes!' cried Orogastus jubilantly, and he swept her into his arms.

The golden bird touched the top of the palace spire, becoming as solidly attached as ever. Anigel and Kadiya slid down from its back and found King Ledavardis, Emperor Gyorgibo, and Prince Tolivar, who had climbed out onto the pinnacle roof to await their return.

'Mother!' the boy cried. 'You will not believe what has happened!'

'Yes, I will,' Queen Anigel said, caressing his cheek fondly. 'There have been wonders and there will be sore pain, but in the end all will be well.' She touched her abdomen and felt a gentle flutter. Her three babes would be born into a strange world indeed, where magic and science would be allied. Would the boys be princes – or would they be something else?

Well, that was in the hands of the Lords of the Air. Offering her arm to Ledavardis, she started on the long walk down.

Kadiya shot an amused glance at the two who were still aboard the bird. 'I think we'll leave them to their conjuring,' she said to the new Emperor of Sobrania. 'I must find my aboriginal friends Jagun and Critch, who were left on a small boat in Brandoba harbour. Do you suppose you can lend me a fronial to ride?'

Gyorgibo bowed with a flourish of his tattered and dirty sleeves. 'Lady of the Eyes, I'll drive you myself in the imperial chariot – if anyone down in the stables recognizes me.'

'If they don't,' Kadiya told him in a comradely fashion, 'we'll steal the damned thing.'

When they had gone, Orogastus helped Haramis to alight. She still held the Sceptre as they stood together, looking down on the city. 'There will be so many hurt people to tend to.'

'We can summon sindona from the Place of Knowledge and the Moons,' Orogastus suggested. 'They can come through the viaduct out at the villa. You can use the Sceptre to transport them here –'

'No, love,' Haramis said to him. 'Let the sindona walk into Brandoba by themselves to do their good work. The Sceptre must be disassembled here and now and never used again.'

He bowed his head in chagrin. 'Of course you are right. And you must take charge of the three talismans.'

She took the magical instrument to pieces, tucking her own amber back amongst the now-empty wings of the Circle. 'I have a better idea.' She handed him the coronet. 'You keep the Monster, Archimage of the Firmament.' A mischievous smile touched her lips. 'For more reasons than one!'

'Thank you.'

'I will retain my Three-Winged Circle, and we will bond the Three-Lobed Burning Eye to Iriane. She is such an easy-going soul that the people – and the Unvanished Ones – might occasionally require reminding of her authority.'

He settled the coronet onto his head. 'I'll fetch the star-box. I hope the Blue Lady will forgive me for the freezing, and for the shameful way that my Guildsmen treated her small Mere Folk.'

'We will go together to the Hollow Isles, release Iriane, and tell her everything. I think she will want to come back here at once and use her new talisman to assist in the healing. You and I will share that work – but first, we must go to the Moons.'

'To begin the awakening?'

She smiled at him. 'Among other things.'

He took her hand. Side by side, they looked into the west. The Sky Trillium was setting, but she had no doubt that it would rise again the next day, and each succeeding day until its work was done.

THE END

SHIPS

rec. 1/4/05

WEAPONS

7-12-00